Through The Windowpane
CS HAGON

I0563199

Through The Windowpane
by CS HAGON

Published by CS HAGON
ISBN: 979-8-9917154-1-6
Second edition, paperback, 2025.

Author's Note

To all my early readers, editors, and supporters, I offer my deepest thanks.
This book has been a journey, filled with many drafts and late nights.
I could never have seen it through without your
insights, encouragement, and patience.
I want to express my heartfelt gratitude to my Front Range inkling group –
particularly the talented writers PJ Winter, Marina Noelle, and Ben Winter –
who inspired me to dig deeper, and helped tons with edits, developmental clarity,
formatting, and vision. To Robert for your invaluable wisdom and enthusiasm,
shared often halfway up a mountain. To all my amazing 1st-draft readers for your
support and critiques. And Valerie: your patient feedback and belief in me carried
me through it. Your notes were stellar, too.
To those who supported me...
It takes a tribe and a whole lotta love.
Thank you, all of you, for having my back
& helping me bring this tale to life.

Death taunts inches away. One small step is all it'll take – one step to not feel anything.

One more step, I'm gone.

At the edge of Cal's boots lies open air, a precipice between tall buildings. A fall towards the tapestry of lights and balconies and parked cars making it a certainty – fifteen floors down to the cold streets of his district.

Fifteen flights to the end.

It'll be quick. Down to those twinkling lights, the ones bringing warmth to the alleyways and shopfronts below, holding all the memories shared with her. Each light seeming to beckon him to forget forever – shining away, urging him to take the plunge.

The dark humor of it...

On the edge, he contemplates not just the rush to his end, but the descent into the memories that make life without her unbearable. Colliding with every sharp, jagged irony: the restaurants, the streets, the pubs, all bound to the hard corners of the city. The places where they once burned for each other, and the places where they burned out.

Gradually, until it was all at once.

Her packing her bags, throwing each item into her case with force, tearing back and forth from the bed to the closet.

The shame of it. The despair mingled with rage.

"Don't speak to me," she said, pushing past him, "And don't call me, neither."

"I won't. Just go. Please."

"I am, I'm going," she snapped. "Good riddance."

Seemingly a lifetime ago, those words echoing in his mind, haunting him, but not that long really in the grand scheme of things... the destruction of it so final with his front door slamming shut behind her heels.

And just like that, in a matter of minutes in relation to the years spent together, she excised herself from his life with the precision of a true professional. No - not just going. Diane was gone.

The pain of it now, thinking it over in the cold wind – beyond raw. Neither allowed to scab nor scar. A cultivated injury.

Yes. Tonight is the night I do it.

Tonight. No going back. Don't be a coward. Not this time.

Cal steadies his head and takes a deep breath of the frigid air, every beat in his chest echoing the weight of his next step forward: the point of no return.

The cold cement against the soles of his boots, the beads of sweat running down his back; the wrought iron fence he grips onto, his fingers coiled tightly to it in the freezing wind. The engravings pressing into his palms as he leans forward, inch by inch, over the chasm. Over the dangerous side of the rooftop. This swansong of a gargoyle moments before the final dive, decayed off its ledge at last.

Then dizziness strikes him. Vertigo.

His head lurches forward and he pulls back. He takes a moment. Breathing fog, steadying, taking stock. He peers down again. Down from his ledge. The wind whips around him.

His rooftop – this special, hidden place discovered in the days following his fiancée's leaving. Or at least after she made the end so final, so destructive, that there was no doubt the relationship was destroyed for good. And that's when it started...

A couple of months or so ago, just before December, after another fight over money, priorities and goals, and a great many other broken things in life where their opinions not so subtly differed. And the dam broke and his heart was torn to pieces in the worst way possible, the schism as unexpected as it was exacting.

There's no denying it: Diane was gone forever.

So, unexpectantly spending the Christmas holiday alone, battling his broken heart, Cal finds refuge from the echoes of laughter and merriment of the season high up on his building's rooftop. Alone with the ever-gnawing wound in his chest, staring out at the cold skyscrapers in the distant blinking black of the night's sky - nobody following him, nor thinking to look up there.

A somber, muted perch, not that easy to get to after all. Cold from the wind, icy from the frost, and remote enough for him to weep and think of her – and all else he's lost and wasted over his thirty-something meaningless years.

So much time now, down the drain.

It feels good to be above it if only just in height. A place to eulogize, sift through the gaping hole in his life. Try and remember and try and forget...

And time passes up on the rooftop.

And a bit after the new year ticks by and the seasonal cheer fades into the biting banality of early January in London, another thought at last occurs to him up there, during the fits of a particularly frigid cold spell.

Descending upon Cal, swaying in the snow – alone and muttering to the sky, guzzling a bottle like a sailor on port call – a singular feeling, menacing and rising with pointed thoughts like the tips of daggers. So insidious that it's nearly impossible to get rid of once the poison plants itself. A sudden shift– a gut punch.

A reframing of his entire life up to now.

My whole life and everything I've been moving towards all these years has been a waste. A wretched, terrible waste. I'm a wasted person.

In this cold thought soon comes other, colder thoughts, building in volume in the sad quiet recesses of his sad quiet flat. Thoughts like how he possesses neither the momentum nor the capability to move any higher in his career, and how he's too weak, too tired to try...

Too bitter to meet anyone else, too broken. Too undesirable. Too depressed.

And most painful of all is that he will never find the kind of love he's lost with Diane again. That when she walked out of his life, so too did his one chance of meaning something to someone, having a family, and with that chance now spoiled, it is even more painful in how he views himself.

The wrath aims inward. His hope diminished. There is no coming back.

The finality is absolute – it is plain to see he's a timebomb, and like any bomb, he means nothing to anyone until he's detonated as intended. Nothing to hold on to. Nothing to go back for...

Of course, his accounting job in the city feels like a sham even after all these years given to it. A way of surviving but never more fulfilling, and he can't think of anybody who will recognize his absence from the cubicle or "highly synergized" video meet-up. Even his closest teammates will forget about him, as he will them quicker still...

And then there's the local dwellers in his district of the city: the many ships passing on the many nights, on the way home from his commute or out and about.

Like the corner mart's checkout woman, Greta: an elderly lady with a crooked back and a kind heart towards everybody she encounters. Who always asks him genuinely, kindly, how his day is whenever she sees him, and he responds "it's truly fine" when she insists that he answer her.

Even she, he recounts bittersweetly, would fail to register that he wasn't buying his usual cooking ingredients twice a week. Almost certainly so. Because why the hell wouldn't she? He's just another face to her.

And his favorite judgy bartender Karalana, around the corner most nights at the smelly pub called the Old Hound, with all her tattoos and wisdoms and stories-for-every-story, would sooner realize a missing tab on a pint guzzled across the room than Cal's ghoulish Friday night presence. His habit of buying too many expensive single malts and blearily watching from the corner of the bar as the drunks try to dance...

And when Cal arrives at the point where he tries to talk himself out of the inevitable conclusions to these thoughts, well, it is even bleaker still. Because if he stays above the ground, above the street, the outcome will be even worse: he'll only lessen into a worse version of his potential; a greater disappointment to himself and the few that know him. Grow older and lonelier still, more bitter to everyone around, devolving like one of the elder residents of the building – the ones that live above and below him – solitary, crabby, forgotten by society and family alike, limping into the courtyard atrium to check the mail in the mid-afternoon sun only to recede again, muttering and utterly invisible really; no more or less than any other fixture of the building. As forgotten and meaningless as the creaky piping, the clanging boilers, or the peeling paint.

It's in these moments that he believes doing this might be the best and only option, the outcome so inevitable either way you examine it... always with his feet dangling over the perch's edge in the icy evening breeze, as they do tonight.

And it only takes a few weeks of these demented thoughts churning around – marinating in the dark recesses of Cal's skull – in his headphones, on his early-morning commuter train into the city, or during the solitude of cooking in the evenings and the sleepless nights spent staring at the digital numbers on the clock, waiting on his alarm – for the whispers of death to assure a new course. Establishing themselves as attractive, even enticing, luring a promise of escape in place of pain: a better destination.

Once this point arrives, it only comes down to a time and place. Luckily, that part is already worked out for Cal, as it is where he conceives the idea to begin with.

A fall from his spot. Off the easement to a swift end.

Gone. A release. Nobody to miss him, nobody to fuss.

If it's timed right, he shouldn't hit anyone down there.

Around a three second fall, give or take. Quick. Fifteen flights.

Just that simple. An escape from an otherwise unasked-for, thoroughly unnecessary, and brutally lonely existence. The escape from missing her. Missing anyone. The ultimate trick of the universe: a crucial opt-out plan to never be alone again.

Cal relishes the finality of these thoughts as the monotony of the winter lingers on, and it takes no time for the feeling to become the only idea in his head.

At last, the night arrives after just one more particularly bad day and he cooks a large dinner of steak and kidney pie for himself, paired with drinking an entire bottle of a lively Côtes-du-Rhône, a leftover engagement gift from Diane's side of the family. He then decides he won't do the dishes as he usually does but instead, this night, he dresses up in his finest suit (which isn't all that nice), combs his hair, and makes sure his tie is straight in the foyer mirror.

The tired blue eyes, the unkempt mahogany hair, that older sadder face staring back – he takes it all in. A moment passes.

He smiles as he messes the knot up, recalling when Diane playfully slapped his hand away, insisting she tie it for him before leaving for a date in this exact same spot years beforehand. He sees them kissing again in that foyer. The two of them. Her smell, the warmth of her skin close to him.

"You'd be hopeless without me," she giggles.

"Lucky I have you," he replies.

The love of his life, there for a moment then gone. Ghosts evaporating into hurt. He swallows and pushes the memory aside like a malformed spike in his chest. He tugs the knot tight, getting it correct. This time, this night, unlike the other times before, he doesn't plan to return to this foyer.

No more ghosts. I'll leave that pain for the next sod.

And really the only thing he does leave behind when he turns the key to his door's lock (more out of habit than necessity), is a note for some distant relatives who reside in America and with whom he hasn't spoken to in years. Nothing else. He doesn't even leave a letter for his brother who recently moved to France.

What's the point? I mean, really.

Everything that should have been said is said.

To all of them.

Stepping out into the hallway, he puts on his jacket and takes the lift to the top floor of his building where he ascends the ladder up to the roof as he has so many times over the past few weeks. He counts the rungs as he climbs. A dozen, never changing. The decisiveness of it all feels strange, almost assuring. He feels weightless like a bird as he closes the hatch door behind himself on the rooftop and makes his way to the icy edge.

The wind's picked up a bit and carries sounds farther than usual, and he hears car horns and indistinct voices from far below. His stomach drops slightly as he peers over, seeing all fifteen flights, and then slowly he puts a foot up and then another and climbs over the iron fence to the edge. Light snowflakes fall from the sky as Cal stands there – swaying.

Fifteen flights, all the way down.

He feels like his entire life leading up from birth has taken him to this moment, and he feels comfort rising in that certainty.

Tonight is the night, Cal. Tonight is the end. At last.

Relief, in place of fear - once more he allows it. His mind washes over with memories of her, things said, interwoven recalls now leaving him feeling a collection of sharp edges torn so roughly that they will never be a part of the whole again.

But it's okay. The weight of another day soon will be an afterthought – no more. This unbearable weight of living alongside these devastated remnants.

Cal nods and loosens his grip on the wrought iron.

No more having to bear the weight of how I failed to find happiness. How I failed not to be alone. And how I failed in being alone too.

He feels hot tears sketching down his cheek and he allows his own weight to take him forward, leaning, feeling the tug of gravity. He knows that all he must do now is let the fall take him – just let go...

Devastated remnants...

And he does, opening his eyes just as his fingers disconnect – and in that moment, he sees something he hasn't before...

His fingertips grasp, hesitating a second longer, seizing back to the cold railing.

What was that?

A movement or motioning directly in front of him, out in the adjacent building about a hundred meters away. A dim flickering of light in a usually dark series of windows.

Something in the stillness.

He gazes into the soft glow of what looks like a living room through the wall, barely lit and mostly shadows, and peering closer he makes out the outlines of a chair facing the glass, and the body of someone sitting in the chair, pale like paper in the darkness. A part of them moving ever so slightly.

A chill comes over him, and he pulls himself back from the edge, gripping the wrought iron even tighter as he suddenly becomes dizzy with how high up he is.

He glances down, pushing through it, righting himself, then looks back at the dim window.

Someone's watching me.

Mortified, deathly still, holding on for dear life in the wind, he realizes the movement hasn't subsided at all – it keeps going.

After several moments, he turns around, one foot over the other on the edge, and climbs back from where he came. Back to his solemn perch. Once back on solid ground he turns and looks back at the window again, squinting.

Was it just in my head or was someone really there?

Then within the shadows of the living room's windowpane, his eyes adjust inward, and he sees the motion again, and he realizes for a fact that there is a person there.

His ears burn, and rage fills up deep within him, acid-tasting, a bitter fury.

Even my last private moments stolen from me.

Cal ducks below the half wall and curses – "Shit!"

He crawls along the roof to stay out of sight of the window. Quickly opening the hatch, he descends the ladder and makes his way back to the lift, fists clenched.

"How dare you think I'm just going to be your fucking show. Your snuff video – my bloody suicide," Cal mutters to nobody as he throws open his flat's door. "Let's see who you are now, shall we? Let's see who the hell you think you are, treating me like your nightly program. Broadcasting me to the world. Let's see how you like it."

Pushing aside piles of bills and some brought-home work reports from years ago, as well as a week-old takeout box, he digs around his office until he finds them at last in a drawer.

He grabs them: the once shiny pair of binoculars now caked in dust, a legacy of his old bird-watching days in the park nearby when he first left uni, thinking the new hobby would help him meet people. Finally, a real purpose for you, Cal thinks as he uses his dress shirt's sleeve to crudely scrub the lenses of dust. He leaves his flat again, locking the door carefully this time, and bounds back up to the rooftop hoping to catch the voyeur still in the act.

Up the ladder and out in the cold again, the biting wind on his face, and he pulls up his scarf and then begins focusing the binoculars on the window.

It's blurry, so he adjusts the focus, rolling his thumb on the knob beside the lens. Suddenly the image concentrates, the view finding a subject, and he gasps.

Bathed in shadows and ceiling half-light, Cal realizes the flickering movement in the window is an elbow, revolving on purpose, moving rhythmically, leading to a hand fixed like a hose between the skin of two wide open legs. A sheer curtain billows at either side of the silhouetted woman, sitting in the chair, doing little to mask her actions in front of the large glass window of the ornate penthouse.

Her knees wobble, back and forth, and Cal sees her other hand move nimbly along her belly button and upwards to the dark outlines of her nipples, touching each in turn, and he can see her ribs and the groove of her shoulders moving as she pleasures herself slowly but rigidly defined in the shadows and the dim light.

He sees a mound that he recognizes as her panties crumpled around a shaking ankle and the determined rise and fall of her bare chest, the way her mouth moves with her breathing, opening and closing as if she's praying, and the way the little light in the room reflects against the porcelain wetness of her thighs; the anticipation of her face up towards the ceiling as she closes in. He can tell her lips are painted red, and the grooved dark around her eyes looks like she's been crying.

The shocking spectacle of this – this woman's unexpected nakedness and exhibition – hits Cal harder than he imagines the concrete would moments before. He considers breaking off the view and heading back but remains nonetheless transfixed, his body locked in.

Frozen. Breathlessly trying to focus the binocular's view closer to the window's occupant: to her face and to her body...

And then, quite suddenly, the room illuminates, and Cal sees a door behind the woman opening.

A light switches on in what looks like a decorative foyer at the far side of the room. Cal sees through the binoculars a man entering behind the woman, and he sees her whip her head around at him like she's being startled, covering herself with her hands.

Something is said, and then the woman springs to her feet. Moving to the window, she draws the curtains at once. Cal sees the lights stay on underneath, seeping out as just a sliver below and nothing more.

The wind gusts around him, but he doesn't stray from the ledge. For several minutes he just breathlessly keeps the binoculars trained on the concealed windowpane – waiting for the very second, the very instant, the naked woman will reappear.

More time passes.

She doesn't come back. The curtains remain closed.

After a while, well past midnight, he feels heady exhaustion mix with the fatigue behind his eyes, and the wind's gusts become more biting. Yawning, all his plans dashed, the desire too numb now, Cal climbs down the ladder and takes the lift. He trudges back to his place, falling onto his couch into an unconscious sleep – his suit and tie still on, wrinkled and unkempt, and the binoculars hanging around his neck like a medallion.

2

The frigid rain falling over London's commute does little to stave off the sun breaking through the clouds by midmorning, burning contrasts of light and shadow into the cubicle desks. At his own, Cal pours over rows of numbers and spreadsheets beneath the buzz of the fluorescent lights and the muted clatter of keyboards that fill the sterile space where he has given the last decade or so of his life.

But today, he can't think about his deadlines, or his special client requests, the quarter goals, or his looming review (which he's been banking on not being alive to attend), because despite appearing hard at work, Cal is doing next to nothing except reliving the events on the rooftop the night before.

The view in the binoculars... her fingers at work on herself... her skin in the shadows, moving up and down with her efforts... the way she must have moaned in that room, thinking herself totally alone... as he sees her... that moment of seeing her with the breath catching in his throat, his gaze tuned completely.

So entangled in the memory of her silhouette, he doesn't hear his colleague Andy saying his name until the younger man leans over the side of the cubicle, holding a ream of documents.

"Hey, I'm speaking to you."

"Oh, sorry," Cal says. "What's up?"

"Didn't you hear me?" Andy raises his eyebrows, exasperated.

"No," Cal says and stares blankly at his screen, then looks again at him, then back to the screen.

"You hear my question?" Andy scoffs.

"No. Sorry... on a roll," Cal says. "What is it?"

"Just slow it down, alright?" Andy shakes his head, a tinge of disbelief in his voice as he tosses the documents onto Cal's desk beside his keyboard.

"How did you miss this? You taught me these calculations for Christ's sake. Elementary mistakes here, Cal, really. Pay attention, come on."

"Right," Cal says. "I'll take another pass."

"All I'm saying, mate."

Then Andy asks, after a moment, his tone softened: "So, what's going on? Couldn't be nothing."

"Don't know where my mind is today, honestly," Cal replies, rubbing his eyes with his palms.

"Don't ask me. You know they're looking for a reason to sack folks this quarter," Andy says and peers around. "Twenty-first-century pendle witch, over there, our lovely Janice. Don't need to tell you that though. You're going to bring her wrath 'pon us all. Can't have that. Right?"

"Hey, okay? I said that I'd take care of it, didn't I?" Cal replies.

"Yeah. Guess you did," Andy sighs. "Bloody Mondays."

"No need to fuss about it. I'll take care of it."

In kinder words, piss the hell off, Cal thinks.

He opens the folder of corporate tax documents, and then looks blankly back at his computer screen, his mind recoiling effortlessly to the window in an instant...

Unmoored, floating back close to her in the darkness...

Her movements... her hands... her lips moving... him standing in his spot on the rooftop.

The binoculars completely zeroed in, so close he can almost touch her. Can almost see the droplets of sweat moving lazy down her skin... so slow... each one of them...

The hours pass and the sky adopts a palette of red and gold across his cubicle, and he realizes the day is nearly done and becomes excited at the prospect of leaving the numbers and monotony.

An hour later, the rhythmic swaying of the train carriage, and the blur of the passing tunnels, does little to distract him from the images of her soaking thighs in his mind. He peers through the train window and wishes the reflection staring back in pale disbelief was hers instead of his own.

He fantasizes about her catching him watching her, his eyes married to her skin, touching themselves from their respective perches...

And he realizes suddenly that he is getting aroused in public, on the damn Southeastern line nonetheless. He tries to shake the image from his mind and readjusts himself in his seat. He turns his music up and closes his eyes.

A half-hour later the train begins to slow for its stop, and Cal springs up to be at the front of the Tube's exit queue. He leads the rush through the turnstiles, up the stairs. And a bit later, after the ten-minute walk in the cold evening rain through his flavored corner, his few blocks of familiarity, he takes the lift up to his tired flat and begins cutting onions into a hot pan for dinner.

Yet his gaze moves from the sink to the couch to the window, and before he even registers what he is doing, he grabs the binoculars from his desk drawer and wraps his scarf around his neck. Minutes later, he climbs up the ladder into the cold night air of the secluded rooftop. Up to look in her window again.

The southeastern districts of the city sprawl below him like a living organism, and below he can hear the faint laughter from cafes, pubs, and restaurants; the patter of raindrops from the puddles on the rooftops, the hum of traffic weaving the wet streets. The distant wail of sirens. The breeze tousles his hair and carries the smell of curries, steaming vegetables, and cooked meats upward to the stoop.

Cal ignores all these things, not glancing down at the street at all, but instead training the binoculars only on the adjacent building, towards the window his mind has been looking through all day.

Leaning against the parapet where he stood the night before, the cold stone pressing into his elbows, his gaze snapped like a magnet there, finding focus in the lens. Her window. Gleefully he sees the same dim ceiling lights, and he smiles seeing the curtains pulled back in the same way.

The world narrows as he zooms in.

Time stands still. Focusing, rolling his thumb against the dial.

Come on, come on.

And in the soft muted shadows, he spots her silhouette forming out of the darkness suddenly, and the breath sticks in his throat – all the patchwork of his fantasies falling miserably short of witnessing her doing it again.

Yet again – the sheer luck of it astounding him almost as much as the sight itself. Naked, sitting in her chair, facing the window a few feet back, her legs spread wide open.

Cal is spellbound. He stares.

Every contour of her body seems sculpted with artistry, a delicate care, and he watches the gentle curves of her collarbones give way to the smooth expanse of her chest, her fingers running down her waist, along the flair of her hips, and lower still to the ghostly dark where her legs meet and flutter, pulsing with her breathing.

Time passes invisibly, and Cal keeps watching, desire awakening within him, a burning heat, as her breasts rise and fall with each breath, seemingly unaware of his gaze... or anything else for that matter.

Soon, she shifts and takes something – a toy – from the ground, long and colorful, and then stands and moves her way to the glass, backing closer to him.

And he sees that her hair is light in the gloom of the penthouse, blonde maybe, and that as she leans into the cool barrier, the winter moonlight paints her starkly, almost like a statue, a contrast to the imagined warmth of her skin.

She is silver – skin and hair alike.

A car horn goes off below, and Cal realizes he is smiling ear-to-ear. He sees the glass window fog for a moment when she turns around facing him, and she presses her breasts into it, and ghostly clouds form in front of her face, and he sees her nipples like two pink buttons in the darkness.

Intoxicated, Cal stares at the gentle give of her flesh, her golden hair tumbling over her shoulders, the way her hips plunge into her fingers, and the way she presses even more harshly into the ceiling-to-floor windowpane, brushing all the keys of her melody.

Does she want to be seen? Does she know?

He imagines so, and he imagines he can hear her, hold her, taste her...

But then, Cal sees the front door swing open behind, adding new motion to the room.

Not again.

Swiftly this time, like an ambush, the room interrupts.

All the lights turn on at once, and he sees the naked woman spin around to face the foyer. There is a charge of friction in the way she carries herself, and then Cal sees her roll the toy to the floor quickly under the couch. He focuses the binoculars inward, to the far side of the room.

The shadow of the man enters. Cal can see he is in a suit holding a briefcase.

With the lights on, Cal also sees the room is exquisitely decorated: Italian marble floors scattered with Persian rugs with several chandeliers that cascade from the high ceilings like waterfalls, illuminating the space in a shimmering glow of gold and crystal prisms. He sees that there is a magnificent fireplace near where her chair is, and a carved mantel above with many framed pictures on top.

Expensive-looking art of varying sizes adorns the walls, as well as floor-to-ceiling walnut bookshelves, large exotic-looking plants hanging, and an exquisite glass coffee table with what looks like a crystalline bowl on top. A gorgeous, long leather couch establishes dominance over the center of the room with throws and brass floor lamps at either end of it. At the far side of it all, near what looks like the bar: a gloss black grand piano.

It doesn't take a genius to see that the penthouse is designed with luxury at the foreground of every design choice – a room meant to be so untouchable, so unlived in, so curated in immaculate presentation, that it appears perfect down to every detail.

Well, almost every detail.

He watches even more intently as the woman's movements change, her back tightening, in fear or defiance he can't be sure. The woman and the man speak to each other, and it appears that he is shouting at her, his finger pointed towards the window in accusation, before she is shaking her head and then yells something back at him.

"Oh, come off it, leave her be," Cal mutters to his binoculars. "What's the problem, you meddler. Leave her the fu –"

The words freeze in his throat.

Without warning, he sees the man take a threatening step towards her and sees her instinctively step back to the glass with her hands raised. They both appear to be yelling at each other, and there is a fleeting moment where it seems the tension might dissolve, him looking away as if pacified.

But then it happens in a flash, the hope shattered, as the man closes the gap between them, his body twisting, and his hand connects with her face in a sharp and abrupt slap. The impact causes her to recoil, and her own hands fly to her face as she stumbles back into the window behind her. The glass catches her.

Thank God it doesn't break.

Somehow, she stays on her feet and the man pushes past her and abruptly the curtains are yanked closed, hiding the unfolding situation out of sight.

Nothing moves.

The ambient noises of the city, as well as the momentary intoxication of witnessing her in her act again, twists into deep, churning nausea. A cold rush descends over Cal, far icier than the gusting of the wet winter evening.

His mind reels over, questioning himself and what he just saw, the gravity of it. His fingers clench involuntarily into the binoculars as he stares at the closed curtains. His nails digging into the rubber grips. He feels a rage swelling up in him, fierce and boiling, and he can't begin to understand where the intensity is coming from.

After a while, he makes his way back down to his flat, stories below. The air is chalked with smoke when he opens the door, the alarm beeping, and he realizes he's left the stove on burning the onions. He opens a window, his eyes watering, coughing, and he can't help but look up at the window in the adjacent building again.

Her living room is way up by the fifteenth floor, far above his, and from this angle he can't see much – but enough to tell that the curtains are drawn, and that it's still dark inside.

A lump forms in his throat and his mouth feels dry. He opens a bottle of wine, slowly turning the corkscrew of his pocketknife. He pours a glass and sips it carefully as he begins cleaning up the burnt pan and working on dinner.

As he goes through the motions, a powerful urge wells up in within him, from behind closed doors he thinks perhaps he shouldn't open.

Eating, he replays what he's seen over and over again.

The smack in the face, the way she stumbled into the glass.

The way she pressed into it.

The way he so casually hurt her...

And as Cal falls asleep, he doesn't dream of Diane for the first time in a long time, nor of killing himself, but instead of the woman in the window: her naked body standing behind him, face bruised, eyes determined, her arms outstretched and thrusting him forward with her voice repeating – urging him:

"Protect me."

3

Days begin to unfurl at a breathless pace, hours counting down to the opportunity of returning to the nightly perch – his sanctum. His professional life and its daily servings of jumbled malaise, the commute northwest and southeast feeling somehow longer now each day, and everything else a reminder of the bitter past or an exhibition of present pain and dullness. And because of all this, inevitably perhaps, Cal begins seeking her out in the dull patchworks of his life, trying his best to get through his regular distractions for another precious glimpse – another look at her.

What is her name?

Who is she?

Why is she there in the window?

He looks for her day after day, sometimes even without noticing he is, scanning every crowd and face bobbing around their shared neighborhood in the otherwise boring moments of his day. And a fascination and worry take grip each time he goes out into the neighborhood.

Will this time be the time I bump into her?

It's silly, really, when he takes a step back. He scarcely knows what she looks like for starters.

Maybe tall. Rich, blonde, fit – and probably bruised.

But would he recognize her if he saw her up close?

If he saw the colors of her eyes... smelled her perfume...

Yes, he thinks, probably.

And he seeks her out, his eyes interloping here and there through his daily ritual.

With each dimly similar profile to these descriptions – on the Tube, in the streets, the market alleys, the shops and stands and pubs – his heart alights when someone appears similar, only to sink again when the realization comes that it isn't her at all. Just another commuter. Another face.

Another deadened denizen like me.

But gradually, with his heart ache lifted ever-so-slightly, his routines shift around such notions: into a purposeful curiosity.

One morning, Cal gets up thirty minutes earlier to cook his dinner instead of breakfast, placing it in tupperware, still steaming, and back into the refrigerator to have it ready after returning from work.

The idea sticks as one worth repeating, and he begins taking the prepped food and the binoculars up with him, night after night to the perch to scan for her silhouette in the window. Same time every night getting up there, as soon as he gets home, and then for hours at a time from there. Out in the cold, alone. As always.

And alone on his perch, Cal sips his drink, the weight of Diane's loss never far away. Yet, this night, like previous nights, there's the faint quiver of hope that the curtains might pull back at any moment to draw his focus outward, away from his ex's memory.

Away from the deep wound within him.

It's strange not to feel it like he has just days before, but the curiosity of the stranger in the window beckons louder than the pain from Diane. And for that, he's grateful.

Yet night after night, despite his routine or because of it, the darkened panes give nothing back, so he returns down the ladder and then down the lift where he lays in bed, and tortures himself with thoughts of the stranger instead of his ex-fiancée, dreaming up ideas of how to save her.

Ideas, wild ideas.

Restless, he tosses and turns, the sheets either too warm or too cold, his mind incessant, utterly infiltrated with each plan and each strategy more intricate than the last, breathed in and out of existence moments at a time.

Spiraling, cascading, deafening thoughts.

He stares at the ceiling and talks to himself. "I'm here for maintenance," he repeats in varying tones and accents. He envisions knocking on the woman's door, holding a toolbox. "I'm here because of a leak in the owner-occupied flat below. Mind if I look, ma'am?"

Okay. Maybe.

Possibly... she lets you in, then what?

What now?

Measuring the situation, he gives her an escape route. Maybe a hidden phone. A burner. For emergencies.

No. Not that way. Bloody stupid. Asinine, really.

This woman has all that, has everything you can ever give her and more... right at her fingertips, he thinks.

She doesn't need some fifty-quid burner phone. That won't work.

Then call the coppers. Anonymous tip. Untraceably done.

Seems reasonable, given what you've seen.

Right... then, just alert the authorities, they'll come in and arrest this guy. This abuser. This putrid coward of a man. Help this woman get out of there without putting her in danger... without putting her at risk. And justice prevails.

Unless it does put her in danger.

Unless it does put her at risk.

Who knows what will transpire once that ball is set in motion.

Maybe she defends him. Maybe she can't go through with it. Doesn't want to. They could have been called already, for all you bloody well know.

Maybe she has leapt before. This could be her last straw with him. Or maybe she keeps on defending him. There's a name for that... can't remember... or if he's been released, maybe a day or so later, and next he comes back at her, that last straw gone now.

He jumps an injunction. Could happen. Anything could...

Maybe he's crazy. Maybe he's a bloody psychopath.

Maybe he's already had an injunction from a time before and doesn't care about dropping in on her at all, unexpected or otherwise, cause the bobbies in the matter are reactive by nature and he is not supposed to be there anyway... and he knows they'll never get there in time to catch him, right?

He's got it sighted. He's figured it out.

He knows this and so does she. He's threatened it, even.

Shit. Probably, he has.

Maybe he lives there. Maybe she's just staying, a visitor.

Or worse, she's his wife.

His prisoner.

Could be anything. All you know, sticking your nose where it doesn't belong, is little more than actions in a moment. Right?

Actions in a moment not meant to be seen by anyone.

But it was seen...

I saw it... can't be changed, that.

So, don't get her hurt again... that's something that can be changed, not interfering, or... no... think... think...

And Cal's mind continues to race unabetted.

Guilty and layered machinations, coupled with daydreams of heroic, cartoony and spiraling outcomes, swinging from realistic to felonious.

At some point, he imagines himself renting a safe house, a sanctuary where she can escape if needed... when needed.

Somewhere discreet across the city and unassuming from the outside street. Ambiguous yet still filled with all the comforts she has at present.

The carpets and plants and books and furniture. The art. The shiny black piano. The toys.

A place where she feels safe in the dim light and can sit on her chair, knowing full well the door won't be thrown open behind her.

Knowing full well she won't get struck in her face.

A place that man won't find you.

A place where you can be free of fear.

"No," Cal says to nobody in the black stillness of his bedroom. "I can't afford a place like that."

4

Days and nights pass and a North Sea-borne storm hits London one Friday evening, driving an uncharacteristic amount of snow to the ground in only a few hours, keeping the usual avenue and alleyway dwellers indoors. Even the Old Hound has less smokers idling and chatting outside.

In the eerie dim, crunching past the raucous pub, walking home in the flurries through the streets, something ticks backwards inside Cal.

A familiar despair creeping up slowly in each cell of his bloodstream, moment by moment, step after step, as he plods through the pelting snowflakes. He doesn't look up at her building as he enters the courtyard, the way he has each evening after checking the mail, and for the first time in the past few weeks he stays in his tired flat instead of going to the rooftop with his dinner and binoculars.

He makes dinner instead at a normal hour, watches television, does the dishes, and then turns the lights off without a word. Before going to sleep, he doesn't glance upward to look from his bedroom window to her living room window as he usually does. And most of all, for the first time since seeing her, he doesn't dream of the naked woman in the window. Not at all.

In fact, he doesn't even dream; his mind is a black pit as if he were dead.

And the next day, a Saturday, his heart is heavy, and reluctant thoughts turn to Diane as he blinks awake in the silence of the cold morning.

Walking beside her that afternoon in Saint James Park so many years ago, her face dappled in the shadows of the autumn trees, hands entwined with his own. Her contemplative eyes and auburn hair, her mouth spun and laughing at something, eyebrows cresting in mirth.

A small pond nearby, its surface shimmering with gold foliage floating on top of it, coming up around the path. Diane bends down and picks up a flat stone like the schoolgirl she was when he first met her, and then she tosses it precisely into the water, grinning in challenge.

"Bet you can't."

Four, five, six skips. Maybe it was more.

Who won that?

It doesn't matter.

The lightness in her laughter that day... his own laughter.

The weightlessness in the memory: a strange thing. Like an unspoken promise of many more days like that.

Points. Scores that don't matter – lies we tell ourselves. Days that never come to be.

The memory fades at the edges.

Cal gets up in his icy bedroom and trudges in his robe to the kitchen in the mid-morning light to make breakfast. The living room is still, and the frosted windows perspire. Rubbing his hands, he checks that the radiators are working before going over to the kitchen and peering into the cupboards and then the fridge. Out of eggs and milk, he curses and returns to the bedroom, throwing on some clothes and his jacket, his cap, and then grabbing his keys and wallet on the way out the door.

Even if only around the corner, a break from this place will do me good. Better than hanging off the edge of the building...

For now, at least. For now.

Under the gunmetal sky and down the courtyard, amid the relentless gray brick of the sprawling neighborhoods, Cal hears the muted cacophony of the city, and he imagines the desires and despairs within that noise, and the heaviness that he feels in his heart from Diane's memory weighs even more acutely than it did when waking up.

The bleakness of it all.

He walks into the neighborhood and hears the car horns and sirens and soft thuds of boots on the snow-dusted grounds, and conversations of people, their voices hushed by scarves wrapped snug around their faces. Cal's teeth chatter and he pulls his cap lower and then, pushing his hands deep into his jacket pockets, presses forward into the sea of people congregating around the nearby market square. He notices no one but keeps walking towards the entrance.

Another face.

Like a morose whisper against a symphony, without awareness of much at all around him, burdened with the thoughts of his own failures. His own regrets. His past.

He shivers at last and looks around as he gets closer.

Why does this month have to be so bleeding cold?

It makes everything so much worse.

As he nears the indoor market, the air's icy tendrils sharpen to the smell of freshly baked bread, meshing with pungent scents of cheeses. Above the entrance, a weathered sign lists back and forth in the wind, announcing the day's deals in chalk. Beneath it, the large glass doors that are speckled in grime and frost present a glimpse of the bustling aisles and ceaseless, humming commerce of Saturday morning shoppers. The panes route the light of the overcast day into almost a glow, creating ever-shifting patchworks of brightness and shadows in the snowy streets outside, as if the ground has a restless energy about it. A life of its own.

And in one such moving patch of light, quite suddenly, like a vision revealing itself, Cal sees her... and his breath catches in his throat.

Not like the other times. No, no.

It's her – that's her!

He's certain of it the moment his eyes fall on her.

Some ten, maybe twelve meters away from where he stands, she steps out of the passenger side of a dark arriving Range Rover, near the curbed entrance of the market building. Pulling her elegant purse around her shoulder, carrying herself with a particular blend of grace that beckons his attention out of the fog – a gilded shine above the mundane.

Her cascade of light blonde hair defies the gray of the morning: wild, untamed, like waves crashing a shore and catching the market's glow in a way that sets her apart, elevating her above the throng and blur of all others.

He notices she doesn't wave to the driver who pulls off sharply towards the underground parking entrance the moment she shuts the car door. Instead, she turns and steps through the market doors, out of sight in the span of a moment.

It was her.

He is so sure of it that he will bet his life.

And it strikes him: a sudden tug deep within him. An inexplicable, indescribable force pulling him towards her.

And so, without another thought, he quickens his pace and follows her through the condensation-streaked doors, the warmth from inside rushing over them each in turn as they enter, only one aware of the other.

By the long displays of chilled fruits and vegetables branching out from the main aisle, he catches sight of her face at last. Close enough to see where the man hit her.

Moments go by. He chances a second look.

Beneath the veil of applied concealer and foundation, the bruise on her cheek is almost imperceptible. A muted yellow, leaving only the faintest shadow hinting its presence on the side of her face. If he didn't know what happened to her, Cal would have missed it, as most others probably will today. But despite the makeup's seamless blend, even from a dozen feet or so, there's a raised texture that betrays damage underneath. To him, at least.

And then she moves again – turning. He follows.

Cal's eyes travel over her as she examines a carton of eggs, and his heartbeat quickens. Her high cheekbones, her sculpted narrow nose.

Her full lips, painted boldly in a somber winter red.

He continues following, staying at a distance where he can, trying to appear distracted whenever her gaze glosses in his direction. Lost in the banality of shopping – the everyday dance – while being anything but that.

He sees her maneuver around the selections, taking each in turn, scanning the vegetables, meats, and fruits.

He notices her eyes have an enigmatic color shade about them, something that dances between emerald-green and gray.

He sees the way she moves her body, her stride, checking her phone at times as she goes, sometimes a list, and he sees all her mannerisms displayed in the presumed anonymity of the market's crowd.

The way she brushes her hair behind her ears, adorned in intricate piercings, and the way her fingers glide across things, absentmindedly playing with a pendant around her neck, grabbing items, yearning for something before reaching for something else.

And the subtle arch of her back, the tilt of her chin as she peers at a shelf's jars, the way her breasts press against her blouse as she reaches up for something, and the soft biting of her lower lip as she considers two competing products, one in each hand. The way she cocks her chin with indecision.

All these nuances he sees, and they pull him in. Further and further into her orbit, and he keeps on following her, his gaze discreet yet fixed.

He sees the elegant clothing: the tailored dark blazer draping perfectly over her silk blouse. Her striped, form-fitting skirt ending just above the knee, showing several inches of her bare legs, dedicated and toned. A dancer's legs, maybe.

And her elegant jewelry, beautiful but discreet, conveying an understated parlance of finer things. And her black-leather heeled boots, pointed, seemingly an audacious choice for the icy streets of London this time of year – a touch of defiance to her as she moves from one display to the next.

He follows. Every unaware gesture, every flutter of fabric, every evaluated item put into her basket or placed back, every expression her lips convey – each little hint painting a narrative for him to record, to decipher, to decode.

Cal keeps her in his sight, and his pace attunes to the rhythm of her movements – lingering in places, rushing forward in others, mirroring her, her quiet cadence, all the ways to the end of the market.

Her market.

At one point, she pauses to read a label with a slight furrow in her brow, then moves onward, and Cal stops and looks at the item, not understanding what it is that made her do that.

Sesame oil. He shrugs, putting it back on the shelf.

Later, he sees her chuckle softly at something, seemingly a private joke, while she chooses a bottle of wine. After she moves on, he looks at the wine rack and can't begin to guess what she's thinking about.

Is she buying the bottle for herself, to drink alone, or is it for the man she lives with?

The man that hurts her. Who is he to her?

As he follows, Cal can't help but think how he's never enjoyed shopping, especially with Diane who was a control freak with such things. Who sucked the fun out of anything like that with her anxieties and authoritarianism.

Nevertheless, he's never been so present shopping for food now, in this moment, and as an outsider, there should be no reason for this. No small or big thing has changed about the market. Not for decades. Indeed, ever since he moved here after uni, the Saturday market has been as it always is - this late morning dance of life in its rawest, most routine form.

And yet through Cal's eyes, each of this woman's actions has changed everything. Magnified, imbued with weight and wonder, time seeming to stop as he follows her to each of the stands, viewing her choices after she does, each hinting at a deeper understanding of who she is – her true identity.

What she likes. What she eats. What she passes by.

Each item springing forth a new part of her mystery. A mystery Diane never possessed.

Because Diane and I had no mysteries. Until we did, Cal thinks.

This is nothing like that, he realizes.

Then he catches her perfume and he forgets Diane entirely. A stitch pulled from the tapestry of someone else's existence.

Lilacs and the sweet smell of jasmine.

A hint at a complete stranger's life.

He follows so transfixed by her everyday ballet that he registers nothing else. Tethered to the invisible thread between them, bobbing behind people, hanging in the background of her, watching. And eventually, she gets to the end and checks out, paying with a card, and the teenage bagboy says something and smiles to her, pleasant maybe even flirting, and Cal sees that she smiles back – a striking, gorgeous smile.

It begins in the corners of her eyes, a soft crinkle hinting, and then radiates out into the curve of her wine-red lips. Subtle dimples etch a presence on her cheeks like an artist's signature mark, making him feel almost dizzy with desire for her, his heartbeat slamming in his chest.

As she leaves the market, and the doors automatically initiate to her exit, remarkably something else catches Cal's eye. A very small thing, so quick that most would miss it.

His vision narrows.

Through a twist of fortune or inevitability, a piece of paper slips from her fingers in the gust of the twin doors opening. The paper drifts to the ground just behind her boots as she leaves.

Before he rushes to it, Cal looks around for anyone watching him like he's been watching her. After a moment, quietly assured nobody knows he exists (for once, welcomed), he walks to it and stoops, plucking the paper off the concrete.

A receipt, as insignificant as any other.

But not to him.

To him, a revelation.

Outside, the winter shimmers with promise as he ambles beneath the dense gray sky again, along the patches of icy pavement and through the frigid wind that's risen since he last left it. He's no longer cold in it, nor does he even feel it that much.

He simply stands, hands in his pockets, and waits.

A few minutes later, he sees the SUV emerge from the underground. The brake lights and the dark Range Rover merge onto the street at the far end of the block, turning out of view.

After a bit of time, he starts walking back in the direction of his tired flat, the opposite way, renewed vigor in his steps. Holding neither eggs nor milk, he keeps walking and stares down at the receipt, feeling a strange but punctuated sense of accomplishment.

Something he hasn't felt in a long time.

It's a strange thing. A sudden feeling that comes upon him, washing over like warm water, the risks and rewards of it all sinking in at last; the narratives he's been cultivating intertwined with these insights, his mind sifting through the millions of tiny events from the past hour.

Over and over again.

A strange thing – an electric feeling in his bones rising further up within him as he reads the neat impersonal print on the piece of paper – line by line, item by item.

Appearing at the bottom, most important of all, scrawled next to the asterisks of her obscured payment information, he finds what he wants – what he's been yearning for all these nights and days since he first laid eyes on her naked body through the window.

"Sarah Jones," he reads aloud.

5

It's Spring again.

The warm Dutch breezes rustle her fussed-over hair as Cal follows her out into the Keukenhof Gardens. The soft light catches the auburn strands as she leads the way into the colorful fields.

All as planned – make it last, now.

"This better be worth the fuss of dressing me up," she teases, gripping the ruffles of the dress to keep it above the wet grass. She can barely contain herself; he can tell.

She's really happy to be here. This is good.

"Get some pictures of me holding up the dress."

"I will," Cal replies, wearing his best suit. He surveys it. Not as wrinkled as it should be, considering its final, disheveled placement in his suitcase. "Trust me, there will be time for all that," he says.

The two of them pass the hedgeline and bank left into the fields with the long beds of tulips. Past the streams and along the curated pathway beside them. Then it opens into a clearing surrounded by flowers. Millions of them in every possible color he can conceive. So many bright sunny yellows, lively reds, and deep violet bulbs as far as the eye can see.

He hears her gasp as she takes it all in, and he smiles as he comes up beside her.

"You love it, then?" he asks, peering out across the tulips.

It's exactly as stunning as he'd hoped when planning this trip. How the pictures showed it. It's exactly as he wanted it to be.

She laughs at something, and he looks but can't see what it is.

That sound in her laughter, a fond joy he remembers. Her eyes sparkle when she looks back towards him.

"It's beautiful," she says and smiles, then keeps walking.

The air is warm, rich with the smells of the blooming flowers and her perfume as he follows her. Her dress sways as the breeze picks up.

"Well, come along babes," she commands. "You brought me, for this here, yes? So, let me stroll with you, sir."

A sense of peace overwhelms him.

A weight lifts from his shoulders.

Here it is. The moment. All coming to a head.

I'm doing this. I'm actually doing this.

Cal watches her, then reaches into his pocket, feeling the reassuring shape of the box as he has so many times over the past few hours of planes, trains, and automobiles. The anxiety of carrying it so far, finally lifting.

This is the moment he's been waiting for.

Cal walks towards Diane and she turns and smiles again at him, a beaming smile; the one he's adored most of his life, since meeting her all those years ago, the year before uni.

"Diane," he begins, his throat feeling like it has a pebble stuck in it, his face suddenly on fire. "I've never been more certain of anything in my life as I am with you..."

"Baby," she says, eyes narrowing, not understanding. "What are you doing?"

The air grows still between them.

He gets down on one knee and takes her hands into his, carefully looking up, his eyes moving to hers slow but steady. The weight of the moment presses. Nothing moves but the wind.

"Diane, will you marry me?" he at last asks.

"Will... I..." she stutters.

"Marry me?" he finishes.

The sunlight shifts and he squints and her eyes open with joy he thinks. But then something else, too.

He sees it. Something different. Fear, maybe.

She opens her mouth as if to respond and Cal feels her hands clench cold around his – painfully tight.

The air becomes icy, his breath biting in his lungs, appearing as a fog in front of him, and the flowers in the garden wither as if sped along the dial of the seasons at full speed. Thousands dying in seconds.

His heart races, a cold sweat descending over him, his head whipping around in each direction.

"What's happening?" she calls out, her hair rising behind her.

The grass and hedges and bulbs turn to ash. The sunlight falls away to a midnight black, a gaping sky above them. Her hands grow even colder, integuments hanging off his arms. Coiling then. Grasping him, her grip tightening. A pincer of crushing force.

"Let go! Let go of me!"

"I can't!" she screams, a terror in her voice, an echo of what it was moments before.

A chilly emptiness fills him to his core.

Not her voice. Something else.

Someone's...

She melts away, peeling off with the shrubs, the flowers, the gardens themselves, the remaining bulbs fettered to ash, withering upwards like burnt tissue paper.

"I can't now, I can't ever. You already know that. You know that..."

The ground beneath them gives way and he feels himself falling into it, sliding down where the world opens.

Nothing but air, the cool wind rising below him, gaining speed towards the end. An invisible ground races up from somewhere below like an ocean crashing against rocks. The ring slips from his grasp, falling away into the depths, swept from his fingers into the shadows. He reaches out, claws at the roots on either side of the chasm, scratching the soil for something, anything, grabbing out to break his fall.

But there is nothing out there. The ash tumbles in. The air becomes a whirlwind of sound.

He can't breathe in the soot falling around him. But he keeps falling deeper and deeper still. Into the dark. Spiraling into the endless hole. The freezing shadows devouring him. A voice echoes above in the black: "I can't now, I can't ever – I can't now, I can't ever –"

Cal awakes with a start, gasping for air, his heart pounding in his chest like a freight train.

He stares at the dark of his room, not comprehending.

"Shit," he sighs, breathing out at last, relief flooding in. His head swivels around. He realizes he is drenched in sweat even though his skin is cold with goosebumps, hairs on end.

"Christ," he mutters, rubbing his eyes. He gets up to dress, shivering, and moves to his closet then back to his bed.

Need to clear my head is all.

He pulls on some pants and socks, then finds a shirt on the floor nearby and pulls it on.

Too much. Way too much.

Moving quickly, he slips his shoes on by the foyer and throws on a coat.

"What time is it?" he asks nobody, realizing he's left his phone on the bedside table. He closes the door behind him without it, keys and smokes in hand.

As he steps onto the rooftop perch a minute or so later, the cold wind hits and he realizes that he's dramatically underdressed to be up here at this time of night. The last of the delirium sucks away as the cold ensnares him and he shivers.

Snow comes down sporadically in disparate pellets, and the rooftop has a thin blanketing layer of white and some dark patches of ice that he crunches around as he makes his way to the edge.

The night is quiet and he hugs the coat tighter around his body, glancing down at the streets below, and fishing out the lighter, striking a smoke to kindle. He coughs and breathes it in deep, realizing at once that he feels naked up here without the binoculars around his neck.

Against his will, his eyes wander, and he looks her way.

Up to the window. Nothing but dark glass.

Nothing to see anyways.

Cal takes another pull, staring at the windowpane. The smoke swirls up in the wind and snowflakes, and he says, "Who are you, Sarah?"

I mean – who are you really? What do you want?

Can I even help you?

The wind picks up and Cal curses under his breath and leans over the railing at the edge, staring out over the covered streets, cigarette shaking.

"What do I need?" he asks to no one.

If I'd just jumped that night... none of this would have changed...

So, what's stopping you? Why hesitate?

This cigarette, presently – I guess. Stupid.

Cal scoffs and pushes the notion from his mind.

"Nightmares at my age."

He rubs the bridge of his nose.

Stop and I won't have to jump maybe, he thinks.

Keukenhof of all places. Those tulips...

Will I ever forget her? Will I ever find peace in it?

After a moment or so, the icy chill seeps down deep into his bones and Cal flicks the half-burned cigarette over the ledge, and regrets smoking it in the first place, clearing his throat. He watches as it falls, counting the seconds until he thinks he sees it hit the pavement far below.

Could have been me.

"May still be," he mutters.

Feeling dizzy all of a sudden, he turns and heads back to his flat. As he opens the hatch, he gives her window one last look, whispering above the breeze: "Goodnight, Sarah."

The following morning, Cal meets with his manager for his monthly review and then gets his second refill of coffee, with a dash of brown sugar, as he likes it. The meeting doesn't exactly go well so it's going to be a different kind of day, he's determined in quiet rebellion.

Opening his browser incognito, he types: Sarah Jones, London.

Far too much comes back, as expected, and a few minutes later, feeling overwhelmed, he refines the search closer:

Sarah Jones Lewisham age 25 to 35.

Familiar articles. Older women, brunette women, women of different races. No one appearing like the woman he's seen.

Dating profiles. Some paywalled. Some silly influencer types.

None her. Nothing there.

He keeps searching.

Sarah Jones blonde - more dating profiles.

Social sites. Profile after profile. None her.

Unbelievable. Bloody common name, Sarah Jones.

He keeps looking, occasionally doing the odd work task here and there. A couple hours in, Andy pops his head over the cubicle.

"You good on last week's compliance reports?"

"All good," Cal says without looking up. "Sent."

"Just checking." And without missing a beat, leaning over further, he says, "Oy, anything fun planned this weekend?"

"No. Course not."

"Really? Come on mate. Give a little, no harm."

"It's Tuesday, Andy."

"No time like the present, right?" he says, looking around.

"Right," Cal replies, reading. "Right you are..."

Andy shrugs, "Well, I'll leave you be then. Seems you're in it today. Don't wish to distract, oh mighty one."

"Piss off," Cal replies, smiling.

"Alright," Andy chuckles.

"See you."

"Hey, wait," Andy says, turning around. "Doing anything for lunch?"

"Not today."

"Craving oxtail. Island spot round the way."

"Alright. Let me know how it goes..." Cal says, his mind elsewhere.

A suggestion appears in the search engine list that catches Cal's eye: Sarah Jones upcoming exhibit. He follows it and results flood in with articles about a gallery and reviews, a chorus of fuss describing an opening next year somewhere southwest of the city.

Cal leans in, clicking and reading and clicking, his eyes scanning for any new detail, any overlooked clue that will tie this artist and art dealer Sarah Jones to the Sarah he lives by.

Then he finds a mention of a previous studio in Wandsworth. Closed several years ago. Following the thread to an older news piece, a glowing review of the studio's opening around the time Cal first got his place with Diane.

A proclaimed haven for contemporaries: *a sanctuary of creativity, revitalizing a rougher section of Wandsworth...*

Below the segment, Cal finds a small grainy photo accompanying some text about the studio's old building interior, showcasing a group of artists standing proudly in front of the doors. HISTORY REIMAGINED FOR ARTISTS NEW AND OLD it says above.

He zooms in and his heart quickens, recognizing a younger Sarah among the couple dozen of them, her smile unmistakable, radiant as ever. Early twenties – a few years ago. She's holding a painting out in front of her. One of her own, evidently.

It captures his attention with its intense shading: a central figure shrouded in violet colors, the posture heavy, with a background of chaotic swirls - midnight blues, blacks and silvery grays. More violent streaks of crimson and gold lightning towards the top right, and on the other side, the direction the figure is walking, Cal sees bursts of light breaking through the painted storm clouds. Blending oranges and soft pinks, casting an outline around the despair of the figure. Flowers by the silhouette's feet.

"Gorgeous," Cal mutters looking at its artist.

"What's that?" Andy asks, popping his head back over.

"Oh," Cal says, startled. "Nothing... thought you'd left."

"Got yourself a lady there, Calvin, have we?" he asks, craning his neck around to view the monitor. Cal minimizes his browser.

"Driving me mad today."

"Alright, alright," Andy waves. "Your secrets are yours. I'll leave ya alone, mate."

When he's gone, Cal pulls up the tab and glances around before saving the photo, emailing it to himself along with a link to the site. A few minutes later, he finds a social media profile linked to the older studio webpage.

Ephemeral Canvas, it's called. What a name. Clicking it, he hits a privacy wall. Just a faded image of a colorful gallery, used as a background shot. Another dead end.

The website pages are shut down, too. Dead links –404.

Looks recently shut down, too. The plug just pulled.

Ephemeral Canvas yanked from the digital world.

Lunch comes and goes. His coworkers shuffle around. Some bring back food. Others go to meetings. Cal keeps searching. He doubles back and continues examining from the art angle.

Several mentions of her work in exhibits across London – a night here, a showcase there with some Shoreditch types; nothing tangible except the single old picture and mentions of a new place to come. No other photos.

He checks art schools next, from the most prestigious on down. No pictures to go on there either. Too many *Jones, S*'s to sift through. Compounding things is how overly vague the art websites are: haughty and secretive, as if purposely done. Just initials under pieces. Scarcely any artist information.

Cal refuses to be deterred – he keeps clicking, keeps reading.

Time flies by until finally, nearing the end of the day, his efforts bear some fruit. Returning to the previous searches, he finds a press release dated back to last fall, a few months before Cal first laid eyes on Sarah.

On first glance, it isn't much more than a statement that the building was under new ownership and was being renovated. But Cal missed the downloadable symbol on the first pass, and this time he clicks it.

Opening the file, the colorful brochure details the recent renovation of the old Wandsworth studio, praising its improvements and its coming new exhibit facilities with the expected eccentric detachment of an art investment group.

Cal checks the date. Nearly a couple years ago. He keeps reading. The following pages showcase paintings and sketches, as expected, but Cal's eyes narrow as he reaches the end of the statement, where a single line makes his blood run cold:

EPHEMERAL CANVAS GIVES SPECIAL THANKS TO OUR CONTINUED PATRON, DAVID JONES, PARTNER OF OUR SHOWCASED ARTIST SARAH, FOR RECENT CONTRIBUTIONS. WITHOUT YOUR GENEROSITY, WE WOULD NEVER ACHIEVE OUR LOFTY GOALS.

Cal scribbles *DAVID* on a sticky note, and then the address of the new studio renovation.

He looks around and suddenly becomes aware of how alone he is. The office is quiet and still. He collects his breath. After a moment, he powers down his computer, packs his things, and heads out.

Catching a different train, Cal makes the detour to the address on the way home, next taking a bus and then walking the rest of the way. About a half hour later he finds himself standing in front of an unlit modern three-story building, surrounded by caution tape.

There's no evidence of any gallery in the site's future, at least from what he can see outside of the construction blankets, tarps, and scaffolding.

What did I expect?

To see her working, hosting an auction?

Of course not. It's closed.

Under renovation another couple months, at least.

He takes it all in and after a few minutes makes his way back through the dim and the cold rain to the Tube.

It's not much, but it's something – the monster has a name.

Two days later it's early evening and Cal gets home exhausted after a grueling day at the office, making up for his procrastination with some overtime towards a client deadline. Far more stressful than necessary, the crunch of it, but he's righted the scales and paid for his sins.

Stepping off the lift, he opens the door to the overpriced, slightly dingy flat, and he's met by the same thick solitude, the same messy diminutive space as always, and he trudges in, casting off essentials and kicking the door closed behind him. Rather than turning any lights on or going to the kitchen and grabbing his dinner from the fridge as usual, he trudges to his room and collapses on the bed, his computer case falling to the floor.

He stares at the ceiling above, feeling numb with exhaustion.

In the muted light, and the quiet and stillness, his thoughts weigh on him, pressing him deeper and deeper into the mattress.

The room's darkness feels like a cloak, both suffocating and protecting, and his mind anguishes and fusses it over.

There, in the dissonance of these ideas and feelings, desires overlapping and screaming their summaries in his mind, one image alone pushes its way to the forefront, breaching the surfaces beyond the noise.

He sees it close.

The seductive pull of her imagined embrace, him drowning in the scent of her perfume, the lilac and jasmine, his tongue running along her skin, and the sensation of her breath brushing against his neck. The smell and taste of her.

Maddening, the thrillful buzz of it, sensations, imaginings as vivid as reality...

The feeling of her pressing her lips into his, his hands tracing the curve of her shoulders and hips, fingers grazing over the expanses of skin he's observed only from a distance, but not now – not here in the darkness with her hungry eyes staring back and the gold strands of her hair pouring out between his fingers as he leans in, gentle at first, and tastes her tongue striking his...

Sarah...

In the room's hush, he undoes his pants, each of these visions repeating and expanding: the fevered aching wants... the imagined softness and yearning...

And then, quickly, a light shines behind his eyelids, flashing in the window from the outside. The disturbance of it shatters his inner fantasy like a rock through a glass window. He lets go of himself and the moment passes.

He opens his eyes, a trickle of shame welled in the place where her vision resided moments ago.

What was that? Did I imagine it?

Curiosity overriding sensation, he stands and pulls his pants up and moves to the bedroom window. He looks down at his familiar street, before turning his attention to Sarah's living room.

So instinctively peering there now... What the hell?

His eyes open wide, astounded to see all the lights on, glowing through the drawn-back curtains.

Oh my God!

His mind jolts into overdrive. He scrambles.

With hurried steps, Cal puts his jacket and shoes back on and races to his office, his fingers pulling open the drawer and wrapping around the binoculars strap, before bounding out of the flat, not bothering to lock the door behind him.

It's as if she wants me to watch her – as if she's telling me to come.

"Come on, come on," he says, tapping his foot impatiently in the lift.

The doors open, and he squeezes through before they do fully. Then he's up the ladder – a dozen rungs – and through the rooftop hatch as he's done so many times before, on all the other nights, but never quite this quickly, with this much urgency.

Each step on the rooftop feels both too slow and too hurried, racing time and his spiraling wonder, while also wanting to not give himself away like a careless fool.

He reaches the ledge and the wrought iron railing at last.

He spots the outlined silhouettes of two people stepping from the window's view. Raising the binoculars, he pulls the lenses to his eyes, focusing on the golden-lit penthouse, its luminescence stark and warm, distinguished against the winter air.

As it's always been. Since first seeing her there.

He finds the drawn open curtains in his view and then pulls the zoom back to see the entirety of the room.

The room is empty, but along a polished wall Cal can see shadows moving like wraiths, pointing at each other, pacing – ghoulish figurines.

Moments pass.

Then, Sarah emerges into his view, her face flushed.

Cal holds his breath.

She's wearing exercise attire, perhaps just getting home. He watches her as she faces the glass before swiftly turning back in the direction that she just came from. Her hair is pulled in a ponytail, and she moves taut with defiance, the tension fixed into every line of her back. She appears to be yelling at the man, pressing her thumb into her chest, then jerking her hands violently down to her side, fists clenching. Cal sees her scream something at him, and he thinks he can see that she's crying.

Then the man comes into view of the windowpane and Cal finally gets a good look at him, and he sees the twinkle of a gold band when the man points at her.

Was she wearing one in the market? Wouldn't I have noticed?

No, she wasn't wearing one.

I would have, certainly...

Cal focuses on him. The cobalt hue of his suit contrasts sharply with the soft tones of the room, and that jacket, with its sharp lapels and polished buttons, clings neatly to his torso, hinting at the broad-shouldered athletic build beneath. His shirt is a crisp white, punctuated by a thick, blue, meticulously knotted tie that cascades down his chest.

David.

His imposing ensemble coupled with his slicked-back hair and square-jawed countenance oozes calculated dominance, and Cal sees him yell something at Sarah, taking a step forward. She then screams something back and points at what looks like the foyer. The man shakes his head, making a dismissive gesture, and all at once he moves around the couch towards her.

Cal's breath catches in his throat as he sees Sarah stiffen, every fiber of her bracing for the blow. And then, with an abruptness that makes Cal lurch his focus, the man's hand cups behind Sarah's neck, just below her hairline, and pivoting he slings her straight into the floor.

She lands beside the couch's leg, her face turning sharp to the side as she hits the marble. It looks like her forehead misses the corner of the tinted glass coffee table by inches. The man continues yelling at her, pointing, and Cal aims the binoculars at Sarah and sees her push herself to her feet, a sudden burst, and in a rush her hand darts to the table and her fingers wrap around the crystalline bowl.

She appears to scream something, and when the man steps forward at her again, fists clenched, she reacts by hurling the crystal at his face.

Time seems to stretch as the bowl sails through the air.

But her aim falters, or perhaps he sidesteps in time because the bowl sails past and crashes into the black piano at the end of the room.

Cal sees its ruin erupt in all directions, scattering shards across all the segments of the penthouse floor, each at last coming to rest and glittering beneath the chandelier's light.

For a moment, Cal feels like he's in the room with them, his bones frozen just as Sarah's are. There's a chilling stillness.

Then like a predator leaping at her, the man rushes forward, and Sarah scrambles out of the window's view. The man follows, and for several desperate moments, both invisible, Cal watches – harshly gripping the binoculars, zooming in, and darting out.

"Come on, come on. Where the hell are you?"

The stillness pervades, and just as Cal determines he's going to get his phone and dial the police, the man returns into view. He crosses in front of the window and walks to the piano, using a sleeve to brush glass from the top of it. He seems enraged, swiping at pieces like hornets, and then kicks more glass away from the piano.

Turning back around, he stares at the tall windowpane for a second, then punts a shard across the floor towards the base of the couch. He then walks back to the window and abruptly leans into it, cupping his hands over his eyes to block out the living room light, his silhouette suddenly becoming dark.

"Shit!"

Instinctively Cal ducks, his heart pounding against his ribcage, the cold gravel of the rooftop seeping into his knees and hands. The world shrinks down to only his breathing – in and out, in and out.

Did he see me?

He counts upwards, and after a couple of minutes, peeks up over the ledge. The penthouse's lights are out now, a void against the city's surrounding nightscape. However, this time around, unlike all the other nights when the pane is black, something looks different. It takes Cal far too long to realize what's changed, but when he does, a chill creeps up his spine.

The curtains are still open.

He ducks his head down below the ledge.

The feeling of dread envelops him more than any suspicion, starting in his gut and teeming outwards. The prickle of someone's unseen gaze ambushing him with primal, urgent warnings; the intensity magnifying each passing second.

He hesitates but then, slowly again, crouching, he peers over the ledge again.

Through the darkness, Cal feels a tethering to the man in the shadowed penthouse window – each aware of the other staring back.

Each dissecting for the other.

And then the thoughts hit him in menacing charges:

I'm no longer the only watcher here.

Someone else is looking back – I am out of time.

7

The buildings appear like pale sentinels above him as Cal glances up, ensuring nobody is awake and watching. Beneath the fog, dodging the uncaring deathly green lights of the lampposts, he starts out, enmeshing himself as low in the gloom as he can.

He moves slow, clinging to the corners of the courtyard. Creeping his way out of his building complex and crossing the quiet street, then pausing at the other side, staying in the shadows, checking his watch and listening.

Nothing moves.

Some of the adjacent tired lamps have already switched off with the encroaching dawn. He moves around the parked cars, shadow to shadow, getting closer. A cat scurries by, startling him. He waits a moment and keeps going. Along the side of the building, maneuvering around the hedged and gated partition which sits a dozen feet high between his building and Sarah's, the sharp points strutted upward like the menacing spikes of one of the castles he visited on school trips.

He moves into the position he's planned for the past few hours.

Slowly, carefully, Cal reaches the unlit corner beside the ramp to the garage doors.

At last, he sighs in relief, then listens again, holding his breath. He hears nothing at all. Nothing but the whistling of the chilly breeze and the low urban serenade of distant highways.

So far, so good.

Her pristine building lays silent in the frozen morning air. Gradually, dawn's light spreads, and he sits and waits.

Nothing else to do except wait and listen. He checks his watch again. Ten 'til five.

The idea had occurred to him when he got back to his flat, hours ago, thinking about Sarah's husband – or whoever he is – and moreover, the kind of clothes he wears. With social media and online searches turning up nothing besides the gallery's mention, it's all he has to go on – the man's expensive suits. Every time Cal sees him, he wears the same gaudy ensemble. That material, that fit, easily more luxurious than anything Cal can afford on his salary. A cost that only the elite can carelessly stomach at quantity. The kind of people who donate to gallery restorations, no surprise.

And Cal has now seen this man in several suits of such caliber. Who knows how many he really has. The tailored jackets, the arrogantly sharp lapels, the seams of the trousers ending just above the polished, likely Italian, leather shoes. It all screams Jermyn or Mayfair.

And so, the assumption is he's either a corporate attorney or some kind of a wheeler-dealer – maybe a Lombard Street broker, or some Canary Wharf finance exec. A white-collar wolf, whatever it may be, making the trek daily to hunting grounds downtown, then returning at night, laying his head just outside the maelstrom of proper London. Bringing his violence back on Sarah.

Whatever this man does, whatever the case may be, his habitually worn power suits voice he more than likely doesn't come from immense wealth, but rather works for it. The way he flaunts himself all but proves this theory. He's forsaken much getting here, whatever that may be. Maybe even gladly so, and even if it all begins with his privileges – affording him the fancy education that sprung him up the ravenous ladder where he currently resides – he still requires the suit to make it real. Make it feel like permanent power, reminding him of his excellence. Reminding him of the distance he's exceeded ahead.

And all this likely means that this man, this abusive monster of a man, is a stratum of man who probably rises early, quite early perhaps – a habit born more out of desire than obligation.

Out for blood and glory, all before the rest of the world even has their sugar-laden caffeinated swill of choice.

The kind of man who makes it a point to get to the office before the sun gets above the horizon, and hopefully, as such, will be leaving his fancy penthouse and driving to work soon, even earlier than most others so he can beat traffic on the A20.

If I were that kind of man, that's what I'd do.

And Cal thinks about this momentarily, huddled in the shadowed well, sitting and waiting for the slightest noise from the heavy garage door.

What kind of man am I?

Do I even know?

Do I even want to know?

The kind that nearly throws himself off a building to start with... the kind that had it coming, and the kind who didn't even see it until it was impossible not to see... sprinting headlong into it... into the heartbreak.

That one terrible morning...

Cal recalls the joy bubbling within him, months ago. His boss summoning him in...

The director of the department, a guy named Mike Rollins: a hard-nosed man who's borne a palpable grudge against Cal since his onboarding; a penchant for exacting his demands on Cal and his coworkers during frequent mood swings. But not this day...

Instead, he surprised Cal in the best of ways, calling him into his office via Janice, who at that time was his administrative assistant.

"The quarterly numbers are in," the pudgy man said matter-of-factly, sitting behind his massive desk and looking Cal over in his usual, critical way.

"Not going to draw it out. Your team has exceeded all expectations. Amazing, I know. Look, it's against better judgment, all judgement perhaps, but with performance goals like these exceeded, it'll bring morale low if I sit on my hands. However much I'd like to, to be frank. So, cutting to it, I'm working on getting bonus checks from corporate. For you and the other blokes. A bonus - for good work. Job well done."

"Wow, fantastic!" Cal responds. "Thank you, sir."

"Oy," the man raises his palm, "I said I'm going to try. No guarantees. Right? We'll see what they say. Still, no matter the outcome or how that scuffle goes, see, I'd like to show my appreciation today for you and the lads. Log off and let the rest have the day off. Okay? I'll see you lot on Monday."

"Sir, you sure?" Cal asks.

"Don't look a gift horse in the mouth. Get out of here."

And so, Cal did that. Not another hesitation. Just a quick thank you and he's walking as fast as he could back to his cubicle.

Returning to his sub-habitat corner of the large office, the half-dozen men and women of his team soon were jubilated with the news. And a few minutes later, Cal clinked coffee mugs with the rowdy few packing up, each giving silly toasts to the others in turn. And on the way out of the office, someone proposed getting real drinks, some well-earned pints, but Cal declined them. He was eager to share the news with Diane and to find a fancy place to take her out to eat for a celebratory dinner.

The promise of an unexpected afternoon together felt like an exquisite gift.

Racing to the station, he was able to catch the eleven-fifteen train going south.

Unlocking their shared flat an hour later, he was met with the unmistakable sounds of Diane's moaning and a dawning horror overtaking him. He dropped his bag and the bouquet he'd purchased at the atrium, pushing the bedroom door ajar.

The scene cut into him like a dagger slipped between the grooves of his ribcage – a scene he'll never outrun.

Never be able to forget.

His feet stuck to the floor, his body frozen in place, all the air locked in his throat. Paralyzed.

The sheer normalcy of the room: the sunlight streaming through the half-drawn blinds, the scattered clothes reminiscent of their own many mornings together — all making the betrayal that much more piercing as Cal's eyes finally comprehend the scene in front of him: her shoulders quivering up and down, wildly, the sheets pushed off.

The way she cried out, her auburn hair disheveled. The way she was so delirious that she didn't have any idea that he was standing there, a couple meters away, until after she finished, rolling over.

The moment their eyes connected that morning.

God, that stung.

Cracked something deep inside your skull that day. Something you can never unbreak. Questions you'll never answer.

The unanswered questions that haunt him.

The ones following him to the rooftop in the dead of the night, lingering behind his eyelids in bed, sitting beside him each day at work or on the train. Questioning every moment shared, every whispered promise, every unanswered detail that may have been a clue.

How did I not see it?

How was it so easy for her?

Did she ever see this version of you? Did she ever think you could be someone like this? Confronting a man like you are about to, a man like this? This malignancy of a man...

The horizon begins to smolder, and the dark tapestry of the night gently unravels in the sky, and from the shadowed alcove, Cal sees the thinnest streaks of gold and fiery yellow pierce through the eastern clouds. He sighs.

Or did she only know the version of you who shied away from everything; who sought refuge in his home almost every minute he wasn't at work or commuting, too scared to really connect with – or contend with – anyone, least of all her?

No matter how much I wished for it to be different.

To be better. To be more. Was that all she ever saw in you?

And did you ever see her either?

Is that even possible, truly, for anyone to do?

Even after years together?

Deepest attractions, aversions, secret sins. All the thousand quiet infidelities committed with eyes alone – dancing day to night, place to place – across rooms to other eyes that don't belong to them, yet whose shine back just the same.

Do we really belong to anyone, or do we simply rely on them, our chosen other, in little and big ways – hour by hour, night by day – biding our time? Waiting for something more. Anything...

Seeing what we want to see. Hearing what we want to hear.

Before he can consider this, at once, Cal's thoughts are interrupted by a sound, and he jolts back to the present.

A metal clinking; a chain being pulled.

A surge of adrenaline hits his bloodstream. Scrambling to his feet, he readies himself.

After a moment, the garage door peels off the ground and Cal waits with bated breath, the weight of his decision bearing down heavily. His tired eyes fix intently on the door, waiting for the unmistakable hood of the Range Rover to emerge from the confines of the building. Every inch of his body tingles in anticipation, every muscle coiled and tense.

I hope I'm right about him.

His mind focuses, feeling hyperalert. Beneath it all rests a burning anger, a rage fueled by the repeated horrors he's seen – the senseless pain this man dispels on Sarah, the fear.

For what?

Does it even matter?

Of course it doesn't. He's got to pay. And now he will.

Then, he hears it, the roar of the five hundred horsepower engine, and the dark Range Rover emerges up the ramp, its headlights cutting through the morning fog like the beacons of a lighthouse.

Cal takes a deep breath, hunches over, and breaks out in a jog right toward where the ramp meets the street. As he approaches, he sees the car coming into view, and Cal picks up his pace, the vehicle's approach feeling almost cinematic, every detail magnified – the tinted windows, the spinning rims, the glint off its dark, recently polished surfaces...

Just at the moment the SUV slows to take a left onto the street, its blinker engaged, Cal slams into the passenger side of it.

He strikes the door with a very loud thud and takes the brunt of the force in his shoulder before falling back into the concrete. The car jams on its brakes before the echo of the impact has even faded in the quiet street.

The driver's door swings open with urgency, leather soles hitting the pavement, and the man that Cal has seen attack Sarah comes around to the front of the vehicle, his face pale, focusing on the front of the car before his eyes narrow over the hood, spotting Cal further back.

He moves through the headlights, his suit looking almost jet black in the beams. His face twists into a mix of surprise and rage as he comes around to the other side of the car and sees the dent in the door's metallic frame.

"What in the hell is the matter with you? Huh? And don't even think to say I hit you, you little twat. I was going straight, this dent's on the side. So don't you dare. Now, what's the meaning of this?" he bellows at him as Cal staggers up to his feet.

"Look at this," the man exasperates, gesturing to the door panel. "Are you bloody kidding me? Speak, goddamn you! Why the fuck did you hit my car?"

Cal's hand goes to his pocket, trying to summon up some semblance of courage.

"Well? the man growls. "Anything?"

Finally, Cal finds the words, and once they start, he can't stop their outpour:

"I've seen what you do to your wife. To Sarah. The way you hit her," he begins.

"Wha -" the man starts. But Cal doesn't give him a chance.

"Chasing her. Terrifying her. It needs to stop. You need to stop. You fucking hear me? You're fucked in the head, mate. Now. Listen. Leave her the hell alone. You hear me?"

Cal watches him. Silence pervades between them.

It feels like the fuse of a bomb has been lit linking the two men and all that's left to do is watch it spark down to the explosive.

A moment passes before, at last, slowly, a sneer forms across the suited man's face: a look of pure contempt so familiar to Cal – having experienced it most of his life across a great many faces – that there's no mystery at all in its malice.

"You have some nerve, you know that? Who the hell do you think you are telling me what I can and cannot do with my own wife? Huh? Hey – she's my wife. Not yours. I can beat her black and blue if I damn well choose, and it'll be no matter to you, now will it? Not that any of the rubbish you say is true. But what is, is I saw you on the rooftop last night – up there, that's right," he nods towards Cal's building, "Up there – and you know I did, don't deny it. You little, sceeving fucking peeper, you. And now, here you are again, running into my bloody car – another matter entirely. Childish little bastard aren't you? Look at you. Don't suppose a bottom dweller sort like you has any insurance now, to sort this out, do you? I'll have my –"

"Oh, for godsakes, just shut the fuck up already," Cal interjects, his heartbeat quickening, his face feeling flushed. The man stares aghast, clearly not accustomed to this kind of treatment, perhaps ever.

Cal looks him straight in the eye.

"Hey, listen," the man snarls, pointing a meaty finger, "You don't get to talk to me that way, you hear me? Now, stop. You don't want to be talking to me like that. We can work this out cordial-like. You ca-"

"I'll say whatever the hell I want to you, you inflated, imbecilic, entitled prick," Cal exclaims. "What, you think, because you go to the gym, because you lift some heavy weights, suddenly it's okay to go around beating your wife – hurting Sarah, that it?"

"How the hell do you know her name?" the man snaps.

"That doesn't matter. I know yours too, David. David the domestic abuser."

Cal sees by the reaction in the man's brow that the name fits the culprit.

"Point is, it isn't okay. Got me? And I'm watching your abusive ass now. And fuck your stupid car too. It's a heap of shit gas-guzzler, you know it, and so do I," Cal nods at the dent in the door, enjoying it a bit now. "Only a tacky, larping asshat like yourself would be caught driving something like this around a metropolitan fucking city – a ludicrously priced, offroad vehicle like that, give me a laugh, for the commute to London? You're a joke. Nothing special about you. Least of all, this heap. But the dent's all right, I'll say, to that end. Personality, we can call it – make up a story for it. You're probably not too bad at that either, considering what you do to Sarah's face on a nightly basis. Must require lots of lies. Lying should come naturally. Nice work, wife-beater. So, fuck your car..."

Cal's voice feels like it's coming from someone else: a thrilling, daring energy he hasn't felt before. His heart is a runaway train.

The man's icy blue eyes harden, and Cal knows he's hit some mark. Looking at him squarely, directly into his eyes, Cal continues:

"And, most of all, you lowlife in a suit, listen to me cause this next part's crucial..."

Emphasizing each word as he says it, Cal raises a middle finger: "Fuck. You. Too."

No sooner are the words escaping his mouth than the man lunges towards him like he's lost his mind, his heels smacking the cobbles in strides, closing the distance with a predatory swiftness so fast that Cal scarcely gets the canister out of his pocket in time.

David springs forward to grab him, his hand outstretched, and in that moment as planned, Cal shoots him in the face with the mace and the acrid spray streams towards the man's eyes. He shrieks out and his voice bounces off the buildings around them. And then, incredibly fast, the man twists and swings a fist half-blindly, and the sharp punch lands, connecting with a snap into Cal's jaw and sending him staggering back.

The pain radiates up through his head like he's been run over by a truck.

"I'm going to fucking pummel you!" David shrieks, and presses his advantage, his eyes squinting through the swelling, and Cal tries to retaliate, pulling up the fetid bottle again and blurrily aiming at his approach, but the man sidesteps this next shot and counters with a brutal combination of body hits to Cal's torso.

Maybe he hits more than the gym and Sarah, Cal thinks.

Maybe... he fights...

Each strike is like a sledgehammer and the air refuses to come back to Cal, and the cold ground meets his face as his balance is kicked out from under him. Then another blow catches him in the cheek and his face strikes the pavement.

He feels the man roll him over, his weight pressing down on his chest, hands moving around his throat, squeezing.

Cal tries to squirm, to move upwards, to resist the tightening grip, but his fingers won't seem to obey. He tries to cough, but nothing rises from his chest, just a feeling of cold finality in the emptiness of his body.

The emptiness of the streets. His consciousness drifts ... standing up... battered ... then another punch lands, almost abstract in its crashing connection to his face, and the pain becomes a haze, surreal, and the world around him spins with unlit edges – but somehow, he holds on, his fingers gripping outwards for anything. He hears a pattern of footsteps, distant-like, far away.

A voice. Someone cursing, slamming something metal. The gliding sound of heaviness, rolling. Drifting. Farther from him.

He holds his ribs, and his diaphragm spasms – no air, his body weakening all over. The pit of his chest burning, molten pain. His throat filled with shards of glass.

Somewhere, deep down in a separate place in his mind, he finds and clings to her – some part of her. A naked silverish form: a specter, gazing back at him. Bemused. Diane... Sarah. Someone...

Gradually, one bit at a time, he feels his misery rush into the hole where she's fading. The absurdity of it all. A wave. Repeating – rinsing. Slapping into the current of his bloodstream.

In and out – in and out.

And in that moment her silver form vanishes entirely into the dark and the sadness in his chest bursts through like the splitting of a great dam.

Freezing air rushes into him, his lungs starved and coughing. Rolling to his side, the copper taste of blood finds his lips and he gasps the first rays of dawn.

8

The blood lingers in his mouth no matter how much he drinks. He takes another sip.

Overcast light filters through the dusty windows, highlighting patches of his bruised and bloodied face in the harsh clarity of the midmorning. He wishes they would close the damn shudders. He wishes for the dull thumping in his head to stop.

Cal slumps over the mahogany bar in the Old Hound pub. His ribs throbbing with every breath. Every cough. Every lift of the glass.

It could be worse. He could have killed me, he thinks.

He nurses his fourth whisky, staring at the tawny liquor for a few minutes before bringing the glass to his lips again and down again in one swift gulp.

"And how many is that?" Karalana asks, rounding the corner at the far end of the room, appearing slightly shocked, maybe even worried, to see him here.

She's wearing her usual get-up. A button-up uniform with the hound's face on the back and rolled up sleeves so her works of art are on display – the colorful tattoos adorning every inch of her arms, wrists to shoulders. She has her dreads up and is in cleaning mode, gloves on, clearly expecting an empty pub.

"Morning, Karalana... another please, and can you, maybe, close that window, please?" Cal asks. "The light is... killing... my head..."

Ignoring him, she stoops and opens a package under the sink. She pulls up a bottle of cleaning product and sprays, then wipes down the bartop nearest her.

"You're a headache, know that?"

"Come on, Karalana. I'm polite about it."

"Morning to you, too. Early, isn't it?" she asks.

"Yeah. Well. First of everything. Never known you here this time neither..."

"It's mornings now for a few weeks," she replies. "Classes started. Freddy's back. Takes Laney to school... Bloody hell – wow."

She stares at him.

"Yeah?"

"You look terrible, man. Long night?" she asks.

"Long, you could say that" Cal replies, his stiff bloody eyelids awakening wider. He touches his face, tapping his fingers on the swellings.

"Ice?"

"Sure. How bad?" he mumbles.

Karalana wraps some ice in a serviette and hands it to him.

"Like you've been through hell," she replies with warmth, glancing at him and then motions to the bottles. "Can't you see the mirror there? Horrific man."

"Was trying not to look. The window closing would help," Cal says.

"Demanding," Karalana retorts. "Not touching the windows. Got to see what I'm doing. Listen. I'll call you a ride."

"No. Another drink, Karalana. Come on now. Live across the street, you know."

"It's middle of the morning, you know?" Karalana retorts. "Just past ten."

"You said it. Isn't this a pub?" Cal waves around him, his bloodied hand shaking.

"It is... You sure?"

"Yes," he says. "Doing much better here. One more."

"Finale," she sighs. "That's it."

Karalana pours the smallest splash of Jameson into a glass and takes a full look at him.

"You're bleeding all over my bar, y'know man. Look at you." She tosses him another serviette as she gives him the drink. "Who served you so many this early anyways?"

"David."

"Who?" she scrunches her face. "Lori, you mean? This morning?"

"Helped me off the road. Let me come in – unlocked it. After him. Kind of her."

"Great, so the bar owner pours a bottle down your throat," Karalana says, rolling her eyes, cursing the woman. She prints Cal's tab then leans in. "Well, she had the good sense to ring it in anyways."

"Of course," Cal says, burping. "Sorry. I told her on you."

"And what happened to you worthy of her pity, then?" Karalana asks, looking at the bruised patches on his face. "Well? Aren't you going to tell me?"

"What do you mean by that?" he asks, sipping.

"Someone had their way with your face, Cal. Obviously, man. Must have done something special, right? Said something wrong to someone nasty?"

Cal takes a long sip, wincing as the alcohol burns his throat.

"Just... ran into a bit of trouble is all. Defending someone."

"Unlike you," she says without missing a beat. "And do I know the bastard?"

"Doubtful," Cal slurs back. "Too prim for the likes of... here, this."

"Idiot," she groans. "Anything else to tell?"

Karalana waits but when nothing arrives, Cal just sipping and watching her through swollen eyelids, she doesn't press. Time ticks by.

"You know, you used to tell me stories about your family. Right?" she asks after a spell.

"Yeah, I remember."

"Well, you were always sad and it cheered you up. Round Christmas time, remember?"

"Sure. Bits. Bad timing... blurry."

"So, tell me something then. Since you won't tell me about the fight. If you're going to haunt my morning, that is."

"Tell you... what?" Cal asks, touching his cheeks carefully.

"A story. Like the one with your dog. What was his name?" she asks, grasping for anything to crack his walls and alleviate her boredom. She wipes down more of the bar.

"A dog?"

"The dog you had. The little dog you told me about. Killing me, Cal. Come on."

She keeps wiping.

"Nelson?" Cal asks, a bitter smile pulling at his lips. "Lord Nelson ran away, far away, and Evan blamed me... told you this. Said I left the bloody gate open. That's the story. That what you mean?"

"Right. That's the one, I suppose."

"Well, not much to it. Even though I didn't do that. Never did that. Aunt believed him, course, never believed me – then gave me the shoulder. He never told her either. Never said sorry. And you know what?"

"What?" Karalana asks. "New dog?"

"No. No. Didn't let me go to the seaside, cause of that. Was the end of the year, everyone going, but nope. Not me. Cause Evan lied. Cause Evan lied about me... Why? Tell me why."

"Siblings, I got ya," Karalana shakes her head, "I've got some too. And the fight this morning?"

"No, you don't see it," Cal says, taking a sip – missing the bait entirely. "If I'd gone, I wouldn't have met Diane... at all. It was that summer. Staying in town. I could have gone another way. Could have been at the beach. Could have saved myself... her bullshit... her trauma... Swam out and avoided it, like."

"That's reaching a bit, Cal... enough about her anyways, bloody sick of it man, heard enough," Karalana says, raising her hand. "And the other thing. The fight? What happened there? Your face. Who did that?"

"Dog wasn't that bad," Cal mutters, lost in thought. Karalana rolls her eyes. He continues – "Came back, months later. Someone fed it. Kept it the summer. Then I guess he got out one night while I was away at school. Couple, some... well, months later. Never came back... Probably dead to be honest."

"Cal, you're a mess. Forget the stupid, bloody dog. Are you going to tell me about the fight or what?"

"No. You asked me about the stupid dog, I'm telling you about Nelson."

"That's not a good story," Karalana sighs, wiping down the last of the bar, then throwing the rag in the sink. "Come on man, let me call you a car. Don't you have a job you're missing today?"

"Called in, off. Obviously. Look at me."

He points, and looks at himself in the mirror, slightly horrified at the person staring back.

"Well, you're cut. Cut before ten-fifteen," she says. "A feat you shouldn't brag about, man. Bit of advice. Mums the word here, okay? But you're cut."

"Alright, cut, got you," Cal slurs, and finishes his drink in a single gulp and pushes himself away from the bar, standing slow, holding on like he's on the deck of a ship in rough seas. Then, fidgeting in his jacket pockets, he pulls out some bills, and after crudely counting, leaves far too many notes on the counter.

"See you Karalana. I'll head out. Walk it home."

"You sure?"

"Sorry about... the mess," Cal says. "Morning mess..."

"Not like me to have to worry for you," Karalana replies, her eyes concerned. "Worrying me, really, all of this."

"Well, sorry. And the windows – that was demanding. Bit demanding of me."

"Just get home safe. No pitstops."

"Right," Cal slurs back. "Okay."

"Hey. Wait," Karalana calls after him, putting down the glass she's drying and grabbing the wad of cash a moment later. "Your change?"

"Quid for... the tattoo fund," he says, running his hand on his arms, "...the next one, meaning."

She grins and waves him off, "Go get some sleep. Shine the light in your flat when you're home so I know you got there."

"I'll send a postcard," he mutters, waving back.

"Drink some water too," she says before disappearing behind the bar and Cal stumbles out of the pub into the drizzled gray morning. Cars whiz along the streets and people splash through the puddles hurriedly; the world is set to a different clock than him.

Pulling his coat tighter, ignoring the pain, he ambles his way down the causeway towards his flat.

His mind drifts as he goes, eventually settling back on that day he first met Diane, the summer that began with a lie years ago.

Sneaking away with her to a park during a day out with friends. The two of them, kissing under a blanket for minutes that seemed like an eternity. So new and overwhelming. Shimmering, the beginning of something.

Something all wrong.

Crossing the street, Cal slips on the wet pavement, teetering, righting himself at the last second. A car leans on its horn, blaring, and his skull feels like absolute mash. People give him a wide berth as he moves sloppy through the crowd, their eyes darting away as they catch the state of him and the smell of booze.

Hesitating, he then stops by the corner mart on the other side of his building. He squints, the fluorescent lights beaming down harsh against his assaulted skin and bloodshot eyes. He tries to not crowd anyone and waits his turn, quiet, and then buys a bottle of midgrade scotch, the cashier not hiding his contempt as he looks down at him from behind the glass. The man says nothing and takes Cal's money.

"It's Lewisham – piss off," Cal rasps at him as he leaves, the bell on the door ringing. The man curses something back at him in a language Cal doesn't understand. He shrugs it off.

A few minutes later, riding the lift to his flat, his thoughts shift back again to his aunt. His teenage years. The stern woman who never gave him the benefit of the doubt, believing whatever nonsense Evan would come up with.

Lie after bullshit lie. On repeat.

Why did Karalana even ask me about that?

Why even ask about my brother's bullshit?

Not her business.

Almost absently, Cal opens the bottle before he gets into his flat, taking a long swig as he pulls his keys out.

Numb that deep. "To Nelson, the first casualty," he says to nobody.

Inside finally, he opens a cupboard and takes out a glass. The ice cubes clink and he pours a proper drink. Three, no, four fingers.

Who's driving? Don't even own one, constable.

He presses a bag of frozen peas against his face, the cold numbing the pain almost as much as the scotch.

Another gulp down and he feels calmer at last. Warmer.

A half hour or so passes – pacing, sitting, listening to music. One record, then another. One skips and he tosses it across the room, watching it break against the wall, shattering to pieces, and he laughs like a maniac.

He bandages his cuts crudely, leaving bloodstains here and there – the counter, the sink, the fridge. Another half hour passes. Maybe more time than that. Losing track now. Where's the day gone?

Eventually, the record skips over and over and he pulls the needle off, then pours another glass and thinking of his brother feels a compulsion to find his knife, the one given to him.

He searches through drawers, pulls things out throughout the office, nearly giving up before blurrily catching sight of its handle on his living room bookshelf. He grabs it and pulls it out with a flick of the wrist, the Damascus steel glinting in the light of the room, and then – losing grip – he drops it by mistake and the knife clatters down and misses the center of his foot by an inch or so, sticking into the floor.

"Christ!" Cal swears, and stumbles back. He suddenly feels sick.

Abandoning the knife, he staggers around and puts the glass down and takes hold of an arm of the couch, wincing, then pushes it out into the center of the room. Standing straight, he pauses and then curses, unable to stop it from coming... running to the kitchen...

He throws up in the bin and after a few minutes of retching and coughing, returns and lies down on the floor. Beneath the drafty windows, looking up towards Sarah's curtains.

Up, far above. There it is. "Fifteen," he mutters.

Listening to the rain's patter. Watching the drops slide down.

"Failed," he murmurs out loud. To whom, he isn't sure.

He closes his eyes at last, his vision rotating black.

Old wounds, painful wounds, reopened, and far newer ones too. Out there. Spinning adrift behind his eyelids. Down and downward still, twisting to a place of no dreams at all.

9

It's a couple days before Valentines when amid the dark, almost spectral glow of his bathroom, all the lights turned off, Cal sees Diane's face reappear in front of him.

He stops scrolling.

His fingers hesitate on the lone light in the room: his device floating above the steaming water.

I shouldn't. I really shouldn't.

But he can't resist. He clicks into the profile anyway.

Shadows play across his face, the hollowed pits of his eyes and the bruising that frames them. And there, dancing on the screen, is Diane – his Diane, her hand held high by a tanned shirtless guy wearing an island outfit. Straw hats, smoking joints. A sunset.

Her with empty drink glasses and rowdy friends for New Years, out by the South Bank in a slim, sparkling dress. A gorgeous dress on her.

His mouth goes sour.

I shouldn't be looking at this. This won't do me any good at all.

Another encircled by friends, some of whom Cal recognizes from past double dates and brunches, all laughing at what looks like the center of a housewarming party, a long welcome ribbon hanging in the background.

Is it her housewarming?

Did she buy a place? In this market? Couldn't be.

He studies each face in the photograph, the anger and hurt rising ever so slowly inside him. Feeling small betrayals in each smile.

She's been having the time of her life without me. She hasn't thought about me at all.

Scrolling further, a picture of her with another familiar face, and the pain hits home. Together on a beach in Ibiza, kissing by the shoreline – uploaded yesterday. Mere hours ago.

Them dancing in another, with other men around. And another. Pictures on pictures - lots from this trip. Public pictures.

Another swimming, and another on the back of an electric scooter, and another and another, each carefully framed.

Her new life, rebuking him with every pixelated laugh, every smile with friends, every carefree kiss – feeling as if it was captured almost purposely to hurt him.

To drive the dagger even deeper into him.

And it's working. A sharp gasp escapes him, like a silent scream, and his ribs throb in turn from his injuries several days ago.

How is it so... so easy for her, moving past it all? Getting over us?

It's just as he knows it to be. As he's always suspected. He means nothing to her. He never did. Isn't it obvious now? No more running from it.

The hate rises inside him; hot, wicked feelings born of pain. He's a ghost witnessing a life he can no longer, and should no longer, see. One he's exiled from. One he no longer affects. No longer breathes, nor touches, nor feels. No longer anything...

Suddenly, every bruise, every wound, every insult from David's fists, resonates cruelly with this new deeper pain in front of him.

Old wounds mixing with new ones.

And then the bathroom, with its stark minimalistic tile, seems like it's closing in on him. A well of tears springs out, alone in the dim. A world of dark reflection, wrath, depression, and within its confines, new pain from the feelings of betrayal seeping into the hot water. Further embittering the ruin of his heart.

He sits alone with it. The undertow of despair spiraling deeper into that room, that place where his hope is a murmur.

He can't break its grasp.

You really thought watching her would save you, that it would pull you out of it. But watching has only destroyed you more.

She is not your life raft.

You thought it might save her, too, and now you've possibly hurt her worse than yourself.

You goddamn fool.

Enraged, at once he throws his phone into the side of the bathtub, and it bounces back into the steaming water with a splash, the light cutting.

Fuck it. Fuck her. Fuck all of them.

He listens to the ripples broaden and tries to breathe. The room is an impenetrable black with just the sound of the water lapping the edges of the porcelain. He feels as if there is no balm in his fractured soul, just a rawness. Even worse than before, the weight of existence bearing down on him. Ruthless and heavy.

His depression, a terrible whispering voice in the back of his mind. Pushing, twisting, pressing him. Self-loathing, encompassing every part of him.

And then it's back – that lure, wicked in the darkness. Hooking him into a willful self-destruction.

Like it never left at all.

And as this thought becomes an urge, Cal moves up out of the water, slow and delicate. He dries off and gets dressed, almost in a trance.

Locking his flat's door behind him, he makes his way up to the rooftop, his eyes distant, taking his time with each step, each rung of the ladder painful and requiring effort. The hatch to the rooftop swings open revealing the sunset over the buildings and a flurry of fire in the sky behind them. The cold wind whips across the perch, howling as it does, and Cal shivers as he steps into it.

In the dusk, he makes his way to the edge, and sees the familiar window, dark as it has been.

Always dark now.

Sirens and car horns blare below, and in the blinking expanse beyond the buildings, the world bathes in the final radiance of the streets and office lights, seemingly infinite as it always feels, pulsating against the tired numbness within him and the tired cold windy surroundings without. The nothingness.

The devastated remnants... of you.

Then, without warning, Cal stumbles a bit, tears finding him again, and he slumps back against the cold brick wall, its chill biting through the thin material of his long sleeve shirt.

His heart feels like it is breaking all over again...

"Hey!" a voice calls above the wind. "You okay?"

What was that?

Someone shouted it. Nearby.

Grimacing, he rubs his eyes.

"Hey!"

The voice carries from a distance, somewhere overhead –

a woman's voice. He looks around, stepping up and off the wall. His head whips around to the adjacent buildings, her window, and around the others too.

Abruptly then, his heart skips as he spots her: the bright strands of hair reflecting the crimson blaze of the sky, blowing in the breeze and the night, meeting the last ambered kiss of sun behind her.

She's standing against the railing of her own rooftop, usually vacant so far as Cal can tell. She leans with her silhouette visible, and waves down at him from above his perch. His heart lurches like it's been tapped into a thousand-volt current with the sight of her –

Sarah.

He lifts his hand, waving back, awkward, unprepared, standing straight now.

"Hey. Thank you. Yeah," he calls back. "Fine."

She says nothing else.

The wind blows and she just watches him.

He wants to say more but can't think of anything at all. He feels frozen. Muted. He wipes his eyes. Time seems to stretch. Moments pass. The sky fades into shades of garnet.

She sees me, he thinks to himself. It's all turned around.

All of it.

For better, or worse, she knows where I am going – where I have been observing her life. Where I've been hiding up here.

Watching her.

Her most private moments. Her worst moments. With him.

But does she know all of it? Everything I've seen?

The weight of shame crashes down, yet amid it a slender thread of connection makes him feel the despair lessen for the first time since intercepting her husband outside the garage. And curiosity replaces it. And excitement.

The alluring captivation sinking in, so profound once again: a magnetic force drawing him further and further to her with every gesture. Every glimpse.

He gazes back at her. And the tiny fire rekindles somewhere deep within him – a fragile thing, easily snuffed – but casting away the darkness in his heart so vividly that he can't help but smile at her with the realization.

Like spotting a beacon. Like it's intentional.

Like she's leading me. Has been. Isn't it obvious?

How didn't I see?

Down from the ledge. Off the rooftop. Away from my shadow days – these ghosts.

Like she's been saying all along: you can follow me. Away from yourself. Back to the land of the living. You only need to know where to look. And now, we're both looking.

10

Sometime after her profile recedes from the rooftop's edge of her building, and the sun sinks below the horizon in a collage of bruised purples and blues, Cal returns with his own bruises to his flat and begins making dinner for himself, feeling a bit better. His hollow blue eyes peer in concentration as the minutes pass, steam rising from the pots and pans casting sinuous outlines upon the ceiling in a hot haze.

He stirs and chops and boils, only occasionally pausing when the pain in his ribs strikes. He does another circuit of icing the swelling and bruises with bags of frozen vegetables – his jaw and ribs especially – and then he returns to his cooking, leaving the half-drunk scotch bottle alone.

His heart lifts with the warm smells of the low and simmering garlic marinara, and Cal leaves the kitchen for a moment, wiping his forearm along his brow, and steps over to the living room window he slept beneath in his stupor a few days ago. He cracks it open, as he often does when the building's radiators collectivize and turn the place into an oven.

Peering out, breathing deeply, Cal glances first up to Sarah's sleeping window, and next down to the street itself. Loud and bustling. Alive. Drunks cackling outside the Old Hound and the alleyways fill with weekend warriors and those out for a bite.

Suddenly, he freezes in his place, spotting a specific SUV below amongst the usual comings and goings of the city's inhabitants. There, at the corner intersection near the decayed entrance to the Old Hound, waiting for the light to turn green, right blinker ticking idly: Sarah's husband's dark Range Rover.

Cal eases back a bit and watches it, staying somewhat out of sight in case he happens to look up.

When the vehicle Cal mocked so brazenly mere days ago finally speeds down the street and out of view in the dusk, Cal forgets to stir the pasta sauce, instead moving into his office as fast as he can – the urge to reach out to Sarah beyond overpowering now.

I can't delay this any longer. I have to. She knows.

He pictures her alone in that vast penthouse. He wonders if she is thinking of him, in this moment, as he is thinking of her.

A mirror to his isolation. To his solitude. As she was on the roof.

Your gut says yes, doesn't it?

But he hesitates as he scatters his things, making room on the disheveled desk. He sits down, turning on the desk lamp.

How do you approach this?

What words can be written to bridge this gulf between two people? Two strangers?

He takes hold of a sheet of paper within a small journal beside the computer monitor, and carefully tears it, inch by inch from the book's spine. He then glances out the window at the street, watching the comings and goings. Keeping an eye out.

I'll write her a note, a simple gesture. It's all I can do.

An introduction of sorts. An offer.

He reaches for a pen and then his hand hovers over the paper. The tip touching the sheet and pausing, the words suddenly eluding him.

What to say? Where to start?

Absentmindedly, he starts writing things on various pages as he collects his thoughts.

Do I love Sarah?

Next page.

Am I obsessed?

Next page.

Call cops?

Next page.

Fuck David Jones.
Next page.
Kill David?
Next page.
If only.
Next page.
How to ask someone out on a date...
Next page.
How to ask someone to leave their husband?
Next page.
How to ask someone how to help with domestic abuse?
Next page.
How to tell if it's stalking.
Next page.
Domestic abuse intervention services...
Next page.
Thought about that already.
Next page.
Useless as coppers.
Next page.

This goes on for a bit, his mind elsewhere, lost in his own spirals, as he thinks and thinks with many false starts. At last, after what feels like hours but probably is more like minutes, Cal arrives on a some-versus-all approach to his letter.

He begins etching out a few lines, beginning with him expressing his concern for her without going into the details of where the concern comes from, then a couple of lines about himself (even more vague), and concluding with him extending friendship in probably the most convoluted way possible:

If you need someone to talk to.... And knows
No....

If you want someone to talk to. Someone who has seen what you're going through, let me know.

I can get you help. I can help you. – Cal

He rewrites it several more times, changing minor structure things here and there before he is fully satisfied with it. At least for a few moments. Doubts rise within him as he reads it again one last time.

She may already know your appearance, what you look like, where you live, generally speaking – and even so, this is a risk. No denying it.

Sticking your nose in others' business. Business you barely understand.

It could end up even more sideways.

You're exposing yourself to this. Dipping a toe in someone else's pond. You know that, right?

You have no idea how deep this thing could go...

But what else can be done? Haven't I already put her on the line here? After all the sloppiness, however well-intentioned?

Sure, but do you believe he told her about what happened that morning a few days ago?

Why else would she have been up on the roof tonight?

That's far too much coincidence, isn't it, Cal thinks. He nods. Far too much bloody coincidence.

The alternative to doing this – more silence, more regret, more pain – even more daunting. At this point, not swimming is sinking. I'm too deep into it. I need to try at least.

I have to.

Like you tried last time?

"No, not like that - like this," Cal says to himself, and he chuckles and his ribs ache. He writes down his building and flat number. Slipping the little note into an envelope, he licks it and presses it closed, and then writes her name on the front: *Sarah*

Such a beautiful name.

Glancing outside the window once more, he feels confident that David has not returned, sure that he would have seen him come down the road from his office window's vantage on the intersection.

It's now or never. Do it.

Cal turns the low-burning coils off on the stove, giving the sauce a quick stir, and then grabs his jacket. He locks the door behind him and makes his way down the dim hallway to the lift, his heart pounding in his chest, all the way across the street to her building, catching someone exiting who holds the large brass door for him when he motions, jogging up.

"Cheers," Cal says, stepping in.

Ambling across to the corner of the ornate and empty lobby, the envelope in hand, he reads through the legend and then pushes the envelope through the slit in her mailbox, as quickly as he can. Set in motion – bound for one of the three Jones residences in the building.

The only one on the 15th floor.

11

The sterile lights compound the inky splotches of bruises around Cal's eyes and head, and even Andy, giving him his habitual fist bump, saying "Welcome back!" in his overly enthusiastic way, can't hide the mix of curiosity and concern in his eyes. Cal tries his best to avoid the weight of the gazes he encounters, moving to his cubicle as fast as his hurt ribs allow him.

Groaning, he removes his bag from his shoulder, setting it down on his desk and unpacking. The low hum of chatter and the rhythmic keyboard noise only amplifies his discomfort as he sinks into his chair and powers the computer on.

I should have taken more time off. I look like hell. People notice.

Nevertheless, he gets to work, catching up on emails from the previous week.

Shit, I missed a lot.

It takes an hour or so before a pop-up blinks across his screen, breaking the concentration he's desperately trying to maintain. He clicks it open, seeing it's coming from Janice in Human Resources.

PLEASE COME TO MY OFFICE – J

Cal feels a twinge of unease. Anything with Janice is seldom a good thing, her head so far up upper management's ass that her serpent-like reputation is recognized company-wide; it's known best practice to strike a wide, professional berth whenever possible. And now, given his current state, he suspects the nature of this beckoning could be a bit more uncomfortable than usual.

They don't like my face. Clearly. Can you blame them?

"Where you going, Cal?" Andy asks, looking up as he stands. "Let me wager..."

"Think you'll win that one. Summoned, as you like to say. Wants to speak about something."

"Uh-oh, whatever could that be," he jokes, uneasily. "Hey, nice knowing you, friend."

"Wow, Andy. Thanks for the support." Cal shakes his head. "Loyalty these days."

Though obviously not intentional, the callousness, coupled with the many surreptitious glances he receives as he walks, gets under Cal's skin. He crosses the open floor and hears an audible hush of whispered conversation. A couple of the salespeople hide their eyes.

Every bruise, every stare, a slight – screaming louder with each step forward. This day. This aching, battered ego.

He knocks on Janice's office door.

"Ah, Cal," the stern, middle-aged woman says, feigning surprise. "Come in. Sit down."

Janice's office is a sterile, neutral space with a killer view of the business park's ice rink. Like the ice below, the room is all austere paleness and modernity, save for her small desk plant that presently struggles for life. Cal glances at it and commiserates, closing the door behind himself and sitting down.

"You wanted to see me, Janice?" he asks, feeling dumb.

"Yes, thanks for coming."

She stops typing and then looks at him, leaning in.

She adjusts her glasses and clears her throat. "Calvin, listen, there have been some concerns raised. To me, and others."

"About?" he asks.

"About your appearance today."

Cal shifts. The room feels colder, more impersonal. Like someone's cracked a window.

"Oh really?" he asks, trying to appear earnest. "Who?"

"You know I can't disclose that. Suffice to say, multiple coworkers have voiced... well, discomforts," Janice continues, choosing her words meticulously, as if plucking them from a memorized handbook. "It's just... well, the nature of your injuries, and your story, or lack thereof. The bicycle accident you claim... It's fairly thin, you know? To be clear, regardless of validity, this whole thing..." she stifles herself from motioning, "See, it's distracting the office today. And not in a good way. In an inappropriate way, rather."

Cal feels his jaw clench involuntarily.

Another humiliation by these people.

"So, it's come to this? My trauma, my pain, you're saying it's a... distraction to you? Is that what I'm hearing?" Cal asks, trying to keep his voice level, composed, and somewhat failing. "You can't be serious..."

Janice sighs, removing her glasses and rubbing the bridge of her nose, as if she's had this conversation a million times before, with a million other people with pulverized faces who decided to go to work before they'd healed.

"It's not about what happened to you, Calvin," she explains. "It's about the environment, the culture this company gives its people. We aim for safety above all else."

All else. Right.

He shakes his head, an angry smirk breaking through.

She looks at him scrupulously. "Something funny?"

"No, of course not."

"The point is, Calvin, it's bigger than you," she continues, folding her hands. "Then all of us really. You've been here nearly twelve years. You of all people should know this. People are worried. Anxious, even. You've had a pattern of acting strange. Since the year started, in fact. People want to help but don't know how and it's taking time away from pressing matters. The quarter's objectives. Namely. I can't have that, of course, and neither can management. Productivity is down, as are profits."

"Okay."

"Do you understand what I'm saying to you? Some of your coworkers are, well, frankly scared of you, Calvin."

He suddenly is fully beyond the mask, his brow furrowing with it – contempt mixing with indignation, swelling up within him.

"Scared? Of what? That I'll, what, break? Lose my mind? Start smashing things? Like some bloody film?"

She looks at him cooly, then responds, "Yes. Maybe that's what it is. Are they wrong?"

Before Cal can reply to this slight, Janice's desk phone rings and she picks up without hesitation, listening for a moment, and then looking at Cal with a resigned expression behind her glasses. She hangs up the phone and places it back on the desk.

"Mr. Rollins would like to see you. Right now, actually."

"Alright. I've heard enough anyways."

"Look. Calm down," Janice says, her voice level. "Call it simple optics if you will. Collect yourself before going up there if you need to. Don't say something you will regret. I don't want to see this escalate in the wrong direction for your sake."

The wrong direction. For your sake.

A not so veiled threat if he's ever heard one.

Ignoring her backhanded cautions, Cal stands up, feeling the world's weight on his shoulders. He makes his way to the director's office, each step fueled by a mixture of anger, embarrassment, and a rapidly dwindling sense of self-worth.

"Calvin, come here!" the big man says, his face redder than usual. "Close the door and listen to me, right now. I'll just say this once..."

The subsequent confrontation with old pudge Rollins goes downhill immediately, like a pressure valve bursting off with the slightest crack of a hammer. Cal gets in a few disparagements long marinading and gets a few in kind, both men shouting at each other. The suggestion to leave for an indeterminate amount of time bringing forth Cal's outburst about inherent nepotism and lazy management. Years of resentment flooded over, making it all seem almost far away. All a bit surreal. Even cathartic on some level.

"Useless twat!" his boss yells back after him.

"Should have happened long ago!" Cal retorts, meaning it wholeheartedly.

"That it? Okay, without pay!" his boss yells as Cal leaves the office in a tirade, slamming the door behind him.

Long time coming.

A nightmarish culmination of every tiresome event leading up to now. Every passive aggressive undercut. Every disrespect. All the years spent fantasizing about slamming that door just didn't do it justice, Cal muses.

And as he waits for the lift down – freshly suspended, the barren lights flowing over him along with the hushed glances of his coworkers – he is consumed with another singular thought, alone and repeating in his head: how the hell did it come to this?

12

The clock reads just past three a.m. He lays in bed and listens to the quiet vibrations of the city, invading the stillness of the night periodically with a siren, the muffled sound of voices, or the rattling of the pipes in the old building. At one point, a car alarm rings out for half a minute or so, before it falls silent again. The only light to speak of is the occasional ambient reflections of a passing vehicle below, casting transient shadows along the walls of Cal's dim bedroom, the shades undrawn.

It is just him and the shadows – as always. And he listens to the noises and watches the gloom dance about, sleep remaining an elusive thing.

Thoughts of all that's transpired in the past few days spinning around his mind, he lies in the darkness with a frozen bag of peas, alternating between various aching ribs.

Sleep so far away now.

But then, he hears something – a noise.

A sudden, soft rushing sound disrupting the stillness. A sound so faint that at first, he questions whether his own mind is playing tricks on him. But then he hears it again, resonating through the silence. Somewhere in the other room.

He sits up and slowly, painfully, swings his legs over and opens the drawer beside his bed, feeling around in the darkness, and pulls out the collector's pocketknife his brother gave him for Christmas years ago. The one he nearly stabbed himself with on the bender. He holds his breath when he hears the noise rustle again.

In his foyer. Near his front door.

The cold touch of the wooden floor beneath his feet sends shivers up his spine, a sense of vulnerability descending over him. His nakedness feels stark, and as he hears the rustling again, he moves silent across the bedroom to his closet, knife still in hand, and grabs his robe, wrapping it tightly around him. Quick as he can manage it.

With hesitant steps, Cal turns the corner, his knife at the ready and he approaches the door. The hallway light casts the feeblest glow under the entrance, and in that light, staring, he notices a shadow not usually there. Moving closer to it, he realizes there is something placed beneath the door. Something thin.

His heart pounds in his chest. An envelope. Unmarked.

He bends down and retrieves it. Looking through the view hole of the door, and folding the knife away, Cal slowly starts unlocking the bolt.

He eases the door open and looks down at each end of the hallway. There is nobody there, just the greenish light and the hum of the overhead bulbs. He closes the door again and locks it.

Moving into the living room, he turns on the lights, and runs his thumbnail beneath the envelope's fold, carefully tearing it open. He produces the note from it, the paper around the same size and color as the one he wrote on the other day. He unfolds it and holds it up to the light.

It's handwritten, the letters flowing elegantly across the paper:

Cal,

It's rare that buildings like ours, which cloister so many souls under a single roof, can allow for any kind of connection. It's even rarer that one of its inhabitants feels moved enough to reach out when another is in trouble. But then, here you are. And here I am.

Firstly, I need to extend my gratitude for your note. It arrived at a moment that can only be described as a bottom for me. On the edge of my own despair, you seemed a little like a much-needed lifeline, a confirmation that humanity can still surprise even me.

However, there's something unsettling about knowing my life isn't as private as once believed. It's peculiar, this mix of gratitude and vulnerability I feel towards you. Yet, I can't help but believe that there's more to our silent acquaintance than voyeurism.

You've seen my struggles with my husband, the worst parts of my day, my moments of fear and pain, just as I've observed yours, your nights, the weight of the world upon you. I don't claim to understand – but I've seen it.

When I saw you the other day, after your row with David, I knew I must say something to you. And so I did.

Perhaps we're both watchers, each in our own way, our whole lives. Feeling alone amidst millions in a city like this is a peculiar sort of loneliness, but I can tell you it can be even worse isolation when the feeling poisons your home. It's a silence filled with knives. One I have never felt able to break out of, my entire life.

I believe you understand, as I've seen the weight of solitude in you too - in how you watch me. Your place on your rooftop.

Your letter, as unexpected as it was, says what we've both been feeling: that amidst the little distance between our buildings, maybe we aren't alone. And we don't have to be afraid about that.

All this to say, I'll take you up on your offer, Cal. Not here in this neighborhood, our shared little enclave, where walls have proven themselves porous and windows revealing, but how about a bit further in the city. Somewhere public. Perhaps a coffee shop or a park bench. Someplace neutral where we can unravel this.

Do you have a place in mind? – Sarah

Cal reads the note again, a flood of emotions sweeping over him. Each word she's written seems to pull a different thread in his mind, and he feels the edges of himself fray, the words cleaving through him, his pulse racing.

How much of his loneliness, his own sorrow, has she witnessed? Clearly, some of it.

"Whatever it is," he repeats, "... we aren't alone."

The weight of the decision hangs heavy, yet within the whirlwind of feelings, a sense of clarity at last overwhelms him: that his quiet fantasies and suspicions are correct in many ways about Sarah.

He's met with an uncanny sensation of being seen, truly seen, a counterpoint to his interest – perhaps for the first time since he fell in love with Diane all those years ago.

It's unsettling and invigorating in equal measure.

He re-reads her note one more time, absorbing not just the words, but the unspoken assumptions beneath them. Trying to glean every little morsel hinting who she might be.

He wonders about the exact moments she might have watched him besides what she chooses to divulge in the letter, what aspects of his life she's pierced through and pieced together silently, as he has with hers.

Did she witness his despair that first night? Or other times on the roof in liquor-fueled introspection?

Did she see him drunk in the streets that morning?

Did she see him at the market?

Did she see his torment, the agony leading up to the night he decided to end his life? The night he leaned out over the edge.

The night you first saw her moving in the dark.

Was that the first night for her, or were there many more beforehand?

How much does she understand? How much does she know?

Sarah's voice, though only known to him through her handwritten words, and the several she called out to him on the rooftop, carries a depth he isn't expecting. There's an authenticity – a vulnerability that strikes a chord. He can nearly hear her say it.

"Feeling alone amidst millions in a city like this is a peculiar sort of loneliness," he reads to himself in the stale light of the living room.

Words resonating with an all too familiar clarity, an all too familiar accuracy.

You've felt that loneliness – lived it day in and day out, most of your life – to one degree or another.

You were right about her. You were dead right.

It was the right move, reaching out.

He moves over to his living room window, looking up at her dark windowpane a moment, and then down at the cold, sleeping streets, feeling solace and a strange, assuring tranquility overcome him.

A confirmation that humanity can still surprise... even me.

Waves of expectation and hope rise within him, and he turns and steps into his office. He switches on the light and tears another paper out of the journal. Staring at it for only a moment or so, he grabs a pen and begins to write.

13

Peering into the embrace of the winter twilight, Chelsea bares its characteristic pulse of trendiness mixed with history. The lamplights reflect off the cobblestones and the many shoppers and tourists stroll on each side of Kings Road and down the crowded alleys, pointing at restaurants and stores and pausing. Others sitting on benches, deep in conversation, waiting on buses or rides. Bicyclists riding home. Parents out with their children.

Exactly the view from the restaurant that he hoped for. A flood of commotion and, so too, privacy.

He watches the fluttering pigeons and the little corner boutiques switch their lit arrangements for the night, the displays of fashion changing over to dim. The skeletal trees line the roads with etched outlines against the high-end eateries, their wiry branches and strung edison bulbs swaying in the damp and the gusts.

Cal watches all this in a corner of the swank Italian bistro Cucina del Cuore, listening to the quintet play jazz songs, peering at the street for the past twenty minutes. Purposely taking small sips of his drink, he's doing his best to steady his nerves as his eyes peel through the activity, waiting with bated breath for her to arrive.

Where is she?

Even though he got here early, he's antsy, and can't help wondering whether she's not showing up the exact moment the eight o'clock hour comes and passes.

He checks his watch again, lost in his anxieties.

Did she not get the note?

Did he check the mailbox instead of her?

Cal's fingers drum on the table, on the crisp tablecloth. The band mixes with the conversations, as well as the whiskey in him, petitioning him to sit back and relax. But for every person that enters through the restaurant's entrance, the little bell chiming heightens his anticipation that much more. And he feels the same disappointment he once felt when looking for her around the neighborhood, realizing, once again, it's not who he hopes it is.

He swishes the liquid around the glass, wanting the hints of dried fruits, chocolate, and peat smoke to distract him, lingering with it, staring at the candle in the center of the table.

Where is she?

At last, savoring the oaky afterbirth of its long passage from Islay, he finishes the glass, and then a shimmer of gold catches in the periphery of his vision. And he hears the bell.

He looks up at the door, peering – it's her.

Sarah stands at the entrance of the dimly lit restaurant, her eyes scanning the room, waving off the well-dressed maître-d with a smile. Cal sees her elegant figure as she takes her damp overcoat and scarf off and hands it away, accentuated by the sage-colored dress she wears that hugs her curves delicately and flows just past her knees. A hint of silver at her collarbone catches the ambient light, drawing Cal's eyes to her slender neck and along her shoulders. He sees light blonde strands escape the confines of her loose bun, framing her face.

Smoothing over his gray button-down, his blazer, and making sure his dark slacks look alright, he leans out of the booth and waves in her direction. His heart skips a beat.

Here we go.

Sarah's eyes continue to travel, chin swiveling, and he sees the soft light catching the many ear piercings that dot her ears, a constellation, delicate gold and silver loops, interspersed with tiny studs, shimmering subtly, echoing the same golden sheen as her wristwatch. At last, she sees him and nods, the clack of her heels on the stone floor rhythmically marking her passage through the restaurant. Each step calculated, graceful, like a dancer's.

He remembers having similar thoughts in the market, seemingly forever ago.

She keeps walking up, and Cal thinks he sees waitstaff and diners alike stealing glances at her, but she seems almost oblivious to the attention, her focus singular. He swallows and stands up.

Their eyes meet as she approaches him — a jolt of recognition, an acknowledgment of the weight of it maybe, the silent observations, the moments they've unknowingly witnessed. All converging to this first real moment.

Sarah's slight smile broadens into a warm, genuine one, revealing her dimples. The nervous energy she carries transforms into determination as she closes the distance, the surrounding din of the restaurant fading into inconsequential background noise.

"Hey you," she breathes, and he detects a hint of excitement in her voice, laced with a subtle undertone of relief, as if a weight has been lifted in finding him amidst the sea of unfamiliar Chelsea denizens.

Her eyes are a rich shade of green tonight, emboldened by the jadestone intensity of her dress. The soft upturn of her lips suggests an air of expectancy. She smiles at him.

"Hey, Sarah. Wow - you look incredible," he says, his own eyes not leaving hers, taking in every nuance of her face, every glint in her stare, and every strand of golden hair that frames her.

The world outside their little bubble seems to blur and recede. Sarah extends her hand, and he takes it, feeling the cool smoothness of her skin, surprised by the strength of her grip, and the slight tremble.

The paradox is not lost on him—the awkwardness and its source: this formal, close-up gesture between them feels strange, given how intimately they've observed each other from afar. It's all backwards.

"It's nice to meet you," she says, her words tinged with a hint of playfulness. A knowing. Her lips purse, the same blood-red color they were the last time he saw her up close.

Cal chuckles, his nerves settling slightly, "In person, you mean? Not from the rooftops or windows?"

She laughs: a soft, lilting sound that harmonizes with the ambient murmur of the restaurant.

"Exactly. Much better close," she quips. "Anyway, shall we?"

Her perfume wafts towards him, and he detects the soft, floral whispers of jasmine and lilac. Just like in the market.

"Yes, of course," he says, gesturing to the seat across from his as she sits, and he notices how the fingers of her left hand delicately push a stray strand of hair behind her ear, and that she's only wearing a single ring on her middle finger.

No wedding ring.

"So, this place comes highly recommended," Cal begins, trying to cut through the initial stilt – the shifting energy of her arrival.

Sarah nods, scanning the menu, "I've heard. Honestly, to be real with you, I'm more interested in the company."

"Yeah?"

She glances up, her gaze direct and searching. "I've been excited about this."

"Me too," he replies. He feels a slight flush rise to his cheeks. It's been a long time since he's been on any semblance of a date, especially one charged with such intricate layers of meaning.

"Have a chance to talk," he says.

Not to mention how stunning she is...

"So up close," she smiles.

"Well, good, here were we are," he stammers, matching her gaze. Stumbling, he tries again, "It's good to meet you. In this beautiful restaurant. Ah, you get it."

Ugh, come on Cal, you can do better than this.

Don't be graceless, you prat.

"It's a lovely place," she smiles politely, looking around. Then she leans forward, looking at him, her voice much lower.

"Here we are... Two souls together by the simple act of me fingering myself in front of my little window... all for you to watch me like a simple twist of fate. And it's Valentine's Day. Nonetheless." She pauses. "I'm not here for the food. So to speak. So," she eyes him over, lingering.

Her forwardness takes Cal aback, and he decides instantly he should play along.

"Oh, me and your window," he smiles at her. "We're just getting started."

Hardball. Call her bluff.

"So you say," Sarah shrugs, sitting back. "Shouldn't we cheers or something first? Before getting mired in the broad strokes and the nitty-grittys?"

"Obligatory flirtations?" Cal offers.

"Obligatory you say?" she raises her eyebrows. "My my. Bit dire, phrased like that."

"How about a bottle of wine instead?" Cal asks, shifting in his seat.

"Smashing," she responds, placing her purse beside her. "What you thinking?"

"A cold night like this? Hm. Something with plum, maybe spice. Something full-bodied?"

"Mmm," she says, smiling. "Alright."

"Do you like French Côtes du Rhône?" Cal asks, surveying the drink-menu.

"Yes, course," Sarah chuckles, flashing a look at him, "And, by the way, if anyone ever answers no to that question then they're an absolute twit and can't be trusted."

"Can't be trusted, huh?" he chuckles. "I'll remember that."

The waiter comes to fill water glasses and Cal orders the bottle.

"So, where are you from?" Sarah asks as he leaves. "Originally, I mean."

"Essex, actually. Maldon's where I did primary... some secondary; Southend-on-Sea for a bit too... was thirteen. Moved there," Cal replies, pausing, considering how much is too much to say, then moving it back. "How about you?"

"King's Heath, believe it or not. Before I went to uni that is," she says. "Then back to the city. Abroad on the summers."

"Lucky you," Cal smirks, closing his eyes and nodding. He thinks of the art gallery picture.

"Out with it then," Sarah gazes at him, accusingly.

"Nah. Forget it."

"What? Tell me!"

"No," he chuckles, "Nothing. I just thought your accent was a bit different. Now I get it."

"What? Tell me. Different how?"

"You're a Birmingham girl."

"I don't have any Birmingham accent. What are you on about?" she frowns.

He laughs. "Hey, I'm only teasing. Half-teasing."

"Okay, fine," she looks at him, eyes narrowing, "Maybe a bit of one. But I wasn't just there. And you don't have to call it out. I've only just sat down, Cal, believe it or not."

She look intently at him, accusingly.

"Hey, for the record, I like it. You don't look like other Birmingham girls. Don't talk like them either – that accent. Took a moment."

"Cause I don't have one!" she admonishes, trying her best to withhold a smile. "Besides, my dad's Sicilian. Like to think that plays a part in the looks department. Maybe that's what you're hearing."

"As you said. I believe you now," Cal laughs again. "Sicily. Exotic."

"Do shut up," she says, rolling her eyes.

"Fine, fine," he raises his palms in defeat. "Only saying."

The wine arrives, and the waiter uncorks the bottle and pours it into each glass before placing it down between them beside the flickering candle.

"Cheers," Cal says, raising his glass towards her with a half-smile, the wine catching the soft glow of the flame. "To our situation."

"Situation?" Sarah furrows her eyebrows. "Really? Bit weak, isn't it?"

"It's a unique thing, you have to admit that much."

"I mean..." Sarah smiles, examining the wine before she takes a small sip, her eyes lighting up. "Yeah, that's one way to put it. Upside-down, inside-out.... Here, hm. How about this one. Try this..."

She raises her glass to him, clears her throat.

"Every new beginning starts from..." she sings, gestating with her other hand, head cocked and waiting for him.

"Some other beginning's end," he intonates, clinking her glass. "Love that song, actually."

"Again – suspicious of any who don't." She smiles and takes a sip. "At least you passed the 90s test. If not the Birmingham one. Fan of Gallagher then?"

"More a Yorke guy. Were you even alive in the 90s?" Cal remarks playfully.

"Hey, you!" she exclaims. "Of course, I was. Caught nearly half of it, thank you very much."

"Just wondering," Cal smiles, sipping, taking her in. "It's just that it's all backwards, isn't it?"

"No more or less than any other decade, I think," she muses.

"No... I mean... All I'm saying," Cal says. "Is I'm rusty with this sort of thing, even when it is absolutely, one hundred percent straightforward."

"What do you mean by that?" Sarah asks, watching him.

What do I mean by that? Cal thinks.

He shrugs. "I don't know. I snuck into your flat's mailroom to ask you out. Twice in fact. And, you know, you're also married."

"To a bloody psychopath," she says.

"Your words," Cal replies.

"But you agree with them?" she asks.

"Don't you?"

"You first. How long has it been for you?" she pivots effortlessly, not missing a beat as she swirls the wine in her glass, watching him. "Doing this kind of thing, I mean."

"What, in Chelsea?" he asks, looking at the people moving by the window on the darkening street. "Bloody dreadful place."

"No, silly. Out with a woman. A beautiful one... my sort."

"How modest you are," he smiles.

"Only when I try," she says, her expression neutral, pressing the point. He considers her question and how much he wants to disclose to her.

"It's definitely been a bit."

Sarah raises an eyebrow, missing nothing, and her voice is silken and slightly tempting, "And, Cal, historically speaking, when was it ever straightforward for you?"

The question feels barbed. The way she specifies the word *you* at the end, her voice lingering. He notices her fingers fidgeting against the stem of the wine glass.

"Good point," Cal replies. "Suppose never really."

Sarah nods as if affirming something to herself.

"Me neither," she says. "To tell you the truth, I'm not too fond of first dates. I used to get very drunk for them when I was younger. Was the only way I'd ever agree to go anywhere."

"Well, I think we can call this whatever date we want to, at this point," Cal replies. "You know?"

"I kind of think so too," she says, glancing around. "That's the reason I agreed to come to be honest. That, and the sheer, morbid curiosity of it."

"The morbid curiosity," he repeats.

"Yes. And, of course, it's Valentines. David's not taking me anywhere, now is he? A girl must eat."

Cal chuckles, enjoying her playfulness, and then he notices her lost in thought for a moment, considering something, her face tightening ever so slightly in the candlelight. The waiter comes, delivering bread, and she smiles and then looks at Cal. He sees the corner of her mouth twitch as if grappling with the weight of the words she is about to say.

Her eyes dart to the street outside the window, momentarily watching something, seeking an escape, but then they lock back on him with unwavering determination. The slight furrow in her brow and the hesitant parting of her lips signal discomfort, but she presses on.

"Tell me something. Something that's been on my mind for quite some time."

"Ask away," he replies, a little too quick, and he feels himself tense. She leans in a little closer to him.

"You were going to kill yourself that night, weren't you? That night you saw me a few weeks back. When you were leaning over, holding on to the railing, looking down at the street."

A bead of sweat emerges on his brow.

She did see me that night.

"Well," Cal replies, quietly, "Usually, someone gets to know a person first, then shares something like that..."

"I do know you," she says. "Maybe more than a lot of people, don't I? And I know that's the case, the subject flipped." She cocks her head slightly, staring at him, her eyes narrowing and digging for answers. "Does it bother you? Me being this blunt with you?"

He thinks about this – "No. I don't think it does. Not with you for some reason."

"Well?" she asks, eyebrows raised expectantly. "Tell me."

His lips part, hesitating, searching for words.

What can I say?

He sighs, at last giving in to her.

"I was going to do it that night. There'd been times before, but that night, well, that night... I was close to the edge. It wouldn't have taken much of anything at all to let go..."

He notices that her hands now lay still, processing.

"But you stayed. Held on."

"I did. Clearly," he forces a smile.

"Well, hey," she says, her mind churning, sitting back in her chair. "Good."

A long moment passes between them.

"How about you? Does bluntness bother you, or should I sugarcoat what I ask tonight?"

It sounds meaner than he wants it to.

"Well, no, don't sugarcoat anything with me," Sarah says back. "I will be honest with you; I appreciate you doing the same with me. It's refreshing."

She smirks, a mischief in her eyes, toying with the stem of her glass, her fingers lingering. Then she says: "But yeah, if your style of doing things bothered me Cal, of course, I wouldn't be here. And to tell you the truth of it, I've always been a girl who's preferred diving into the deep end of it anyways, so... I had to meet you, see? Though you might be a serial killer. Still hovering around fifty-percent..."

"Just fifty? I was going to say..." Cal grins, "That's kind of a little dangerous, isn't it? Not that I'm disappointed that your baser instincts prevailed."

"Hence my pleasant life," she shrugs, then after doing a mock bow, she raises her glass to him. "Salut, to fifty-percent then?"

They clink glasses.

"It was a bit daring for me, too. Writing you..." Cal says and takes a sip of wine. Sarah looks at him, flatly, a smile emerging across her face.

"Perhaps not as daring as shooting pepper spray into my husband's eyes. Telling him to keep his dirty little hands off his own wife. Quite... bold, that. Not that I don't appreciate it – I do, actually. In this day and age, bit archaic, some may say excessive, but can't argue with the good nature of it."

"If nothing else, it had that going for it," Cal sighs, feeling his face grow hot.

So he did tell her. Or she saw it. Heard it. Who knows.

"I can see that it also wasn't, well, an easy thing to do," she continues. He feels her gaze floating over the bruises on his face, her eyes conveying some kind of small test. He recalls seeing the bruises this man left on her face not too long ago, too.

"He's not the strong and gentle type," Cal replies.

Sarah snorts. Cal smiles, loving her laugh.

He then asks her: "And has he?"

"Has he what?" she asks.

"Kept his hands off you? Or did I just make it worse?"

Sarah shakes her head, clearly not anticipating this, her smile fading and downplaying a bit, "I'm surviving." She shifts in her chair. "Look, life hasn't always been gentle with me, but I believe in facing my challenges, you know? And I'll keep doing that as long as I can. Doing what I need to."

"Yeah. I get that," Cal offers, trying to alleviate the tension a bit. "Look, I can't imagine how it is living with it though. I'm sorry."

"Don't be. And you can more than most, it seems," Sarah sighs, her sharp eyes fixed on him.

"I'm just saying that I don't claim to understand," Cal says, "Just from seeing it happen."

"Fine," Sarah replies, her tone brisk. "How about you, then? What drove Cal on that rooftop? I've seen you in pain. I've seen you nearly kill yourself. So, tell me why."

"Does it really matter?"

"It absolutely matters," Sarah exasperates. "Don't play coy now. What do you think about all those hours up there, out in the cold? Even the times when you weren't hanging off the edge. What are you looking for up there, you know, pacing... all alone? I came tonight, didn't I? You can give me that much."

He hesitates, a shadow crossing his face. He takes a sip of his wine.

"Searching, maybe," he says at last. "For meaning, a connection, trying to heal somedays, trying for a way out others. Thinking through it – again and again. I don't know. Something... real. Something I could hold on to. Some real reason to stay."

He pauses, staring at her. "I've got a lot of pain, Sarah, honestly, and I'm still finding a way to work through it. It's... overwhelming, sometimes. So, I've gone up there. That's why. For the longest time, I thought I was all alone, too. All I needed. You know? Clearly not."

Sarah reaches across the table, her fingers brushing his.

The contact is brief but charged.

"Yes, of course I know. Partly why I came."

Her lips purse slightly, and she hesitates, biting her lip. "I've been thinking," she says, "How sometimes it's what's right up there, too – you know? People like us. What we need the most. In the dark, stripped alone, where we least expect to find it. Not plain sight or anything, but near us, right? We just have to be low enough and mindful enough to see it. And brave enough to reach out and grasp it. And the truth is not so many people are up for all that effort. It's a lot of effort... to risk it. A lot of pain, maybe. Too much for some, for most even. That risk. It's easier to just be miserable..."

"But you are?" Cal asks slowly, almost a challenge. "Up for it?"

"What do you think?" she says back.

Their gazes latch to one another, the candle flickering.

"I think I want to find out," Cal replies after a moment, his voice low. The moment stretches on. She lifts her eyebrows as if daring him to elaborate.

Then the waiter comes by – "More time?"

"Please," Cal replies, remembering suddenly he has a menu.

14

The conversation flows on smoother as the minutes tick by, each adjusting to the energies and touches of humor of the other, and by the time the food arrives they are speaking with the ease of friends. Cal's initial nervousness dissipates, moment by moment, and they delve into topics from their favorite books to their shared love of old movies, to countries they have traveled to and far-off cities they want to someday see. Then a touch of politics – a shared anxiety and pity – followed by stories from growing up.

"I used to be a cliff diver as a teenager," Sarah confesses between bites. "Bet you didn't see that coming, did you?"

"You're lying."

"No. Stone serious. My sister and I'd sit and time it. Wait for just the right big one. The waves that is. Then hold hands, and off. Jump as the waves waned out, then once they stop, you know, by the time you hit the water, splash, a soft landing."

"Absolutely nuts. Are you one of those adrenaline junkies, by chance?" Cal chuckles. "No, I'm serious!"

"Nope, nothing more out of me," she grins, dimples beaming, eyes eager from laughing. "It's your turn now. Trivia fact, numéro trois. Don't hold back."

"Fine..." Cal groans, eating.

And as the time passes, Cal feels more and more comfortable with Sarah, and his guard drops, little by little, piece by piece. And so does hers he thinks.

At last, as she finishes another story about growing up, he feels the time is right to ask her the question burning within him since they sat down.

"Sarah," he begins.

"Cal," she says warmly back.

"Okay, you don't have to answer if you don't want to, but..."

"But?"

"Your husband. All the hell he puts you through," he pauses, looking her over. "How did it get that way? Just curious, is all. You don't have to answer if you don't want to, of course."

She chews her veal and swallows, considering the framing of the question. Then, taking a deep breath, releasing it slowly, she replies:

"Guess it was bound to come up. Kind of shocking it took this long actually – knowing what you know, that is. Sometimes I don't even know myself to be honest, but I'll do my best for you."

She sighs, sitting back.

"It started like it always starts. David was charming when we first met in uni. Friend of a friend, at a party, like everyone used to meet. And he had charisma, you know?" she smiles, recalling, looking at the tablecloth. "It's what made him great in sales, starting out. Of course, it's also what drew me to him. Me, twenty-one, third year, what the hell did I know really, and he was twenty-five at the time, finishing a business program. Of course, I saw potential and the stability he offered, the quid he'd throw around, talking about moving up. His business taking roots. But I was also just mad about him. The butterflies. You know. Stupidly in love. It had nothing to do with money. It had to do with familiarity. That's really all I saw, in retrospect. The affection of it. The romance - being swept off my feet, you know. Young, like I said. You have your reasons. Well, that and his physique, of course. Godly, let me tell you."

Cal rolls his eyes, and she enjoys his reaction. He refills her wine glass. Her fingers fiddle with the stem, her gaze fixed on the crimson contents.

"But as time went on," she continues, "moving in together, particularly as we were married," then she hesitates, looking away and then back to him, "Little over three years ago that charm began to wane a bit, as he showed me more and more of his temper. This boiling anger. Resentment. This rageful side of him. Screaming at me... over such small things. Dishes. Laundry. A bad day at his job. Smashing things. More... volatile than anything I'd seen up to that point... Out of control, really. The early days of it. And then, overnight, I started simply living on eggshells. It was like it had always been that way. Like the flip of a switch. And that was the way of things after."

Cal nods, encouraging her to continue but hoping she knows there's no pressure. She takes a long sip of wine.

"And now?" Cal asks.

"Now he's just more of that possessive man, worse... He likes to act as if he holds all the money, too, but it's mine, really. My family's, at least. His import-export business has always been up and down, never steady, never that profitable," she goes on, her voice barely above a whisper, almost as if she's talking alone to herself, choking the words out. "At first, it was just that, fighting about money though, his rights to more of it, bouts of envy, jealousy, access to things, an occasional cruel word. Whatever. I dealt with it. But as the months turned into years, five years now all said and done, it's a lot more... well, you know. Physical. He started coming back late at night. Always pissed. Nothing ever right. Never enough. I started calling the police, at first at least. They'd come down. Ask about it. Take a report. Talk to him a bit. Leave. He'd come back at me. Shout some more. Then the hitting started. He only used to hit me if I rang the police."

Cal sees tears welling in the corners of her eyes.

"And what would he say if he saw us now?" Cal asks, poignantly. The grip on his fork tightens as he asks it. He thinks of the violence he's witnessed in her husband, time after time, the rage. The blows struck down on his face, and those struck down on hers as well.

"Impossible. He won't," she replies, quick as if she's considered it. Because of course she has.

"He's not even in the city. Up in Edinburgh for some shipment renewal thing until the end of the month, thank God," Sarah responds, and then, noticing his graveness, offers a weak smile.

"Look, I know, it's a lot to take in. And I don't want to paint it all black. Spoil the night. There are good moments too. Were once, I guess. Times of passion, tenderness. It wasn't always this bad. But the darkness in him... it overshadows everything. I've reached the breaking point with it. I've been so checked out for years, too scared to know how to get away."

"Was there a point when it all changed? When he became this person?" Cal asks, taking a sip of his wine.

She ponders this for a moment, having another bite, chewing through the question, before saying: "I think he always was this person. Perhaps, in the beginning, he was just better at hiding it. Or maybe I was too young, too blinded, to see it."

"I get that. You know you don't deserve any of it, though. The guilt of it."

"Of course I don't," she says. "As I doubt you do, with whatever happened with you and your ex-fiancée. Of course, I know that. I'm not some doe-eyed victim, Cal."

"I'm not saying you are, sorry," he replies, "I just mean, you know. It's not right is all. The way the people you sometimes trust the most almost take pleasure in how much they damage you."

She takes another bite of her food, the pain evident across her face. "No one deserves his shit," she says, chewing. "But it's my reality. And it's a reality I fully intend to change. Soon, hopefully. I live in it, you just stumbled onto it. Remember. From across the way."

They sit in silence for a moment, bristling, the gravity of her words sinking in before she spears some of her penne with her fork and leans in towards him.

"Here, try. Pesto's to die for. You'll love it."

Not knowing what else to say, he leans in and takes the bite.

The tension lifts.

"It's amazing," he hums. He then feeds her some of his risotto.

Her eyes light up with joy and he smiles at her.

"Bit amateur in my opinion. You know, I'm something of a cook myself," Cal brags.

"Are you now?" she says, chewing, covering her mouth with her hand. "I'm so aroused suddenly."

They laugh – loud and boisterous, and she snorts, and they laugh even louder. A few in the restaurant glance over but both are hardly aware. The conversation drifts to lighter topics: on to recipes, cookbooks, and then just the books they love.

More time passes and the tiramisu, cheesecake, and coffees arrive, and they continue to share, slowly navigating through the layers of each other's lives. He tells her more about his childhood. She tells him about her paintings. He plays none-the-wiser to her mention of the coming gallery, which she finely hints around but never quite presents to him.

Modesty, perhaps, he ascribes it.

Eventually, the band packs up and the evening winds down, and the candles on their table burn lower and lower, casting a dimming glow across their faces as they chat. Sarah chuckles, her dimples deep shadows in the light, her eyes like shiny emeralds.

Even in the dim, Cal can tell her face is a little flushed from the wine.

"Oh, so now I'm the spy, am I? I seem to remember someone being quite interested in my windowpane, too. You, your binoculars, trying to hide, snooping. Think I didn't see that?"

"Hey, I don't know what you saw," he says with a playful grin, feeling the wine himself. "I needed a reason to use the binoculars, okay? And I know what I saw..."

"That's what you're going with?" she jabs. "Boredom? Really?"

He laughs again, like he hasn't in ages.

"Touche. Hey, in my defense, your life looked far more interesting than anyone else's. Some dull neighbors, you've got. The lot of them. Your window looked... simply much more intriguing."

"Simply," she repeats and giggles, and raises an eyebrow, the undertone evident. "Only looked? How about now, seeing this up close and personal?"

He leans in, voice low and husky, poorly imitative of a French street painter.

"D'accord, far more clothing... Now, I'm determined to find a canvas suitable for ze tres belle, uh, comment do you say, j'en sais quoi."

"Awful French." She shakes her head, smirking, "Just awful. You're bloody ridiculous, you know that?"

"Maybe so. Maybe it's just the wine. Who really knows anymore."

"Not me, to tell the truth. Hated French lessons. What do I even remember?" she asks, looking at the ceiling. "Bon chance, bon jour, bon soir. Bon vin. Far too much vin to remember much more than that. Let the vin breathe. Important. What else..."

He laughs and they watch each other for a moment, wondering who will be the one to do it.

She smiles at him, and he smiles back. The air thickens.

"Anyway, should probably get going," Cal says. "Getting late."

"We're the worst – practically the last ones," she says. "These guys must totally hate us."

She nods to a couple of waiters on the far side of the room who are staring at their phones. Cal motions one over. The last of their dessert plates are cleared, and then he makes a proposition to her, trying to elongate the evening as much as he can – hoping, truly, that it will never end.

"So, hey."

"Hey," she says back.

"Want to walk around a bit?"

"Where a bit?"

"I don't know. Chelsea is beautiful this time of night."

"Is it really?" she asks, feigning shock.

"Maybe. I'm sure of it."

"Oh, jeez," Sarah rolls her eyes. "Smooth as vinegar."

"Well?" he asks, after a moment.

"Hm," she pauses, looking out the window. "It's bloody cold, you know?"

"I know," Cal says.

"Alright," she nods after a moment, "I'll use the lady's room and meet you outside. Wait for me."

15

As they meander through the alleys of Chelsea – its narrow alcoves and stairs down Paradise Way, with the three-story Victorian buildings juxtaposing starkly against the luxury homes and fancy boutiques – Cal catches a hint of melancholy in her eyes.

The night deepens, and the streets and passing cars cast soft glowing lights on the brick buildings, and then on the Thames itself, as they walk down to it, wandering beside the cold river with the wind blowing fiercely along the running path.

"So, you're excited for opening?" Cal asks, descending some stairs, out of the wind. "After all this time?"

"It's going to be a beautiful new gallery. Yes, of course I am. It's always been my dream to own an art gallery. My own gallery. My work on the walls. Others too, you know, people who I admire. Pieces I love. Pieces the world should see."

"Can't imagine how excited you are – to have something like that," Cal replies, thinking about standing outside the exact gallery not long ago. "Something you've wanted so long, almost in your reach. It must be an incredible feeling."

Didn't the brochure say the renovations started over a year ago? He resists the urge to ask how long.

"I'd like to see your paintings sometime, you know, hanging on the walls in there," he says, pivoting. "If it's okay with you, that is."

Was that too forward?

"Can make that happen," she says, flashing a cheeky look at him. "If you'd like."

"The name – Ephemeral Canvas," he asks. "Where'd you come up with that anyways?"

Her smile fades ever so slightly. She shrugs and shakes her head.

"Oh, I don't know. I'll tell you some other time, okay? Bit of a story."

"That's alright," Cal says. "I have the time if you do."

"Too unkind for tonight," Sarah insists, looping her arm in his. "It's a sadder kind of story. Another time, okay?"

"Sure. Okay."

They continue and Sarah grows even quieter as they amble along the route, as if she's lost in thought. Past a big bridge that runs out across the black water, the ice still nipping their faces until he points to her, and they take a left again, crossing the road and going up some more stairs, then back into a glowing cobbled alleyway. The lights twinkle in the branches of the winter trees on either side of the road as they walk. They follow the trees along and the surroundings change when they round a corner, finding themselves suddenly in front of an old cathedral, its Gothic architecture dominating the end of the street in shadow.

"Something on your mind?" Cal asks at last, not sure of what else to say, staring at her as she stands with her hands deep in her overcoat pockets gazing up at the church now. After a moment, she looks back at him, pausing, and then outstretches her hand. Her fingers brush the rough stone walls of the old building,

"Beautiful old building," she says. "I love things like this."

"Me too. And yes, it is," Cal says, looking up.

"Strange thing, how history has a way and clings to these kinds of places, you know?"

"Here specifically?"

"All places really," Sarah says, pulling a strand of hair back. "But the more history, the more clinging."

"Yeah, of course... it's kind of ancient," Cal jokes, and she cocks her head at him as if saying: really?

"Sorry." He clears his throat. "Go on."

"Violence, for instance... any violence" Sarah says, her head nodding. "It has a history, right? Its lineage, passed from one generation to the next, one hand to another. We all know that."

"A cycle. Certainly. Look at the Middle East."

"Right. Look everywhere, really. And just like this old cathedral has seen ages go by, probably eight-hundred years or so, possibly, give or take. Lots of things. Lots of violence. And, what I'm trying to say I guess is, Cal, I've felt the weight of my own pressing down on me, too. My violence. My whole life, really. Two inseparables, really."

Sarah clears her throat, looking around. The square is empty besides the two of them. She keeps walking and Cal watches and follows her and senses the depth of what she's about to share, urging her with a nod as she glances at him.

"Sometimes, it's impossible to escape things that have happened to you," he offers. "I understand that. I've lived it too."

"Cal, my family," she explains, her eyes distant, looking up the parish walls again, "They weren't strangers to it. Ever, really. And it's in me. Since I was little. You see, my dad was – how do I put this mildly – well, a quick-tempered man, one that let his rage get the best of him. And when he drank, which he didn't much, but when he did... well, you get it."

"Shit. I'm sorry Sarah," Cal replies.

"To this day, I don't know how my mother endured it," she continues. "But she smoked herself into an early grave, that much was for sure, and I've always bet that's why. And well, David now... you see, my husband, I'm sure he saw it in me, too. This woman who's been wounded by someone close to her. Who, by the shit end of the draw on the family lottery, whatever you may think about it, was made to learn how to take a hit when she was young. Very young. Whether David even knew that's what he was looking at that first night or not... I'm sure he sensed it, right? Deep down on some level."

"The cycle of it, you mean?" Cal asks. "That you'd felt it."

"Yes. That. That I would take it. And maybe he embraced it then or fought against it. Either way. Same outcome – right? It was cruel irony, but very fucking real for me. I married him hoping to escape the shackles of this, but instead, I was just reliving it. Over and over. Another person now. But still. Tying myself to it tighter each goddamn year I stayed with him. Because he had trauma in his past, like me. And I justified it with it. So did he. And I was too young getting with him to know how volatile that combination could mix... these two damaged people. Two people coming up from violence. From that cycle... bound to it, really. And each and every year, I thought things would get better. And they didn't. Of course they didn't."

Sarah's fingers play with the lone ring on her middle finger, spinning it round and round.

"It started... as an outburst. Something tiny. Calling me things, breaking a dish, a shove, pushing me into the wall. Testing. Like I told you. Just like how it'd been with my dad, and from what he told me the same with his. Well, when I was young, I thought I could control it as I know my mom did too. With David, I mean. But it breaks free. It becomes more frequent. Like he knows, on some level, I'll just take it as I said. And I had to work even harder to control it and not get hurt. Even though I was getting hurt, I didn't really think that I was."

The two continue walking around the cathedral, slowly, and Cal takes her hand in his own for the first time, intertwining his fingers with hers, and the wind picks up as she continues.

"One night, in a really brutal, shitty argument, he just punched me right in my face..."

"What the hell – why?" Cal asks, as delicate as he can, regretting it after the words escape him.

Sarah shrugs, as if contending with a minor inconvenience: "I brought up our issues with having a child. Which was something I thought could fix me. But, the child, I mean. Stupid. And it was something he blamed me for not happening."

"What a piece of shit," Cal says, shaking his head in disgust.

"Categorically – he is. But it wasn't me. The tests weren't looking good on his side is the thing," she continues. "And they were fine on mine, really. But he didn't care about facts. Not David. He called the doctors terrible things. Even directly to them. It wasn't the first time either, but he hit me at some point. Again. Like really hard, I remember, when I reminded him of one test. Punched me right in my nose. And then," she exhales. "Well, it hurt like hell... it's my bleeding nose... and something in me just snapped, Cal."

She stops and looks at him, squeezing his hand a bit.

"I punched him right back. Like a lot. Like a crazy person, and then we struggled, and then he just threw me down... walked away. Left for a couple days. I thought gone for good, but no, never that simple. Never that lucky. And when he came home, after that, and really moving forward, he started hitting me every time he got angry. He hit me whenever he wanted to, really. Whenever he felt it was justified. It was like me in that moment standing up for myself, gave him permission to go all out – to perpetuate the cycle. Training wheels off."

"Jesus..." Cal stares at her, the anger rising in him.

"Maybe now he feels I'm as guilty as he is," she says, looking away. "Our flat was once my safe place... more mine than his, anyway, because he would just stay downtown to do God knows what... well, it turned into my prison about a year or so ago. Because he started doing the full commute a lot. There and back. Everyday. Everyday after that fight. And he started being home a lot more. Investing in my gallery now, taking control of things. And that was the moment I think when I really lost all control over it. The violence, the cycle I mean. If I ever really had any at all. Because he got all the power. He got my art. My passion. My name... I got nothing."

Cal's grip tightens back. "Sarah..." he starts. "That's not –"

"It is, though," she interjects. She looks up at him, her eyes damp. "I'm not saying all this for sympathy, okay? I just want you to understand and see what binds me to the situations you've seen me in – the relentless fucking history that holds me there. This way you can understand that it's not black and white, and how hard it's been to get free. I'm not a weak person, okay? I'm really trying not to be. But there are layers..."

"Hey, I know you're not," he swallows hard. "You're the farthest thing from a weak person, Sarah. But what about now? What will you do with all that realized? You know it as well as I do. He isn't going to change. He'll never stop."

"Now?" she takes a deep breath, sighing. She looks at him curiously. "Now I'm truly going to break free of him and rewrite my story. I'll be twenty-eight in a month. I'm not beginning this new year of my life with him. It's not going to be easy. History, as I said," she wipes her eyelids carefully with her thumbnail, "it clings to you."

"I know it," Cal says.

"But I have to do what I have to do. For myself. To break the cycle of this. For me. Or it's going to kill me. I realize that now. It's going to kill me."

"Sarah," Cal says quietly, struggling with his own emotions. "Whatever you decide, know that you're not alone. I'm here for you."

"I just met you," she replies, looking up at the gargoyles above their heads, and then glancing back at him through a strand of hair, a sheepish smile forming across her face, "and yet somehow I know that's true."

They continue walking around the dark shadow of the old cathedral, in silence. Tiny snowflakes begin descending from the inky black of the city sky, down across the forgone arches and the somber stained-glass windows, down to rest on their shoulders and the streets.

The weight of Sarah's story, the raw openness with which she shared it, beckons equal honesty in Cal, feeling its exposure lifting within him, like a layer peeling off his heart. Something deep down.

He takes her hand again and leads her to a bench in front of a shadowed, quiet park, across the street from the old church. They are illuminated only by the lavender light of a lamppost and the slick gleam of the cobbles.

Sarah's vulnerability is so infectious, Cal feels it strongly: the compulsion to unearth a wound he's too long kept buried from the world. Taking a shaky breath and exhaling, the fog of their breaths pouring out in front of him, he turns to her.

"There's something I've never told anyone, not fully anyway. About me."

"Okay," she replies, sniffing, looking at him. "Showed you mine... right?" She cracks a crooked smile to him.

"Yeah, you did."

He chooses his words carefully at first, starting slow.

"You know about Diane now – the little I told you at dinner."

"Yes..." she replies. "The cheating bitch."

He pauses, ignoring her disdain, chewing through his feelings. Sarah, perhaps sensing the gravity in his tone, moves closer to him on the bench, her hands finding his as he did with her minutes before. He swallows hard, his eyes staring into the distance, far beyond the square.

"It wasn't just any man I found her with, Sarah. It wasn't just some boyfriend she had on the side. Or some guy she'd met in a pub. Not like that would have made it better. Of course not. But still. It couldn't have been worse. He wasn't a stranger in our bed."

Cal's throat tightens, the image reappearing in his mind. The two of them. His heart quickens to a gallop, and he feels his hands growing sweaty.

"When I walked in on them that day, I saw who she had been with the whole time, behind my back..."

He pauses, takes a deep breath.

"Sarah – it was my brother. My older brother, Evan. She was riding on him in our bed when I caught them. When I walked in that day. And I never can unsee that."

The weight of the revelation makes the air around them grow dense and still. Cal's hands tremble but he continues, his voice raw, pressing on.

"I haven't spoken to him since that day. Since telling him I never wanted to see him again. For both to leave. Shit, now he doesn't even live in the country anymore. Which is good," Cal says, trying his best to keep his voice steady. "But my whole life, he's punched down on me. And that betrayal, Sarah, that one moment, was the single most destructive thing that's ever happened to me – to my entire being. Every childhood memory, every shared secret, every bond of trust was obliterated with him. Every warm moment, few as they were towards the end. She wasn't just the woman I loved betraying me, breaking the promise of our future, which crushed me brutally. But my past was broken too. Everything that made me a person. I'm a broken person, Sarah."

Sarah's face is a mask of shock, her eyes searching his. And there's something else, working its way behind their gaze. Cal can't quite figure out what it is.

"Cal..." she starts.

But he continues, his voice breaking at the edges, "I've always been a bit of a loner. My parents died when I was young, barely a teenager. A car accident; I was in secondary. Had just turned thirteen. Moved in with my aunt next. You know, it was just Evan and I for a long time as I told you at dinner. She was disinterested, so he was my rock, looking for me in the new school. My older brother. But he picked on me too. Made my life a bit of a hell as well, with his lies and his blaming. Probably dealing with our parents' deaths badly, I suspect now, well I see it now, but still. I was too. I was hurting too. And then he moved to the city to work and got mixed up. Would check up on me on the weekends, sure. Now and then. Less and less. But you know. Made sure I was still okay with my aunt. Just... I'm sorry... I don't know any more how to..."

Cal feels tears welling and he places his head in his hands and then runs them through his hair, overwhelmed by the memory of those visits.

"No," Sarah says, assuring him, resting a hand on him. "Take your time."

"Just to have the two people I loved most ripped out of my heart like that... so unexpectantly, violently... at the same time... just a loneliness I've never known, Sarah. The second time in my life. The pain... unbearable, sometimes. Worse than even my parents, really. At least," he pauses, trying to collect himself. "Well, it was an accident, at least."

He looks down, ashamed. "Yeah, I spiraled, Sarah. That's what you saw on the rooftop that night. That's what you were asking me at dinner, I know. But it's not easy to tell."

"I was," she says, her eyes affirming and searching his. "And now I know."

Cal shakes his head, "The misery of losing them both consumed me. The isolation wasn't new, sure, but its... It became like an echo in my head, no trust and love. No one to talk to. And then," he breathes out deeply, pausing, looking at her and then out across the square. "Things got really dark for me. It's why I was up on the edge of my building that night, why I was about to jump. In that moment I was so determined to just let go cause I couldn't take it anymore and I was tired of fighting that. I couldn't live in a world where people I cared about – so much about – could do something like that to me... I still don't know if I can. It's grieving, I know, but..."

"I don't blame you," she says, just above a whisper. "Not one bit."

"Look. You're not the one who's weak, Sarah. I was the one who almost did the most selfish thing anybody can do. Because I couldn't take it anymore. I am the weak one."

And then somewhere, deep down, Cal feels himself easing.

The wind rises and he takes a deep breath.

A cathartic weight rising from within, deep down. Off his heart. Little by little.

He feels lighter. He looks at her. Sarah's face is pale, her green-gray eyes widened as the weight of Cal's confession settles in. She doesn't move. She holds his hand. Her gaze, intense and searching, processing in her telltale way, locking into Cal's eyes. She squeezes, and when she finally says something, her voice is low in the breeze, gentle and sincere.

"Cal... I'm sorry."

"Yeah," he nods, wiping his eyes with his sleeve. "Yeah."

He exhales. "It's... fine."

"It isn't," she replies. "It's really not fine. At all. It's fucking rotten is what it is. They deserve what's coming to them, if you ask me – everything coming."

"You believe in karma, then?" he asks.

"Not really, but it has a way, doesn't it?" she replies. "People who screw people over, people fucking up the world, getting their comeuppance, right? All bends towards justice, as they say, right?" and she cocks her head, flashing a look, humor in her eyes.

"If only saying it made it so," Cal sighs.

He thinks about it, and she looks away for a moment. They both listen to the sound of the cold breeze blowing around them in the derelict square.

Then at last, leaning into him, she says, "No matter what you do, this life is going to hurt you, Cal – leave you bruised and heartbroken and... bleeding. That's the cold truth of it. And even if we choose the best of people, which we never do, but if we do they can't protect us from that truth. And neither does being without them. Because that breaks you just the same, in a different way. You know it and so do I. So either way we break ourselves over it all. And we are wired for it. By nature maybe, against our wills, and our history and these terrible phases we find ourselves in to us are just part of that package, I think. That deal we didn't know we were signed up for. That game we can't quit."

"So, what," Cal stammers, "we have to keep just standing up? Risking this... this crushing misery, for a chance at... bare minimum love?"

She laughs at his phrasing, and, after a moment, it becomes contagious.

"You know, I think that's the case. Bare minimum love," she giggles. "Bloody depressing when you put it like that, morbid even, but maybe that is what the universe is telling toi et moi. And we just have to listen a bit better. Accept that."

"Well – you're not bare minimum," Cal says, composing himself, glancing at her. "Mean that."

"Neither are you to me," she says back.

"Look. I didn't want to go into all of it –"

"Hush. It's been a good night," Sarah interjects, sitting up. "Don't ruin it with apologies. And you did – you needed to say it. And there's nothing to apologize for – seriously. Absolutely nothing. These are terrible things people have done to us. But that doesn't make it who we are, right? They're just terrible things. Things we must escape."

"I know you're right. It's hard to remember that sometimes." Cal says. "For listening. For hearing me out. Thank you."

"I'm glad we can talk about this shit together," Sarah replies. "We both have our lashings to share. Least we can do is flaunt the scars to kindred spirits, right?"

"Right. I mean. Of course, you're right."

"The least we can do," she repeats. "But not all we can do."

Cal shivers a bit. He looks back towards the river, feeling himself calm down. Then he looks at her, resting her hand in his hand.

"Seriously. Feels good to say all that, Sarah, to anyone. But especially to you."

"I'm here for you, too. Okay?"

"Okay Sarah."

She glances around the empty square.

"But now, I'm getting cold. I told you it was bloody cold out here. Not a soul in sight for ages."

"Yeah," he grimaces. "It's a bit eerie, isn't it?"

"I should be getting home too," she says. "Want to split a fare back before we have to pay the drunkard fee?"

"You don't want to take the Tube?"

"Hell no," she snorts. "I want to get to bed before I turn into an icicle."

"Same amount of time either way, I think," he replies.

"Nonsense. And one is far more comfortable. And safe. I hate the train this time of night. Weirdos abound."

Cal can't help but agree to this, and he gets to his feet with her.

"Besides, we'll be cutting it close with time," she says. "Nearly midnight."

"Yeah, let's go. Get you home and warm."

"Warm, huh?" she replies, tightening her scarf, and he feels his face flush and he's grateful for the shadows.

"You know what I mean."

After a minute or so walking, she takes his arm, and they step into the long, peering reflections of another old square, a sleeping fountain in the center of it, and he feels the tender weight of her head against his shoulder as they move across the empty cobbles.

Then at some point, waiting for a cab with a yellow-lit sign to pass down Kings Road, they huddle against each other in a storefront door stoop out of the flurries and the rising wind.

Their breaths fog and mingle, a rhythmic dance of hesitance and desire between them. Pressed close.

And then, in an exhilarating moment that seems to drag on forever and be over too soon, Cal leans in and places his fingers delicately beneath Sarah's chin, the smell of wine between them, and looking at her, his thumb on the dimple of her cheek, he leans in and kisses her for the very first time. Far beyond any fantasy he can imagine, she kisses him back, her lips exploring his, gently at first, before running her fingers into his dark hair as she pulls him closer. He presses his arms around her, and it feels natural.

The world seems to fade – first the cobbled streets and people on them, the wired frames of the trees; then the storefronts and the steeply pitched rooftops, the gables and alleyways; the parked cars and sleeping bicycles and icy patches of pavement, the snowflakes – and then, at last, there is only the two of them, enfolded in the sensations of something new and profound – feeling the motions intensify and blossom between them like radiant flares in the dark.

16

The lights of the clustered London skyscrapers glow on the horizon, becoming increasingly distant behind them as they near the exit. The hum of the hackney's engine mixes with the white noise of the motorway – a mechanized lullaby.

The causeway's lights skip past, one by one, flashing their faces. Their bodies. A soft murmur from the radio in the front is the only sound that fills the space, with the two passengers scarcely saying a word since being picked up twenty minutes before.

He kisses her neck in the shadows of the backseat. The sporadic lights reveal the contours of their faces as Sarah's fingers run along the nape of Cal's hairline, and then around the bruises on his head, jaw, and eyebrows. Touching the swollen spots. Lingering.

"Your poor face," she whispers to him.

"Is it so bad?"

"It'll heal. You'll be handsome again, just needs time," she whispers as his lips trace her shoulder blades, the flutter of her pulse echoing the beat of his heart.

"Thanks for that."

"Just a little more time," she sighs, a wicked look in her eyes, daring him.

"When we get back," he says, leaning in to kiss her, between breaths, feeling the warmth of her lips against his own, tasting her, "We can get a nightcap at the Old Hound if you want." She pulls away slightly, her eyes like emeralds flashing in the moonlight, reflecting the street's rhythm of lamps. She fixes them on him.

"It's too public. We live here. Word will spread like wildfire."

His face flashes disappointment but is quickly masked as he pulls a lock of hair back behind her ears, his thumb running along the metal grooves of her earrings.

She's right, of course.

You forgot that little detail of this arrangement, didn't you? Kind of a big part of it.

"I just don't want this to end is all," he confesses, looking at her, desiring her, running his fingertips along her forearms.

She leans in and kisses him.

"Guess there's only one thing to do."

"What's that?" he asks, his lips moving to her neck again.

"Take me home with you."

And a few minutes later, the world's a frenzy as the front door flies open, its momentum matched only by the urgent swiftness as the pair stumble inside from the hallway, pressing against each other, kicking it closed. Forcefully. Once, twice – Cal cursing, Sarah giggling – and on the third try, the door finally clasps.

Cal pulls Sarah, their lips hardly parting. They move in a dance of desire, a give and take as they shed layers. Sarah's heels click against the wooden floor of the foyer in the dark, echoing like a metronome before she pulls her feet from them and slings them off, one by one.

The space between them diminishes with every staggered step into the dark flat. Rapid breathing punctuates the silence, their movements filled with urgency, insistence, rushing. No time. Cal's hands pull her deeper, fingers gripping the curves of her waist. He trips over the living room rug, catching himself on the side of the bookshelf, sending a few forgotten volumes cascading to the ground.

They laugh nervously in the dark together and then kiss again. She sucks his lower lip into her mouth.

The dim lights through the blinds of the window silhouette their intertwined forms, cutting stripes across their bodies as they move. Sarah's fingers fumble with the buttons of Cal's shirt, her nails digging into his skin, and he slides her jacket off letting it fall to the floor, revealing the delicate fabric of her sage-colored dress beneath.

They leave a trail of clothing, piece by piece, discarded like old memories as the soft carpet underfoot gives way to the wooden floor of his bedroom.

"Light a candle," she commands as she slips her necklace off and places it in an empty glass cup beside the bed. He fervently stumbles around in the darkness and then finds what he needs, striking it to the flame, and then placing the lit candle beside the glass.

Sarah's hands move behind her to the zip of her dress, sliding it down deliberately slow, teasing, and smiling as her eyes flash a hungry shade of green in the half-light. Cal's fingers brush hers, taking over, the sensations making her gasp as he touches the skin of her lower back for the first time. With a newfound boldness, she reaches for Cal's belt as he does this. The remnants of his clothing join Sarah's dress in the pile, underwear and all, and the cool air of the room brushes against his skin.

Their eyes lock in the flickering light, the intensity unwavering, a brief pause.

Then she moves to him and Cal feels a whirlwind of emotions engulf him as he takes her into his arms. Memories of the times spent longing for her flutter across his mind - stolen moments when he imagined and placed her at the center of every fantasy. His curiosities, his obsessions, a driving force against his pain. The images of her from across the way, through the windowpane: the mystery stirring the very essence of his most hidden desires and somehow, someway, keeping him alive.

Does she know that? Does it matter? No, not now.

Now, that very same desire builds itself fully, bridging the chasm between fantasy and reality, and he feels almost dizzy as Sarah climbs into his bed with him.

He can feel the frantic beat of her heart in her lips as he follows her in, his fingers tracing the band of her bra to the clasp at the back.

Her skin quivers beneath his touch and Cal also feels like he's shaking. His fingers struggle to unfasten it. It finally gives, a moment later than he'd like. He slides the fabric off her and sees her flushed skin, the warm glow, under his gaze – a blend of nervousness and excitement in her eyes as she watches him back. Then he sees a bruise, just below her collar bone. It's smaller than his, much smaller, but dark enough to plum above the makeup she's applied.

He swallows hard, struck by the vulnerability and beauty of the moment with her. He touches the bruise with two fingers. She smiles at him, reassuring him, seeing him, and she takes his hand and guides him down across her stomach and beneath her breasts. The soft contours fill his fingers as he glides upwards, feeling her taut nipples brush his hands, dragging them across his palms. She moans slightly, and he feels her skin cover in tiny goosebumps and soon her hands travel his body as well.

Little by little, they map each other with careful fascination, enthralled in the vast expanses of nakedness and skin. Sarah's gaze, intense and yearning, stares back at him in the flickering shadows. And her stare remains fixed on him as he ventures lower on her body with his lips kissing each inch of skin – from her neck to her breasts, down her belly button, her hip bones, the inside of her thighs – drawn to the apex of her legs.

Her fingers clasp the hair on the back of his head while he delicately grapples the edge of her underwear, hesitating at the juncture before easing them past the crest of her hips. As he delicately pulls the fabric down, a fine trail of her hair unveils itself, looking almost silver in the candlelight and leading to a well-tended patch of softness. Descending further, his lips still on her skin, the moment feels eternal, as he touches the edge of warmth and is enraptured by how wet she is.

She moans loudly and arches her back, pushing herself against him relentlessly. Minutes pass with little else but their hastened breathing and her soft cries. And then the sheets rustle, and he crawls up to her, slowly again, kissing her skin, charting her freckles with his lips, sucking on each of her nipples as he passes in his ascent, taking his time, and then up further still, kissing her deeply when his lips at last find hers.

Time is lost in waves of overwhelming pleasure as he moves in Sarah, her breath gasping out, the world ceasing to exist. All that remains is the rhythm of their two bodies in tandem with each other. Her legs wrapped around him. The air between them becoming a force – electric and charged – gradual, their synchrony manifesting in every movement, every sound, every moan, every jagged breath. And Cal feels attuned to the shifts in Sarah's breathing, each arch of her back, her hips, as he slips out and she pushes back into him.

Sarah's whispered pleas become more insistent, her nails digging into Cal's back as if trying to moor herself, and he responds, ever so slightly. Cal slides forward, and Sarah finds each peak; the urgency of oblivion so close, before he pulls back again, leaning in then, his tongue attaching to her nipple, kissing upwards along the sweat-slicked skin of her neck and shoulders.

Their movements a mixture of raw need and emotion, and they lose themselves in the delirium and the radiating pleasure. The heat between them becomes an engulfing flame, their breathing harmonizing in ragged, unsteady patterns, and Cal feels the tension coiling. So close. The air is heavy; her hips hinting as the crescendo approaching, and her legs constricting tighter around his back. She pulls even more, as she cries out and kisses him, letting out a joyous whimper, shuddering – and Cal matches her, finding his own, his hands clutching hers.

The intensity – shaking, breathless, as they ride over the cresting wave together.

Colors blend eternal – the world stops spinning.

The dim candlelight casts an airy glow across their glistening skin, accentuating the contours of the panting forms and the languid ease with which their spent bodies roll over and rest against each other. Time seems to stretch into infinite as they savor the smoldering embers.

Eventually in the dim, he feels her eyelids and chin move on his chest and then her fingers tracing idle circles. He softly brushes a large strand of golden wet hair from her flushed face and he looks at her.

"Did I hurt your bruises?" she asks, somber, staring back, eyelids half-closed.

"No," he smiles lazily, his voice seeming far away to him. "Did I hurt yours?"

"No. You were wonderful."

The rigid loneliness, the pain of the past, the uncertainty of the future – all these fears faded away. Their eyes speak without words, without measurement, staring at one another – the connection they've experienced. No more barriers.

The vast blank spaces that Cal knows exist between every person overflow in his heart, renewed and filled – a single continuous blend of harmony stirring between the two of them. He holds her close to him, relishing it, running his fingers softly up and down the damp of her back, along her spine.

A bit later, with the candle blown out, his lips find hers again – sucking each into his mouth in turn – and then she tells him her mouth is dry and he gets up and fills a glass of water in the kitchen. When he returns to her side of the bed, he hands it to her, and she drinks from it and goes to the bathroom.

"Want some?" she asks, as she gets back to bed.

He finds the glass in her hand in the darkness, chugs some, not realizing how thirsty he is, and then gives it back to her. He hears the retort of it on the coaster and then a rustle, and he feels her body press against him, kissing down his chest, slow, renewed energy. Her soft lips pressing against him. He closes his eyes and tries to relax. Then he doesn't think about anything and after some time he pulls her up and kisses her in the dark. Holding her close. Tender, careful not to lean into his ribs, Sarah takes him in her hands and climbs on top.

17

The morning sunlight sits high in the sky and spills neat rays of light through Cal's bedroom window, and dust hangs in the stillness. It kisses the crumpled sheets of the bed where the two of them slept, before gradually moving over Cal's foot hanging out from beneath the duvet.

After the heat of it starts burning his toes, he groggily opens his eyes and awakens to a sensation unfamiliar to him. It takes him a few moments to put his finger on what it is. Then he realizes it.

The strange tranquility: the usual weight that has always pressed upon his chest in the mornings since it all went down is absent. A lightness, much like the one felt in front of the cathedral, but far greater, fills him as he blinks through the fog.

Sarah.

He looks to the side for her. He then looks around.

She's gone – her effects and clothing missing around the bedside.

He smells her perfume on the sheets and smiles, sitting back.

Lilacs. Jasmine.

He imagines the warmth of her skin in his bed, closing his eyes. Replaying the night back. Each moment.

The feeling of her breathing in his arms as he fell asleep.

The sensations of her.

The way she kissed him. The way she tasted.

At last, he gets up and showers.

Sarah's absence barely registers as a pang to him, his spirits so uncharacteristically high as he washes off.

Last night was one of the best nights of my life, he thinks.

And even if there was the fleeting potential for self-questioning, it is soon displaced with the discovery of a note she's left him, affixed beneath a magnet to the center of his refrigerator as he walks into the kitchen. The small rectangular paper is the same as the ones he's torn from his journal to write to her.

He unfolds it carefully and reads her handwriting:

I will never forget it. My place for dinner – same time? Bring vin. Let it breathe first. I'll cook.

He beams, shaking his head.

Luckiest guy in the world, I am.

He takes it and puts it in his robe pocket. Pure joy bubbles up within him, and he begins singing "Closing time... one last shot for alcohol..."and then, on impulse grabs a duster from the pantry cabinet and dusts off the record player. And he hunts down the correct LP in his office shelf, putting it on the turntable, needle down – volume knob set nice and high.

With newfound zest and the old single blasting, he gets some coffee going and a frying pan on some heat. He scrambles eggs and savors the noises of them sizzling, chopping up garlic, tomatoes, and spinach – his omelet coming together – the delicious aromas filling the flat.

Suddenly, pouring coffee, he realizes that today is a workday. For the rest of the world, that is.

Not me. Not now.

Maybe not that job again.

I should get the scoop. Reach out to Andy...

But that would require getting a new phone. Not today.

"Whoops," he says out loud, chuckling to himself. "Destroying your own phone. That'll be a Janice improvement plan."

And that nagging weight, persistent in the back of his mind since the day he first started making money, is oddly absent.

It will all work out, one way or another.

Today's about living, not working.

His food cooks. He cleans out his office next, throwing away junk and organizing his desk. Unburying himself. And the world seems quaint and vibrant as he sits and eats on the windowsill a few minutes later, taking periodic sips of his black coffee with brown sugar, and looking out through the glass at the people of his neighborhood. Watching them go about their mid-morning routines.

Such a rare thing for him to see. I'd be at the office by now.

He finishes the food and glances at Sarah's window before washing the dishes. The curtains are characteristically drawn.

"I've been granted a break," he says to himself through the toothpaste, in the mirror as he brushes his teeth. "Today, I will be my own muse. Today, I will be happy."

Now, to that end, what should I do with myself?

It doesn't take long for him to find an answer to that question, his boyhood curiosities beckoning.

It takes a little under an hour before he's stepping out of the Tube and strolling the distance to the British Museum. Stepping through its grand doors, Cal feels the weight of centuries of history and suddenly thinks about what Sarah shared with him the previous night, standing by the cathedral.

He thinks about her again as he stands in the queue to buy his ticket, her naked body moving against him, the depths of his affection and desire for her feeling limitless.

His heart races and he takes a deep breath.

He finally gets his ticket and steps into the giant atrium of the renowned museum. The vastness of the place is awe-inspiring, and he soon loses himself in learning about things that he hasn't in ages – reading each display, observing each relic, and feeling a rush as he enters the various exhibitions.

He drifts through one that plots the cultural and political changes of Burma to Myanmar; another, the fall of Rome. Then a history of Shakespeare's Henry the Fifth, and another exhibition showcasing the antiquities of stars and planetary scientists, and various astronautical photographs, all making him feel minuscule in the best of ways - connected in this inexplicable web of existence where his pain is just another constant with every other living thing in a way. Something across many outcomes and stages of human life. Nothing more or less than anybody else that has come before and no different than everything still to come.

Just life. Something every single thing in the world must tolerate, resist, and hold on to.

He finds comfort in the camaraderie of these thoughts.

Then the mummies captivate Cal the most of all, as he recalls they used to back when he first came to the exhibit, some three decades ago. He considers their age-old secrets, wrapped in layers of linen. The way they removed the organs. The way they spent their lives planning for death. He reads and reads.

The hieroglyphic markings. The black-and-white photographs of the tombs. Allegations of curses from disturbing the dead. Pharaohs and the workers alike. The indiscriminate nature of the ancients drawing intellectual parallels. Disparities of classism. Self-obsession of a different nature.

Well, maybe not entirely different.

Then he reads that the pharaohs were buried with their slaves, many of whom were still alive as they were sealed in the great tombs, a fact he'd forgotten. He leaves the exhibit thinking about closing podgy Rollins in a sarcophagus and hearing the protests of his boss cut out as the lid clasps for four thousand years. The fantasy makes him smile like he's six again.

At a quarter til four, Cal stands in front of the massive, 37-meter-long skeleton of something called a Titanosaur. The gargantuan stature of the dinosaur is breathtaking. And then nearby he spots his favorite, the towering Tyrannosaurus skeleton, which is not so subtly reconstructed to appear as if it's chasing the larger herbivore across the backdrop of some primordial wetland. An uncomplicated world of survival. A hunger so much more obvious, unlike the hidden appetites and ambitions of us.

Who so often obscure everything until the bite is vital.

Until the poison is deep.

Who tear each other apart on the inside, not out of base hunger – just selfishness or ignorance or both.

Killing for pleasure. Killing for greed.

People who let you wander your life after they damage you, after they lacerate you, tearing you down to a fraction of who you once were. Completely unbothered by the wreckage they leave behind in their wake. The broken pieces – the pain.

Unbothered by anything but their own relentless search for appeasement. For indulgence. Power. Recognition or satisfaction; the restlessness of it all. The unquenchable thirst for more, more of everything, more resources, trapped in the heated agency of these quick, little lives. Never stopping until the entropy takes hold and they toss some dirt on top. Revenge and envy and hurt at the forefront, pooling underneath.

Paranoia. Lust. Obsession. Vanity. You name it.

The destruction of who we claim to love...

And never looking back.

But always... always more than simple survival.

Cal looks at the teeth in the T-Rex's open mouth, each the length of a boomerang, monstrous and black and vile in their intent. Nothing subtle about the creature. It was what it was.

No lie in it. Not even one.

He looks again at the massive plant eater and believes that maybe, just maybe, this one would have had a fighting chance, even considering the obvious advantages of the prehistoric predator. All you get, really. A fighting chance.

Did I have one? Maybe now.

Yes. Maybe I'll have one again.

Cal thinks about Diane, their love during the good times, the little things – sweet things. The way she loved cooking extravagant breakfasts in their tiny kitchen every weekend; the way she felt hugging him every night as he got home after the long commute. The pride he had for her when she finished her graduate degree. The way it felt the day he asked her to marry him. The day in the tulip fields. How warm and wonderful that had felt, that specific day.

And then feelings about Evan, too. Memories together, growing up. The way his older brother comforted him the night of their parents' death. Some of the many nights thereafter. The way he assured him that things would somehow persist and get better. Somehow. Just hang strong. Moment to moment. Day by day.

"Just hang strong, Cal," Evan's voice echoes in his mind.

This cycle. It'll never end. The breadth of the pain the two of them caused. I'll never heal – not fully.

But that doesn't change the fact that I miss them.

Both things can be true. And neither feeling absolves the other. It is just the way it is now. Forever, maybe. Nobody ever knows how long grief lasts. Anticipating it... stupid maybe. Maybe it doesn't end until you do. Maybe grief outlasts us all.

After a bit, the memories dissipate and he realizes he's been alone in the exhibit, sitting on a bench for quite some time.

He looks around. The room is drafty with its immense high ceilings. He checks his watch, standing, and follows the echoes of voices out through the rooms and towards the main staircases, heading towards the exit. He purchases two annual passes from the kiosk on his way out then heads through the doors to the busy Bloomsbury district. In his heart, he's happy he made the trip, and as he gets back to the crowded station, he pushes through and boards just in time to catch the train before the last doors close behind him.

18

The neighborhood around his corner moves in its rhythmic, characteristic chaos. People lost in their own worlds, smoking and shuddering in the wind – talking, staring at their phones, cars honking in cacophony, buses unloading commuters and bringing others aboard. Bars and restaurants winding up for the night. Waitstaff turning on heaters, wiping down tables and setting up for the rush; filled pint glasses clinking between slouched, tired groups.

Teenagers and children running on pitches in the park, laughing and screaming amid heated matches, unfazed by the cold. Birds flying overhead as the shadows grow longer in the streets, the sky an exaggerated violet, and darker towards the southwest with a storm coming in.

It's the same district it's always been, on every early evening of every season as he emerges from the Tube on his way home. But tonight, it's earlier, and he's in a much different frame of mind than every other time he's returned.

He feels almost as if he's discovered some ancient secret, some formula, feeling his path righted.

New eyes, new ears – new senses.

Cal moves past these things as he rounds the corner to his J-shaped road. He briskly walks the distance to his building's courtyard in the waning light, the lampposts discordantly humming alive one by one nearby.

Back home, he doesn't linger. A quick shower, a shave, a change of clothes. The heat of the water on his back, the tendrils of steam rising – all just precursors. Formalities. Rituals before being with Sarah.

Maybe even better than the last.

Half an hour later Cal looks around the flat, ensuring he's not forgotten anything, before turning off the light. Locked up, he goes down the lift and back onto the street. The night is gusty with heavy clouds in the sky, the waxing moon half-covered, and he walks down a quarter mile in the gusty breeze and stops by his nearby corner grocery mart. In the wine section, Cal hesitates for a moment, contemplating the vast array of choices.

A red again, like last night? Hard to say... not knowing what we're eating... Just choose something.

You don't want to be late. Do you?

What we got here? Something bold, rich.

A bottle of Malbec catches his attention on a midlevel shelf, and he examines the label.

Ouroboros. New Zealand.

A pair of intertwined snakes, one black and the other white, consuming each other's tails around a silver tree. An ancient symbol below it, engraved on the roots.

Well, the artwork justifies a try, doesn't it? Next, the flowers.

Not roses – too trite. Overplayed. Need something more fun. Something affectionate but not too on the nose.

Unable to find lilacs or jasmine, Cal chooses a lily bouquet.

This will do.

He forsakes the self-checkout stand for Greta's queue, and once it's his turn, she throws him a curious, world-weary eye while retying the loose bun in her wispy white hair – probably noticing his fading bruises. But he realizes as he steps up to her that it's not that at all, but the flowers that has her attention.

"Who's the lucky lady?" she asks, her tone sweet, laugh lines crinkling around her eyes. She takes the flowers from him and scans them.

For a moment, he considers playing his cards close to his chest. He thinks suddenly that nobody else in the whole world knows about his connection with Sarah, except she and him. Why change that?

But something about the soft, knowing glint in Greta's eyes makes him want to give up something to her. Anything. A morsel of his joy.

"Someone who saved my life," he replies. "Someone special."

He smiles. Greta's eyes search his, looking for the tale beneath the words.

"Well, then. No small thing, is it?" she says, cocking a toothy grin back at him. "Haven't seen you this cheery in a bit, tell you that. But still, hun, mind you, if she's got cats. So you know. Lilies a toxic flower."

"I... didn't, actually," Cal pauses and nods, considering he doesn't know whether Sarah has any pets or not – it never came up and he's never seen any pets through her window.

"Appreciate it. I'll keep that in mind. Place them high after I get them in water," he says.

"Very lovely, aren't they," Greta beams and scans the wine bottle, ringing it up, and Cal pays with cash, taking the change in silence. He lets the mystery hang in the air, offering nothing more. Greta nods at him as she hands him the receipt and his bag of things.

"Have a good night, deary. Be good, now. And a gentleman."

Cal smiles and wishes her a nice evening.

He checks his watch and his heart races as he leaves the store, stepping out into the gusty night, clouds closing in above.

Not because he is running late, or because the distance is far, but the weight of the sheer anticipation. Seeing her again. So soon.

To hold her. To kiss her lips. Those sexy, full, beautiful lips.

To hear her voice again. That sultry voice. Hear the way she moans his name.

Feel her mind at work. Her stories. Getting to know her all over again. All of her. Every last, succulent part of Sarah Jones.

His entire day has been leading up to this point, his cheerfulness snowballing wider each hour as the instance of seeing her grows nearer. Each step toward her building, each moment closer to being in her home for the first time; he sinks deeper into the mire of possibilities, fantasies, and the fragile hopes of another evening with Sarah. And he cannot help but feel giddy... for the first time in years.

19

The indigo-red sky begins drizzling freezing rain as Cal steps up to the building's auto-attendant beside the lobby's entrance doors, and he scrolls down to "J" in the registry, calling the "Jones" residence. He looks back at the street and the passing people in the moody twilight pay him no notice. The box rings and then clicks over.

Sarah's face doesn't appear on the computer screen, but her voice comes across the line: "Cal? Hey. 15-04. Ready for you."

The door buzzes and Cal heads in, making his way to the lift, avoiding eye contact with the few people he sees by the mailboxes.

Word will spread like wildfire, she'd said.

He checks the dials above the lift doors and sees one going up, another heading down. A moment later, doors open at the far end, and he is relieved to see the lift empty.

Ready for you...

His heart thumps in his chest.

As the doors glide shut, Cal surveys himself one last time in the brass reflection of the lift's ceiling as the floors tick upward.

Eight... Eleven... Fourteen...

The doors open on fifteen and he checks which way the flat's numbers are oriented. He follows the ruby-red carpet of the hallway around the corner. When he gets to her door, he takes a deep breath. Seeing this place from the inside instead of across the street and through the window will be strange, he thinks. Maybe even stranger than the first-time looking in.

Doubtful, but maybe.

Once more unto the breach.

He rings the doorbell beside the large mahogany door, and after a few moments, he knocks and it opens on its own, squealing and folding inward ever so slightly, and he realizes it's the weight and not a mechanism carrying it, and that it wasn't fully closed to begin with.

"Hello?"

When Sarah doesn't come to greet him, he pushes it all the way open, the weight of it surprising him, and then steps inside.

Cal closes the door behind him, and then turns the lock and moves through the foyer.

Cal can tell that the lights are off and the fireplace is lit in the living room by the elongated shadows that dance and meld on the pristine floors ahead. He sees the lights are also dim in the adjacent side room nearest him, an area he never could view from his rooftop perch. He glances in it for a moment and sees an incredibly ornate kitchen. The cabinetry is dark mahogany, the appliances top-tier, and all contrast impressively with the gleaming white marble countertops, matching backsplash, and textured ceiling tiles.

Oh, the meals I'd make here. Perfection.

Instead of entering, he steps further down the entrance hallway, hearing the muted melodies of some classical music playing somewhere on the other side of the walls.

"Sarah?" he calls into the flat, walking slowly beneath the chandelier. Nobody answers, and he steps along the plush carpet, past the giant gold-framed mirror and hanging potted plants, the lavish baroque paintings of Dutch windmills, and into the lambent, expansive living room space.

The fire crackles in the fireplace illuminating the grand marble in red, almost out of place in the remoteness of the room. Its flames lick hungrily at the artificial logs, the only living entity in the darkness. It distorts the shadows of the decorations, the sleeping pristine furniture, the vases of fresh flowers, the deep patterned Persian rugs and shined glasses on the bar cart, contorting them as much as it illuminates.

The many paintings. Sarah's painting, probably.

"Sarah? You here?" Cal calls out again, feeling unsettled.

He walks over towards the shiny black piano sitting proudly in the dim half-light at the far side of the room, the edge of his rooftop view. He thinks about Sarah hitting it with the crystal bowl and runs his palm along the top of the instrument. The surface is marred by some scratches and a single chipped piece of wood, grooved inward, a silent memento to her act of defense. It makes it somehow even more real to him, now touching it – the glossed feeling of it. A current of violence, seething just beneath the tranquility. The beauty.

Around every corner here.

He notices the art adorning the walls by the darkened hallway to his right; extravagant and expensive looking, with abstract swirls of black and starkly monochromatic portraits and landscapes. He imagines the price tag motivating the purchase more than the sentiment, since they don't look anything like Sarah's style.

The cold detachment from the space they inhabit is palpable.

Corporate art – his art. Cal smirks, rolling his eyes.

But then another painting too, amongst the clinical stuff. One he recognizes immediately. Though smaller than the pieces around it, it's far more commanding on the wall – its aggressive brushstrokes in the darker sections, contrasting with the fluid gentle tension applied in the light. The figure, shoulders stooped in despair, standing, facing the far away storm clouds. The purples intense and dominating. Within the light too, Cal now can see by the figures' feet hundreds of delicate outlined flowers in emerging light.

It sits in a great, gold-plated frame, about two inches deep against the wall.

Sarah's painting. No mistaking it.

The one from the brochure he found.

"Incredible," Cal murmurs to himself, taking it in.

He looks around after a moment.

Where is she, anyways?

Every shadow dances like a menace from the light of the fire, relentless from across the room.

More like a mausoleum than a home.

The sound of classical music grows louder and clearer, guiding him as he heads towards the hallway. He recognizes the reflective, haunting melody as one of Chopin's nocturnes. He ambles down the echoing corridor with its stark walls, feeling as if he's walking through a gallery that's had its exhibitions hurriedly removed all of a sudden. He opens the door at the far end of the corridor.

The grim spill of the hallway falls away in the opulence of the fully lit master bedroom: the enormous bed, its posts tall and dark, hung with drapes, the sleek lines and profiles of the sheets and duvet, creased like they've never been slept in.

Looking around, he sees the walls, painted in muted tones, hosting more abstract art – broad strokes and bold colors – but few photographs, if any.

Not one. Vast blank spaces of nothingness. So strange.

Maybe she tore them down. Or he did.

Or maybe nothing was ever put up at all – insight in itself, he thinks.

Beside the floor-to-ceiling windows that twinkle with raindrops snaking down the glass sits a low-set chaise flanked by bookshelves, its fabric a stark grey, both inviting and distant in the room's curated light. A massive flat screen television leers on a wall too, screen black. There is another large Persian rug in the center of the room, beautifully patterned, and several big potted plants in each corner.

From somewhere invisible, the melancholy of the music fills the space – maybe from the ceiling – emanating the piano playing, each flair and pullback seeming to be everywhere at once, both past and future, melding with the impression of the room.

A curated introduction. Intentional.

One she's thought about.

At the back of the room, past the elegance of this, this gilded cell, something else draws his attention to the far side. It takes him a moment to tell that it's steam, escaping and rising out of the slightly ajar bathroom door in the dim light.

An invitation. He smiles.

The thought of Sarah in there, naked beneath the water, waiting for him, stirs a heady mix of anticipation and desire. His fingers move for the buttons of his shirt but pause.

He looks at the wine bottle, the snakes winding against one another.

Let it breathe first, she said.

Good idea. Who knows where it goes from here.

Cal steps out of the bedroom and back down the hallway, retracing his steps through the grandeur of the living room, the poignant stirring still hanging in the air as he enters the kitchen again. He hums to himself and absentmindedly, he places the bottle of wine on the pristine marble island and begins searching for a corkscrew in the nearby kitchen drawers. So many appliances and utensils, all gleaming in the ambient light as he searches until finally, Cal finds one sitting on top of the counter of all places, beside the sink.

As if she anticipated helpless me, he thinks.

He turns back to the bottle, wrenches the tip into the cork, and curls it out with a pop. As he sets it down again on the counter, there's the soft chime of the glass clinking, the deep red of the bottle starkly offsetting the pallor of the stone, and Cal closes his eyes and breathes in the earthy aroma, evoking memories of happier times irrevocably tied to the smell of the grapes.

Times that may never have existed. But they do in the rose-colored moment.

His eyes open. Regaining focus, and he sees it – his smile fades.

His eyes fix like a hawk's gaze across a field, the glint of light coming from the center of the island's tiered, empty metallic stand. Just sitting there, where fruit should be. Alone beneath the hanging focus of the ceiling sconce.

The folded knife.

His knife.

A cold chill spills over him.

It must be his. There, in its cold and muted Damascus steel.

Gathering a breath, he touches the hilt, memories flooding back to the day Evan presented it to him in his car after they'd left the mall nearest their house, last-minute Christmas shopping. Cal couldn't have been more than fourteen at the time.

"Go on," Evan said, nodding to the small box in Cal's lap. "Open it."

"It's not even nighttime yet."

"You can't follow every single rule all the time, Cal. And besides, we'll wrap it up after. Just lie to her that you haven't seen it, come on. I want to see what you think. Afraid of something? What are you afraid of, you wanker?"

"Cut it out. I'm not afraid. I just want it to be a surprise."

"It is a surprise! You don't know what it is now, do you?"

"No. How could I?" Cal stutters.

"Come on. It's got scissors, a corkscrew, and the sharpest knife I've ever felt. Open it, or I'm taking it back. Open it or I'll stab you with it. Come on, I'm only kidding. Just do it. There you go..."

And Cal withdrawals the shiny knife at last, deploys it fully, and the blade glints in the dimmed light of the kitchen. Worn now, but it still bears its spiraled engravings: the leather-wrapped hilt displaying the same slight fraying at its ends as his. And at the base of the blade, almost hidden, the same tiny notch in the same place – the remnant of the time Cal used it to unwind a screw, assembling furniture with Diane years ago.

The pocketknife is not that different than the winter afternoon Evan gave it to him, but it now has visible scars, visible tells—memories from more than half Cal's life.

Things that only Cal can see.

This is my knife.

But how in the hell did it get here?

The opulence of the kitchen takes a differing hue, the sheen growing cold and impersonal, shadows deepening, stretching out like old memories clamoring to exist.

Old memories he'd rather not remember. Questions spiraling in Cal's thoughts.

Why would she take this? Why steal it at all?

And when did she take it?

While I was asleep last night?

Before she left this morning?

While I was out today? Somehow? It makes no sense.

His throat feels dry, all the moisture in his mouth suddenly missing. The knife appears almost accusatory in his palm, summoning something in him, an old ghost from the past, whispering preservations, urging self-caution. Awareness. Fear.

He walks over to a cabinet and opens it, then another, finding the glasses and taking one. He fills it up with water from the sink and drinks.

Should I go? Yes.

No – wait. No, not without an answer.

Too many questions claw away in Cal's mind. He can't.

He gathers himself and folds the sharp blade back into its hilt and puts it in his pocket. Leaving the wine and flowers behind, he makes his way back to Sarah, walking the thin line between anger and the desperate hope that he somehow, someway has it wrong.

Chopin's haunting notes ring out like a mournful requiem, furious and rapid, and an acrid taste forms in his mouth, beginning as he crosses the dark living room again, his throat dryer than before he drank the water. Half a moment later, he swings open the bedroom door and moves around the bed towards the sound of the running shower.

"Hey Sarah?" he asks, pulling open the door, the steam and heat rushing over him. The pallid lights of the overhead bulbs refract through the rolling mist, casting a nebulous glow that obscures his vision as he moves to the shower.

Then, Cal's breath catches in the humidity, standing disoriented near the large sinks. His eyes search the mirror where the message is written in large lettering, her handwriting unmistakable.

It takes Cal a moment to process what he is seeing as the swirling fog encloses around him, and the only movement and noise in the decorative bathroom comes from the relentless pattering of the shower.

BON CHANCE

There, written by two fingers' touch against the damp – Sarah's two fingers.

Good luck.

Summoning courage, he wrenches open the shower door, half-expecting to still see Sarah there, her skin soaking beneath the stream, or maybe some other twisted clue she's laid out for him.

Some other strange, unnerving symbol.

Instead, there's nothing but the gilded showerhead gushing hot water; its rivulets splashing, converging, and spiraling down into the drain. Cal's heartbeat pounds in his ears, amplified by the close confines and the steam surrounding him, the relentless gush of water, and the growing feeling of being played.

This game she's springing.

The world, or at least this water-logged, steam-filled segment of it, tilts off its axis and an embarrassed rage starts building in Cal's breathing. Everything feels like a cruel farce tonight, despite his

elaborate hopes. His wants for the evening and the rising affections...
his desires...

Enough is enough of this.

Cal rolls up his sleeve and twists the tap to staunch the flow. He
takes a breath as the last of the water drains, the anger bubbling up,
replacing the initial shock of it.

These puzzles are no longer charming.

It's time to go.

He feels mocked, hurt a little even, and with a fervor that betrays
growing agitation, Cal turns and leaves the bathroom, his damp dress
shoes squeaking on the polished tiles.

As he moves down the hallway and reenters the flickering living
room, the expansive sterile elegance seems even more suffocating.

The glinting surfaces, the high ceilings, the soulless art, the
scratched piano, the stark white walls – all persisting with judgment,
skipping around the room in shadows, staring down at him.
Menacing cold.

I shouldn't be here.

Then he hears the creaking of the front door, the sound of it
groan heavy on the hinges as it opens.

Cal goes for his cellphone, but then realizes he no longer has one.
He freezes, listening for a long moment before calling out, his voice
an odd mixture of defiance and pleading:

"Hey! What the hell is going on, Sarah?"

But the reply isn't the sultry voice that he's been waiting to hear
all these hours.

The front door's heavy thud echoes through the flat as it closes,
suspended in the air, followed by footsteps.

Slow, deliberate footsteps.

20

D avid appears around the corner emerging from the dark obscurity of the entrance. He stops moving as he takes sight of Cal standing in the living room.

They stare at one another.

Moments pass in the solemn, flickering light.

He is wearing one of his dark tight-fitting suits, the picture of weary elegance, his tie loosened, briefcase in hand, ready for the sanctuary of his home. The confusion that strikes across his face is immediate, his eyes narrowing in the dim as he sees Cal around the corner. As if he's a traveler who has just encountered a squatter on his doorstep.

Their eyes lock onto each other, two worlds crashing through the nexus of Sarah's entanglement. Again.

Once again.

David's icy blue eyes ignite with recognition, then in the span of a moment anger. His briefcase drops to the polished floor with a muted thud, the echo seeming to reverberate through the entire living room.

"You. Again. In my fucking house," he snaps, his professional demeanor crumbling. "I left you breathing that morning, and this is how you fucking repay me? You break into my flat? That it? You have no fucking idea who I am do you?"

The air freezes in Cal's lungs. Time seems to elongate. His heart racing as the realization of how absolutely cornered he is sets in – a rat ensnared in the swift catch of a trap. A nightmarish maze with no clear exit.

The polished wooden floors, the art depicting vague and twisting human forms, the flickering from the fire, Sarah's purposeful absence, like sets of dominoes falling down into one another, all things conspiring against Cal at once.

His thoughts are a tempest, and his muscles lock as each one contends for attention, dissolving in rapid succession and indecision.

Should I try to reason with David?

Will words even matter now?

What did Sarah mean with her message on the mirror?

Was this all part of a twisted game?

"Wait a minute," David says. The suffocating layers fall away; his chest heaving, taking a step closer. His voice lowers, "You're fucking her, aren't you?"

Adrenaline bristles into Cal's veins. David takes another step into the room, disturbingly calm.

"My wife Sarah," he says. He raises a meaty finger, "See, at first I thought you were some deranged stalker, but no. This is more, isn't it? You can't keep your little eyes or hands off her, can you?"

The ambient light casts a shadow over his face, and gradually he sees the man's form strip his jacket off, and step again closer – slow, like he's walking in water.

"You simply can't resist, can you? Coveting what is mine. She's very beautiful, isn't she? My wife? But you don't know her like I do. She's not what you think about her. Far worse," his face twists. "She's a real cunt, when you strip all the dazzle away. Let me tell you. A real sunk-cost bitch."

"No, she's not," Cal says. "She's the most incredible woman I've ever met."

David scoffs, rolling his eyes, "So you are fucking her then..."

"Why are you laughing?"

"Oh, I'm just going to enjoy this, mate," David smiles sadistically, and he advances again, moving around the large couch, each step predatory now, the distance between them shrinking. Cal's hand moves towards the weight of his pocketknife, slowly, smoothly, not wishing to cast attention to it in the fire's glinting ambiance.

"Listen, I don't want to fight you, okay?" Cal says. "I love her. I love your wife. You don't. We know that. It can be that simple."

"It's not that simple," David replies. "She's mine."

"I've been falling in love with her since the moment I set eyes on her," Cal stammers, his heart swelling. He nods his head towards the floor-to-ceiling window in the center of the living room between them, the rain lapping against it quietly.

"When I first saw you step in and scare her – it changed for me. Seeing her in that window. The night I was going to kill myself. Right there. Through the glass. Look, I saw it. I'm not joking when I say Sarah literally saved my life."

"I don't give a fuck what you think she did or didn't do, you sick little twat. She's mine. It's simple."

"You beat the shit out –"

David yells, "Stop your babbling. I don't care about any of it. I don't care. Come here. Come on – little closer."

"I mean it, David," Cal says, taking a step back. "She's not yours anymore. She's done with you. You wasted that chance, long ago. You betrayed her. You hit her. You hurt her. You don't deserve her. That's it."

"Shut up I said!"

"After all you've done to her, all the damage. It's over, okay? And it's your fault. Not mine. Yours. Blame yourself," Cal says.

"Don't you say another goddamn word," David barks, pointing his finger at Cal, getting closer to him, step by step. Cal backs up some more.

"You hear me?" Cal yells to him, his heart a freight train through his chest. "Sarah's leaving you, asshole! It's over between you two, like it should have been the moment you ever touched her!"

His words hang in the dark spaces between them, but David's face doesn't register hurt or pain or contemplation in the shadows –

only a twisting, exploding fury. His brow furrows and Cal sees his fists coil.

There's no way out of here but through.

Cal braces himself for whatever's coming. And he sees a cold clarity overtake the slots of David's eyes, like someone pushed too far, too many times.

A look Cal knows well.

And then, without warning, as it was during the last confrontation by the garage door, David springs forward and lunges towards Cal – his tall frame propelling him around the couch at surprising speed. Practically leaping towards him.

"I'm going to fucking kill you!" he screams.

Despite Cal stepping back, their bodies strike, colliding harshly, smashing into one another. The force of the impact sends each man crashing to the side, into the nearby coffee table, with an explosion of glass as it implodes beneath their weights, shards scattering in all directions across the floor and carpets. Pieces of the fragments tear into Cal's cheek as his face strikes through the pane into the floor.

After a moment, he pushes David to the side, disoriented, his hand reaching for the sharp sting in his face and blood registering on his palms in the firelight.

"Ouch," Cal groans. "What the fu..."

The glass scrapes and crunches against his hands as he starts getting to his feet but the larger man retaliates again, pulling himself up faster and delivering a ferocious punch that connects upwards into Cal's jaw. There's a vicious snap as his view turns to the ceiling, and then over again. Tumbling. The pain smashes outward in the tightness of Cal's skull – white hot, blinding, as he feels himself hit the floor again, glass peppering his skin like bites from tons of angry insects.

Cal's fingers brush against something in the haze of motion, reaching and pulling for it from his pocket: the leather-wrapped hilt of his knife escaping out as he groans and slides over, rattling the glass away from him on the floor, trying to open his eyes through the flaring and blinding pain in his head.

"Okay... okay..." he hears someone say, and then realizes the words are falling out of his own mouth. His heartbeat resounds in his ears, a staccato gallop of fear and survival, echoing through anguish and anger alike. He feels the familiar leather in his palm.

Then there's Sarah's perfume.

Her words painted temporarily on the mirror. In the steam.

The memory of Evan – laughing without a sound as he glimpses the knife come out of the box for the first time. "Hopefully you'll never need it for anything life or death," his voice echoes. Life or death.

The cold touch of its handle as he fumbles to deploy it, finding the edge, pulling the blade as if his fingers are laced in a viscous wet. At once, from behind him, David grabs him by the back of his torn shirt, reaching beneath Cal's armpits, looming over him with his onslaught and pummeling down on his face, and then pressing his knees into between Cal's shoulder blades. The world fades to black as his elbow sinks deep beneath Cal's chin.

He will not stop trying to suffocate you until you die here.

The thoughts, enraging, boil up in Cal's gut and all at once he twists over, yanking the knife's brutal edge across David's constricting arm.

The fire's glint catches the steel as it slips open the flesh of his forearm, and the opening folds of skin look like loose, hanging cloth at either end of a zipper. The carved red line appears behind the blade a moment after, deep, and blood leaks out from the grotesque cut, David's crisp white sleeve turning dark almost instantly.

He howls clutching his arm at the elbow. When Cal tries to break around him, David pins to his feet, swings, misses, and then feigns another punch before kicking him straight in the ribs. Cal stumbles and collapses back, managing to hold onto the knife as he falls.

Through smeared vision, the room's opulent remove is utterly shattered now – Cal struggling to his feet just in time, only to be kicked again. Painfully, he tumbles back into the black shiny piano, its ivory keys shrieking out as his bloody hands collapse onto them for support, discordant notes spiraling.

David's face, framed by the gloaming fire, looks like an old Roman bust — timeless, calculated, devoid of mercy – as he approaches Cal each time, relentlessly, his shadow looming forward in the firelight.

"You should have listened to me and stayed the hell away from her," David says, his voice low. "That chance has passed. Now you're just an intruder in my flat. I'm justified. You see?"

Cal points the knife at him, glancing around.

With the wrath of a wounded beast, David snarls and grabs a small porcelain statue, swinging it wildly towards Cal's head, as he rushes towards him again.

Is this how it ends?

Over love? Betrayal? Sarah?

Cal dodges the projectile, twisting to the side, and hears its loud smash against the wall behind him. Anticipating the grab, he swings the knife in David's direction again, and he feels the grip sink home – a wet smack into the man's arm just above the elbow as he bears down upon him.

He hears David scream.

Call pulls the knife out and stabs again. And again. Blood, warm and sticky, spurts between Cal's fingers as the blade stabs deep into David's flesh and muscle.

The gravity of the fight shifts almost imperceptibly but also in an instant – the brutality of what just happened smashing in, and David's face contorting into a scream as he grasps for the blade wildly, out of reflex, both men fighting for their lives with the weapon between them.

And Cal rips the blade free from him once again, and David punches at him with his wounded arm, flailing almost, but then he switches and his good fist catches Cal in the face, just below the cheekbone. Stumbling, Cal swings out with the blade, this time missing, both men slick with blood.

And the man keeps coming for him. Dodging, side-stepping, and approaching just the same. The taste of iron fills the air, metallic and heady, as the walls seem to pulse in the death struggle; the paintings dripping with shadows, absorbing the grotesque arena playing out beneath them.

The fight continues its brutal dance: a whirlwind of punches, dodges, stabs, desperate flails and feigns. The men grapple, crashing into each other, blocking with bleeding forearms, smearing with each strike, each kick, cursing; a macabre wake of destruction following them as they slip and grapple and smash through the once immaculate room.

Desperation imbues David's movements as the blood drips from his arms, and Cal feels the man's strength surge into him as the two lock into a fight again for the blade in the dim. David shoves Cal off and sidesteps.

Attacking and retreating. A blur of motion, smashing, crimson speckles dashed to the white walls. A hit to the face, and Cal feels the hilt loosen away from him as something crashes into his elbow.

Then David finds Cal's wrist and rips his fingers open, painfully, taking the knife at once, and in the fierce struggle Cal feels something reach up and bite him in his shoulder, sharp and quick, and he realizes at once that the knife is in him... a fire deep in his flesh. Pain radiates with the recognition – dizzying, blinding, pulsing outward, with a surge of adrenaline erupting in him: the deep will to survive a siren in his ears.

21

C al headbutts David as the larger man tries to pull the knife out of him, and his forehead smashes into the man's nose with a sickening crunch. His frame stumbles backwards with his hands going to his face, and Cal screams out, not thinking, ripping the blade from himself in a blinding flash of pain and slashing at David in the blinking dim.

Cal feels hot liquid leaking down his right side from the wound, down his shirt, the small of his back, feeling wetter each time he swings. The first slash misses, as does the next, David dodging and stumbling backwards further, tripping, kicking glass, more things smashing around them, his arms flailing up. But then Cal presses forward and connects in a shallow arcing cut across David's abdomen and the man shrieks – the line between predator and prey blurring.

"Goddamn you and your fucking blade!"

Stepping back, David grabs and slings a vase at him, and as Cal moves around it, mid-air, David steps to the side and kicks him square in the chest.

The blow knocks every ounce of breath and strength from Cal, and he falls backwards into the bloodstained couch, coughing harshly, his vision narrow, his diaphragm in spasms.

Then, in a blur of motion, Sarah's husband moves up and connects his knee right into Cal's side – once, twice, three times – pounding strikes, each of them into his damaged ribcage.

He keeps going. Four, five. Each one harder than the last.

No air.

Six.

Cal feels his energy collapse away, and his consciousness slip slightly.

Seven. Eight.

Can't... let go...

But then David regains his grasp on the knife, one hand around Cal's wrist, pulling it from the grip of his fingers as Cal coughs blood out of his pulverized lungs, wheezing. David takes it from him.

Not good.

Cal's mind recognizes this and frantically scrambles as he realizes he's lost possession of it again, but unable to breath he can't get his forearms up in time to block the swings coming his way, and the knife closes the distance like the thrusts of a seasoned butcher, utterly invisible in the semidarkness until he feels it first slash across his torso like a burning lance, and then sink into the deep of his thigh with a nauseating smack. The pain sears through him like he's been lit on fire, the blade thrusted into flesh and the hardness of bone, and his gravity falters, twisting beneath him as he goes down with his own knife in him.

And Cal screams. His head slams into the hard floor and the shards of glass from the coffee table stab beneath him. His vision tunnels, smeared with blood, outer periphery blackening; only seeing David's manic fury come down upon him, icy eyes glinting and bearing, hands clawing for his throat.

He is going to kill me.

Cal can do little to stop him as David gets on his knees, on top of his chest, pinning him onto the floor. The irony of it all, Cal thinks to himself, a strange calm slipping over him in the thrashing, pulsing wallows of the pain in his leg.

He tries to breathe but can only get gasps in beneath the weight.

Maybe shock. A detachment from everything happening, as if he's an onlooker witnessing it all, the destruction and sprawled figurines below...

How many nights I must have stood there on the precipice.

How many nights craving that fall...

That abyss. That escape. That pull of oblivion.

The gates begin to open, inviting so loudly to step through.

No more pain.

Each memory – the solitude and cold of the windy rooftop, the echoing void left by heartbreak, despair, the loneliness; the porcelain outline in the dark: the sight of her that night for the first time – surging back and culminating into the present. This agonizing moment under his crushing weight.

David on top, squeezing his hands around Cal's throat.

Cal chokes, unable to breath. His life sputtering out, swiftly from somewhere, colder, moment-by-moment. A pulling feeling. Sinking down. Departing.

Let it... a voice whispers out.

Embrace it. Take what you've wanted all along. It's yours.

This remedy to your useless existence.

You wished for it and now you have it. In your grasp. Not his.

So, let it.

As David's hands tighten even more around his throat – the room nearly gone, out of focus – another memory emerges up: another thought springing out of the desperate wellspring firings of Cal's dying brain. He can almost feel its warm glow on the skin of his face.

A memory. A feeling.

A temporary vantage of the world painted in brighter hues. The precious possibility of another sunrise, another laugh, another kiss, another chance to find a fragment of happiness here, in the cruel world he realizes he's only seen from one point of view.

His entire life.

The truth crystallizes in his slipping consciousness. The truth of why he's still alive. Why he didn't step off the ledge that night.

It wasn't Sarah.

No matter how much Cal wants it to be.

You yearned for it before you met her.

Before she helped show you what you needed to see.

Not at the hands of another.

But what you needed to see deep inside of yourself. The strength you thought didn't exist. To struggle. To overcome. To stay alive.

You aren't a wasted person. That was a lie. Your lie.

Not without hope. I just needed to see...

Low enough and mindful enough to see it.. brave enough to reach out and grasp it...

His feet twitch against the floor, scooting upwards, trying to find holds. Cal's hand falls from David's wrist to his side.

And the last of his adrenaline dumps, fueled by the sheer desperation surging within him at the end...

Now, for the first time in a long time: an end against his will.

His fingers reach out into the blackness, determined, slick with hot blood – soaking, grappling, desperate – finding at last the hilt of the blade embedded in the thick cold of his right thigh, just a few inches above his knee. He pulls.

The tearing sound, drawing at it, wrenching it free, his muscles burning without air, his bone splintering; almost inhuman in the searing pain rising through his hips and spine, his ribs mangled, stomach cut, and he tries to scream all at once – the sharpness breaking free of his bone with a snap, a grotesque internal symphony of agony, spilling out. A determination sears into his every nerve's ending with the blinding pain. Then a slicing noise out of the shivering coldness – and Cal feels the knife slip free.

"Just die," David grits through his teeth above, somewhere, his hands viced around Cal's throat even tighter, and when Cal's swollen eyes open at last, he sees David smeared and looking right at him.

The murder in his eyes – how they widen in shock as Cal's right-hand lunges up from the shadows of his side, angled and aiming in.

The stab is desperate but thuds home, knocking through the grooves of two of David's ribs. The grunt that escapes his lips is almost a sigh, a soft gulp, yet he continues to strangle with feral determination in his eyes, unfazed. His strength's not lessening, Cal panics.

He's going to kill me.

Cal feels his own eyes bulging out of his skull, knowing death is just seconds away, vision dancing dark bloody spots. The light's nearly out. Red, everywhere. One last go.

Cal yanks the knife free of David's torso, and – with the remainder of his willpower – thrusts the blade higher. The hit resonates with something soft: the smack of wet. A moment passes and a series of gurgling grunts follows and a hot wave of liquid cascades with heaving motions in the space between them.

Cal opens his eyes, this time seeing the outline of the knife's hilt protruding from the side of David's throat. The man teeters some of his weight to his right side, listing. Weakening. He gulps.

The clutching grip around Cal's windpipe loosens swiftly, oxygen flooding back into him at once, and he gasps in air, his chest heaving. Coughing.

A frozen moment is shared between the two men, breathless, looking at each other in the firelight, horrified by the extent of it as new marks of blood pour between them in surreal, vital pulses.

Cal turns to ice as he sees the fear in David's eyes.

David chokes, sputtering, and his hands move off Cal upwards, panicking, to the knife's hilt.

Cal scoots back on his throbbing elbow and leans in before David can get a hold of it, grabbing the soaked leather handle, and then jaggedly ripping the blade out of him.

The knife separates with a liquid-sucking noise, and an arc of blood spirals across the destroyed debris and living room carnage. David clutches at the gushing hole in his throat, trying to stop its downpour, his body shaking in frantic motions. His eyes wild, darting helpless around the room, blood pouring down his lips and the front of his shirt in heavy splashes.

And Cal groans, shifting his weight in this moment of respite, and he pushes back and extends against the floor, anguishing, screaming out, and channels every ounce of power through his hips and into his legs.

With an explosive force, his feet thrust into the bulky shadow above: one single kicking blow, his heels striking the center of David's mass. And in that second — it happens so quickly Cal barely sees it —there's a blinding, scorching pain in his leg, and David stumbles backwards from the couch.

He falters to catch his balance against the momentum, grasping out, catching nothing, and then there's an immense crash of glass, petrified muffled screams, and his form vanishes through the space where moments ago there was a windowpane—disappearing into the blackness.

Swallowed with the cold rain in the inscrutable chasm below.

22

P ulling, entwined...
     ... ebbs and flows...

Laced in the folding midnight hue of it.

The moon half height by the nightscape – the owl's hour.

Time a haunting specter; hope not foreshadowed.

Dimly now. The past, nonexistent. Love not bearing the tarnish of guile or guilt. Anguish or avarice. There he is – right there. In the bliss. The middle. In the mellow syrup. The coddled wake of it. Right in that intersection where the dunes meet the tides...

Diane's standing there too, wearing the dress that first night. By the splashes of the ocean's edge, the sea lapping at her ankles, washing her impressions away in the wet sand as she strides forward in that dress. The blue one kissed with little white blossom patterns, flittering like fireflies in the midnight.

Moving. The smell of the salty breeze, the lilt of her laughter, faraway, carrying back and following her with her perfume.

Lilacs. Jasmine.

Her dark red hair. Her head turning back.

Lips moving. Her breath.

But the words, if any, are swallowed in the sound. The soup of it. The wind is rising. A roaring white noise. A fluttering abyss.

Then many of them. Muttering behind the flow.

Words, words, more words – some hot, sticky. More of them.

Weaving through Cal's thoughts with the noise.

Someone's breath on the slick of his skin. Someone's mouth, moving. Saying something.

With the coldness. With the echoes. The ache. Fiery, shifting below it.

The threading instinct, a foreboding, rising within him, through the grains of time that pass. Through the splashes of water, tides in and out. The thin veil between all his dreams and everything else.

The flittering fireflies of youth...

A sharp pain catching in his throat, sudden, brutal, cutting through the fog of the beach, anchoring him back again, down into his dying body. The husked sensation of being drained, expended, comes upon his semi-conscious mind as he becomes aware of the forceful pull of life away from him. So weakly aware, but he can feel the absence of it there. Like a phantom. An outline of his body's frame.

His eyelids flutter and the dreams of Diane collide with darkness and disappear into someone else's face entirely. A new outline. Someone's eyes – almost green – etched in an intensity baring determination and despair at once. Staring into him.

And something else too, a mouth below.

Moving. Words. Something.

"Can you hear me?" he thinks he hears.

"Where is he?"

Murmuring, too far away, the voice only a whisper above the sounds of the ocean's waves, kissing the sand, and sirens too... approaching... not so far.

Really close, he can tell. Somewhere out there.

Cal tries to speak, to say something, anything, but he can only suck in air. His throat is gripped closed – a hole filled with cement. Only enough air getting through to breath. He tries to say anything.

As if understanding, she nods, saying something else, and then Cal realizes what it is.

"You saved me."

I don't... believe... you. She says something else.

Her voice is only the faintest counterpoint above it, the waves crashing down in the moonlight, and something impending. Not far off. The suction of it. The feeling of sand in between his toes. From somewhere out in the blackness, the shadows of the face watching him, her hands beneath his head. Holding him.

Sand in my hair.

"But they mustn't know. To them, we've always been just friends."

A voice, close. Hers. Whispering in his ear.

Close. Warmth to the cold.

"Nothing more. Can you hear me Cal? Can you remember that? They can't know." Her face turns, sitting back. He thinks he sees her looking at his feet in the shadows, maybe his legs.

She's moving then, blurry, a strange, twisted form in the darkness, her hands around her own waist as she pulls at something harshly from herself. Shaking. A vague pulling sensation and then he feels a biting clench of something wrapping around his ruined thigh.

"Owww!"

The pain is blinding, the beach gone in a harsh flash of agony.

Her fingers work deftly about him, the sound of a buckle. Tugging. Stabbing.

More sharpness. Cal's screaming out, in his mind or the room he can't be sure.

Memories, futures imagined and lost, all pooling around him in that molten flooding pain, seizing every cell in his body in total agony. A dripping, crimson, pulsing rhythm in his leg – boiling liquid and clasping like a tightening noose made of razor blades. The teeth digging into his flesh.

"I know it hurts, but it will save your life," the voice says.

The shadows beckon him, and he sees the starlight reflecting off the tireless expanse of the ocean in front of him, dark blue, calming, drifting in like ripples, his feet dipping into the water as he steps forward—a warm sea pulling him in. And in the distance, the pier stands as a monolithic outline against the horizon's precipice. He watches it.

A cold, wet sensation beneath him, the metallic tang in the air. The lapping of the tide. Sand between his toes again. As it should be.

Drifting out. Ocean bobbing him.

"... just friends, okay?" the voice whispers above him.

A peaceful voice. One he's fond of.

The world recedes - becoming this, repeating – a fervent plea, a promise. Her voice. Then the ocean's waves. Crashing in. Fading at last to a merciful absolution, nothing more.

23

He gasps in processed air – the silent lullaby gone. The midnight, faded. Sounds of fluttering curtains against a wall.

Heaviness. A stale, sour taste. Commotion.

Beeping. Voices. Papers shuffling. And a static fan.

Some footsteps.

Cal's body feels warm, stiff as if asleep. As if frozen. Buried. His eyes squinting open. Blinding light pours in. The sterile fluorescent bulbs glare down on him through the crevices of his eyelids as he blinks. Slowly becoming aware.

He sees sheets, bleached beyond any normal white, draped across him, and he hears more beeping and buzzing of machines. Footsteps, distant chatter. Following the sounds, he moves his head slowly and sees tubes and cables attached to his arms and legs. Like an insect's limbs. He stares at them for several moments, not comprehending what they are.

Moving slightly as he adjusts himself, Cal realizes that he is not only tethered to the machines but also to the bed itself. On his right wrist, shiny handcuffs reflect back at him in the pallid light, anchoring him to the bed. He jostles and they rattle.

Clink, clink, clink.

"What..." he mutters.

His skin feels raw on his arms and back. His throat is swollen. Belly throbbing. Damage everywhere. He grits his teeth.

Somewhere, in the muted distance, he hears more footfalls and voices talking. The sound of an intercom saying something in another language he's never heard.

Or maybe he has. He can't think.

My head... what the hell happened? What is this?

Panic overwhelms him as he rattles the handcuffs and tries to sit up. Then, suddenly, he feels it—the brutal bite in his upper thigh.

The blade being pulled free all over again. That same blinding pain.

He remembers. The burning fire from where the knife lodged deep into the meat of his leg – the leg that now suspends above him in a massive cast and brace. And he starts to remember other thing too, suddenly. A cascade, flowing in.

He starts to remember all of it. Scene by scene. Through the miasma, the anesthetic fog. Piece by piece.

Cutting past the resistance. The recoil.

The scrambling. The screaming. His mind reeling back, resistance against the pull of it, a fighting in his mind - the insane violence of it, but he has to press into it now. No other way. He has to know.

Stitching the chaos together, all the savage moments, trying to bind the serrated edges of what happened into something coherent. Something singular. Each memory floating in Cal's mind, fading in and out; each desperate kick, each cut, each stab into him, each punch, pain rising again like shards of glass, scraping his insides onto the floor, his head feeling heavy and tired all at once.

The smash of the table. The scream he made when I put the knife in his arm. Or was that me screaming?

Some time passes, and he lies there with the incredible weight of all that transpired. The blood. The brutal blows. The thrust into his throat. The fear in his eyes as he lost his balance backwards, smashing through the glass.

Sarah. Oh my God. His eyes open suddenly. Not a dream.

Not before – it was real.

She was there. Afterwards. When it was all done.

He tries to sit up.

When I was dead. Almost dead.

After, when I was just lying there. She was next to me. Holding me.

And... she set you up. Sarah. She set you up.

Bon chance.

Good luck written on the mirror.

The knife. Her absence. The lucid, haunting look in her eyes, her promise to him, her vice-like grip on the belt around his leg. Her words, asking him.

No, not asking – telling.

"Just friends," he mutters, his head slouching back into the pillow. Eyes closing.

Fatigue overtakes him, and the room starts to spin.

All the events crash down again and again.

Why would she... why...

Just as Cal begins drifting back to sleep, something moves, and his eyelids catch a motion by the door to the hospital room, and he hears a knock and looks to see a blurred figure step into view.

He's a tall man with a big beard, and a grave-looking face.

"Who are you?" Cal asks weakly, still trying to get himself to sit up a bit.

"Glad to see you awake and alive, Mr. Beckley. May I?"

Before Cal can give a response, the man ambles in. He's wearing a suit beneath a damp beige trench coat. He's towering with graying temples and an ashen complexion, and the worn-out look of a man who's seen too much yet never enough.

His face is a series of deep-set lines, his gait deliberating as he crosses the room, taking his time, looking through the medical charts, page by page; at last, pulling out a chair to sit near the bed, his eyes focusing on Cal like some kind of bird of prey.

"I'm sorry, you are?" Cal asks, feeling slightly delirious.

"I don't expect you to recognize me. Apologies for any confusion," the man begins, clearing his throat, and presenting his Warrant Card. "I'm Detective-Inspector Elliot Grant of the metropolitan police force. Call me Grant if you'd like. Most do.

You'll forgive the delay, Beckley - been unable to make your acquaintance due to, well, your surgery. Each of them, as a matter of fact. Then the morphine. Long couple of days for you. So, anyways," he clears his throat. "All that to say I don't want to waste much time getting down to a statement from you. As there hasn't been one collected yet. You understand, of course, yeah?"

"I'm, just sort of mist–"

"Very well. This is an incredibly grim affair, as you may recall. Well, you know. At least, a general outline would be most useful in corroborating the evidence at hand, you understand," Grant glances at Cal's casted leg, suspended above the bed.

"I see," Cal replies. "Now though, really?"

"Yes, if that works for you," he says gruffly, sitting back in his chair, once again not waiting for a reply.

The two study each other for a moment. Then Grant looks at his phone.

The man is clearly enjoying interviewing someone who can't move or protest much, Cal thinks.

"Well, can't find the app. Must have deleted it."

Putting a finger up, he fidgets in his jacket, removing a small silver recorder.

"The old fashion way. Less fuss," Grant says and places it on the bedside table. He then presses record.

"So, getting started – how you feeling?"

"Not my best, if I'm to be honest."

"You've undergone surgeries, yes, Mr. Beckley?"

"So you just informed me," Cal says.

"Do you know why you're here?" Grant asks.

"Where is here, exactly?"

"Sorry?"

"This... place?" Cal asks.

"Lewisham Royal Hospital, critical care unit," the detective-inspector says, his tone impatient. "Been here for the past three days. Since officers found you on the scene, that is, Jones Residence of Victoria Vista Towers, barely alive," Grant nods towards Cal's leg, suspended in a cast above the bed. "Nicked the femoral that, doctors say, the lower stab wound you got there. Quite nearly killed you by its lonesome. You're lucky if I say so. Seen others take something like that another way. Back in the service we'd call that a timer wound... seen some bleed quick. Five minutes or so. Lucky, Beckley."

He looks at Cal and his dark brown eyes harden, pressing.

"So, point is, you barely survived," the detective-inspector says, and something about his continued familiarity is unsettling. A long moment passes. Then, as if asking the weather, he goes on:

"So, do you know why you're here chatting to me? Now that we've established that much and where we peeled you up from..."

Cal looks at him, his face expressionless, trying not to let him get under his brutalized skin.

"I imagine it has to do with the fight, course," Cal says. "In Sarah's flat. What else – accident on the Eye?"

"What else? I think it's a bit more than a laugh from you," Grant replies, "Your blood's all over the place. Living room, foyer, the ceiling. You know all the major details here. And David Jones's body, found outside, right? You probably already know that too. Right?"

"Dead?" Cal asks, perhaps a bit too enthusiastic in tone considering he knows the answer.

"Severed on each side of the wrought-iron fence between his building and yours."

Cal closes his eyes. Worse than he could think of. All of it is.

"Horrible scene," the detective-inspector continues. "Well... from my viewpoint. Same the neighbors who happened to find him. Horrific barely describes it. This is a major crime, Beckley."

"Jesus Christ. I know that. Of course, it's a major crime," Cal scoffs, wincing.

"So. Cards on the table. Want to tell me what happened to David Jones?"

Cal hesitates, the weight of the night's memories bearing down on him. The blooming revelations that have resided in a place of his mind for days now, waiting for the energy to examine. And now he must. There's no more denying any of it. The painful obviousness of it all.

Sarah. She walked him into her place with the knowledge that her husband was coming home. The only explanation for her answering the intercom and buzzing him in, then writing the words in the mirror, as well as being absent at the crucial moment.

The moment each man walked into the flat.

And, of course, the planting of the knife.

Now, of course, it was her. It had to be. It was all her.

Knowing he'd find it as he went for the corkscrew. Opening the wine, as she requested. Asking to bring the wine in the first place.

Step by step, detail by detail. Layer by layer. The knife.

The stolen knife. The one Evan gave you. Given back just before, to tip the scales in the mortal struggle. By the only person who could have taken it from the drawer in his nightstand.

Now, so plain to see. Now, no longer in that kitchen, realizing it all with the feeling of dread coming on like a tidal wave. Each little clue, leading back.

And now realizing that Cal's dread in that moment was intuition, trying to scream at him to get out of that kitchen, out of that flat, before the impending confrontation with her husband – notions that he had desperately tried to avoid in favor of confronting her instead. In favor of seeing her in the shower.

A complete fool - I should have died there.

"Sarah," Cal begins, stuttering at first. He tries to sit up but a sharp pain in his shoulder flares and he gives in, realizing at once it is another stab wound.

"Take your time."

"She invited me over," Cal says, wincing again. "Asked me to bring her wine. She wanted to eat."

"Okay. It's not a far walk. You step around the big gate. Off you go for dinner. You make your way up. Then what happens?" Grant asks. "At the door?"

"What do you mean?"

"She buzzes you up? You and the wine bottle. What happens that gets you in?" Grant asks, his eyes peering down, unblinking.

"I... I'm not sure. I think it was her, but I can't remember, really."

"Can't remember? Did you buzz at all?" the detective-inspector asks.

"Yes. I... yes. Check the cameras, mate. It's difficult -"

"This is a statement, Mr. Beckley."

"Yes, I realize that."

"Anything else?" Grant asks without missing a beat.

"I don't think there was a face in the screen, come to think of it," Cal replies.

"But Mrs. Jones, did she speak?"

"No," Cal lies. "Maybe. I don't know."

"Alright," Grant presses. "So just a buzz in, as you recall. Not her giving you the code or anything like that, right?"

"No. No code. Buzzed. Maybe I followed someone in?"

"We'll return to this," the detective-inspector says, motioning with his hand. "Go on. Continue. What next?"

How much should I say? How much does he know?

Shit – there's no time to think at all.

Cal's voice shakes as he continues: "I came upstairs. It wasn't supposed to go down like that. Obviously. The fight. I was going to meet with her. Dinner..."

"Meaning what, exactly?" Grant asks.

"What?"

"Not supposed to go down like that," he repeats. "That mean you didn't expect David Jones to be there?"

"No, of course not. He came in after me – you know, bit after, that is. Confronted me. Misread it all. What it was. We struggled; he outright attacked me. Basically charged me. I fought for my bloody life."

"When?"

"When he came through the door. Wouldn't let me leave," Cal answers.

"Wouldn't let you leave," Grant repeats, lingering on each word.

"That's right. He cornered me. Then went berserk. Mental. Charged at me."

"Alright. Charged at you, you say," Grant types something on his phone, eyes narrowing as he leans in and looks at Cal. "And Sarah Jones, David's wife? Where does she fit in all this? This berserk encounter, you call it."

"How do you mean?" Cal asks, trying to buy precious seconds to think before the next rapid-fire question.

"Her orientation on the matter. Was she in the flat when her husband attacked you?" the detective-inspector asks, "Sarah?"

"No," Cal responds, his voice weak all of a sudden. "I'm not sure..."

"No?" the detective-inspector asks. "Or she was som...?"

"No," Cal repeats. "I didn't see her."

"Alright. How can you be sure of that?"

"I looked for her."

"Looked for her?"

"When I arrived. But I think she'd stepped out," Cal responds.

"Could she have been in another room, maybe one you didn't check?"

"I'm not sure, okay?" Cal says meeting the man's glare.

"And your relationship with Mrs. Jones?" Grant asks. "Were you two romantically involved? Were you having an affair?"

"No," Cal retorts. "No. We were just friends."

"Just bringing wine over to your friend then? For dinner?" Grant asks, a hint of patronization in the way he cocks his head while saying it.

"Is that illegal?" Cal asks.

"Flowers, too. For friends?"

"Lilies... easy. She's been... going through a lot... Never come empty-handed..."

"That's it? A single man off to see a woman he knows has a husband. Simple as that?" Grant asks, matter-of-factly.

"Did I say that?" Cal's eyes narrow.

"Probably," Grant shrugs. "We can rewind the tape if you'd like."

"I don't think so."

"Well did you?" Grant asks again.

"We were friends, detective-inspector. Neighbors," Cal says, feeling his heartbeat even faster, the man's eyes staring at him. Still hardly blinking.

I don't have the strength for this much longer.

He's withering me down.

"So, you make your way up," Grant presses on, his foot firmly on the gas now. "Then what? You're telling me this man finds you in his own living room, the nerve, misunderstands the scenario, and attacks you? Tries to kill you, nonetheless. No questions asked. That it? That how it all happened?"

"There were some questions, I believe," Cal says. "Yes. Mostly how it did..."

He must know these painkillers are going to knock me out soon.

"Okay. What questions?"

"She invites me over for wine."

"And?"

"And we are neighbors. I... I didn't expect David to be there. I'm not sure she did either."

"Why would that be? He's her husband."

"Because I thought he was out of town," Cal says.

"Based on... something Mrs. Jones told you?" Grant asks.

"Maybe I just saw him leave. My office window looks down on their parking garage... did you know that?"

"I did know that," Grant responds cooly.

Of course, he does, Cal thinks. *They've probably turned my place upside down by now.*

"Go on."

"I can't remember. I don't think he was supposed to just come home," Cal says. "Because he didn't like her friends over."

"But then David showed up, unexpectantly," Grant presses. "While you were there, waiting for Mrs. Jones. Implying you didn't particularly want him to see you there, right?"

"Correct. That's right."

"And why is that exactly?" Grant asks.

Has this guy not read any of the domestics?

None of the prior history there?

"He has a violent psychopathic way about him," Cal says at last.

"Really? He seems to be quite the accomplished investor. Businessman."

"What does that say about his business," Cal replies, his voice wavering.

"Not for me to decide," Grant snaps. "Nor you. And, what, so he just attacked you? For being in his flat? Seems a bit understandable, really," Grant nods, feigning consideration. "Even reasonable, one might say. Considering. You know, I might even understand, I come home tonight to a stranger in my living room. Bit different, sure – have little ones. Not much different though. Not really. A stranger in someone's house."

"It was more than that, detective-inspector. I was invited. Then he tried to kill me," Cal retorts, feeling sweat now on his brow. He hopes Grant doesn't see it, but he is pretty sure he does.

"Tried to kill you…" the detective inspector repeats.

"Not just throw me out, a stranger," Cal says, "No, the bloke didn't like me. He didn't ask me to leave – he wouldn't let me leave. I tried. He didn't like what I had to say about him hitting Sarah, neither. Seems a bit self-evident, no? I'm sure you have reports… on his shit. On the domestics. The charts. The abuse between the two of them. Their history, don't you? Come on."

"Some," Grant nods, as if conceding a point he'd rather not have to give up. "I've read them. A couple of them. But what interests me more are your charts, Beckley."

"What do you mean?"

"Over there," he nods his head behind him. "Saying some ecchymosis, bruising, older than the newer ecchymosis. On your mug, mate. Explain that."

"Bruising," Cal repeats, playing dumb, biding time, mind spinning as he's unprepared for where this is going or how to stop it when it arrives.

"Meaning… to me," Grant fills in the gaps, "Me who's done this a few too many times, mind you, that there's been other altercations in the past. Correct me if I'm out of line here. Am I wrong in this deduction, Beckley?"

"No, not wrong," Cal answers him, hoping to sidestep with a morsel. "There was me telling him to stop hitting his wife. To stop hurting her. And there was him punching me and nearly choking me to death. Right out in the street. Violent psychopathic tendencies, every time."

"No reports of this. Any witnesses?"

"Not that I know of..."

"And that would make it two encounters. Correct?"

"First, more of a scuffle, but yes," Cal admits.

"And when did this first scuffle happen?"

"Bit before. Not too long before. Can't totally recall. The bruising will have to do... carbon date it, whatever."

"Right," Grant fidgets, his eyes narrowing in seeming agitation at Cal's impudence, and he checks his phone for a moment before looking up. "Even still, you brought a knife, didn't you? Brought your knife over to the flat. The murder weapon."

"Murder?"

"Expecting a fight, perhaps? Expecting to confront this man, in his own gorgeous living room, about his own gorgeous wife? Premeditated, even, one might say – having that knife. How do you explain it being there, Beckley?"

"Premeditated." Cal swallows, "Please... that wasn't it..."

He feels the cold bite of the metal needling in his arms, the IVs and painkiller administering, and the even colder gaze of the detective-inspector. He thinks of the knife, the weight of its handle, the pattern on it etching an old, perhaps intended tale, his brother looking out for him.

And worse – stained by him, along with everything else.

Stained by his betrayal. And hers. And now a bloody death to boot, another notch to it. In the defense of another unfathomable betrayal. Damnable. The irony of all is not lost on him.

"It was for protection," Cal responds, his voice hoarse, as he imagines the flashing events of the fight that carried across the flat that night – the stabbing, clawing for life, the wind cutting from his lungs, the blade between David's ribcage, then up into the meat of his throat; the kick, his form crashing into the windowpane. Sarah leaning over him, the tourniquet tightening– all of it, blending in a tortuous maelstrom behind his eyes.

"I always carry it. It's legal to have."

"Only just legal," Grant scoffs. "Nonetheless, ill-advised to carry about."

"Our neighborhood isn't the safest."

Not the safest. Not at all. Even between neighbors, Cal thinks.

If she set me up, then why save me? It makes no sense.

"That's interesting," Grant says, pausing, cocking his head.

"What is?"

"Mrs. Jones claims that the knife is hers. What do you make of that, Beckley?" Grant asks, his eyebrows raising a bit, his weatherworn face appearing only slightly less stoic.

"I'm confused, maybe," Cal replies, his mind spinning like a top.

How much to say, how much to say...

He rubs his eyes, taking a moment. Sighing.

"Maybe so. Maybe. I can't... I don't remember. Maybe it was mine. I know... I know she invited me over. You'll have to show me," he stutters, then hesitates, yearning to defend Sarah, but the doubt sinking ever deeper, shadowing his ability to lie for her—a piercing self-doubt, too. Born of frankness in his own memories.

"I don't know why her husband just attacked me like that, detective-inspector. But the knife wasn't some premeditation thing. I don't understand what happened. Except that I told him to stop hitting his wife. He wouldn't let me leave. So I gave him a piece of my mind. I told him to stop hurting her. Like I said, there's a pattern with this man. Was... a pattern. He was hitting Sarah."

"So, you were trying to protect her, from him hitting his wife?" Grant asks, eyes like daggers, relentless, cutting deep. "And in return, so I understand it, later, she protects you, tying a tourniquet, is that it?"

"You're implying some sort of alliance. Some sort of quid-pro-quo. That wasn't the case, detective-inspector."

Grant glances at his phone again, as if he's taking notes, although he isn't typing.

"I don't know why she tied the tourniquet, but I'm grateful. Obviously," Cal continues, looking at his inert, wounded leg. Out of nowhere, he feels his eyes dampening. The agony of the wounds, both physical and emotional, constricting his voice. Tightening his swollen throat.

"I want to believe it was her that saved me..." he begins. "But..."

"But?" Grant asks, peering at him.

"But the truth is, now, everything's twisted in my mind. I don't know what's real. I just know what happened before I was stabbed..."

"Alright," Grant nods, as if expecting Cal to say this. "But it's a tangled mess, you must admit, yeah? One you're right in the center of. So we're going to need to think about that. And we're going to need an explanation that absolves any motive in you bringing that knife on purpose to kill David Jones. We are going to need a real explanation, you hear me Cal?"

"You don't think I know that? I'm giving you that," Cal snaps. "Right now."

"A better one than what you're giving," Grant responds cooly. "To reframe it: clarify your intention in that penthouse."

"Look, I was attacked in the middle of their living room. The middle of their flat. After being invited over. I barely made it out of it alive. Look at me. I barely fucking survived."

"I am, Beckley. I am looking at you," Grant nods his head. "Self-defense. Got it. But you have to understand something. A man is dead. Regardless of the circumstances leading up to it, there's a responsibility to be shouldered. Now. I understand you've sustained injuries. And you've had surgeries because of them. I'm mindful here. I want you to be lucid as we sort this mess out. So – now, rest up. I'll be leaving you with that. And I'll be back tomorrow when you've had some more time to... remember things a bit better. Right?"

He clears his throat and checks his phone. He then slides it into his coat's pocket, along with the recorder.

"For your sake, I hope these are truthful things, because as of right now, Beckley, I won't lie to you, things are not looking good."

"You think I don't bloody well know that?" Cal spits back.

"Well," the detective-inspector says and stands. "Maybe you don't," he shrugs, picking a callous on his palm, "But either way, you will soon enough. Mark my words."

"What the hell is that supposed to mean?" Cal asks.

"Nothing – truth prevails," he flashes a mock grin, pushing the chair to the side of the room. The bearded man shrugs as he goes. "I'll have a bobby outside if you need anything—all night. Let him know. He'll contact me if you have any epiphanies... anything you want to disclose. Any details, big or small. All of it helps. I assure you. Otherwise, tomorrow... you and I will meet here, just like this. And from the beginning again, we'll talk through it. Alright? Want to make sure I have a full picture of how things played out from the one survivor in that room that night. So, think it through. Right?"

"Sure thing," Cal mutters, feeling numb, his voice far away – his mind shifting elsewhere, whirling in the memories of the fight with Sarah's husband... each horror of it sinking in, rapid now, with enough remove to examine each brutal action and each bloody, painful result. Each violent, horrendous moment.

The pain of being stabbed. The steel piercing deep into his flesh. The gasping for air. Feet kicking the floor. Glass slicing into his skin.

The sweat mixing with his blood, salty against the cuts in his mouth.

The impacts of slamming into the piano. The sharp edges. The floor. The couch. Through the coffee table.

The firelight shimmering on the spatters of carnage in blackened patches and dancing shadows. The acute coldness of his skin being pierced in many different places all at once.

The guttural howling sound David made when the knife slit his forearm into folds of bloody skin.

The retort in the handle of the knife as it sunk into Cal's body.

The hot gore flowing down over him from David's opened throat. Life pumping out of him. His gulping and grabbing – his panic. The fear.

"Have a good evening, Beckley," Grant says, looking at Cal as if he can see the same recollection, that same terror in Cal's eyes, as he turns away. "We will talk soon."

And the detective-inspector leaves, and Cal is left alone with nightmares, haunting either side of his eyelids – a dreadful reality sinking in.

24

Painkillers swell hot in his bloodstream, floating bliss in a sea of agony, his thumb pressing the self-administration button, again and again. The pain lessens to a murmur, a siren underwater, deep in his bones. Held at bay for now. Just for now. His face. In his shoulder. In his throat. In the meat of his thigh, most of all.

Because of her.

Because of her, I've ruined my life.

Because of her, I killed a man.

Because of Sarah... or because of me.

Which is it?

Her voice echoes in his mind: I have to do what I have to do. For myself. To break the cycle of this. For me. Or it's going to kill me...

He feels dizzy, a disassociating nausea attaching deep within him. And silently, lying in his hospital bed, Cal wishes to himself that he'd never seen her that first night.

"Why did I have to? On the... the binoculars..." He groans.

"Why did I have to go back up?" he mutters again to himself. Take a closer look. Knowing what I know now, I wouldn't have let go of that rail.

I wouldn't have died, he thinks.

I would have pulled myself back up, climbed back over again.

Slept it off. Maybe. Maybe so.

That was the history of it. Up to that point, right? Why should it have been different? I didn't need her. I didn't...

He floats away on the warmness of the drugs. He sees her touching herself in the window. He pulls away from the edge. Floating, grasping for answers in the delirium – waves and scenes in the black.

Snowflakes falling down on him. Cradling a dark nothingness.

He sleeps, catapulting in the jetty inked miasma of his thoughts. Skirting above the horrors. But not far above.

And Cal tries to roll over at some point, about an hour later, forgetful, wincing awake, the brace holding his leg hostage. The clock staring down.

Sarah – just thought I did. Thought I wanted her. Thought she was everything I needed because there was nothing else.

His brow is soaked. He wipes it with his good forearm.

Clink, clink, clink.

Because I was broken. So broken by Diane. By Evan. By all of them. So broken. Hurt. My parents too. Not having them.

Gone. Like everybody. Needed therapy. Not Sarah.

Needed real help. Not Sarah.

There's more. Another way past it. Not falling... Pressing ahead through the blues of it. Through the bullshit. And now, I can't...

All she has done is destroy any other path to take. Destroyed any other way forward. For herself - and for her fucking problems. For her path forward. Not mine. And now, it's too late for me. Too late for anything else. I have to live with it, whatever happens, for the rest of my life...

"Why should she get away with it?" Cal mutters to himself, maybe a couple hours later, waking up, a bit more lucid now. He hears thunder grumbling outside from behind the closed curtained windows. He notices one of them is shattered with glass on the floor in front of it. Or is that the dream? Was it all one?

"What's that, dear?" a woman asks, her hands on him, and Cal opens his eyes to see nurses. He feels wiping on his skin through the blurriness.

"Nothing," he murmurs and when she has cleaned his bandages and left the room, the clock ticks and he watches it for a while before the painkillers take hold again, warm, settling, and his eyelids dip into the black once more.

And then, at some point, hc realizes he's been asleep with a start and he notices someone has turned the lights low in his hospital room. It's the middle of the night and the night feels like an eternity. He feels hot, flustered. Trapped.

His heart begins to race. His fists clench and he joggles the handcuff absentmindedly, over and over against the rail.

Trapped.

Clink, clink, clink, clink, clink.

"Because she's rich? Because she's beautiful?" he asks the ceiling.

Because she convinced me, somehow?

Manipulated me?

Clink, clink, clink, clink, clink.

Because she needed help, and I threw myself on the sword? So eager to die. Just the right person to do so, showing up at just the right time. Through her window.

Why should she just get to go on with her life, while my life ends? Why?

Clink, clink, clink, clink, clink. Clink, clink, clink, clink, clink.

Cal lies awake and senses himself trying to hate her, and the hours continue to drift – him trying to detach and pull his feelings for her in an opposite pathway than the direction they want to go... as he has so easily and so many times done with his ex-fiancée.

But with Sarah, his heart wavers, even after all of it.

Fighting back. Defiant and digging its heels against the idea of betraying her to the detective-inspector - that sod Grant. Cal can't even explain it fully to himself. But the resistance is there no matter what reason he applies.

The same way she digs in... the way she fought back against her husband... The crystal flying at his face.

Defiant. Stubborn. Angry.

Relentless to not be beaten down. Both physically, landing her own blows, inviting the torrent that followed, and through her schemes. The schemes that led to David's brutal death. Her victory in the end. The long game of her resistance against him. David's vice grip on her at last lifted.

And Cal can't budge the resistance within himself now too, no matter how much he tries – the facts always coming back.

She saved your life. Even after all.

"But why should I defend her? I don't owe her anything..." he says aloud in the dark.

I killed that bastard, sure, but it wasn't like I wanted to.

The detective-inspector should know her game.

He probably will soon. But she saved your life.

Cal tries to move his leg, forgetting, and the pain is so unbearable – so blinding and fierce that he almost screams.

She nearly got you killed to save herself.

Wake the fuck up!

It's called being loyal. Clink, clink, clink.

"You should try it sometime."

They should know what Sarah's done.

Will it even help, betraying her like a coward?

Either way, I killed him. Didn't I? The feet that kicked him through the window were mine, not hers, right?

She didn't care if I lived or died going in there. That part's on her. Either way, her husband ended up a murderer or he ended up dead. Both great outcomes for Sarah Jones.

She keeps her money. She keeps her penthouse fifteen flights up. She keeps everything. Maybe even some life insurance, should the investigation work out for her. And then what? Then she is finally free.

Free like she told him she'd be. Twenty-eight. A new year.

Brilliant, because no matter how the dice lands that evening, she gets her escape. No matter what. The perfect maneuver.

But why now? Why me?

Doesn't matter. She wanted to escape. The details of why are irrelevant.

She betrayed you to die. She saved your life.

And you, hers. David is dead. His threat is gone. Forever.

But she could have just as easily left you to bleed out after he died. Why didn't she?

"It doesn't make sense," Cal says aloud.

Why wouldn't she let me die? She would have benefited the most from that, right? Being alive complicates things. Legally, and otherwise. Now it's two stories, instead of just hers.

Yes. It would have been better for her if you died. Right there. In the flat. If both of you were corpses and she walked away. Walked over the carnage to the door.

Clink, clink, clink.

Away from the aftermath, apparently none-the-wiser.

The point is all she had to do was do nothing to push the outcome that way. And yet, she did something. At the crucial moment when I was about to die, she saved my life.

There is no denying that.

The paradox – the endless loops of his torn emotions fighting head-on against his desperate petitions for rationality. A losing game as the memory of Sarah grows in the darkness. The memories before the bloodshed, before the cataclysmic trauma. The fight to the death.

And at some point, just as dawn's light breaks through the sides of the curtains, Cal resigns himself to the truth he's struggled with for hours.

None of this would have transpired if it wasn't for Sarah's manipulations. And none of it would have happened if he'd stayed away from her in the very beginning.

If he'd not followed her through the market. If he'd never left his flat that early morning. That morning he confronted David. The morning he purposely brought the canister of mace – a weapon, really – to a confrontation with a stranger. His role in this.

Clink, clink, clink.

His hand jangles the handcuffs as he thinks it through. Both facts are true. Her manipulations and his blind pursuit. Her guidance of his self-perceived mission to save her.

A fuse lit for destruction.

And deep down, no matter how long he lies in the hospital bed listening to the heartbeat monitor, his inner debate raging, Cal knows he won't say a thing to the detective-inspector, or anyone else that asks for that matter. He's said enough and won't elaborate more about the details. They'll have to piece it together for themselves, if they can. Not another word. Not at least until Cal can hire a solicitor of his own.

Clink, clink, clink.

One thing is for sure: I won't talk to Detective-Inspector Grant again.

Ambushing someone who's just survived another ambush. What a move. What a saint. The man's a predator in his own right - defending his ilk, even. The death of one of his own.

Clink, clink, clink.

No, Cal isn't talking, and he isn't lying anymore by doing so.

No more lies – least of all to myself, he thinks. It's impossible to frame Sarah: this woman he's been falling in love with since his eyes first fell on her across the space between their buildings on that cold night.

This woman he's been so intoxicated with that he can scarcely breathe without thinking about her. A feeling steadily increasing every moment since the first thought crossed his mind, what feels like years ago, but only really a handful of weeks.

From the moment his eyes found her by accident across the street that night, their night, his fingers gripping him loose to the edges of the wrought-iron – the edges of his miserable life. That night he knew he wanted to die.

That night he didn't. But now he knows something different.

Cal knows his self-destructive urge was not him. Not in totality. A damaged point of view in the kaleidoscope of apertures and vantage points that makes up living – anguish, yes, but joy too.

A part of his grief. Only one part.

A possibility for more than that.

Happiness, to some degree within the odds... lingering out there. A chance encounter. Or not so chance.

And he knows at last that he has a better chance of standing up and walking out the entrance of critical care with a couple dozen wounds in his body than he does betraying his suspicions about Sarah's con of him. Her twisted little play. That collision course she meticulously plotted which killed David and nearly killed him. Cut her husband in half across the divide. And the fallout now. Cal's unexpected survival. All of it, in some way, by her own hand.

No matter how much he tries to reason against it, no matter how much he tries to talk himself towards self-preservation, he knows it's not going to happen.

Not to her. Won't do it. Not now.

So, it's the hard way. The only way: standing by her and seeing this twisted thing through.

In the end he has no other choice.

25

Detective-inspector Grant curses at Cal, utterly furious by the time they approve him for discharge over a week later, the orderlies with police escort moving him out of the hospital for transfer. Down the shrill hallways, past door after door of people who aren't prisoners and won't be discharged with metropolitan police units in escort. Then the lift to the top of the parking garage where the rest of them wait with a squad car idling.

"You'll regret playing it like this, Beckley, you have no idea," the tall, bearded detective-inspector threatens, glancing down at him in the wheelchair at the doors of the hospital, thoroughly bristled over being stonewalled for days on end.

"Given numerous opportunities - but no, why try and save yourself? Not being forthcoming is not how to handle a self-defense investigation, tell you that. It's not difficult to speak to me, tell the truth. Is it? I'm not so bad. Don't risk tossing your life in the bin. You hear me? But you can't, can you? Not for something like this – and you'll regret that. Fucking 'ell. You're young enough, now. But you'll see that, mate, what a mistake you've made. Guarantee that. You'll regret this."

Cal stares mutely ahead, his face robbed of any expression. Pale and removed. When they get to the waiting car, the detective-inspector asks him again, one last time, over the sounds of the rainfall on the cement nearby:

"Was she involved – yes or no? Just answer me that, Beckley. That's all I want to know. That's it."

Moments pass. The two men stare at one another. Each refusing to back down. All that can be heard is the rain, the murmuring thunder, and the sniffles of one of the policemen. With nothing else, Grant gestures for the car's door with a nod and commands his men:

"Get this wanker out of my sight."

The detective-inspector shakes his head and leaves.

Cal's refusal to provide any account since the first interview with Grant has made it difficult for the man to catch him in any further lies about the details of the night. This clearly bothers him, and, all things considered, it gives Cal the smallest bit of satisfaction. They are scratching at a door they can't open.

He smiles, watching the man storm across the exposed rooftop-level of the parking lot, breaking into a jog for his car.

I don't deserve to smile. Stop it.

"Up you come," one of the escorts says. "No trouble."

Then the uniforms get Cal out of the wheelchair and into the back of the waiting police car, with his leg out of the cast and in simple bandages now, and his arm out of the sling, still sore but functional.

They can throw me away. Whatever. They can try. I know what happened that night. It wasn't what they think it was. If it's going to be the hard way for me, it's going to be the hard way for them.

So long, Detective-inspector Elliot Grant – for now.

The jail cell's claustrophobia is almost welcoming as he arrives at his specific bunk a couple hours later. No more unannounced drop-ins by voracious, inquisitive officers. No more nonstop humming air units and beeping medical equipment. Nurses pestering. No more sponge baths and painful physical therapy.

Most of all, no more questions from Grant.

He's been pushed through intake, told his few rights. Then given the rules. Then his prisoner number – B4671DE.

Then a day or so passes. He sleeps some more.

More than he thought possible. Until he can't at all. And then Cal begins to settle into the sights and sounds of his grim reality. The cold concrete and iron bars. The routine of it.

But with the case and the world closing in, the bars don't really change much, and his unkempt cellmate scarcely says a thing the first few days Cal sits and sleeps in the bunk above him. Cal says hello a couple of times before the man finally acknowledges his existence, greeting him back out of the blue the fifth morning there.

"It's Cal innit?" is all he asks.

And it doesn't take long before Cal realizes it's not a relationship that will require much from him. The long-haired, gangly man in his late forties is awaiting his trial for a vehicular homicide case, drunk driving over a teenager after leaving a pub in Shoreditch one night. With the trial postponed for vaguely conveyed reasons, the shared cell in Southwark is now all he's got moving forward.

So long as Cal doesn't talk too much they'll be fine, Ben repeats several times – a joke or threat, Cal can't be sure.

"Fine by me," Cal says, shaking the man's hand from the top bunk. Ben looks him up and down, his eyes tired yet curious.

"Better than m'previous cellmate. Name of Imran. Obvious reasons. All gone downhill, really. Overflowing, the whole country is. Brexit did nuffin', course. Lettin' 'em all in. Even the jails. The bloody jails. See it here course. Pissed it away. Once an empire, you believe that? Funny, innit. Now, we got this."

Lucky for Cal, further tirades or any other words for that matter are few and far between, and so he has plenty of time to think in silence. Plenty of time to pour over each small part of his crimes in turn. The past few months. The past few years. Sins of a lifetime.

And the ignorant man stays in his space, and Cal stays in his own.

Instead, Cal stares up at the dim overhead bulb from his upper cot, illuminating the scant furnishings of the small room: the stainless-steel toilet, two plain metal beds, above and below, and the small window on the far wall whose view consists of the concrete barrier of another side of the pen.

And, slowly, Cal learns that the days blend into monotony. And he learns that the nights are the time to be with her.

Laying on his thin mattress, when not thinking of the outside world, or his defense case, or the terrible things from the past, it's just Sarah. Only Sarah.

The best place to be. With the memory of her lips. Her hands. Her eyes. Flashing green – yearning.

The soft ease that her voice gives him. The lilac and jasmine smell of her perfume. The slender dip at the base of her neck where her clavicles meet. The curve of her hips. Rising and falling.

The sharpness of her anger. The sadness in her past. The strength of her, her words recounting it. Her torment. The way her lips moved as she said those words to him. Carefully choosing each. Her confession that night in the square.

Her sense of humor, too. Dry, dark humor.

The shadowed couplets of her dimples in the flickering candlelight of Cucina del Cuore as she laughed.

The way that golden strand fell across her eyes all night. The curve of her smile.

The sound of her. Light. Playful. The way she tasted. That night in his bed. Her legs locked around him. The way she said his name, whispered it. Moaned it. His name – his. And a million other things...

The many, many things he's watched, either through her window or much closer, in the brief time she occupied space in his life. In the brief span of time, she captivated every part of him.

It's not the easiest place to reminisce about her, and yet it's these thoughts alone that keep Cal's heart beating each day, each night, as time leads up towards his murder trial. Keeping his head forward as questions continue to swirl around it.

"She's just another one," Cal's cellmate says one night to him, oiling his scraggly beard below with a hand mirror in one hand and castor oil covering the other.

"What did you say?" Cals asks.

"Gash relationship, yours. Real shite, from what you've told. Going down for a trollop. You kidding? What you thinking, mate?"

"Thanks for your opinion on that."

"Ah. Know it too. Don't sulk so much. If she's rubbish, tell her to fuck off right. Better in the long haul, innit. Better for all. Take it from a bloke who's seen a thing. She could testify, you know."

Cal shakes his head. Ben's becoming more conversational as the few weeks go on, and that's not the greatest thing, the depths of his knowledge not extending too far beyond Eastender nightlife and casual narrow-mindedness about immigration policy. And despite believing himself a makeshift therapist of sorts at times, the man mainly just talks to talk.

"Not against me," Cal responds from above, reading Dostoevsky for the first time – the irony not lost on him. "What's it to you, anyways?"

"Think it's dim is all. Stupid. Just get over 'er. It's over from the other side, you better believe me. Long haul, I mean. Can't last, you locked away, such as you are."

"Maybe so, but I can't forget about her," Cal replies, turning over in his bunk. "It's not that easy. Or I'd have done it. Not your business neither mate."

"Ah. Means fuckall. Maybe talk some then, y'prat. Maybe, when she comes to see you, grow a bloody pair. If I had the likes coming to see me, best believe, every other week or whatever, waiting to see me in here, best believe I'd-"

"You don't understand it at all, Ben," Cal cuts him off.

"No, right-o, right on that much."

He continues massaging the patchy, coffee-colored scraggly mound of his facial hair. "But in'it wild, the way you think mate? Wild. Blimey, three-inch shank, too, legal that is. Know that right? Can't hold you for it. Let 'em know. They just can't. The law, that."

"Bit more to it than that, Ben," Cal sighs again. "As I said. They're doing a premeditation angle."

"Bullocks mate. You're good or you're not good. Seen blokes with far more get far less."

"I'll let my solicitor know you think so," Cal says and leaves it at that, rolling over. After a minute or so, Cal closes the book and next his eyes, pretending to fall asleep.

"Tosser," he hears the man mutter below after a bit. Eventually his block's lights shut off and the noises die down.

Cal doesn't care what this man thinks of him – Cal's choices, his obsessions, his case. They're not Ben's burden.

They're mine. My own worries.

The little Ben knows, through the scraps he's been surrendered in bits and pieces, gives him no right to voice anything, least of all advice.

They're my own troubles. Not his.

At least I didn't smear some poor twat down Old Street after a few pints...

Cal doesn't care what anybody else thinks, for that matter. Nobody in this world. Least of all, Ben the bigot. Nobody except Sarah, that is.

And the only reason this fool thinks she's beautiful is because he's said as much...

To that, Cal chuckles to himself unexpectedly, relaxing a bit, and he lets his frustrations subside, shaking his head. All worked up over nothing.

Got to let it go. He sighs. Keep the boundary without being angry. Bloke thinks he's actually helping.

The reality – what Ben can't grasp – is one wrong word while meeting with Sarah might imprison her. A single sign of conspiracy. A single hint could complete a case file on her, fill in a gap, giving them cause enough. Just what detective-inspectors need.

And he sees it in the changes in the police visits, too. New police to begin with now. No more just Grant. Not for a bit at least – couple weeks. The fresh faces bring new phrasing to the same old questions, and new ones as well, the last time around, in particular – moving away from Cal's sequence of events of self-defense, to instead the nature of Sarah's marriage, looking for a new angle. A collusion. A monetary angle, perhaps. An angle on David's businesses.

"What did Sarah tell you about her trust?"

"Her new gallery?"

"Did Sarah ever mention David's investments in the gallery?"

"The debt leveraged?"

"Anything financial, white-collar sort, embezzlement?"

"Heroin? Smuggling?"

"Do you have any idea who David's partners were?"

"How did David acquire funds for undertaking renovations on Ephemeral Canvas? Cal, do you know? Was anything ever confided in you about David's work?"

"Did Sarah ever implicate David in anything beyond his abuse of her?"

"Did she tell you anything?"

And more of the ilk. On and on. Over and over. Continuing to come in, every visit. Once every week or so. One after the other. None being answered. Not even a word.

It's usually an in and out thing. They ask, he doesn't answer.

They don't try as hard as Grant. Not as much intimidating.

Cal's dismayed looking solicitor stays quiet beside him. And stranger and stranger questions in nature keep coming from across the interview table. Cal has no idea about any of it, and while his lawyer takes notes, he offers nothing.

And then one particular question stands out, sparking Cal's curiosity more than the others beforehand. His ears perk up. The temptation to break intensifies, and he feels himself struggling to resist the urge to ask a question in return. One right back at them.

It comes from one of the younger policewomen:

"Do you even know who he was connected to? You could be in danger. Especially in Southwark - in here. Help us help you. We'd be gutted if you don't make it to trial."

Gutted – Cal considers her choice of words.

"Really would be a shame. Think about that, okay? Before our next visit. Think about who you killed, and what that means for your future in here."

Not giving in to them. I won't give in to them. I can't.

Gutted. Their constant threats. What the hell are they on about? His work? Make him out like some type of gangster; a modern-day Kray.

Cal taps his fingers on the table, and looks away, as he always does.

Baiting me, nothing more. More lies. They either find it, find the truth about the showdown in the flat, or they don't. Leave me out of it now. I won't give them Sarah on some kind of silver platter. Nor will I be intimidated. Her husband was her husband.

Cal can only hope Sarah does the same for him and keeps her mouth shut. That she neither tells them truth nor lies. That she doesn't say a word.

Prisoner's dilemma aside, he knows the visitor tables are listened to, always recorded, and talking to her because of this won't do, no matter how many times she comes to try.

Twice so far just last month.

More days pass. More nights. More routine.

Eventually the seasons change.

Spring in full force, underway. Lots of rain. Some pretrial motions. But the case moves slowly. The sun finally starts shining a bit through the small window of the cell. Cal is grateful for that.

The small patches of light. He wakes up early sometimes and watches them glide. Small things made big as the world shrinks.

A bit later Cal decides to fire his appointed duty solicitor, who has offered little meaningful guidance up to this point, weeks in, seemingly only engrossed in other cases. Cal searches for a replacement through the legal aid services given to inmates.

And while he waits, Cal exercises. He reads. He dries and folds laundry for a few hours a day. He reads some more.

He dreams of Sarah, lying in bed, staring upwards.

Her naked body. Her sweet smile. Her earrings.

He exercises. He reads some more. He dries and folds laundry. He sleeps.

He dreams of her. Sarah's laugh, her fork extended to his side of the table as he chews... laying in his bed afterwards, sweat on their skin, staring upwards...

That laugh. Her lips against his.

The way she described her family. The way she confided in him. The way she breathed when she slept beside him. A slow harmony.

Investigators stop coming after another week or so.

His only real company is Ben thereafter. But as days pass, Cal begins keeping even more to himself, the last threat from the detective-inspectors about David's former affiliations (ruse or not) ever-present in his mind as he walks solitary laps around the outside yard, avoiding the eyes of other inmates. He tries to take in some of the sunshine, but his eyes dart around him. Sometimes he thinks he sees someone staring for too long. Sometimes he realizes it's him who's staring. He tries to not linger in any one place, always walking, ready to run if he must, grateful when he is back in his cell, his back against a wall with the barred doors closed.

And when he has visit days, she always comes, the notification coming down from a guard, which tells him of course that she has something to say, but also, subtle and assuredly, that she hasn't been detained. His only assurance Sarah's fine. His only assurance that so far, she's not been tied to David's death. Some sort of transitive implication. Conspiracy.

Even the truth.

He denies seeing Sarah when she comes again the following week, too. The eighth time now. Nearly three months in.

Nothing's that important for her to say to me.

Why does she keep coming? Nothing's worth the risk of her saying it.

She should know that. She should know better. They are both in this case and anything they say to one another will fire straight into the prosecution legal files. Into the stack of evidence against him.

She told you all she needed to when she stopped you bleeding to death. She told you the play. How she wanted you to handle it.

Maybe she wonders if I remember. If I'm cracking?

But by now she must know I'm not. That I've given them nothing. Week after week.

He climbs back into his bunk, the tenth week in it, his heart heavy with the thought that Sarah is close to him. Somewhere in the concrete walls of this place. About to get the news: "Not available this week."

Despite the answers to the questions he wants so badly from her. The questions that keep him awake at night. The questions he desperately needs answered:

Why him?

Why that night?

What now?

And so much more than that, too.

Despite his love for her. His burning desire to see her one more time. Kiss her. Hold her. The possibility of never being able to again haunting him, night after night, alongside her memories.

Difficult in a place like Southwark, but it's the only risk he can take. The only risk he'll allow himself. Never seeing her again, when he very well can, even now. Even here. Each time she attempts it, it's a blessing to him. An offering perhaps. Awakening that same, deadly curiosity within Cal that he resists. The kind that led him each thread of the way to her in the first place. Willing him, step by step, into the twisted webs of her life.

And Cal tries not to think about it – the real cost of denying Sarah.

26

The Persian rugs glide backwards and the living room lies transmuted in endless, warping shapes as the accusing figure follows him – David, with a knife extending outwards, stumbling through the fire around his feet. The blade twisted gargantuan, clasped in both hands, shining out.

Jagged, shifting. A living entity. Drenched in blood.

The blade plunging, over and over, the repeated strikes into Cal's stomach sounding like the smack of a large drum, and David's laughter is deafening, cackling with each stab into him.

Menace, glee, the pounding of it hitting bone, the knife plunging deeper and deeper into his flesh in serpentine, tortuous patterns. Cutting his arteries and organs, flesh and veins, one by one. Twisting. Tormenting laughter surrounding him.

The fire grows higher. He tries to scream.

There is no air in his lungs. He is already dead, iced over...

His eyes open wide.

Shit.

He looks around, panting in his bunk. He sees morning light filtering in through the singular window of thickened glass and bars.

His cellmate snores below and the gray walls whisper the same despairs, thoughts he usually staves off with his go-to blend of memory and fantasy about Sarah. Gradually, the cell block begins to stir awake as the begrudging rays of light break through all the slants in the windows.

Cal lays there, his thoughts traveling as they do, his mind a million miles away until the bell sounds as it has each morning for the past few months. He watches the sunshine patches, and listens to Ben stir awake, cursing before saying "Morning, sunshine," as he does at the beginning of each day now.

And Cal gets up automatically, jumping to the cold floor, his leg and shoulder no longer sore every morning, and he brushes his teeth and heads to breakfast when it is his floor's turn to, the metal doors swinging open with another bell. He eats and listens to the chatter of the other prisoners, his mind with Sarah.

Always with Sarah. In his old bed, beneath his sheets. Holding her panting sweaty body. Her golden hair falling around him. His eyes staring off. Sweet memories of their date together. Their confessions to each other.

Far beyond the concrete walls that hold him – nearly untouchable – he remains in his own walls, too. There, locked from the inside, on his own terms he feels safe, comfortable, and sometimes even guiltless. But most of all, Cal doesn't feel alone when he's there.

Never at all.

After breakfast, a few hours later, returning to his cell from his daily hour out in the summer yard, one of the escorting guards turns and stops him.

"Beckley. Some bloke... uh, Macleod is here to meet with you."

"A who?" Cal asks.

"Don't be daft. Your defender. Legal aid."

Cal blinks through the sweat on his brow, wiping it across his sleeve.

"Your solicitor, you wanker. The new one. He's here for you. Now, come along, follow me."

"Right. Sorry – yeah, lead the way."

Cal, flanked by guards, navigates the hallway up a stairwell and through several more floors of the large penitentiary wing, his ears soon echoing with the footfalls and distant conversations of the other inmates in the rooms with their visitors. They pass by several more visitor rooms but keep going down the long hallway. After a few minutes, one of the guards ahead of him swipes a card beside a flat steel door, and the door slowly opens automatically.

It's overdue, Cal thinks.

It's been a few weeks since the last pre-trial hearing, and subsequently he hasn't met with his legal representation in a bit. Cal's anxious to speak with him.

They enter the consultation room, which is long and narrow, dimly lit, with a heavy-looking table in the center of it and several chairs scattered haphazardly around. One of the guards then leaves and the other stays at the corner a few moments before taking position just outside the door.

Damian Macleod pushes his circular glasses up the ridgeline of his nose as his wiry figure stands to meet Cal, a nicotine-stained hand outstretched. His thick raven-black hair is erratically tousled as usual, like he's been running from his car to get here. The well-fitted pinstriped suit is especially mismatched with his gregarious flower stitched socks today. His typical, eccentric get-up.

But who really cares about fashion or eccentricity? That's not why Cal's hired him. From the moment Cal first met Damian, he saw that there was a quirky brilliance about him – the way he asked questions, drew out potential objections, avenues the prosecution might take, his quick wit and intellect firing away at the angles. Energetic fervor to uncover it all and push back hard.

Cal met him a couple weeks ago when his second representative dropped due to the news that Cal's company had terminated his employment. The legal firm had doubted Cal's ability to financially endure the upcoming challenges, a reasonable assumption given the circumstances. And despite Damian's idiosyncrasies at their first meeting (or because of them) – like his willingness to tell long, unsolicited stories about his law school days in Scotland— lurid late-night study sessions in ancient libraries, and spirited evenings in Edinburgh's gay club scene —and Cal finds himself laughing for the first time in ages. Appreciating his dry wit, his unabashed optimism. And he starts to befriend the man... and next he hires him.

Somehow, in this place, on these humorous offerings, marks the beginning of a blossoming alliance between them. And Cal starts to suspect that this younger man might even have what it takes to fight this fight. Maybe even be some kind of competent solicitor, looking to make a name for himself. Looking for a big win to make his mark. It's Cal's hope, at least, that his case could be just that – so it will make it that much more personal for the man to win it.

An ally in a time he needs it most.

A career win for a career that needs it, too.

"Cal, skip the pleasantries today," Damian begins, motioning towards the chair after the two shake hands. "We have a lot to discuss. Lots. Tons and tons, my boy. So let's not waste a minute of our time. Shall we?"

"Alright," Cal says. "What's going on?"

Both men sit and Damian places his leather briefcase on the table and with both thumbs pops it open. He produces several thick manila files and places them beside Cal each in turn.

"Take a look at the top one first. Before anything else."

Cal looks at him and can't tell if Damian is being his typical dramatic self, or if this is something he should be bracing himself against.

"Damian, look – before that," Cal says, placing his hand on the folder, and looking over at the door before leaning in, "Any word from the prosecution since the plea? I thought we'd have a meeting by now. Why is this taking so long? Months..."

"These things take time. Homicide trials. They are building their case and us, ours," Damian replies, a twinge of impatience in his response. "As I told you, most of my defendants are either dealt with in the magistrates' court, pleading guilty, as we decided not to, of course, or they see the prosecution's case collapse before trial. Well, now we know their case isn't collapsing. So, that's some intelligence, right? This is a good thing, Cal."

"That's not my kind of good thing, Damian," Cal retorts. "You said we'd get approached after they denied bail. To twist the screws. Leverage a more concise confession. Still not a peep. Months. That can't be a good thing. It means they're confident, right? It means they have something, right?"

"I said we might be approached. Might, dear boy. Nothing's certain here, Cal. If they are going to make an offer, it'll be soon, I can assure you."

"Right. Do you think they will? That's my question. Do you think that's a possibility?"

"I'd be lying either way, dear boy. It's not that simple," Damian clears his throat. "Disclosures in progress. We're learning what they have. They're learning what we plan to do with it. And it's not as bad as it could be Cal, okay? We'll review this week's findings in a moment. I need you to open that folder and look at that document, right there. It's the big one. The one just below the top. Okay? Now, if you would please."

"Okay," Cal responds. Exchanging a curt nod as he does so, Cal slowly lifts the envelope up and sees something flutters – a dark square below it. He furrows his brow.

A photograph sticking to the page. The image is faint and a bit misty around the edges, yet unmistakably clear as well.

A sonogram.

Cal's fingers shake ever so slightly as he picks it up. It is as though a tiny universe has unfurled before him where it didn't exist at all before.

A fragile form, nestled within, a beacon amidst the shadows and curves and lines of Sarah. He slowly flips it. On the back of the photograph, in her handwriting, he sees the words:

girl (February)

He turns it back over.

There it is - a tiny speck of life.

Hope. Sleepless nights, lullabies, tiny fingers wrapped around his, first steps, innocence.

"This could be a real problem if she's yours," Damian says, his voice low, breaking Cal's thoughts.

"I don't know about that," Cal replies, blinking as he takes it in.

"Well, how could you?" Damian replies. "She sent it via mail to my office. You believe that? Asserting it's yours no doubt."

"Must be, after what she told me about David's tests."

"Not necessarily. I'll find out for sure, of course. DNA tests, etcetera. This is cause though. You see that, right?"

"Yes. I see that, Damian."

"Motive, even. As far as how they use it. And it is possible, yes? As in, the realm of possibility, however unlikely..."

"Yes. I mean – I don't know."

The weight of the photograph in his hands feels like it bears the dreams and fears of his lifetime, and Cal stares at it a long time in silence and utter amazement, his thumb running along the edge of it. The juxtaposition of the child being his coupled with the reality that this development could sink the case... his life...

Will I be there for this child? Be there to help raise her?

Ever even know her name? Or will I be forgotten, a criminal, die here instead? Will I ever meet her at all?

Is it because of this child's existence that I will never be free?

The thought pierces him, and he lets go of the photograph, tapping the metal of the desk, the brutal irony sinking in. Why? Why now?

To show him the bigger picture: a chance for redemption.

She wants him to know that there's a reason... to focus on that above anything else... a purpose to strive for.

A reminder of the world he might be permanently exiled from.

A world with his daughter.

She wants me to know.

And then he realizes something else, too.

Cal looks at his lawyer. "Damian, she's wanted me to know for weeks."

"Huh?" he asks.

"With the visits I told you about. How she kept coming. Kept requesting the visit."

"What do you mean?" Damian asks, staring over his glasses.

Cal's thoughts race. Despite the chaos, the betrayals, and the bloodshed, this unborn child of theirs is a tether to a world of possibilities. New possibilities. A future – together. An invitation.

"Well, isn't it obvious?" Cal replies. "She wanted to give me this herself, all those times coming here like she used to. She wanted to tell me...Communicating that she plans to fight."

"They'd call that a leap of judgement, from my perspective," Damian replies, his eyebrows raised, sheepish. "Nice to think perhaps, but we don't know that. Besides, is it even possible?"

"I don't..." Cal's heart races. "...yes..."

Sarah's message seems clear, even if unspoken. She is asking him to hold onto hope. To keep fighting as hard as he can to get out. She will be fighting too.

But perhaps something else as well.

"Maybe, she could be playing a silent bargaining chip," Damian says, as if reading Cal's mind. The two lock eyes.

"What do you mean by that?" Cal asks.

Damian holds up his hands. "Just, leverage, dear boy. For what you'll say in court. How we'll play it. Covering her bases. Black widow, on and off the web. Oh, look, I have a kid. Could be yours? Could not be? So... play nice now. Look, Cal, call me a cynic..."

"You are a cynic. She's not a male-eating spider, Damian."

"Hey, if it makes me good at this kind of stuff, I'll play the devil's advocate. The unimpressed poet."

"I don't think that's what's happening here."

"I'll err on the side of your judgement, dear boy, if you insist," Damian says, shuffling a few papers into his briefcase. "But I remain a skeptic, nonetheless, until proven otherwise that is."

"Thank you. And besides, I've told you that's not how I want to play it, how many times again?" Cal asks.

"I know. I'm just saying, considering what we now know about Sarah..."

"Now know... what do you mean by that?" Cal asks.

"Showing over telling." Damian grins. "Look here."

"What are you talking about?"

"Patience, ah, here we go," he shuffles out another folder quickly, pulling out papers within it. "If that's the stick..."

"What?"

"... you haven't seen the carrot..."

He reads a neon-colored post-it before peeling it off the top of the stack of pages before handing them over.

"Here we go. Have a look at these, now."

"What is all this?" Cal asks, sifting through the pages.

"Sarah's portion of the disclosure. Glorious morning, really," Damian grins and he slides over the rest of the stack to Cal.

Cal begins reading page by page, smelling the indelible smoke from Damian's beloved Gauloises on the papers.

"For now, that is," Damian explains. "I don't know if that's the last of her depositions, but probably. Witness statements, police interviews. As a whole we're going to need to look through as much as we can of that today. Familiarize ourselves to make sure there's no vulnerabilities in your recorded testimonies. Then see what we can use from there on the stand."

"With her?"

"And with you, if you feel compelled that is. I know we'd spoken about you not..."

"Okay, fine, sounds great. But what do you know about it?" Cal asks, his eyes narrowing. "You're acting like you've read something. Acting very strange today, I might add."

"Look forgive my theatrics," Damian chuckles, his intense eyes magnified through the frames. "You're not going to believe this..."

"Yes, out with it Damian."

"Look. I did some reading as soon as I got the documents sent over this morning. Listen to me –"

"I'm listening..."

"Sarah is going to testify on your behalf," Damian says and sits back. The revelation hangs in the air.

Silence pervades the room for several moments.

"Well, is that what the sonogram means?" Cal scoffs. "Some kind of a symbol?"

"No, no. I don't claim to know what that sonogram or the symbol means," Damian says, looking slightly frazzled. "However, I'll find out whether that is yours, and let's pray it isn't. But all that notwithstanding, Cal, she's claiming that you acted in defense of her that night, and defense of yourself as things turned ugly. She is corroborating your version of events. Almost entirely. To a tee. Self-defense, dear boy. Self-bloody-defense."

"How to prove it though?" Cal asks. "As it's been since the beginning with the police. They refuse to believe that."

"Well, that's where the details matter. Let's find out. She's submitted new evidence along with all of this. Two hours ago. I'll be getting my hands on it this afternoon. CCTV."

"Video evidence?" Cal's head whips up from the pages. "From where?"

"It's amazing. Some monitor they had hidden up there. Not turned over to the police until now. Heavens knows how it skirted the investigation. Or the search," Damian shakes his head. "Don't get it. No claim on that front just yet. But this could throw the case. Either way, dear boy. May be looking up. Way up."

Cal's mind spins. Where was there a camera?

What did it see? Why now?

"I never saw –"

"And of course," Damian continues, licking his thumb before turning more pages, "Of course, she's still going to run up against the fact that you brought the dagger, and – "

"Pocketknife, Damian," Cal interjects, agitated. "It's a pocketknife, please. Am I the lawyer, or are you?"

"Pocketknife, right. And they'll try to discredit her for saying in initial testimony you didn't – question her motives, even that," and Damian nods towards the photograph, "most likely, a motive. All as a motive to lie. To kill him. But, no matter what they throw, if that video corroborates your story of self-defense, alongside this coming from his wife, Cal, his own wife's testifying that her husband was the aggressor. Claiming she can substantiate that claim with this evidence. This does help quite a bit for us, I think. Yes," Damian says, excitement stapled across his face as he sifts through more of the documents, the gears of his mind spinning, passing paper after paper over to Cal. "This could be good. Depending on that video. How much it shows. Could be very good."

Cal nods his head, his mind still reeling with Sarah's decision to step up on the stand. He stares off.

Damian looks skeptically at him.

"Well, anything? Aren't you pleased, dear boy?"

"I just... can't believe it..." is all Cal can muster back.

"Yes, it is quite the turn of things."

"Why would she wait?"

"I have no bloody idea," Damian responds, chuckling. "None. Sure, the prosecution's livid though. That much is certain."

Always like her. Weaving webs with strands of truth and deceit. A morsel here – a slice there. Then a bomb. A big bomb.

Bon chance.

Playing her cards one by one before the kill shot.

... You don't know her like I do... She's not what you think about her... Far worse...

Maybe. But fuck you David. Sarah hasn't forgotten that I'm here. Or so at least it seems that way. Despite no visits for a couple weeks. She is fighting. And she is pregnant.

"So, you'll stop trying to throw this whole thing over on her as a defense strategy?" Cal asks at last, resuming his reading.

"Hey," Damian says, looking up and then seeing Cal's smirk. "Glad you can still joke around, I suppose. But no promises there."

Cal glances at the sonogram picture again, the unmistakable sign of life. Life within Sarah.

Life she and I created.

He can't help but think about it. Maybe there is a chance in this mess. Somehow, someway. Maybe a little hope at last.

"Want to see the suit catalogs I brought?" Damian asks out of the blue about a half hour in. "Your collection was atrocious. Rubbish mate, it pains me to say it. I went over though; I did try. Met your landlord – nice old chap. Gave him the final check."

"Good, thanks. Hey!" Cal says, realizing the jab a moment late. "Leave my wardrobe out of it. I pay for your legal expertise."

"Consider it consultative and wrapped in the fee."

"Just tell me what to wear to win this."

Damian chuckles, "I'll do my best – we may yet."

27

The sweat drips down his neck as Cal trudges back from the laundry detail, another grueling day of prison work done. Hopefully one of the last ones. His joints ache and his muscles are taut from hours beside the heat of the machines. He passes through the sterile corridors, each step echoing off the concrete walls with the voices of the other inmates. Familiar faces. Many still without names.

How long have I been here now?

Fourteen weeks. And three days.

The faint hum of fluorescent lights above casts a sickly glow on the faces of the weary prisoners and stern guards as he breaks into the common area. The air is thick with the mingled scents of sweat, disinfectant, and food from the mess and he feels the faint, ever-present sense of eyes on him. A feeling he'll never get accustomed to.

Not too much longer. Trial starts tomorrow.

Cal keeps walking, his mind whirling anxious thoughts as he navigates another evening's onset in confinement. He nods to a few familiar acquaintances, but for the most part, he keeps to himself, making his way tiredly, his eyes fixed. The din of the general area is murmurs, laughter, and the occasional shout. Noises he's learned to tune out of his head. The prison alive with its peculiar late afternoon rhythm – the ceaseless pulse of confinement, resignation, goofiness, and rage.

Cal's steps feel heavier today, anxiety washing over him that this may be a permanent view with permanent sounds if things go poorly tomorrow, and the days after.

After changing shirts in his cell, he heads down the stairs and towards the first-floor loo. The need to wash away the grime and fatigue of the day is overwhelming. Pushing open the door, he's greeted by harsh unflattering light across the dirty tiles: the space is cramped, the air caked with humidity and the lemon, eucalyptus reek of industrial cleaning products. He moves to the sink, fills it, and splashes cold water on his face, the chill a quick respite.

Cal sighs.

Will she be there tomorrow? Will I see her in the stands?

Will I see her again?

Probably.

No. Definitely. She'll take the stand... she said she would...

As the water drips down his face, he catches his reflection in the cracked mirror. His eyes are tired, shadows etched around them like plums, dark reminders of the sleepless nights in this place. The nightmares.

Need to sleep tonight. I can't look so strung out tomorrow.

I can't look worried – need to be on my best game. The only game.

He looks himself over. He recalls seeing the bruises from his altercation with David, the weeks after the fight. The purple swellings across all parts of his body, some worse than others. The mauled fingermarks around his throat. His lips broken open in gaps. His eyebrows and eyelids split and bloated.

He sure beat the piss out of you...

None of it still visible – just stark pale skin and tired eyes.

The fear in his eyes, though. The same.

Cal lets out another weary sigh, leaning heavily on the sink, and splashing more water on his face. The door creaks open behind him. He glances up, meeting the gaze of a man he recognizes— a shifty-eyed man always lurking around the yard's far bleachers with similar ilk. He's around the same height as Cal, maybe only a few years younger.

He saunters in, his shoulders low, a smug grin plastered across his face. Having a great day it would seem, despite the place and predicament.

"Got yourself a trial coming up, don't ya?" he begins casually, his voice oiled, dripping with mock friendliness. "So's I hear, anyways. Round the by."

Cal stiffens, his grip tightening on the edge of the sink.

Who the hell is this guy?

"Yeah?" Cal asks, turning to face him. "And?"

The man slinks forward into the space between Cal and the exit.

"What's it to me, that what you thinkin'?" the man smiles. He steps closer, grin widening. "Just thought I'd give you a little friendly advice, is all. One lag to the next."

"None needed. Thanks though. Anyway."

"Give ya some just the same," the freckled man says. "Seeing hows some are real interested in what you might say about the hubby's ventures. In your wee trial."

Cal's heart skips a beat – he tries to keep his voice steady.

"I don't know what you're talking about, mate."

"Eh-eh," the man shakes his finger. His ridiculous smile fades, replaced by a hard stare. He takes another step, leaning in closely, his breath rancid.

"Now, now – don't play dumb. If you spill anything about your cunt's arrangements, a charge is going to be the least of your worries. You got me?"

"Back. Off," Cal says, his voice low.

"No need to repeat," the man replies. "You just mind your little words up there."

"I'm not going up there, fuckwit," Cal replies.

"That'd be a mistake."

"Would it?" Cal interjects, feeling fury boiling up in his guts. "Why's that? Explain it to me."

It feels almost good to give into it a little. A rage he hasn't felt in months.

"Mind your tongue. Right?" the man says. "That's it. That's all I'm here for."

Cal's heart races, the weight of the threat sinking in. He forces himself to keep meeting the man's gaze, refusing to show him fear. Refusing to show him any weakness.

But the confrontation triggers something within him. Deep within him. From the night it all went down. The bloody fight.

"Look, I don't know what you're talking about. Back away from me," Cal replies, his voice forceful, trying his best not to sound rattled.

The man chuckles, a low, ugly sound. "Right, you don't."

"Fuck off, will you? And don't you -"

"Courtesy is all," the younger man grins, bowing his head. "There are people don't take to snitches, pinched or otherwise. Not difficult. Easy as I did it here. You follow me, mate? Just courtesy is all. Keep your knickers dry. Just a courtesy..."

And with that, the man turns and walks away, leaving Cal standing alone, the blood pounding in his ears, fists clenched. After a moment, he looks and stares at his reflection, the fear and anger churning. Pupils miniscule.

What the hell was that?

The restroom feels suddenly smaller, walls closing in.

He grips the sink, his knuckles white, trying to steady himself...

After a moment, he sinks down and splashes more water on his face.

A courtesy, he said. Courtesy from who? The threat so emboldened.

Cal waits a few minutes before he leaves. Back in the general area, the sound of the prison's almost a comfort compared to the silence of the restroom, and Cal makes his way to the fixed-line phones at the corner of the expansive common area. He waits in line, and when it's his turn, dials Damian's office.

It's a bit late... it rings and rings and rings.

He tries again. Staring out at the common area.

The phone gives nothing back, each unanswered loop heightening his anxiety. No answer, just the cold, mechanical report of the voicemail.

"You've reached the legal services of..."

Cal hangs up, frustration bubbling to the surface.

Who was David?

Can anybody tell me?

Who the hell did I kill?

Who the hell did Sarah marry?

Have they reached out to her, too? Threatened her? Is she okay?

He feels the eyes of other inmates on him, the weight of their curiosity and judgment. He forces himself to breathe, to focus. He thinks through the case some more. Dinner time approaches, and he heads to the mess hall, the familiar routine, a small anchor in the chaos of his thoughts. He's on hyper-alert, preparing for an attack from anywhere.

Any of them could be connected.

Any of them could take a stab at me.

But the mess hall is just a sea of faces, the clatter of trays and murmurs of conversations filling the space as it always does.

Only now an undercurrent even stronger, a danger lurking, even more probable than yesterday. From any direction.

He grabs a tray and finds a spot at his usual corner table. He picks at his food, barely eating more than a meatball or two, his appetite lost. His eyes dart around and suddenly, across the room, he spots the man from the restroom lounging with a group of rough-looking inmates, the same he's always congregating with out in the yard.

Cal takes another bite, then gets up, returning his tray, and walks towards the exit. He doesn't make eye contact. He tries not to walk too fast.

How long have they known I've been here? How long have they been watching me? Who are they?

What will they do to Sarah?

Questions, like rapid fire in his mind. The walls feel like they're closing in. So close. He retreats to his cell. A few moments later, Cal rocks back and forth on his bunk and then lies down and Ben comes in after a bit of time and watches him with a curious expression on his face.

"Didn't see you at mess tonight."

"What is it?" Cal says, agitated, turning on his bunk, returning the man's stare.

"Something on your mind?" Ben replies and his voice is low. "Trial?"

"Some shit earlier," Cal hesitates. "Had a run-in today, actually. Weird, some guy threatening about the trial. You've seen him."

"What about your trial?" his cellmate asks.

"Something about Sarah's husband... something he was wrapped up with..."

"Oh right," Ben leans back while holding onto the frame of the top bunk, his expression thoughtful. "That all?"

"What does that mean?"

"Y'know, you being you. Affairs with stunning women. Fights to the death. Let me guess, gangsters now? Narcotics? A conspiracy?"

"What the hell?" Cal's eyes widen. "Why do you think it's that?"

"Why not?" Ben chuckles darkly. "Know the bloody type. Type who marries Sarah. Looks like finance, smells like powder. Bag of chop. Something untoward. Ex. Powerful friends. All that. Let me ask you this, Cal."

"Yeah."

"You really think some Lombard Street muppet is going to be able to fight like that chap did against you?"

"I... don't know..." Cal says. "Maybe if he... trained.. you know? Weekend warrior type."

Ben shakes his head.

"Nah. Weekend warrior or not, fightin' to the death isn't most's cup of tea, mate."

"You never met this guy, clearly," Cal replies. "He was the sort."

"My point, right," Ben clears his throat. "They say you owe 'em something?"

"No, not like that," Cal replies. "Not in so many words, no."

"What then? What'd he want from it?"

"Police just asked me something about a connection to heroin, bit back," Cal says. "When they kept calling me out, remember? They told me I should watch out. That maybe someone knew him in here. Now this guy tells me to watch what I say on the stand. Like he's connected or something."

"Oy, come on," Ben says. "Mate, who cares what it connects to, and everybody knows somebody, who cares what the bleeding coppers say," Ben smacks Cal's mattress theatrically. "If you don' know, you don' know, so you can't talk, right? And they know that too even. Probably, right? Bugger it. Don't fret on it. No different than any other day, far as I sees things. Any other time."

"You do seem very calm about it."

"Nothing to fuss, really," Ben replies, the sarcasm lost on him. "They're always threatening someone here right? Frankly, as safe in here as it is out there. So... right? No need to hide in the bunk."

"I'm not hiding in the bunk."

"Sods I get paired with..." Ben shakes his head, chuckling.

The beeping alert blares above them all at once, signaling an hour before lights-out. After a minute it cuts. Cal hears a jumble of movement in the cells on either side of his. Ben sits down on his bunk below.

He's right, you know.

On some level, he's right. What does it matter in respect to the trial? In respect to the next few pivotal days?

There's nothing to tell. So, it doesn't matter at all.

The man hated me because I loved his wife. Hated me because he hated himself too much to love her like that. Deep down, he knew it too.

And he hated it.

He died for that hate, nothing else.

Cal leans over and looks down from his bunk at his cellmate, seeing him in a new light at once, and a strange, rare sense of camaraderie comes over him.

"What would you do?" Cal asks him, "if you were me?"

"Me? What'd I do?" Ben asks, stroking his messy beard.

"Yeah. If someone threatened you, came up on you right before your trial started? Telling you to not talk about this or that business or something?"

Ben's dark eyes stare up at him, rubbing the castor oil in. Considering this. Savoring it, even. This moment of solicited wisdom.

"Not hard when you don' know. Focus and win the bloody case Cal," he says, shrugging, then breaks a crooked grin. "Don't let 'em shake you, sunshine. Always shite to let 'em shake you. Even I know that. It's the trial – nothing else – here on in, innit... stay focused an' getting set free. The rest'll come, sure enough, sunshine. Mark my words. It'll come."

28

J ust over a hundred and thirteen days after his arrest in the bloody chaos of the Jones's living room, Calvin Beckley goes on trial for the premeditated murder of David Jones. And in the hours leading up to his transport from Southwark to the Old Bailey, the media coverage reaches somewhat of a frenzy outside, flavor-of-the-week hot-takes abound... or so Damian informs him, coming in with the suit in one hand and his briefcase in the other on the morning of the big day.

"Saw you rang last night. Was out early. Everything alright?" Damian asks. He hands over the suit. Cal pulls off the dry cleaner's plastic sleeve.

"Easy now. I took pains. Let's hope she fits."

"Everything's fine," Cal says. "What's that there, literature while I get dressed?" He motions towards the newspaper, folded underneath Damian's arm.

"Hardly," Damian scoffs, then places it on the table between them. "For you, dear boy, while we both wait. A glimpse into the circus that awaits you out these doors."

"Can't remember the last time I read one of these," Cal says, taking and unfolding it – The London Times. A moment later, sifting through the pages, he finds a story about the trial. Shots of the aftermath of the bloody murder scene. Blood and glass, over-contrasted from the photographer's flash; Sarah's bruised face from previous domestic assaults; the tarped remains of David (in two distinct coverings), and Cal on a stretcher; some other arrest shots, populated in a crime collage within the story's texts, basically hitting the basics.

Then, in the opinion section beneath – an inclusion titled TALE OF TWO DADDIES? with several conspiratorial paragraphs below conjoined with pictures of Sarah, stepping out of her car, dark glasses on, her palm pressed to her visible baby bump.

Cal finishes getting dressed in the suit, and later as he departs through the streets to the old courthouse steps – paparazzi swarming behind the curb like locusts, flashing cameras at the backseat window of the car – Cal watches it all unfold before him with the quiet surrender of a man who knows that it's too large to stop. Because, after reading the articles all the way through, Cal realizes that it's bigger than he and Sarah, and his cell, and the prison, and even that pristine flat when he came over that February night.

And the police. Bigger than them, too.

A lot more people know about it than he thought.

A city story. A flavor of the week. It's been broadcasted – in the streets of Lewisham, the streets of south London; in two buildings especially, across neighbors full of candid gossip, as well as in the pubs, restaurants, marts, parks, conversations, the places on the block the three frequented (never together, of course).

Karalana, his old pub confidante, knows. His old coworkers know too, Andy and his boss. And sweet old Greta, at the grocers. And his aunt... of course they do.

All of them. How couldn't they?

His picture is at the top of the story.

The bloody top of it!

People talking about the trial's opening proceedings, their own theories, beliefs of what truly happened that night, what David did or didn't do to his wife, and the various evidence morsels that have come out so far to the public.

Thank God my parents are gone, Cal sighs, feeling a bit mortified.

What would they think of me now? On trial for murder...

Cal reads through more bullet points about the case. None, of course, that he doesn't already know himself. All too well.

"Nearly there," the copper next to him says. Cal's heart quickens as the van pulls up alongside the curb of the massive courthouse.

The police swing the door open, and Cal steps out and hears the expeditious clicks of cameras, and sees a couple dozen paparazzi and news reporters held at bay behind barriers on either side of the steps leading up to the entrance.

"Calvin Beckley, how are you expecting the proceeding to go today?"

"Calvin Beckley, why did you murder your girlfriend's husband?"

"Mr. Beckley, are you nervous for the testimony that'll be presented to the court today?"

"Do you think the jury will buy your account?"

And, as he passes them, he hears one journalist yell to him: "Cal Beckley, are you in fear for your life?"

And another: "If you are freed, how will you live with yourself?"

Damian presses him forward, his hand on his back.

Inside the grandeur of London's Old Bailey, the chaos falls away and the scene is a bit more of a methodical, deliberate energy.

"Why do people keep asking me that?" Cal whispers to Damian as they step through the great doors.

"What's that?" Damian asks and leans in, pulling his glasses down his nose.

"Am I in fear for my life?" Cal repeats. "That reporter back there."

Damian looks around as if an assassin is inbound, then pats Cal on the back. "No need to be in fear of anything if I do my job right today, dear boy. Now breathe for me. Ignore the press. Ravenous swine, they are. Prats mostly. The lot of them. Know a few, myself. Loathsome. Anyway. Quiet now."

A silence falls over the room and just like that, the High Court judge enters and opening discussions start off. Several summary explanations, moving into the heart of the matter, the jury's arrival

– and Cal's anxiety ticks upwards with each passing moment. The wheels beginning to turn on the event that will decide his fate.

He looks around at the courtroom's occupants, feeling sweat on his neck and back. Despite the more composed environment, palpable anticipation can be read on the faces of everyone in attendance as they come in to sit. The shuffle underwritten with nervous glances and whispering.

Courthouse Four. The gleaming polished wood echoing with the footsteps and hushed conversations. He unbuttons his suit's jacket, a shade of navy. Shadows play across his face, outlining the stubble and the worry lines. The sleepless nights spent thinking of how the outcome of the next couple weeks in this room will change the rest of his life.

I should have slept more.

He hopes it's not too obvious. The fatigue. The worry. The guilt. The ordeal of it playing across his face.

Cal shoots a furtive look towards the entrance, scanning for one person, and not seeing her. The courtroom's air feels thick like melted paste.

"Dry off," Damian whispers to him, passing him his lime-colored, silk handkerchief.

"Thanks," Cal mouths back, taking it and pressing it to the hot skin of his forehead and neck. "Nerve wracking, isn't it?"

"I'd be worried if you didn't feel a smidge of trepidation frankly, dear boy," Damian replies, writing on his pad. "Just theater in motion, my friend, nothing more. As we practiced. Same as we reviewed. Theater in motion."

On the other side of him, the prosecution team is abuzz, exchanging notes, writing last minute things on last minute documents, other preparations. Speaking with each other by leaning in and cupping hands around their partner's ears at times, and Cal smirks during one such sighting of this, taking Damian's assessment to heart.

Perhaps Damian's right.

Cupping each other's ears like children. As if anything can be deciphered in the echoing discordance of this high-ceilinged chamber. They're putting on a show, really.

Some weird game - my life at stake in the middle of it.

A large screen is wheeled in a few minutes later, with a laptop connected to its base underneath. Several struggle to get the extension cord unraveled, and then take even longer to get the rest of it set up and turned on. Cal zones out after a few minutes, feeling himself calm a bit, slow in the tedium, fingers intertwined, the muted conversations fading away. Feeling his eyelids growing heavy. Staring off and waiting for the judge to speak again.

His nerves are shot from the threat the night before, the not sleeping much, the dreading this part more than any of the others. Now, those lost hours catch up and tiredness overtakes him, and his head nods when he feels Damian shift beside him, his blazer shuffling, turning to peer back.

And then Cal feels a thunderbolt of energy.

There is a commotion off to the side of the room behind them, and a hush descends over the spectators' seats. Cal looks as well, leaning over, craning to see where the faces are turned, at the group entering. There at the center.

He gasps as Sarah walks in. The first time he's laid eyes on her since fading in a pool of his own blood. Her face hunched above him. Those eyes. Her hands at work. Fighting to save his life.

Sarah's wearing a loose-fitting ivory dress, contrasting starkly against the severity of the room. The gilded soft waves of her hair cascade down her shoulders and are longer than he remembers them. He notices how her poise doesn't betray the slightest hint of turmoil. It's the walk of someone who's known pain but refuses to be defined by it. As she always is. Her chin is high, and she looks straight ahead to where she is going to sit.

This is not someone mourning.

This is someone pressing forward.

Looking around, Cal sees all eyes in the room are on her, and he suddenly feels sorry for her.

To think this all started in the privacy of our own shadowed perches across from each other.

Months ago. One winter night.

Who could have ever thought it'd come down to this?

Would I not have looked up there, knowing this outcome?

Would I not have lingered?

Obsessed over her? Confided in her? Fell for her?

Slept with her?

He sees Sarah sit down on the far side of the room, crossing her legs, with several others sitting around her. She speaks with someone nearby, and smiles at them. She looks behind her and then he watches her lean in and speak with a woman dressed in a pinstripe pantsuit, who then scoots in and sits down beside her. Her solicitor perhaps. The two discuss something. Then he sees Sarah sit upright, silently nodding. Never looking at him. Not once.

A rushing flood of feelings rise within Cal, seeing her after all this time. The attraction. The glee – his wonder of her. His lust. All this anguish, and pain, and legality between them. So many things he wants to say to her, to ask her, to tell her.

To confront her about.

But he can't. He can't even say a word. The distance and spaces and predicament far too vast between them...

I may never get the chance to say what I want to say to her.

But there's no time to reflect on that. There is a shuffle in the room, and a quieting of conversations. Heads turning.

"Here we go," Damian whispers to him, tapping his heel, standing all at once. Cal follows his example. "Chin up, mate. Game time."

The jury enters and the judge beckons the prosecutor and Damian forward to his podium, Cal standing there, eyes glued ahead with fingers intertwined in front of him.

The day I've been waiting for all these months. Here we go.

And lumbering like a train departing King's Cross, Cal's murder trial begins.

29

D iscussions between the judge and the jury take place as expected followed by the opening statements. And a little over an hour into the proceedings, it finally happens – the first major witness of the trial is called to the stand. Cal holds his breath as he hears the prosecutor utter her name:

"Sarah Jones, please arise and step forward."

From the outset. No foreplay. None at all. Not even one witness beforehand.

How many other witnesses could there be though?

Sarah is the main one, perhaps the only one, that counts.

This is good. This is a good thing. They're not wasting time. But, somehow, Cal almost wishes they were.

"I do solemnly, sincerely and truly declare and affirm that the evidence I shall give shall be the truth, the whole truth, and nothing but the truth," Sarah repeats after being prompted. The prosecution team shuffles around, preparing themselves. And things get going from there, the clerk and the court reporter typing away in front of her as Sarah falls into the question-answer flow of the examination.

It begins with her recounting the origins of her relationship with David, the beginning of it – as she had with Cal what feels like a lifetime ago in the candlelit Chelsea restaurant, on their first and only date together. The tale being the same one: love gone horribly wrong, filled at first with whispered threats before devolving into hopeless cycles of explosive confrontations, violence, retaliations... followed by promises and forgiveness. The cycle of his violence.

She tells how police would get involved at times, and how, in the end, her fear of him killing her made her stay.

"Despite, on some level, you knowing it might kill you in not doing so?" the assistant prosecutor asks, flipping her dark hair to the side, gesticulating with her ballpoint pen like it's a conductor's baton. "Leaving, I mean?"

"Yes," Sarah responds, her voice level, reserved. "Even though I knew it might kill me."

"Care to elaborate on how you came to such conclusions?"

"Care to?" Sarah scoffs, shaking her head.

"Might you?"

"People judge so easily from the comfort of their untouched lives, saying what one should or shouldn't do in situations," Sarah says, her voice sharp. "But when you're living it, every day, every night, every moment – it's not that simple. The stakes change. You decide things more on a what-avoids-a-fight basis. What avoids a confrontation, a punch, a slap, worse even, in that moment – much more than how to run from it. More than some elaborate, grand exit strategy. Or whatever else you think you might do. On some level you believe that it's what you deserve a bit – the bruises, the cuts – for what's put on you. It's never as black and white as: I'm out, cheerio, farewell!"

The court audibly chuckles at Sarah's mockery, and the prosecutor doesn't seem amused, tapping her pen against the podium's top. She waits a moment for it to become quiet before proceeding with the next question.

"I didn't mean to imply as much. Apologies. Moving on, Mrs. Jones. What more can you tell us about the fights you and your husband had?"

Each response from Sarah draws a more vivid picture of life under the worsening tempers of David: his drinking, his late nights, his gambling, his refusal to go to therapy, to seek real help for the issues he endured; the abuse she's been led to believe he suffered from his own family. And elsewhere. His growing addictions.

Cal's ears perk at Sarah's remark.

"...began using drugs. Buying, and a bit of selling, the little he told me –"

"Please your honorable justice, hear me as I am reluctant to rise, but I beseech that this be removed from the record and jury consideration as it is mere conjecture, unsupported by intended evidence and findings of this court, or this case," a junior member on the prosecutor's team calls out from the table beside Cal's.

"Yes, yes, that makes sense," the high court judge nods. "From the record. Do try and stay on point, relevant to the questions inquired of you, Mrs. Jones, without conjecture about adjacent criminalities", the wrinkled man says from above. "Understood?"

"Unrelated?" Sarah asks, glancing at her own solicitor towards the back of the room.

"Indeed, only what's relevant, please. Now. Proceed along," the judge says. "Please."

And Sarah continues, steering back to herself, each word drawing a picture of the horrors she navigated living with her husband: nights spent enduring his violence, days spent trying to scream out for help, scream out for distraction, scream out for a lifeline. The marriage getting worse. Less communication. The line between love and fear completely faded, finally, when by the time she becomes friends with Cal, her neighbor across the street, she's hitting rock bottom.

"And it's because of this, witnessing the violence, that Cal reached out with a letter one day, having seen it himself. Having witnessed it from his own place. His rooftop."

Not untrue, I suppose. Truthy. But not all I witnessed.

Not the first thing.

Then the assistant prosecutor moves to introduce Cal's first note to Sarah. It is placed on display for the jury to see. Cal recalls the evening he wrote it, feeling like years ago now. And it's then, in this pause, this brief fleeting moment that the court reads the display, that Sarah's gaze meets his for the first time since stepping into the courtroom. It's a momentary instant, but his heart skips as her emerald eyes hesitate on him in the span of half a second.

Looking for something. Sifting. Searching and finding.

And then she is elsewhere again. But in that sudden moment it's like he's been shocked – swallowed within a world of feelings welled up for her – a lump forming in his throat.

All his restless emotions stirred, pounding the walls within him. The weight of his choices, her words, hanging in the space a dozen meters between them – somewhere in that broken stare.

For Cal, as it's the first time all over again: the room fades and there is only Sarah.

He and Sarah.

Her voice is soft and clear as she presses on, nodding with her explanations, responding to each question with a sort of quiet certainty that demands attention.

"David was not the man you've heard about in the papers nor the one seen in those curated social media groups. Trust me, I've seen them too," and the court again chuckles at her teasing tone, the high judge looking around wearily.

"Those were masks he gave the world. Behind closed doors, David was a storm of a human being."

"And what do you mean by that, Mrs. Jones? A storm?"

"I mean just that. Tempestuous. Outside of his professional life. His network. His import-export business. His precious little empire. He was a mess of rage, paranoia, and possessiveness," she says, her voice carrying an authenticity in its quiet delivery that makes people lean in. "He was terrible to me. Behind closed doors."

"And did you ever love him?" the assistant prosecutor asks, moving to the center of the room, her hands behind her back now.

"Of course I did. I agreed to marry him. But as time went on, his love became an obsession with me," she replies. "And obsessions aren't love. Are they? They are all-consuming fires that in David's case saw only threats."

"Meaning...?"

"Friends, colleagues, even strangers on the street - to David, they were all potential enemies, would-be challengers of his perceived ownership over me. And it only got worse as time went on."

She pauses, swallowing.

Damian throws Cal a look, eyebrows raised almost like he's enjoying this. Like he's witnessing gossip about his favorite sitcom.

"Really," Sarah continues, her voice cracking, and Cal sees her eyes suddenly glisten with tears, resolute, focusing on the jurors, and then the defense table, and settling briefly on him again. "Before Cal came into my life as my friend," she says, "David's suspicions were already volatile. He believed, truly believed, that everyone wanted to take me from him. Take something from him, at a minimum."

"And did you warn your neighbor of this?" the prosecutor asks. "This suspicion your husband had of people?"

"Yes."

"So Cal knew?"

"Yes."

"And can you describe your husband's mental state at the time you and Cal were becoming friends?" the prosecutor asks.

"Again, he thought someone was coming after him. He acted preemptively, out of a distorted sense of protection."

"So, defensively you could say?"

"Yes, in his own mind," Sarah answers, not falling for it.

"That's all for now," the assistant prosecutor says.

Sarah looks around, her eyes seemingly everywhere except in Cal's direction.

"So, Mrs. Jones, there was a pattern of your husband lashing out at others in your life, besides you?" Damian questions her, rising for his redirect examination.

"Yes."

"Other friends or family members, for instance?"

"Yes."

"Such as whom, specifically?" Damian asks.

"All my friends, really. My sister first of all," Sarah says. "I haven't spoken to Sofia for years. That stopped with a blowout she had early on in our relationship. First year I believe that I was dating David. She warned me profusely about him, after the two had a row over something small really, a difference of opinion, and I never listened to her because he downplayed it. I was young. In love. Dumb, really. I thought she was just being an annoying older sister."

"Did she ever relay specifically what David said to her that caused her to feel this way about him? What your boyfriend at the time said to your sister, I mean?" Damian asks.

"No, not really," Sarah answers. "I remember Sofia just had a bad feeling about him. She said he swore at her. Told me that David reminded her of our father."

"Who was, himself, abusive?" Damian asks, taking notes on his pad, even though he already knows the response.

"To my mother, yes, growing up." Sarah says. "At times," she adds.

"And is he still alive?" Damian asks.

"My father?"

"Yes, a –" he glances at his pad, "An Aldo Ciambra?"

"Yes, as you already know, but he is out of the country. Refuses to live in England."

"And before he moved, did your father meet David?" Damian asks.

"He did, yes. At our wedding. One of the only times, I think. The first time, for sure."

"Why did it take so long for your father to meet the man marrying his daughter?" Cal's solicitor asks Sarah, and Cal feels himself tensing. "Wouldn't he want to know who you were getting married to beforehand?"

Why is he even asking that? Damian can't help himself.

"My father and I were estranged," Sarah says, eyes narrowing slightly. "Have been for some time."

"And what did your father think of David?" Damian asks. "When he met him at the wedding?"

Sarah bites her lip, considering this for a moment.

"He never really said one way or the other," she replies at last. "But the two were not close by any means. After the wedding. I think my father thought –"

"My Lord, I feel this line of questioning beginning to trespass on inadmissible speculation," the assistant prosecutor says suddenly, cutting Sarah off. "May we please return to the matter?"

"Indeed," the Judge says. "Move along, Mr. Macleod. Relevant to the matters of which have brought us here, if you please."

"Understood. Let's try another way," Damian says, shifting gears, pacing in front of where Sarah sits. "Cal was not the first by any means, is what you are saying? The first to have concerns with the way David acted?"

"No, he was not the first at all."

"And there were others before him – people David hurt out of suspicion, rage even?"

"Yes. Like I said, my sister, verbally," Sarah answers. "And others too. He always thought other people were bad for me."

"Meaning what exactly?"

"Out to use me, hurt me," Sarah says, her eyes fixed on Damian. "People that had been there for me, way before him even. Years and years of my life. Friends of mine he scared away. Texting them strange things. Acting hostile at dinner parties. Passive aggressive, usually. Moody. Pretty much all of my friends, now that I think of it. Small, petty aggressions, but the kind that leave an impact on people. Just like pumping cold air into my life... but at such a small level that I couldn't tell even while sitting in the room."

"Even while sitting in the room," Damian repeats, cocking his head. "And what kind of impression did he leave with your other friends?"

"Well... half of the relationship was cold. Sabotaging, as my friend Abigail put it once. Like he didn't want to be there. Didn't want to interact with them. Get to know them, you know?" she replies, her eyes furrowing slightly.

"And why do you think that was?" Damian asks. "Him doing that to the relationships in your life?"

Sarah looks nearly serene as she looks at the jury and replies.

"He wanted me isolated. It became so obvious, in hindsight. He wanted me alone. It's funny how something like that can disguise itself so readily in love when it's early on. But it only evolves, never lessens – I get that now. The need for control. And he was getting worse, so when Cal came around, naturally he got it worse than any of the others."

"When Cal confronted him, you mean?" Damian clarifies. "Telling your husband to leave you alone?"

"Right – when he told David to leave me alone. He was confronting the worst version of my husband is what I'm saying."

She pauses, the weight of her admissions pulling her down for a moment. She straightens her chin before looking at the jury.

"I lived in that hell – hoping, praying that things would get better in our home. And every passing day, every glance I shared with another, every laugh, every conversation   it only fueled his paranoia. I was alone, sleeping next to someone who would explode at any moment. At any misstep."

"At what point did you realize that you were in real danger, Mrs. Jones?" Damian asks poignantly, not missing a beat.

Sarah swallows hard and takes a deep breath.

"When he raped me for the first time," she says.

Cal feels nausea rising within him. The thought of it.

This new angle to her misery. This new misery of her violence.

"And that's..." Damian clears his throat. "In the act of raping you?"

Something Cal almost seems to have known but never confronted – an evil implication of living with that kind of man. A man who would never take no for an answer. A man who couldn't be controlled by anyone.

His expectations. His methods. His force. The violence would bleed into sex.

He raped her. Of course he did, Cal thinks grimly.

The last piece she hasn't told, but in many ways she has, too.

"Afterwards, really," she continues. "He'd tell me he wanted to kill me sometimes after he was done. When I was just laying there, praying he'd just go, just leave. He'd say it. That I wouldn't make it far. That he would kill me if I ever tried to leave. I believed him," she nods. "God, I believed him."

The courtroom stirs, a few in attendance clearly uncomfortable.

Damian presses forward: "Mrs. Jones, were these rapes by your husband ever reported, ever documented to authorities?"

"No," she replies, pulling a bang out of her eyes and behind her ear, shifting herself. "Never to the police, no."

She shakes her head. Someone behind Cal murmurs.

"And why was that, as opposed to the domestics which were reported?" Damian asks.

"Because I was too scared," Sarah says. "Rape is different. It's very different."

"How so?"

"Well. It's what he said – he'd say it to me. Rape is worth killing over. So take it. Just shut up, or I'll fucking kill you. Shut up and take it. Like my wife. Like your duty. Take it."

She hesitates, pauses a moment, wiping her eyes with a tissue.

"He said it was his right. Said I was lucky to be alive. And that part was true - I was lucky. If it wasn't for Cal seeing me from his building..." Then she looks directly at Cal and time freezes. "... In his own grief, seeing the violence I endured from David firsthand, taking the chance, contacting me, trying to be there... for me... I may not be here today. He probably would have done what he told me he was going to do. David would have finally done it."

"Killed you, you mean?"

"Yes. He would have raped me, like any of the other dozens of times, and he would have killed me. Strangled me. As he said he would. I have little doubt in my mind. I was trapped in a death cycle with him. I had an hourglass turned over my life. It was only a matter of time."

Sarah's words reverberate through the room in the silence Damian allows, looking at his notes. The weight of her confession palpable to everyone listening. You can hear a pin drop in the large chamber. Every eye in the spectators' seats fixed upon her; every ear leaning forward to grasp the revelations of her torture, the days locked in her brutal marriage of sexual assault, violence, fights, isolation.

"One final question," Damian asks. "One I think we would all like some clarity on, if I do say so."

"Yes?"

"Is David Jones the father of your unborn child, Mrs. Jones?"

Sarah sits poised, her voice unwavering, drying her eyes.

"Yes," is all she says.

30

C al sits with her words lingering over him, the weight of her answers sinking into his bones, his heart floundering. He stares, hearing her say it's David's baby, but his mind rejects it, clinging to the fragile hope that he is the father.

Their one night together.

The many times that night.

She's lying to them all. She must be.

He sees himself holding the child with Sarah by his side. Laying there. As he has so many times on the upper bunk of his cell in Southwark. But the truth gnaws at him – the relentless beast, this disclosure like a spear thrown at him, smacking into his chest, tearing at the dreams he had built around himself; the ones clung to, helping him survive each day in prison.

Even though it is the same answer Damian corroborated weeks ago after the sonogram pictures first were given to Cal. Even though he knows it's the only explanation why the prosecution hasn't weaponized her pregnancy as proof of motive.

Even though all of it – it is something he can't accept.

Think about it – the fertility issues she told you.

David couldn't... he blamed her. He beat her for it.

It was the reason they had that fight.

Unless she lied. But why lie?

"They've tested it, Cal – listen to me. Under duty of witness summons – there's no mistake there," he recounts Damian saying to him, visiting him several weeks before for trial preparation. "A lab. Think about it, they had to do the DNA tests from a criminal evidence assessment, for motive, dear boy. You should be pleased, happy even, it's not yours. Set aside your feelings. This is a good thing for our case. There's no way they can use it against you now."

But Cal didn't believe him then. And he doesn't now.

No. It's not the truth – Cal resists the explanation.

She's done something. And even with the revelation now fully out in the open, from Sarah's mouth herself, soon to be dispelling the conspiratorial gossip columns of London's coverage writ large, Cal still doesn't believe it.

He flatly rejects the notion. It's not true.

I don't know how. But it's not.

Why send the sonogram at all, if that were it?

No. It's our child – not his. Ours. Our night together. The consequence of it. The night before all the other consequences...

Looking around, Cal can see the room wrestling with the immensity of her confessions too, for obviously different reasons. The trauma of it revisited, the past hour or so of relaying these stories aloud, it's clear it's a lot for several of the older jurors in particular who have adopted a pale color and a permanent stare at Sarah.

These memories she's been telling, punctuated by the pictures displayed, each shown in turn from the television screen: images of the blows, shouts, blood, and shattered glass; exhibiting also the various captures from the previous domestic reports. Piece by piece. A narrative exhibited. And in the silence that follows her powerful statements, a shift in the atmosphere can be felt. Across the whole court.

A different narrative emerging, clearly challenging the held feelings and preconceived notions of some in attendance, judging by the shifting and unease in the chamber. As Sarah continues, it's become undeniably clear that her testimony paints her husband David not as the victim, but as the monster.

Good. Cal glances over.

Cold panic radiates from the prosecution's table, shattering the carefully constructed story they've built up until now. As terrible as hearing about the rape is, Damian was right in his assessment that Sarah speaking about it on the stand would only be a good thing.

The impeccably dressed lead prosecutor however, a tall graying man named Mr. Simons, seems to sense the shift as well and Cal watches him scribbling things on a legal pad, furious and intensely, taking a moment to readjust his approach, and his slender tie in turn, before standing and taking the notes to the podium.

"Mrs. Jones," he begins, his voice a deep, commanding authority. The room becomes deafly quiet. "You speak of the violence you suffered at your husband's hands. In great detail, in fact. But isn't it true that you had relationships that also ended tragically before ever meeting Mr. Jones?"

"I'm – I'm sorry?" Sarah stammers.

"Would you like me to repeat the question?"

"I, um. Yes, if you don't mind," she says.

"I asked about your other relationships that have ended with tragedy. Specifically, an incident in Ireland. Glenevin Falls," the prosecutor says. "An ex-boyfriend drowned there, correct? In a lake, Kerry County – let's see. Ephemeral Lake, just a kilometer from the falls."

Ephemeral Lake, Cal repeats to himself, realizing where her studio's name comes from.

Too unkind for tonight... another time – her words echoing in Cal's head from their date, walking around the derelict cobbled streets.

"Was that a question?" she asks the prosecutor, staring back at him.

"Isn't that how it happened, Mrs. Jones?" he clarifies.

"Yes, that is so."

"You were the last to see him alive, were you not? You were swimming with him, in fact, as the report states, were you not? At the time before he slipped, hit his head under the water as the autopsy report states?"

"Your honor," Damian stands, "Your honor, might we beseech the opposing council for an explanation of relevancy in regards to the present matter?"

Mr. Simons throws him the look a hawk gives a rodent when it spots it across a field.

"It pertains to the character of a key witness, your honor," the prosecutor retorts. "This is a documented accidental death case out of Kerry several years back. Nothing more. Contextual."

Cal looks at Sarah.

Sarah's face is perhaps a shade paler than it was a moment before, but her composure remains unphased while all this is occurring. The courtroom stares back at her in silence.

Ireland? A drowning?

The high judge waves them in, calling council to his podium. Damian leaves Cal's side. A whispered discussion ensues.

Ephemeral. The name of her gallery. The long story she declined telling after dinner. Peeling Sarah back – subtle layers only he is witnessing within the trial.

Cal glances at Damian as he returns and sits down, who catches his gaze and nods, holding a lone finger up and closing his eyes momentarily.

"Continue, Mrs. Jones. You may answer the line of inquiry," the judge says at last, nodding to the prosecutor in turn.

"Which was?" Sarah rebukes, looking from the judge to the prosecutor, eyebrows raised.

"Care to explain, Mrs. Jones, the accidental death that occurred in your past at Ephemeral Lake?" Mr. Simons asks.

Sarah replies, her voice wavering at first, "I've faced tragedy before... love and grief make us seek shelter from it, and sometimes not always in the wisest of places. Sam drowned, yes. We were teenagers. It was a tragedy... one of a couple in my life."

"And you two were dating?"

"Yes. It's something I've had to work very hard to move past."

"Yes, Mrs. Jones," the prosecutor lingers, taking a second, choosing his words carefully. "But wouldn't you say this is a bit... unseemly, the word may be. To lose not one but two great loves in the span of less than a decade... each meeting an unfortunate, premature end?"

Silence pervades the room, Sarah chewing on the question, as she stares back at the man - her eyes flat, inexpressive.

"I resent your implication," Sarah finally responds, her voice far away, a side Cal hasn't seen. A wrathful edge boiling to the foreground.

"Both in respect to the obvious, but also that my relationship with David was some sort of great love, as you call it. Rather presumptuous, aren't you, saying something like that. As I have articulated, perhaps not clearly enough, for you or anyone, it was a very flawed love. A wretched love. A toxic, destructive, poisonous, devastating love. Much different than my love for Sam. Which was innocent teenage love. How dare you conflate the two."

"But you do deny it?" Simons asks.

"Deny what exactly, Mr. Simons?" Sarah asks, her lips pursed.

"The unseemly nature of these two occurrences, Mrs. Jones. All within a decade of each other."

Sarah rolls her eyes at the man, and Cal can't help but feel a smirk breaking at the corner of his mouth. Sure, he's trying to get under her skin, but in a strange way she's enjoying it.

A lifetime of trauma – of defending her jugular. Of managing the casual and the spiteful – the blended varieties of cruelty from men in her life. And she's cracked it now. Her methods of defense. Adept at them. At sparring with them. Flawless.

"Of course, I can see how one, with an agenda, could extrapolate such conclusions from two otherwise unrelated events," Sarah replies. "Yes, unseemly, because they were each not happy things.

Terrible things, in fact. Each in its own. Mr. Simons, are you not a happy man? Is that terrible of me to ask?"

The courtroom gushes laughter, the apprehension broken for a sheltered moment or so, before the high judge yells for order, his face red with a large vein protruding out of his forehead.

"Silence, silence!" he yells. "I demand the witness refrain from such ad-hominem outbursts or she will be removed from my court and held in contempt! That is a first and final warning, Mrs. Jones!"

"Understood, your honor," Sarah nods to him, glancing up. "My apologies."

Cal suppresses another grin. Sarah flips a strand of hair behind her ear again and Cal can see the shine of her earrings from where he's sitting. She takes a deep breath, her green eyes flashing a look his way.

"Apologies, Mr. Simons, I don't know what came over me – please continue, sir," Sarah says as the courtroom quiets down. As if under her spell, the world falls back into focus on her.

"Mrs. Jones, is it true that Mr. Beckley here has recently written you about wanting to 'kill your husband?" the prosecutor asks.

Cal looks at Damian, feeling a cold tremor down his spine.

"I'm sorry?" Sarah replies, her eyes scrutinizing.

"Indeed," he says, moving to the podium. "In the very same journal, on the very same pages where he wrote to you this – I quote: if you want someone to talk to, someone who's glimpsed even a fraction of the storm you're weathering, I'm here, and I can help. End quote. Well, Cal also used these sheets to write things he didn't send to you. Worse things, in fact. Things he didn't want you to see, Mrs. Jones. Such as him writing this, and this."

The prosecutor clicks something to the display of the screen, showcasing each of Cal's absentminded scribbles, carefully chosen for this point.

Fuck David Jones.

Kill David?

Sarah hesitates, her eyes darting to Cal in the span of a moment, before looking back at the images. Cal feels his face growing hotter and sweat forming beneath his shirt. The courtroom seems to contract, the walls pressing in as the weight of the evidence bears down for all to see.

"Well," she begins.

And in that moment, as if time has slowed, she catches Cal's gaze again, this time longer, staring back, and there is an intense silent exchange between them. Something the court probably misses. An unspoken plea, perhaps. An acknowledgment of all the truths and deceptions they've shared. The yearnings. An answer.

Don't worry. I got this.

Cal sits back, hands in his lap, fingernails digging into the skin of his palm.

Sarah takes a deep breath, steadying herself, and then shrugs, looking from the prosecutor to the jurors in turn.

"Look, Cal wrote a lot of things in pain. People scribble their darkest thoughts when they're at their lowest – I know I do. It doesn't mean they act on them. Cal only wanted to protect me. He was angry at David for hitting me, yes, but he wasn't a violent man like David. He wanted the best for me. To get me out of a bad place. That's all. To be my friend. To make sure I got help. To make sure he didn't hurt me."

Mr. Simons strokes his chin, then says, "If that is in fact the case, why did you try and cover up for him on your initial testimony to police, stating, I quote – the knife is my husband's knife, Cal must have grabbed it – end quote. Why lie, Mrs. Jones, when you didn't in fact know who owed the knife?"

The question hangs in the air for less than a moment before she strikes back.

"I didn't lie. It was dark. I didn't get a look at the knife when I left my car in the parking garage and went back up. How could I have?"

"Explain that to the court," Mr. Simons commands, as a photograph of Cal's bloody knife is projected on the screen.

"My living room was destroyed. Yet I'd assume Cal wouldn't bring a knife when I asked him to bring wine. And I couldn't find David. So, when they asked me about a knife, I just answered. It seemed much more plausible for David to escalate something like that than for Cal to do it. They never asked me again, either."

The lies pour off her tongue like silk wine. Not a word on how she really found the knife. The morning after they'd slept together, probably. In his drawer – while he slept.

None of that, though. Just smooth, boldfaced lies instead. Each one sold better than the last.

"But you never did leave your flat's underground garage to see who had the knife and who didn't, now did you?" Mr. Simons asked. "During the fight?"

"No."

"And why was that? Why did you wait down there? Staying in your car as you reported to the police. Why stay in your vehicle, Mrs. Jones?"

"I went down for the food. The groceries for dinner. When I came up, it was over, as was reported. I immediately dialed the authorities. Then I went further inside my home, saw..."

"Before or after providing medical care to Mr. Beckley?"

"In regards to...?" Sarah asks.

"Contacting authorities," Mr. Simons clarifies.

"Before I went in."

"But when you came up, you reported that you heard glass break, did you not?"

"I did," Sarah says. "I was coming off the lift and I heard a smashing noise."

"And then why didn't you go into your own flat Mrs. Jones? While standing outside the door? You heard commotion, after all..."

She was right outside...

Cal feels a shiver run down his back.

The sweat breaking out on his collar.

She was there the moment I kicked him... the moment David fell back into the glass window.

"Simply answer, Mrs. Jones," the high judge says.

"I was scared," Sarah replies at last, her voice breaking.

"Scared... of?"

"What David would do to me. When I heard the crash, I thought it was him, breaking things in our living room. I was scared because when he'd left... we'd been on bad terms. He'd thrown me onto the floor. I'd spent the night locked in the bathroom, him threatening to break the door down. Kicking it. Yelling as he did."

"But all the while knowing that your neighbor, Cal," Mr. Simons says, glancing in his direction, "would be encountering your husband in your very own living room, only without you there to try to deescalate the situation. Is that right?"

"No. I thought I'd closed my door. I didn't know Cal would go inside. It should have been locked. I thought it was fine, that I'd catch up with him after unloading the food. And so, I left."

"Is that so Mrs. Jones? But didn't you buzz Cal into your building? After all, one can't just walk into a building like yours, can they?"

"No. They can't. I asked him to bring the wine. I expected him to meet me in the lobby after I brought up the groceries."

"Meet up..." the prosecutor nods, considering this, theatrically appearing incredulous as he draws it out, "... in the lobby. To have wine in the lobby?"

"We exchange letters, but that doesn't mean I'd risk him coming there if I wasn't in. I wanted to freshen up the place. Unload the shopping. It's not much different, meeting downstairs first. As said, the nature of my husband entailed precautions, by now you should see why. Cal knew that. Look before you leap, I'd told him."

"Even for just a friend? A male friend?"

"Considering my husband's temperament, with any friend, to be honest. But especially one like Cal. One who was there because he was worried about me. And who had already told David to cut it out."

The parrying, the lies. The way she distances herself so masterfully from each small exposure, each small vulnerability in her story, each little crack that Cal has suspected exists. That he has lingered on in his own suspicions. Each area he knew the prosecutions would bury themselves into during the open floor examinations.

"And yet, Calvin went upstairs with a weapon, not just wine... why do you think that is?"

"I don't know why he went up," Sarah says.

"But you yourself have stated that you didn't expect your husband to come home, is that right?" Mr. Simons asks.

"Yes," Sarah answers.

"Right," Mr. Simons turns on his heel, pressing and facing the jury, letting his words fester before landing his question. "Returning to it, so the knife is or isn't your husband's weapon, Mrs. Jones?"

"I didn't know who it belonged to at the time – I now know, through the police informing me, that it's Cal's pocketknife, Mr. Simons," she says matter-of-factly, her politeness walking a line bordering mockery.

"Right. Cal's knife. And what do you make of that? Him bringing a weapon in the first place? He didn't think your husband would be there, as you said," Mr. Simons continues. "Yet he believed it necessary to bring a knife, didn't he?"

"It's a dangerous neighborhood. My husband is... was a dangerous man. As I have explained. Plus, as I understand it, being a pocketknife, it possesses a corkscrew. Doesn't it, Mr. Simons?" Sarah asks, her eyebrows scrutinizing in mock curiosity.

"I'll ask the questions, Mrs. Jones," he replies gruffly, and then, looking directly at Cal, he asks: "Bringing a weapon with him, instead of just a corkscrew. Because he could just as easily have taken a corkscrew, yes, instead of a lethal weapon, right Mrs. Jones?"

"Could he have taken just a corkscrew?" Sarah sighs, "Yes, of course. But what some seem to be missing is, had Cal not had the knife, he'd be dead. My husband would have bloody well killed him... almost certainly."

"That's your opinion, Mrs. Jones. The fact remains that Cal was stabbed several times by said knife, so had he not brought it –"

"Like I said, my husband was dangerous," Sarah snaps. "Cal knew my husband was dangerous. Cal had seen how dangerous my husband truly was."

"Indeed, and so it would have been far better to not have brought the weapon, you'd agree?" the prosecutor asks. "It would have been far better for him to have met you somewhere more neutral, without possessing a lethal weapon. Somewhere where this danger was lessened to where a weapon wouldn't be needed?"

"Yes, Mr. Simons, if it could be done over," Sarah retorts, apathy in her eyes as she stares at him cooly. "But it can't, can it?" she asks with a hint of defiance. "And so it is."

"And so it is, Mrs. Jones."

Saying whatever she must. Not giving up an inch.

Not even pausing, considering her responses before smacking the ball back over the net. Not letting him pin her. Just giving him the tiniest of slivers before parrying. Biding time.

"Nothing more, your honor," Mr. Simons says at last, and Cal thinks he can see the slightest bit of disappointment in the man's stern face as he returns to his seat.

And then Damian is standing one last time, pacing out in front of Sarah, who watches him, tiredly, and Cal notices that his awkward gait is sharpened to appear almost natural in the space, as if he's been pacing there for decades – or at least honing his acting skills, his own brand of courtroom flare.

Far better than he's done the rest of the morning in the confidence department. A pep – like he's enjoying it now. Look at him. Maybe he's seeing weakness in the prosecution too. Like I am.

Unable to rattle Sarah.

And Damian begins, clearing his throat.

"Mrs. Jones, did Cal ever harm or show any intention of hurting David before that fateful night?"

"No," Sarah replies, her voice soft, lying with ease. "Cal stepped into my life to help me. To be there for me."

"And did you ever have sexual relations with Cal?"

"No, I did not."

"So, he never felt... compelled to fight your battles?" Damian asks. "I mean from a sense of romantic obligation?"

"I didn't ask any man, or woman, or family member, or friend to fight my battles, Mr. Macleod, whatever the obligation," Sarah replies, her lips curling ever so slightly. "That was for me to do alone. But no... Cal didn't have any sense of romantic obligation."

On some small level, deep within him, Cal wishes that were the reality. Wishes he could roll back time. Roll back these feelings for her.

As he did while in the hospital room, morphine warming up his veins.

"Nevertheless, Cal did fight your battles," Damian continues, tapping his pen against his palm as he speaks. "After all, didn't he... when he had to, Mrs. Jones?"

She cocks her head slightly, looking at Damian, a little baffled, and he adjusts his glasses, his stare betraying back annoyance with her. The lies he knows damn well she's telling under oath. Perhaps even a little disgust, too – just a flash and it's gone. Cal shifts his weight in his chair.

He shouldn't be doing this. Come on, mate. Get on with it. You're not the prosecutor.

As if he can hear Cal's thoughts, Damian continues: "That is, when Cal had no other choice but to fight your battles... Wouldn't you say that's an accurate statement?"

"Yes, as I said before," Sarah answers, slow at first, "Cal was there for me. He didn't quit on me. Not when my husband picked the fight. As he always did – always picking fights. Only he shouldn't have that night."

"And why's that, Mrs. Jones?"

"Because he lost. A first for him..." Sarah breathes, her eyes tearing as she sits back, looking at the jury, her gaze falling on each in turn. "And for me... I was grateful he lost... when I came back home. I found Cal there, still alive. And I have to live with that feeling. Knowing that... well, knowing I felt that way... knowing my husband died trying to kill my friend. That feeling I felt... dialing the police. Gratitude mixed with shame... the bloody shame of it all. That's on me now. For the rest of my life, that's on me. I'll carry that to my grave."

31

The first day draws to its conclusion. At last, done.
One down.

Damian splits quickly after the jury is dismissed, promising an early morning debrief to cover the day's many happenings.

"Thanks for today," Cal says, and then when he leaves, he curses him under his breath. "Couldn't even wait a fucking moment to talk."

Cal sits back, exhaustion setting in a bit behind his eyes. Blinking, looking around, wanting to stretch, exercise his stiff joints. A few minutes later, the prosecution exits, and Cal is told to stand and is escorted out of the court by the bailiffs into the rainy afternoon; past the snaps of the cameras flanking either side of the stairs to the Old Bailey, the people craning their neck to take a look due to the viral nature of the case – back into the seat of a police car, the door slamming behind him. On his way to his cell in Southwark, through the London streets, with his mind firmly fixed on the day's happenings like tidal waves breaking against the sides of his skull, one after the other.

Revelation after revelation. The marital rapes. Her explanations. The baby. Her standing outside the door, presumably listening as it all went down.

He sits with each as they wash over – over his anxieties, unsure of which to pick apart first.

The car grumbles and pulls away from the curb and the curious, shouting crowds. Minutes of silence pass, with nothing but the pattering sounds of the rain hitting the rooftop of the car and the blaring of horns in traffic. Cal watches droplets slither their way along the glass as the car accelerates, merging onto the crowded motorway.

She said it. Just as Damian had said she was going to.

She claimed David was the father of her unborn little girl.

And... now, an implication of rape hanging over that claim.

And then when he fought David. Her claims to have stood there. Just outside. She could have stopped it. Could have stopped him. Somehow, she could have. At any point. Maybe.

But she didn't stop it. She didn't come in until it was over. Until he'd fallen through the plate glass window. The image of her standing there, coming up from the parking garage, watching the blade sink into his leg from the shadows of the foyer...

Cal wipes his eyes, feeling a little sick. His stomach growls. He realizes he has barely eaten anything at all today, his nerves far too racked for an appetite.

Jesus Christ, get a grip. It's not over. Get a grip.

She lied so much today, it's hard to know what the hell was up or down.

Lies in shades of truth. Truths in shades of lies. But she did it for you. At the end of the day. For you.

Almost every lie, a defense of him and a defense of herself, too.

The plan.

Just friends.

But does it matter? If I get out of here?

If it gets me out? Will it matter?

His mind swings to the early part of Sarah's examination. The questions about the drugs. The undercurrent of danger there regarding whatever it is exactly David did for a living, or in his free time. Sarah beginning to explain that her husband was entangled in something...

Something maybe tied up in the gallery, in her business...

Cal thinks of the brochure he read all those months ago at work, the one he found after hours of searching for clues about who Sarah really was. Remembering the passage below the photograph:

Ephemeral Canvas gives special thanks to our continued patron... David Jones, partner of showcased artist Sarah... for the contribution this month. Without your continued generosity, we would never be able to achieve our lofty goals.

Another level of complexity to this nightmare.

Lucky for him, Cal thinks, that there was an objection before it got too far into David's affairs. But the objection itself seems strange, considering it now. So quick and made by the most junior on the prosecutor's team nonetheless – the one who spoke the least during the trial.

In fact, I don't think he spoke at all after that, now that I think of it.

I beseech that this be removed from the record and jury consideration as it is mere conjecture...

Mere conjecture... defending the reputation of a dead man?

Doubt it.

Should ask Damian what he thinks of the conjecture statement tomorrow.

Cal rubs his eyes, his mind swirling back to the fact that Sarah said the baby girl was David's child.

It can't be. It just can't be.

A bit later, the early evening routine upon the prison, Cal trudges back up the stairs and along the labyrinth of hallways towards his cell. The day's strain clings to him like a second skin, and feeling emotionally exhausted, the corridors seem as if they stretch forward endlessly, punctuated by the murmur of the other inmates and clanging of metal doors. He shoulders his way through the throng in the common area, up the stairs, and enters his cell; the diminutive space feeling even more confined after the long day spent in the vacuous rooms of the courtroom chambers.

"Hey Ben," Cal says to his cellmate, who sits on the lower bunk, propped up and reading a National Geographic on Vikings judging by the Norse longboat displayed to the cover.

"Hey," Ben replies, not looking up.

Cal climbs up and collapses onto the upper bunk, the thin mattress offering little support to his aching lower back after sitting all day.

"Well? Spit it out. How'd it go?" Ben asks from below, his voice sounding gravelly tired himself. Dim light filters through the barred window and Cal listens to the rain picking up for a bit before answering.

"It's a mess. Not especially bad. But messy. Sarah's... twisting it... I don't know what to believe anymore."

Ben considers this for a moment, and Cal hears the pages of the magazine turn.

"At least she's testifying for you. That's good, innit? Not bad things."

Cal exhales, staring at the ceiling. "Right. Not bad things." And then Cal hears shuffling beneath him and suddenly Ben is standing up and looking over the edge of the bed, hands clasped.

"Look, mate, might got something for ya, but I'm going to need something, alright? A favor first. That hunky-dory?" he asks.

Oh God. What does he want?

"What kind of favor?" Cal asks, sitting up, curiosity piqued despite his exhaustion.

Ben's dark eyes lock onto his, serious and unwavering, "It's m'mum, Cal."

Cal cocks his head back, "What about her? I'm not shagging her, if that's it..."

"Fuck out of here," he chuckles, slapping his leg. "No. She hasn't filed taxes in years, mate. Need ya to sort that for me. With your accounting knowledge. All that. She's too stressed to even go see someone. Knackered over it, really. Too scared they'll judge her. A professional like."

Cal can't help but laugh and it feels good.

"Fuck y'laughing for?" Ben frowns. "It's not a joke."

"Nothing, man," Cal chuckles. "Nothing. Of course mate. I'll do it."

"What's so funny about it? See, that there is the goddamn response she was worried for."

"No," Cal says, "Not like that. I just thought it was something... you know, more serious-like."

"Not filing is serious-like," Ben says, eyed wide. "You better believe the Crown shall get her due, mate. 'Specially if you're a hard-working family like -"

"Okay, yes man," Cal pats his shoulder, "I'll help, okay?"

"Right," Ben says, looking relieved. "Thank you. I'll get the docs sorted. Then you just tell me what more you need."

"So?" Cal asks.

"So what?" Ben asks back.

"Aren't you going to tell me then?"

"Well the taxes ain't done, innit," Ben says.

"Bloody hell, Ben, where am I going to run to after I weasel you over in the exchange? I live with you in this bloody cell, under lock and key!"

"True," Ben says, considering this, before nodding. "A point."

"So?" Cal asks. "What then? Spit it out."

Ben leans back, holding on to the bed frame, a small, satisfied smile playing at the corners of his beard. "The bloke who confronted ya earlier—name's Ian Toley. I asked some mates 'bout him. Here for fraud, credit cards or somethin'. But his older bruvver Tom, right, he did a fiver, burglary a stretch back, Southwark's big brother Blackridge; now works the door at a spot called the Phoenix Inferno – Soho place, pretty fun club actually, connected though, I hear, to the Fenningtons crew, long time back now, since like a decade probably. Under various names, course. But they got it. Security, I think. Maybe drugs. Girls. You heard of it – the club?"

"Went once. A long time ago. For a stag years back," Cal replies, barely recalling the night, "Back when it was nicknamed Folly. Guess that was true, in light of this."

"Yeah, Folly, remember that," Ben chuckles. "Thought that was the area though."

Either way, not somewhere Cal felt drawn to reacquaint on any given night, no matter what the place was currently called. The nightclub there was now a bit of a tourist trap anyways from what Cal gleaned from younger conversations at his office watercooler.

Former office. Former conversations. Former watercooler.

Ben grins. "Ay, well. Fenningtons, ya know. If not the club."

"I've heard of them," Cal says. "And I've been to the damn nightclub."

He's heard whispers, tales of the London-based syndicate's unrelenting grip on the underworld. There'd be mentions on the news every now and then. Some crypto scam most recently. Usually just back-alley shit. Fixed fights… extortion rumors… prostitution rings and car thefts.

But it was a world so far from his own. So far from everything he knew outside of Guy Richie films. All of it. A world he wanted to steer far clear of. Always had, since his brother's first time being brought home to their aunt in the back of police car.

Evan's world. Never mine.

"I mean, in passing, yes I've heard of them," Cal nods, "But I'm not in that, Ben. What does that have to do with me? Why threaten me like that?"

"Well, if I were to connect it, each dot say," Ben's eyes narrow, calculating. "Lowly lush as I am, unconnected me-self – I reckon Sarah's ol man owed some quid. Now they're lookin' to collect from you or her. But considering the drugs, maybe more too. Somethin' tyin' it up to her hubby, anyways."

"You think this has to do with drugs?"

"Or cash, right? Something. But I don't know. Just figured I'd help ya, get out who sent the sod to speak to you, right? What it pertains to... only speculation, course."

Cal feels the room close in around him, the walls tightening, the air growing thin. It's his deepest suspicions breathed into life. Since the moment the detective-inspector told him to watch out.

Sarah has something they want... Something they at least wanted kept secret...

David was wrapped up in some sort of organized crime element, and now it's lingering.

How much did she know about it? How much is the art gallery tied to it?

Cal's mind races, piecing together fragments of the puzzle.

The renovations. The brochure. The mention of drugs.

Buying... a bit of selling...

The threat of a lifetime in prison looming large, the thought of always looking over his shoulder gnaws at Cal's sanity. In stepping into that penthouse, he came close enough to some part of London's underworld... the Fenningtons territory... a sea of crime. What a fucking nightmare.

"All the more reason to get the hell out of prison," Cal says to himself.

"Didn't know one needed a reason," Ben cracks a grin at him, before saying, "Look, just concentrate on winning the bloody case man, whatever all this is 'bout. All flexes. Again, as I said. Ya don't know anything, anyhow, right?"

"Right," Cal nods. "Right. I suppose."

The mattress creaks and Cal shifts, feeling the weight of it all press down on him at once.

"Eyes on the prize."

"Hey," Cal replies, laying back. "Thanks Ben. I mean it."

"Wasn't attempting to blighter a good day, or anything." He lays back below Cal, opening his National Geographic.

"No, not at all. I appreciate you telling me. By the way," Cal says rolling over, looking over the bedframe at him. "I'd have done the taxes either way."

"Yeah. Figured," Ben shrugs. "But now it's impartial innit? If someone comes pokin' 'bout. He's doing me mum's taxes, that's it. Deniability, they call that. Plausibility. Something like that."

"Only saying. Could have just asked," Cal says, nodding to him. "I'd have done it."

"You better have, you bastard," Ben grins.

32

S hortly after dawn casts its usual patchwork of golden rays across the cement floor of their cell, Cal is taken to his interview room by a couple guards and allowed several minutes to change into his suit – brush his teeth and ready himself – before being taken to a waiting police car outside the gates.

When he leaves the walls behind him, he is surprised to see Damian waiting for him in the back of the car as the stern-faced bobby opens the door.

"Thought I'd ride with you. Save some time," Damian smirks, and Cal feels that reassuring anchor of his friend.

"They let you do that?" Cal asks.

"When you ask with manners, dear boy. Come, get in."

Cal sighs. He's thankful to have him by his side, going into another day in the lion's den of the Old Bailey.

"Morning," Cal says to him, his voice a bit rough from another restless night. He waits for the handcuffs to be reset in front of him, and then he sits in the car and the door is slammed behind him.

"A good morning it is indeed," Damian smiles, smelling like cigarettes and coffee.

A few moments later, the car breaks away from the curb, navigating into the early morning traffic. The city outside is a blur of movement and sound and fury, a stark contrast from the sterile silence of his prison cell in the pre-dawn. The hours spent staring up at the ceiling. Replaying the events of yesterday, over and over.

"Today's another big day," Damian begins, breaking the thought, an urgency in his voice now. "There might be a deal on the table, depending on how things go."

"A deal?" Cal turns his head from the window. "I've never heard of anything like that this late in," he replies.

"A lighter sentence, possibly even time served, if we can show that the prosecution's case is falling apart," Damian explains, his eyes focused on the documents in his lap. "It's rare, but there can be instances where new evidence or changes in circumstances prompt the prosecution to reconsider a case during the trial."

"And why would they suddenly feel so generous, Damian?"

His lawyer scoffs, looking at Cal, sliding his glasses down his nose, "You were in the same courtroom as I was yesterday, dear boy, yes?"

Cal's heart skips a beat. The thought of walking free, of feeling the sunshine on his face again without the shadows of bars, for longer than an hour at a time... it is almost too much to hope for.

"Do you think they're faltering? I wanted to ask you yesterday but you practically ran out..."

"Somewhat," Damian says, his lips pressing into a thin line, ignoring the accusation. "They haven't been able to press Sarah meaningfully, Cal. We both saw that. She's held up well under examination. Today's evidence could be the strategic pivot. The card we both didn't even know was in play until someone remembered to share it with the class."

His eyebrows raise knowingly at Cal for the space of half a moment. Cal rolls his eyes. "Yeah, I don't get it either, okay," Cal says, ignoring the innuendo.

"You ready to watch it again?" Damian asks, his tone genuine. "Reliving it, so to speak."

Cal swallows hard, the memory of the fight replaying in his mind. The raw, brutal chaos of that night.

"I've been thinking. Sarah's husband..." Cal says, not answering him. "What if David was involved with something more dangerous. You know? I mean... before his death."

"No. What do you mean?" Damian asks, looking at him.

"I just think there's more to this than what we're seeing here. The reason why the prosecution objected so quickly when drugs were brought up yesterday. Don't you see that as a bit odd?"

Damian glances again at Cal. "It wouldn't surprise me. The man clearly was a... squalid character. But right now, the focus has to be on getting you out of this, right? The objection they raised was sound. David's not on trial. David's dead. You're on trial, dear boy. Everything else is secondary."

Cal nods, the weight of the situation pressing down on him. He wants to believe Damian, wants to trust that everything will be alright, but the doubts linger, gnawing at the edges of his mind. Something not fully adding up.

"By the way, suit looks great. Good cleaner I have, I told you," Damian says, clearly trying to lighten the mood a bit. He waves his pen knowingly at Cal. "I always know best in that department. Should have been a tailor."

"I thought it was an unimpressed poet?"

"Tailor by day, poet by moonlight," Damian clarifies, smiling.

As they stop at a red light, Damian reaches into his case and pulls out another newspaper, unfolding it to show Cal the third page from the front.

The headline blares in bold letters:

A WRETCHED LOVE: Dubious Widow of Murdered Business Magnate Recalls Brutal Treatment in Testimony.

Cal's eyes scan the article, the words blurring together. Sarah's face stares back at him from the photograph, her expression a mix of sorrow, evidently taken as she left the court yesterday.

"They're spinning the narrative," Damian says, his voice tinged with frustration. "But it's not terrible for our cause. We still have a good chance to turn this around. Today, I suspect, will do even more for that."

The city outside is waking up, the streets filled with people on their way to work, the shops opening, the cafes breathing the scent of fresh coffee and baked goods. Rushed and weary eyes.

Cal watches it all pass by from behind the barred car window. A world that no longer feels like his own.

They arrive at the Old Bailey, its grand façade imposing and austere, the throngs of press and cameras out front even thicker than the day before.

"Ready?" Damian asks. Cal nods, his resolve hardening.

Around half an hour after taking his seat in the buzzing room, he sees Sarah walk in.

Today, she wears a fitted dark dress, the fabric hugging her curves in a dignified and subtly provocative way, exposing the baby bump. The dress falls just below her knees, and she pairs it with sheer black stockings and heels. Her hair is pulled back into a sleek chignon, emphasizing the lines of her face. Her makeup is understated, meticulous, shadowed with a touch of mascara that makes her green eyes stand out even more vividly.

As it always does, Cal feels his heart lurch in his chest like he's been shocked, his eyes gazing at her.

She sits with her back straight, hands folded neatly in her lap. Every now and then, she adjusts the delicate silver bracelet on her wrist, the only piece of jewelry she wears. After everything yesterday, her presence is commanding in the room, drawing the eyes of everyone else too, not just Cal. Yet Sarah remains calm – her demeanor reserved, almost serene - like she doesn't see it.

And just before the courtroom stands for the high honor's entrance, her eyes meet his, and Cal feels the same weight of her gaze – like a physical touch – that he felt the previous day. There is a softness there, a vulnerability she rarely shows; a stark contrast to the poised, unyielding exterior she presents to the rest of the courtroom.

A glance beneath her armor.

And then, as the court stands, and the projection equipment is rolled in, Cal thinks he sees her wink at him, so quickly he thinks he may have just imagined it.

"Day two," Damian says, rising. "Here we go, dear boy. Look alive."

After formalities, and some technical difficulties, the grainy footage from the camera within Sarah's flat is shown, broadcasting images for the entire court to see on the pulled down screen. Someone hits pause after they confirm it will run.

The prosecutor, Mr. Simons, in a crisp navy suit, rises to address the court.

"Your Honor, today we present critical video evidence recorded from the Jones's residence. Footage from the night of the incident. This will show the jury the true nature of the events that transpired as so discussed in yesterday's court proceedings."

Cal's stomach churns. The CCTV footage. The images that will lay bare the violence, the raw brutality of that night. He braces himself, knowing that once those images are shown, there will be no turning back. The prosecutor gestures to the technician, who dims the lights and presses play.

The frozen image flickers to life, grainy footage coming into focus.

Cal's heart races as he watches – his breaths turn shallow.

In and out. In and out.

The video begins, and the scene unfolds in gray, stark detail. And against his will, Cal gazes on, every muscle in his body tense.

It has timestamps flickering in the corners of each recorded segment that the courtroom sees – each bit painting a grotesque ballet of violence. Beginning with the innocuous ambiance: the living room illuminated in the dim light that Cal remembers; the paintings, light reflecting off muted hues of the furniture, a room silent in the muted recording but also as it was.

Then the front door opening, shadows dancing, and Cal sees himself coming in before it all unfurls. Bottle of wine under his arm with the lilies.

He's moving around the house, heading through the living room. Then heading back into the kitchen where there is conveniently no camera footage of him finding his own knife. Then him crossing again, clear across the cameras view yet the panic he felt in the moment not translating into its capture.

Then there is David appearing in the frame a minute or so later, his silhouette outlined in the backlighting of the hallway through the camera Sarah must have hidden in the corner somewhere up high.

The confrontation, muted words exchanged. David pacing towards him. Then the images of chairs toppling, vases smashing, David lunging, the well-placed camera catching the sheer determination and aggression in his eyes.

The footage does a great job of confirming Cal's movements as more reactive, defensively stepping back, saying things unheard by the court but seemingly calmly to David, who is rushing him. Pushing him into the piano, the wall, the floor. At some junctures, the footage blurs, the camera struggling to keep pace with the quick and erratic movements, but what's clear is the visceral, raw intensity of it all.

David's larger frame dominates, but Cal's tenacity shines too, as he pulls out of his reach again and again. Then the knife enters the frame, glinting ominously for a half second, becoming the third dancer in this fatal tango. More and more blood fills the room in darkened spots on the carpet, smearing the walls, staining the men's bodies. It's hard to tell what's a punch and what's a stab as they hit each other.

A sight he can't unsee – himself on the screen, his own face twisted in fear and rage. The fight is brutal, raw, a desperate struggle for survival, even from this vantage point. Without sound, his mind fills it in with remembered echoes of flesh hitting flesh, the grunts of pain, the crashes of furniture, the slicing crunching feeling of broken glass...

It's all there, laid bare for the court to see. Yet only Cal hears it like it was.

And it's not just the violence that strikes Cal. It's Sarah, just outside the frame, watching.

Invisible, but by her own admission there.

She was there. And he knows she was there now.

That was a rare truth provided.

He glances back at her in the darkened courtroom – her face, her eyes, a mask of conflicting emotions as she watches the video.

She could have intervened. Right there. But she didn't.

The living room is transformed by the end: a version of the room he hardly was conscious enough to be aware of at the time. Then he sees David's bloody form wrap his hands around his throat, on top of him. His large body pressing down.

Cal's mind races: the implications crashing on him, each in its own turn – the lies, the deceit, the manipulations. Having that man try to kill him. Her staging it all...

And yet, amidst it, the glimmer of hope. Always, when it comes to her. Hope. He can't tell whether he loves Sarah or hates her for this.

Cal closes his eyes before the fatal blow is depicted on the screen to the courtroom. The blow that stuck the blade in David's throat. The kick. The moment. Right as David fell backwards, blood spewing down his shirt. Stumbling as he did. Back, and back. A second, maybe two. Crashing into the window. Into the darkness and the rain.

Once was enough.

As the video ends, the lights come back on, and the room is deathly silent, the tension palpable. The high judge clears his throat, breaking the stillness.

"We will take a short recess. The court will reconvene in thirty minutes."

Cal puts his face in his palms, leaning against the desk.

Not what I wanted to see again. Don't make me watch it again.

Damian leans in, his voice calm and steady. "We're still in this. The prosecution didn't land that like they wanted I think. That video is our ace, Cal. Trust me. A few more witnesses, and we're in closing range. I wouldn't be at –"

"What witnesses?" Calvin interjects. "Nobody else was there."

"The character variety, dear boy. You recall our discussions on this," Damian says. "Your older brother is next."

"What the hell for?" Cal asks.

"To vouch you are an upstanding citizen. How you were given the knife –"

"Pocketknife," Cal reminds him, shaking his head.

"Minor details... That you would never stab someone without good reason, that sort of thing. Should be good for us, dear boy. Remove some of the narrative around predetermination."

"You think so," Cal exhales, more a statement than a question.

"Don't you?" Damian asks, eyes narrowing behind his glasses.

Cal doesn't answer, his gaze drawn in an instinct to the commotion in the back of the room – his brother appearing through the doorway. Evan taking a seat in the stands. The first time seeing him since the morning Cal found him naked in bed with Diane.

33

C al's older brother takes a seat with calculated composure – his specialty now, it seems. Perhaps he fancies himself to be Parisian, Cal muses, rage rising within him at the sight of his older brother's airs. Evan's hair is slicked back and catches the light with a strange gleam, making the angles of his face seem sharper than they truly are. His suit fits better than anything Cal owns, and the dark brown tweed blazer exudes confidence and charm, two attributes that are clearly newly acquired possessions for him, judging by his indelicate swagger.

He thinks he's the shit. Always has, I suppose.

It's just a bit shinier now. Better disguised. More arrogant.

The Evan I knew didn't even know how to tie a tie, Cal muses.

But his brother's eyes betray him slightly, if only just to Cal, as they swivel, darting around the room, assessing, filled with an air of smugness but a nervousness too.

He doesn't really want to be here. He doesn't want to be on that stand.

Then why the hell is he? A feeling of obligation?

Evan's lips curl into a faint smirk as his eyes fall on Cal, as if he's relishing the moment. A momentary gleefulness at the situation his younger brother has fallen in. He gives Cal a silent nod, and when it's unreturned, leans back slightly. His fingers tap on the armrest, his shoulders possessing a coiled readiness to their posture. He takes a long look at the jury.

He's agitated. Perhaps he doesn't have a choice to be here at all.

This bastard of a brother of mine.

The room grows quiet as Mr. Simons takes the floor at last, the man's eyes set on Evan. After some fanfare and introductions, the seasoned prosecutor dives into the meat of it.

"Mr. Beckley, can you tell us about your relationship with your brother, Calvin, growing up?"

"Well, yes, course," Evan leans in, feigning nonchalance. "Calvin was always... needy."

"Can you explain that to the court?" Mr. Simons asks.

"Yes, um," Evan clears his throat, "He had trouble finding direction. Even as a kid, he was always in and out of trouble at home and later, at uni, so I'm told."

Cal's jaw tightens. Damian shifts beside him.

Is he mistaking me for himself?

"What kind of trouble, may I ask?" Mr. Simons replies.

Evan smirks slightly. "He had a temper. He'd get into fights, break things round the flat. He was unpredictable. You never knew when he'd snap. A strange one, some might say. Loner, they call them."

"So he was angry, you'd say, growing up?" Mr. Simons clarifies. "Had few friends?"

"To a degree. Never got pinched, but he could have," Evan says, looking at his brother, his eyes distant, and removed.

Cal looks away, feeling waves of nausea boiling up in his gut.

Nausea and fury. And rage.

"Like what?"

"Like he hurt animals. Had a black heart," Evan replies cooly.

The courtroom buzzes. Evan's words hang in the air. Cal shakes his head and Damian throws him a look.

"Can you elaborate?" the prosecutor asks.

"What you mean, elaborate?" Evan spits back.

"How could your brother have been arrested?"

"Well, he lost my dog, for starters. And I believe he killed the animal. No proof, but always a belief. Kid was up to no good lot of the time, see. He has a darker side to him, hurts –"

"Your honor, I do not see –" Damian stands, interrupting forcefully.

"Yes, yes," the high judge responds, cutting him off with a waving hand.

"Matter at hand, kindly. Proceed."

The prosecutor doesn't miss a beat: "And do you believe Calvin could kill someone, Mr. Beckley?"

Evan hesitates for a fraction of a second, eyebrows furrowing theatrically, then nods. "What I'm saying, your graciousness. Honestly? I could see it. Yes, 'specially if he thought he was justified. Depressive, he could be, growing up. In his own head. Melancholy, my aunt called him. Yes. Perhaps. Shut me out, that's for sure. So yeah, could see it."

Cal clenches his fists beneath the table.

How could I have expected any less from him? After everything he's done to me. He's never once known loyalty.

To me, or to anyone. Why start now?

The courtroom murmurs again behind Cal and he can feel Damian tapping his leg on the floor beside him.

Evan's words hang in the air, painting Cal intentionally as a volatile, dangerous man. But why? Why is he doing this?

Cal leans over to his solicitor, "The outcome you expected?" he whispers to Damian. Damian ignores him.

Now that the prosecutor has the court's attention the questions fall into more laborious scrutiny of the brothers' shared upbringing. With a grim face, Cal's older brother paints a tale of them reeling from their parents' death; one lost to addiction, making terrible choices, and the other grappling with love and betrayal from the fallout of that. Furthering the anger issues of his younger brother with his own self-described immaturity. A world revolving around the actions, and consequences, of Evan's life. Only Evan's life. His testimony speaks of shared pains, fractured ties, family death, and how he is currently seeking redemption for the terrible things he's done that has made Cal the man he is today.

Not exactly any kind of defense, there.

"If it weren't for me, perhaps David would be alive," Evan concludes, self-righteously. "When you think about it. Not that I played any part. But, removed, you'd say."

Cal stifles the rage for the hundredth time and rolls his eyes.

Finally, the prosecutor steps back, nodding, a gesture meant more for the jury than for Cal.

Even with his mea culpa, he finds a way to fuck me, Cal thinks.

When it's Damian's turn at him, his friend and lawyer stands and wastes no time at getting things back on track. There's a shared fury in his solicitor's approach that Cal can't help but respect the man for.

"Mr. Beckley, you mentioned that your brother was in and out of trouble. Can you give us specific instances?"

"Well, sure," Evan shifts slightly. "He got into fights, vandalized property. He was just a troubled kid, 'specially after our parents died. A loner. As I said."

"A loner," Damian repeats, then presses. "Isn't it true that many of those fights were instigated by you though, the older brother, and others, and Cal was simply defending himself? This is according to a statement from your aunt, mind you, who did in fact raise you both after your parents died. Is that correct?"

"Right, as I said."

"So, you were on drugs, perhaps, during said fights?" Damian asks.

"As always, blaming," Evan scoffs, shrugging, his composure slipping a bit. "Maybe, but the kid still had a temper. It weren't the drugs that did it to him."

"Not your cocaine use at the time, as documented by the Maldon police?"

"Yes, yes. But that had nothing to do with Calvin being a loner, now did it?" Evan snaps back.

"Mr. Beckley, let's talk about your relationship with Calvin. You said you tried to help him growing up. Can you elaborate on that?" Damian asks, not missing a beat.

"I tried to be there for him, ya know, give him advice, but he wouldn't listen. He was always a stubborn prat. Depressive. Victim mentality, you see. Wouldn't listen to our aunt neither."

"But it was you she kicked out of the house, no? You who dropped out from school?"

"No," Evan scoffs again. "I left because I wanted to. Got a job. Odd to stay after I could pay for m'self."

"So you supported your brother growing up, then?"

"By and by. I'd drop in when I could. Lend him some quid. Clothes. Whatever."

"How about after uni?"

"Course," Evan replies. "Why wouldn't I?"

Damian's eyes narrow from behind his spectacles. "Is that so?"

"Yes. Right."

"So you were being supportive when you had an affair with Calvin's fiancée, Diane?"

The energy in the courtroom shifts. Some even gasp. Cal can practically hear the tumblers of the papers pumping out this salacious tidbit tomorrow morning. He resists the urge to groan.

Damian's gone nuclear with my dirty secrets.

Well, maybe more with Evan's.

Evan's composed facade cracks. He glances around for guidance, but there's nobody there to offer it. He taps his fingers on the armrest again.

"Look. Don't know what he's been on about. That was a mistake," he stammers. "We were both in a bad place. Her and I. No need to bring it up, really. The past."

"A mistake? Or a betrayal? Certainly not just the past, Mr. Beckley. You didn't just have a snog, did you? You broke up your brother's engagement and moved to France with his fiancée after maintaining an affair with her, leaving your brother devastated. Isn't that right?"

"No. Not really. I didn't mean for it to happen that way," Evan protests, conveying little emotion. "Wasn't s'posed to at least. He kicked her out. What else could I do? Shouldn't have been like that, admittedly so. But life is a funny thing."

More disgust rises up in Cal. A sick, vile taste filling his mouth.

"But it was like that," Damian presses. "You did that to your own brother. And let's talk about your other recent, noble activities. You've been involved in some questionable dealings yourself, haven't you?"

"No," Evan's visual discomfort grows. "I don't know what you're talking about."

Damian's voice is sharp. "Oh, but you do. Larceny, gambling debts, a narcotics arrest in Porte de La Chapelle months back. Do you deny any of this?"

"Those are rumors and unproven to top it," Evan spits back.

"Bit more than that, Evan. Number of offenses on both sides of the Channel. Bit convenient for you now to be up disparaging your own blood, is my point, isn't it?"

"I don't see the connection... look," Evan clears his throat. "Most are rumors. No convictions. Wrong place, wrong time, right? As I said. I'm not on trial here, he is," Evan looks around the room, striking a forced smirk at the jury. "Here for my brother, sitting right over there."

He nods Cal's way.

"Rumors? Or truths?" Damian asks. "Because the truth is, Mr. Beckley, for context, you were willing to betray your brother for your own gain, and now you're trying to save yourself, perhaps your battered reputation, by throwing him under the bus again today. It's a pattern with you. Isn't that right?"

"No, that's not it..." Evan's facade crumbles, his grin fading from his face, his body shrinking back.

"And you gave Cal the knife as a gift?" Damian asks, repositioning his attack. "Correct?"

Pocketknife, Damian, Cal thinks. Jesus, how hard is it?

"That's right, yes. Long time ago. Not like last year or something. Long, long time. For Christmas. When we were teenagers."

"For the purpose of?" Damian asks.

"No purpose. A gift. Me to him."

Look at him Cal. You can do it.

Cal flashes another glance.

His brother's true nature, sinking into the chair, into his fancy blazer... laid bare for all to see.

The police have him on something. And they're twisting his screws. Has to be. Why else would this lowlife come out and show his face to me?

The courtroom falls silent as the weight of Damian's words hangs in the air.

Cal looks at his brother, the man who has caused him so much pain over the course of his life, now exposed for what he truly is. A lifetime of slights and betrayals, now out in the open. In the blinding light. The asshole brother, for all to see.

He watches Evan, feeling a strange mix of satisfaction and sorrow. He remembers the day their dog went missing, how Evan's tears had turned to accusations. He remembers their parents' death, and the night Aunt Martha kicked Evan out a few years later, the charm that never wavered, even as it wreaked havoc in their kitchen on a nightly basis, him staggering around drunk with his idiot friends. Then the night he introduced Evan to Diane when he was in town, having him over for dinner. An event Cal has poisoned himself with over and over again in his mind since the day he caught them together.

A regret I don't deserve. All because of him.

Now, here he is again, the same brother who flirted with Diane in front of Cal and then said that he was just high, who betrayed him time and time again, up until the ultimate betrayal, getting with the woman he once loved more than anything in the world.

And yet, seeing him unravel now, up there, he feels a flicker of pity amidst the rage and disgust.

It's all come to this, hasn't it? An inevitability for the two of us. An end. A lifetime of lies, of using people like stepping stones. And now you're here, Evan, on the stand, sweating under the weight of your own deceits, as I sweat the weight of my actions. You always knew how to turn a situation to your advantage, but this time... this time, the truth's clawing its way out. In front of everyone.

You came to tear me down and now look at yourself. Couldn't help yourself and now look. You think you're still in control, Evan, but I see it, that crack in your head. You're sweating. You never thought you'd be here, did you? Have it so flipped on you.

Facing your little brother, the one you always put down, always overshadowed, always beat on. Well, now, I'm not as weak as I appeared. Now, you think I'm the one on trial, but maybe, just maybe, this is your reckoning too. For even daring to get involved in my life again. For even daring to show your face to me.

As if on command, Damian seizes the moment, and his questions become more incisive, more relentless. Evan squirms as he asks more about the dog incident and the childish speculation on his brother's part. And how the dog ultimately came back.

You bastard, you.

Not so fun now, is it? Having your lies peeled away – flayed alive off you.

"So your brother, in fact, doesn't hurt animals as you said to this court?"

"Perhaps... I exaggerated, mixed up my suspicions and memories on the matter..." Evan stumbles, "But his heart is black, I'm telling you. Melancholy chap, my brother."

Cal refuses to catch Evan's looks at him thereafter, but feels them – each a bit more desperate as his testimonial authority unravels under Damian's hasty pivot.

Cal doesn't even look when Evan's words at times touch Cal, specifically the bits about how much the two of them relied on each other growing up. The moments he tried to be a good brother, few as they were. Making sure he got to school. Making sure he got fed.

Not even then does Cal care to look at him.

An uncomfortable truth you don't like to think of.

How those you rely on the most have tried to destroy you. How those you respected failed you. How those you loved broke you. All can be true. All somehow forged you, sitting here now.

Evan was at times a good brother, and he was at times a piece of shit. A terribly flawed piece of work, Cal thinks, glancing up as his older brother steps off the stand, teetering, his legs off balance.

Depleted of manufactured charisma for the day. There he goes.

Terribly flawed like everyone. Destined to be forgettable. Anomalous in existence, exceptional in survival. But it can't save him. The endless brawl of ego possessing no victory, no crown of achievement. Just a walking scrimmage match in his head.

Like me... like everybody. Broken but managing it.

And the trial progresses onward with a few more witnesses being called to stand after Evan, but none as rage inducing for Cal.

Some who witnessed David's fall from the Old Hound's stoop, then detective-inspector Elliot Grant (who scarcely looks at Cal), and another who was a member of the responding crime-scene investigators. She goes into belabored detail about the forensic chaos of the penthouse; a surprise to none.

Then building management and security guards come forth for a bit, reporting broad incidentals, and then, lastly, Janice from Cal's old accounting office, who corroborates that Cal was suspended due to personal issues he was going through, something pertaining to a bike crash.

When the prosecution asks her to elaborate, she replies in her characteristically sterile tone, "There's nothing more to say. He argued with us, was put on a performance review, temporary leave, and that was that. He wasn't coming to work looking presentable and the quality of his work suffered. When his arrest became known to us, we terminated employment per policy. Nothing unusual."

Nothing unusual – Cal smiles to himself.

For once the absolute apathy for their employees in that corporate bullshit job is paying dividends: she hardly remembers me. Why would she? She never dug any deeper because she never gave a shit.

None of them did.

And right now, that's as good as it gets.

34

"Members of the jury," Mr. Simons begins in closing arguments, his voice smooth and steady, resonating through the courtroom with his arms outstretched. He looks over each juror in turn, his silver hair slicked back.

"Over the course of this trial, we have delved into the murky waters of passion, jealousy, and violence. You've been presented with facts, with testimonies, with tangible evidence. A murder weapon, even."

Couldn't help himself, Cal thinks, his heart skipping a beat. He tries to steady his breathing.

"And Calvin Beckley, the defendant; a deeply depressed, lonely, anxious man. A man who claims he intended to kill himself after his fiancée left him. A man with nothing to lose. A man who did not get along with his brother, even before the fiancée incident. Who barely interacted with his coworkers, too, or the rest of his family. Who had few friends. Who kept to himself. A man who was depressed. Let's be honest. Who needed help, perhaps a psychologist. This lonely, isolated man who willingly entered a situation of volatility, equipped with a weapon, a knife that ultimately took David Jones's life..."

Cal tries to tune him out, to place his mind elsewhere, but fails.

"... Now, no one here denies that David had his flaws, that he had his moments of rage... That he was rough to Sarah. But does that justify a brutal end in his own home? Arriving back from a business trip... Only to have his throat severed. Kicked out of his own living room window."

Mr. Simons swivels on a heel in the center of the room, pointing towards Cal's table while simultaneously maintaining eye contact with the various jurors, each in turn as he approaches them.

"The defense paints a picture of Sarah, a damsel in distress, and Mr. Beckley, her would-be savior. But let's not forget Mr. Beckley's own writings, his own intentions laid out for all to see. Kill. David. Question-mark. Premeditation, we call that. And the hidden cameras meant to portray abuse by Sarah, also unveil us to this brutal fight, a struggle where a knife was the chosen weapon. Unnecessarily so. We can all see that, too – it didn't have to be this way. But Mr. Calvin Beckley made it so. He is the critical link here to a man who is dead. His actions! He delivered a mortal weapon into that fight. He didn't have to." He points to where Cal sits. "He wanted to kill David."

Cal rolls his eyes. The prosecutor catches this and then looks directly at the jury again, his gaze unwavering.

"In your hands rests the gravity of justice. It is your duty to wade through the complexity and arrive at the truth. And the truth, as the evidence has clearly shown, is that Calvin Beckley made a choice that night, a choice that resulted in the loss of a life of a hardworking, successful, and well-respected man of his community. Regardless of his intentions, a man lost his life because Calvin entered a place he didn't belong. A place where the door was not even closed. And nobody greeted him or said he was welcome to enter. But still, Mr. Beckley entered with his knife. And because he did, David Jones died. Because he went in there, we are here today..."

When Mr. Simons finally sits, concluding at last minutes later, Cal sighs in relief and shifts uncomfortably in his chair. Damian rises, his demeanor a juxtaposition of empathy and stern determination. He adjusts his jacket and Cal sees him throw the slightest of nods to him before stepping out into the floor, beginning.

"Ladies and gentlemen of the jury," Damian's voice rolls out, "We've been shown a tale painted in broad strokes of right and wrong. But life is rarely black and white. At the core of this case is a man, my client, who, albeit imperfect, sought to shield another from violence he witnessed first-hand. From his own home. Through their window. Nothing more, nothing less. Should he have dialed the police instead of going there? Maybe. Did he plan on any of this occurring? I believe we have clearly shown he did not. So as you deliberate, I urge you now to consider not just the act, but the intentions behind the act, and the complex circumstances that led to that fateful night we watched play out on the screen. This is not as simple as a man died because another man entered his flat. The night when my client stepped into that flat, carelessly perhaps, but not with malicious intent, he was attacked and forced to fight for his very life. It was self-defense."

A juror coughs, and Damian pauses, clearing his own throat and collecting himself, before continuing.

"Justice isn't just about punishment; it's about understanding the entirety of the human experience. Are we really to condemn a man who has risked his life, as we saw, his freedom, for a stranger, his neighbor? Is that the message we give society? Or do we still cherish a fundamental truth: that courage is acting when we want to the least. Risking life for another. Whether you have a choice or you don't. Whether my client should have been there or he shouldn't have, no matter, when violence was forced upon him, as we all heard here through this trial, as we all saw on that video, then should we condemn self-defense? Someone who stands against the worst of us, for himself, and for others? For his friend? For his neighbor?"

Little cheesy. Little poetic. Very Damian.

Cal debates how he feels about it. The courtroom also sits in reflection, the weight of Damian's words a tangible presence. Somewhere in that silence Cal hopes that someone is changing their mind about him. That the verbosity isn't estranging them, at the very least. Cal closes his eyes and hopes with all of himself that it's enough.

Damian continues, coiling it tighter as he goes, wrapping up with the prosecution's failure to prove anything more than what is obvious in the footage. That there's no real evidence of Cal wishing to ambush and murder David after only a couple weeks of knowing Sarah – beyond one page in a journal of other sketched pages, and that the footage and testimony show clearly that Cal fought for his life in that living room, and barely made it out alive against the man who his own wife painted as a rapist, a monster. That this case should never have been a murder trial to begin with. That it should have always been a matter of self-defense, against a chronically violent man who would have killed him otherwise. Who would have killed his wife, too, given the time and opportunity.

And shortly after, the judge dismisses the courtroom and the dice is rolled. The jury files out of the room to decide whether Cal is a murderer or just a clumsy victim of fate, and Cal feels like a nervous wreck but feels some relief too.

He realizes why after a moment: it is finally all done.

Each one of these strangers balances his fate now, but no longer him or Damian, or Sarah. Nor the prosecutors; nor the witnesses. There is nothing more to be said or done.

Whether Cal deserves to have his life back is entirely on the jurors – whether he lives, or whether he dies in a concrete hole is at long last out of his hands.

35

H e manages to lower each side of her underwear down the length of her – the tip of the silk in his mouth, between his teeth, each end pulling against her skin and then popping up and over her protruding hipbones. He pauses for a second, then with a tug, he directs them down her legs, dropping them at the end and moving up to kiss her, his hands moving with him, delayed, taking their time. He inhales, running his fingertips along her like this, each part of her, up past her breasts, down her pubic area... her rib lines, the small of her back – suddenly bare, the flesh of her body entirely smooth as he kisses her.

Her belly button and the skin below. The taste of her body lingering on his tongue as his lips find hers.

Blending, melding together down and down between her legs...

"Cal, a chance," she says peering down at him. "Won't you?"

Her emerald eyes usher him inward, deeper – her fingers running along his scalp, her nails digging into his hair, clutching him, urgent and pulling – and he feels her shudder, her legs tight around his neck, senseless. Tighter still.

Ravenous... craving...

Her sweat, sour and exciting, head dizzy with her... No.

"Hey Cal," the voice says again, only it's not her voice this time. No.

Cal opens his eyes as he's shaken awake, alarmed with the bright light beaming down. He's atop his bunk again. Reality setting in.

Ben leers beside him with the morning rays on his face and the last vespers of the dream snapping away. Cal blinks into focus.

"What... what time is it? What, man? Spit it out," Cal says, his eyes narrowing. "Something wrong?"

"Easy. Ease up. Visitor at the gates. Ol' bobby makeshift," Ben says to him, stepping back, nodding his head towards the cell's entrance.

"Funny," the guard snorts. "Beckley, step down, sleep's over, let's go. Got someone who wants to talk with you," the stern facing guard says. "On your feet."

"What now?" Cal asks, rubbing his eyes and sitting up. "Come on, now."

Why would Damian be here today? It's a bloody Saturday.

"That's right. Come on, won't ask again," the guard barks.

"Who is it? My solicitor?"

"No," the guard answers, his voice emotionless, even-keeled, "It's the deputy-inspector. Grant, he said. Now, on your feet, get moving. He's got something urgent to talk with you about. Now, he says. Can't wait."

Cal sits up. There's nothing he can say to me now.

What the hell? It's done. The trial is almost over, one way or another. What the hell could he want?

To intimidate me? To harass me?

"No," Cal says, shaking his head, "I'm not going."

"You sure about that?" the guard asks sternly, looking side to side, his chin jutting into the cell and eyes glancing around.

"Well, can you make me see him?" Cal inquires, his tone pointed, accusing.

"Inspector Grant was insistent," the guard says, his hands grasping his sides, thumbs on his belt, elbows against the sides of the door.

"But can I be compelled, I mean? Do I have to?" Cal asks him. "Legally? Considering my trial's ongoing nature? Its pending nature? Doesn't seem right."

"Doesn't," Ben mutters below him.

"No. I mean – I don't know," the guard cocks his head, considering it. "No, s'ppose not. If that's your bloody choice, fine. Is that your choice, Beckley?"

"Aye, it's his fuckin' choice, innit mate, as he just said, now scram, shit," Ben says from below. "How many times he has to mumble it to ya to get through that noggin'?"

There's nothing good that'll come from going with him, Cal thinks. Nothing good. Done with their threats. Their intimidations. Their antics and dangers and maneuvers. Their little morsels of information. Their insinuations. Done with all of it.

The guard scowls at Ben, "Ah, piss off, you little shit. That the way it is, Beckley, huh?" the guard asks. "Not coming, is it? Going to stay in your bunk? Snivel up there?"

"It is," Cal replies, sitting back, fluffing his thin pillow behind his head. "Don't want to see Grant or any more of them trying to put me away. I've had enough of all of you. I've had enough. I've said my peace. Now, let me be."

"You've heard that?" Ben chuckles. "That means sell your shite elsewhere, lollipop. Out you go. Go patrol 'round. Take some laps. Walls and watchtowers, whatnot. Catch some of that dark stuff comin' in. Intakes needin' a spray down. Cavities to be searched."

"Alright," the guard shrugs to Cal, ignoring his mouthy cellmate. "Fine. I'll tell 'im. Can't say he'll take it kindly, course. But do what you want."

"Can't say I much care at this point how he takes anything," Cal retorts, almost to himself, but feeling defiant nonetheless, and he slings his arm across his eyes to blot out the light. And when he chances a look a minute or so later, the guard has disappeared without a word from the opening of the cell. After another few moments, from down below, Ben asks him:

"What do you make of that, anyway?"

"What's that?" Cal sighs.

Not another dissection, please mate, he thinks.

"Bit odd, them coming to you this far along, don' you agree?" Ben asks. "You know. Considering, is all. Not even an investigation anymore, right? Past all that. Past a deal."

"Who bloody knows. Nothing good, I'm sure of it," Cal replies. "Nothing good talking to that man."

"Right. But didn't want to find out?" Ben asks, poking. "Curiosity sakes?"

"Bugger curiosity sakes," Cal says. "Now, let me sleep, Ben. This trial... I'm dying, absolutely knackered."

"Course. Good beauty rest's important. For any sentencing. Change their minds, last minute with your glowing mug."

"You'll have one soon enough," Cal chuckles. "Sentencing that is. Mug's out."

"Uh huh," Ben replies, chuckling. "We'll see."

"Fear not, man, can't forget you forever. You'll get yours."

"Don't we all," Ben replies, a gloominess taking hold in his tone, and Cal hears the sifting through magazine pages.

He sighs and rolls over and closes his eyes, soon lost again to the world. Before he has time to think why this detective-inspector would visit a man on trial with a deliberating jury. Before he has time to consider what that man would want from him this late in the game. Before he has time to think why the jury has been hung this long. Two full days now.

No time to think of anything...

So desperate to get back to her, he plunges into the shadowy forms of his mind. Into the exhaustion, into the deep sleep he's been craving for so long. Behind the citadel of his thoughts, his dreams, where it's just him.

Where only he goes. Where he's been these hundred and fifty days or so, one way or another, and before that, longer still if he's honest. Back when he first laid eyes on her. The place where only he stays. Alone.

Far away from it – with Sarah. As it should be.

36

C al and Damian sit in the back of the police car, the hum of the engine and the murmur of the city beyond the windows their only companions. It blurs past in shades of hazy summer, the early morning light casting shadows that seem to stretch into eternity.

Cal's mind, as is his habitual routine, swirls with thoughts of the looming trial room, of Sarah, of the uncertain future that today brings to his doorstep at last: the day of sentencing. The day he's been waiting for since the reality of his situation truly set in, laying there in the hospital bed all those months ago.

Damian fidgets with his tie, his eyes darting. Anxious.

Unlike him.

Cal looks over at the man with a small smirk playing on his lips despite the weight of the day.

"What's going on with you, mate?" Cal asks, his voice a rumble over the sound of the road.

"What you mean?" Damian asks. "Just need to smoke…"

"That all?"

Damian glances at him, attempting a reassuring smile that doesn't quite reach his eyes. "I've got a good feeling about today," he says, "Don't mistake me."

"But?"

"But nothing."

But there's something there. Something amiss.

A crack in the facade.

"Hey," Cal raises an eyebrow, his gaze steady and unflinching. "Shouldn't I be the one who's nervous?"

Damian sighs and rubs the ridge of his nose. He lets out a dry laugh, the sound hollow and forced. "Yeah, you probably should be. But it's my job to worry too, right?"

They lapse into silence, the weight of the impending verdict pressing down on them. Cal's thoughts drift to the courtroom, to the faces of the jurors, to the cold, detached expression of the judge as he reads the sentence. The future feels like a dark tunnel, and Cal is hurtling through it, blind and directionless, on a train he cannot stop. Down a track he doesn't know.

"There's something else," Damian says abruptly, breaking the silence as they go around the last roundabout of their escorted route to the courthouse. "There's been a stir with the police on another side of the case."

"And?"

"It's interesting," Damian shrugs, "Simply put they've lost interest in you, Cal. Whatever today brings."

"Lost interest?" Cal turns to him, a flicker of curiosity piercing through the fog of his thoughts. "What do you mean by that?"

Damian takes a deep breath, choosing his words carefully. "Ephemeral Canvas, you remember that?"

"Yeah, Sarah's studio."

"Right. Co-owned with David."

"What about it?" Cal asks.

"It burned down over the weekend."

"Burned down?" Cal feels a jolt of shock, his mind racing. "How?"

"It was raided by the police the night before it happened, and then there's a fire," Damian continues, his voice tense. "They were looking for something, but I don't have all the details. That's all I really know. Came into my office this morning. Everyone's talking arson but I haven't heard it corroborated."

"I don't understand. So, what then," Cal stammers, "now they're after Sarah?"

"I don't know," Damian says, "seriously Cal – I have no idea. But someone burned her studio down and we know it wasn't the police."

Cal's thoughts fall into a whirl. He thinks of the visit over the weekend from the guard. How detective-inspector Grant had attempted to interview him.

He'd declined...

Why didn't I talk to him?

The memory now tinges with a sense of foreboding.

He was trying to tell me something. Maybe he was trying to warn me.

"Listen, detective-inspector Grant tried to talk to me over the weekend," Cal says to Damian. "I told him no, to fuck off, well his lackey, at least –didn't see him, personally. But he tried."

Damian stares at him and then his face twists, darkening with anger. "Why the hell didn't you tell me this before now, Cal?"

"There wasn't time," Cal retorts, his voice rising. "And I didn't want to deal with more questioning. The case is nearly over, I didn't see the point."

"No, it's not. There will be appeals. This is a gross circumvention of me by them," he shakes his head, frustration etched into his features. "You can't just decline interviews, Cal. You should have called me. He has no right. You're making this harder for both of us."

The car slows as they approach the Old Bailey, the massive building looming ahead like a monolith. The hour of reckoning.

The air in the car is thick with tension, the anticipation almost palpable. Damian takes a deep breath, trying to regain his composure. He pushes his glasses up and collects himself, straightening his tie.

"We'll deal with it later," he says, his voice a bit far away but steadying. "Right now, we need to focus on the verdict. It's what we've been working towards. It's all that matters."

"You're right," Cal nods, his mind still reeling from the revelation about the studio. "Look, I'm sorry Damian. You're right. I wasn't thinking. Should have told you earlier."

"It's okay. As for the studio – it's nothing to us. We know you didn't burn it either, right? Got a good alibi, dear boy," Damian remarks and Cal forces a smile. "Just thought I'd tell you, is all. The police are hunting bigger game perhaps."

The car comes to a stop, and the doors open with a score of police officers waiting, and the morning air rushing in.

The two step out. The courthouse stands before them, stone and steel, and up the stairs they go. Reporters and onlookers gather even deeper than usual outside, a sea of faces and flashing cameras and questions.

"Cal, do you expect a good result today?"

"What do you intend to do if you lose?"

"Cal, do you have any message to the family of the victim?"

The cacophony of voices and the blinding lights creates a disorienting whirlwind, a stark contrast to the quiet tension inside the car. Damian and the police escort guide Cal through the throng, shielding him as best they can from the barrage of questions and the intrusive gazes, microphones jabbing forward and being swiped aside. They pass through the doors, the noise outside muffling as they step into the relative quiet of the courthouse. Hopefully for the last time.

Cal's heart pounds in his chest, each beat like a drum that reverberates up into his throat. Damian stops for a moment, turning to face him. His eyes are intense, filled with a mixture of determination and concern.

"Remember, Cal, no matter what happens, we'll find a way through this. Okay?"

"Confidence gone that easily?" Cal smirks, letting out a sigh.

"Shut it," Damian rolls his eyes. "It's a pep talk."

The courtroom is an amphitheater of anticipation. The past days of trial have been a crescendo, and now it awaits the final note – the ending.

Cal sits, feeling the weight of all that's transpired behind his eyes, in his skull, his palms drenched, his deep feeling of fatigue mounted to a siren's pitch at last. The gallery is awash with stifled noise: quiet murmurs, whispers of speculation, dread. The walls themselves seem to be listening, timbers soaking up yet another brief drama in their grain. Cal takes it all in, his head swiveling around.

His eyes at last find her in the throngs of commotion.

Sarah is elegant, subdued, sitting a few rows back, eyes downturned and reading something. Ever so often, she steals a glance at Cal, her gaze conveying an ocean of unsaid words. Something he can't quite read.

He can't help but glance at her as much as he can – both for his nerves, and because he knows he may never see her again. He sees that today she has an escort, a stern looking man in a crisp gray suit, sitting beside her. Then there is a shuffling noise at the far side of the courtroom. Sarah looks up and they exchange a nervous look at each other.

"You ready?" Damian asks, leaning over to him. "Hey, Cal?"

"Yeah?" Cal says, looking at him, steeling himself.

"Just remember to breathe. No matter what happens. As I said."

The jury files in. The room grows deathly quiet.

Their somber faces reveal nothing, a collective mask of duty. Cal scans each one of them hoping for some hint of the coming moment. The foreperson hands over a sealed envelope with Cal's destiny on a small piece of paper in it. The judge, today his figure and robes seeming more like a cloak, takes a moment that feels like an eternity breaking the seal. Opening the paper. Reading it.

The courtroom's collective breath catches.

"In the matter of the Crown vs. Calvin Beckley," the judge intones, voice steady, "on the count of first-degree murder, how do you find the defendant?"

The foreperson stands. The silence is almost unbearable, a vacuum in which every possibility hangs suspended in front of him.

Cal closes his eyes, hearing only his breathing.

Slow. Concise. In and out. In and out.

He clenches his fists. Time slows.

"We the court find the defendant... not guilty."

A shockwave! An exhalation.

His body feels lighter. His world, contracted to the pinpoint of the verdict, explodes outward.

Damian leans over and hugs him and Cal's eyes, brimming with emotion, jump around the room, from face to face, some angry, some overjoyed, finding Sarah's at last. In them – turmoil, gratitude, lingering shadows of the ordeal. She raises her eyebrows at him, smiling hopefully. Her eyes conveying something, a message –a sliver of hope. Not outright optimism, but close to it.

Whispers spread like wildfire. Some disbelief; some approval.

Cal hears scoffing at the decision, too. Maybe David's family members, somewhere behind him. Maybe David's coworkers. His employees. His notorious partners. He dares not look.

"One more," Damian whispers to him. "One more, dear boy."

"Order!" the judge calls out. "I'll have order!"

And after a moment, when the room falls silent again: "And on the lesser charges of involuntary manslaughter, how do you find the defendant?"

"We find the defendant..."

Please.

Oh God, please.

"Guilty of the charge of involuntary manslaughter."

The words seem far away, as if he's witnessing them spoken through a telescope. Damian curls his palm around Cal's shoulder. Cal feels his knees go weak.

His heart sinks, yet even then, there is a tinge of gratitude.

"It's not the best outcome, but it's far from the worst," Damian murmurs beside his ear, just audible above the noise, and Cal knows he's right.

The judge stirs, nodding and accepting the judgement.

Not the freedom he'd hoped for, but a lesser charge, a lighter sentence, maybe a chance to someday rebuild his life again.

Maybe, eventually, be happy.

"We'll appeal, of course. Try not to worry. I'll get the papers going as soon as I'm back at the office."

The judge begins discussing sentencing and legal procedures, and Cal looks again towards where Sarah sits. Their eyes meet. No words are exchanged yet a thousand unspoken sentiments linger in the spaces between them.

I love you. I'll miss you.

He can see that her cheeks are stained with tears. She throws a reassuring smile at him. And he tries to commit her face to memory, to capture every glimpse of her, drink it in – the warmth of her eyes on him, the way the curve of her lips put him at ease – but there isn't enough time before she is lost from view and he is ushered out of the courtroom, passing the howling paparazzi and onlookers in the hallway, camera lenses' glaring, flashing in his eyes, and then into the shadow of the waiting police van, the heavy doors opening for him before slamming shut.

It's a ride back to his cell. Plenty of time to think about her.

How she looked at me.

He knows there will be plenty of more time to think about the rest of it, too, and he exhales out into the darkness. Slow, and unexpectantly, he feels himself calm down. And then relief arrives like a wave... finally knowing his fate. A cold flood of it. Washing over him.

He feels the rumble of the engine, and himself rocking as the truck moves away from the court's chaos. In the shadows and privacy of the back of the van, Cal feels tears coming on, overwhelming, and doesn't stop it – his chest welling up. All the pain over all the months, spilling to the surface in this moment. This tired moment of cathartic release... he lets himself cry for the first time in what feels like ages.

And then, suddenly, for reasons he can't explain, the tears rain from him and he is also smiling at the same damn time, and then laughing, howling, bawling like a child.

And it feels magnificent – Cal feeling himself again.

He's sure it's the greatest feeling in the whole world.

A deranged, liberating type of joy elating deep, deep within him back to his prison cell. And he laughs and cries the whole way there like a madman.

37

E ight months and a few days later, on early release with time served, the iron gates of Belmarsh open in front of him. Cal stands just behind their shadows, the late-afternoon spring's breeze feeling almost alien on his face after the long winter spent mostly indoors.

He watches the gates swing before him and rubs his beard.

All said, over a year since feeling the warmth of freedom, of sunlight flooding his skin, the kiss of heat. He rubs his wrists nervously – his hands unsure of their newfound freedom, hovering near his sides afterwards as if waiting to be restrained again.

He looks around, anticipating word from the nearby guards. He is not trying to get shot this late in his stay for misunderstanding when to go. The sun sits halfway low in the sky casting long shadows across the prison's tall slick walls. The nearest guard nods and Cal squints and steps cautiously onto the unkempt gravel as directed, and then down the pathway to the road and past the towering iron gates, the inner fences with razor wire on top of them gleaming in the sunlight. He feels neither relief nor reluctance flowing through him as he goes. He just keeps walking. Not sure what he is expecting, or who he will meet.

Within the prison walls that confine him, he has unexpectedly crafted a new identity. In one of England's most notorious prisons, he has created a space he calls his own—a makeshift classroom where, for the past few months of his life, he has been offering hope to others in his own way. And in doing so, he has found some hope for himself as well.

Cal teaches accounting to inmates, many of whom barely completed secondary school. A project suggested by Ben, inspired by his mother's success. Although Cal was initially reluctant, his skills flourished, giving him a sense of purpose during his confinement.

Slowly, he has begun to see a future that is less bleak, more promising, and even exciting. And at night, before sleeping, alone in his bunk, he starts to count down the days again.

Week after week. Month after month.

Things arrive for him in the mail to pass the time: newspaper snippets from Damian when the case is mentioned; a note and photograph from his favorite judgy bartender Karalana (wearing reindeer horns) when Christmas passes and he misses the Old Hound's annual drunken bout.

And even a certain wedding invitation from two of the worst people Cal knows. Suppressing rage, he simply throws it away. Not worth lingering on.

But the letters from Sarah, those matter the most of all.

Those he does turn around and around in his mind.

Those keep him going on his lowest days and nights.

Letter after letter. Word after word. Telling stories of her paintings. Of her life by the sea, somewhere far away from England. Telling him stories about their daughter, Lucy. Photographs of her and her mother, taped to the wall by his bunk.

During the days, he sits with his friends, reading these stories, exercising, and preparing his lesson plans. He takes pride in his lessons for his students. He gives it his all like he's never done before at his old job. Diligence - something he hasn't felt in years.

It feels good.

And Cal finds himself teaching other subjects too, from time to time. History. Rudimentary personal finance. It keeps him preoccupied. And his popularity in doing these self-determined tasks keeps him surrounded by people that care about him carrying on doing it. So even in the dangerous prison yard, he has people around him. It keeps Cal safe.

And on his last day, some of this mutual gratitude is evident in his pupil's earnest scribbles, attentive gazes, respectful nods. A few even wishing him well on their way out the door. Shaking his hand. He smiles as he watches them go.

Ben's the last of them, having finally been sentenced and transferred in about four months into Cal's stay at Belmarsh. A light in a dark place.

He gives him a warm hug. The man has grown on him, against Cal's better nature, and he's sorry to say goodbye.

"Catch ya out there, huh? Few years, innit. Nothing really, thinking on it. Not too long," Ben says to him.

"Not too long at all," Cal says, knowing that even with appeals Ben's got close to ten years before he'll get his own exit.

"Oy, Cal," Ben calls to him as he walks away. "A sec."

"Yeah?" Cal asks.

"Not much. Just... stay away from her. Your bird. One that landed ya here. She's no good. Right? No good at all."

Cal waves him off.

"I tried, okay? Deniability. You minger, you," he hears his old cellmate call back to him as he's escorted away down the hall.

A few hours later, Cal is presented with a package during his discharge procedures. The guard hands him the large manila parcel with his name written on it in a squiggle he recognizes from the many squiggled legal pads of his past. The contents of the package – a crisp black suit, pressed shirt, stylish tie, goofy socks, his old watch, and a newly bought pair of elegant wayfarer sunglasses.

Chuckling at the memory of Damian's pre-trial jests about his pedestrian suit collection – how he insisted on renting them for him instead of letting him wear his own to trial – Cal enthusiastically dons the new outfit, piece by piece. Taking his time, feeling like it is his to spend as he wishes.

Because it is.

You got this – (tailor info included, just in case) : the accompanying note says. There's a smiley face, and then some more written on the other side of it:

You could leave life right now.
Let that determine what you do and say and think.
Marcus Aurelius said that, not me.
But still, rather applicable that, I'd wager.
What I'm trying to say is may the future be yours, my friend.
You've earned it, dear boy – now, cheers, drinks soon.

- (solicitor by day, poet by night) Damian

He finishes reading it and then folds the paper and puts it in his pocket, smiling.

Cal's boots press into the gravel until he reaches the asphalt of the road. After maybe a kilometer or more, passing cabs and busses, he reaches a shopping district's busy street. The city's hustle and bustle audibly surrounds him and welcomes him back like a warm blanket of noise. He crosses and steps onto a curb. Cars zip past him, people shuffling along sidewalks, and the symphony plays out in full force.

Where to go? What to do now?

Each honk, each shout, each distant siren sparks an inner joy within him, despite his confusion. He keeps walking. Farther and farther still. His boot heels resound on the pavement amidst the cacophony of urban life. He feels London's pulse around him. Its lifeblood.

Cafes and pubs brimming with chatter, buses announcing their destinations and people flooding on and off them, tourists taking pictures and reading guidebooks, weary eyes over fresh pints, the trains below the streets roaring, pigeons fluttering in garbled flocks, the distant laughter of children playing in parks, airplanes flying overhead, and so much conversation – all these sounds, taking him back again, embracing him. Reminding him. Filling a longing that he almost forgot he possessed.

And he continues to walk and amidst the noise of the early evening he hears a distinct purr, an engine, becoming more pronounced behind him. Louder, until he knows it is right behind him. Moving very slow.

The metallic sheen of the black Mercedes slows down as it passes. Cal looks up at it. And he sees the baby girl's gaze meeting his through the windowpane. Drawing him closer: a little girl with light green eyes and dark hair. Cal's heart catches in his throat.

The elegant car looms to a halt a few meters in front of him, and slowly the front door opens and he smells jasmine in the breeze. Jasmine and lilacs. Familiar and intoxicating.

Sarah steps out of the driver's seat, her hair now well below her shoulders. She looks at him for a moment, studying, hesitating, as if trying to figure out who he really is again. But then her dimples appear suddenly in the evening glow.

"It's a long way to walk, you know, and not very safe," a mischievous glint rests in her eyes. "Care for a ride?"

Cal takes a deep breath, the city's vigor filling his lungs. The street stretches out in either direction. Teeming with possibilities – chances and choices. Other roads not taken. A moment passes.

He shouldn't – but he wants to.

The breeze lets off and he hears her voice for the first time, coming in through the open car door.

Slowly, he walks up and looks through the glass, seeing the tiny girl staring up at him with earnest little eyes. Cal looks to Sarah, and she nods, watching him in a way he's never seen her look before. The sunlight plays on her features, her golden hair, tracing the contours of her jaw, settling warmly on her lips.

The distance between them shrinks. Cal's fingers brush the softness of Sarah's skin and she closes her eyes, leaning into his touch.

Their faces draw nearer, lips inching closer, then meeting – the soft press, exploring slow at first, a reacquainting of two weathered souls.

The passion rises, and he pulls her closer to him.

"I'm sorry," she gasps, just above the rising breeze. He sees her eyes flooding with tears. "I'll never forgive myself. I can't forgive myself."

He pulls her back. Their foreheads resting together.

"All the letters. The photographs. The imprints of her little hands you painted," he replies, a bit unsure. "I... I forgave you a long time ago."

"How can you, though?" she sniffs. "How can we ever be normal again? We can't stay here. They're looking for... well, both of us. But mostly me. Who knows. You too, probably."

"I want a new beginning. So do you. We're not that much more or less fucked up than anybody else."

"You think that's actually true?" she asks.

"Yeah, frankly – I kind of do. And we can't stay here, right?"

Moments pass and Sarah nods and kisses him and they stand beneath the buzz of the streetlights until she cocks her head, saying slowly, "You ready to meet Lucy?"

"I'd love that – more than pretty much anything."

"Okay. Let's go." Sarah turns to get back in the car, glancing around the street before getting in. "Buy you two dinner on the way to the airport."

"You sure?"

"Least I can do," she smirks, and hesitates before getting into the car. She looks at him, her eyes grave suddenly.

"Sarah, it's time to run," Cal says to her. "No turning back."

"I've been running," she replies, "waiting for you."

"Well, now together."

"As long as you're sure about this."

"I'm sure."

Without another word, she nods and gets in.

Cal walks around the back, forcing a smile to his daughter in the glass as he does so, wiggling his fingers, and then opens the back passenger door to scoot in next to her.

Taking a deep breath again in the dusk, he pauses, looking around for anyone who might be watching or sitting in a car nearby, and then instead closes the door softly and gets into the front seat by Sarah.

The city's skyline stretches out before the car as it purrs to life, gaining more and more speed, winding up, before breaking at a stop sign with the sunset in both their eyes. They take a right, and she signals onto the next on-ramp that comes along, accelerating harshly again, joining the motorway winding westward towards Heathrow - the windows an inch down with the wind and the muted sounds of the outside world creating a lull between the two of them.

After a few miles, he turns on the radio, changing stations, settling on some nineties rock.

Sarah starts singing with it and she glances at him and reaches over. Cal takes hold of her hand with a nervous smile and leans over to look back at his daughter.

38

The wheels strike tarmac and his eyes open for the first time since departing Zurich, the plane having landed for fuel just before midnight. Just before he finally allowed himself to get some sleep. Now, a few hours later, the slim interior of the older Learjet bounces and rattles and Cal sits up and peers his head around dizzily, forgetting where he is for a moment until his eyes focus on the paneled lights of the aisle.

In the dim cabin, he makes out Sarah sitting across from him, strapped in her own chair with the baby pressed against her chest fast asleep in the carrier. Sarah's arms lay around the base of the little girl, and her head tilts to the other side as the plane finishes its landing, braking harshly. Somehow, she stays asleep through the jostling and Cal checks his old watch and dials it an hour forward.

It's early morning. Sitting up now, he adjusts himself and then peels the window shade away, bit by bit, letting the saffron tinted sunlight filter into the cabin and peering through bloodshot eyes at the island's introduction.

Dawn light dances across the waves in the Tyrrhenian Sea, shimmering liquid gold, then up across greater Palermo as the city awakens in a slow deliberate rhythm – an ancient energy so unlike London's incessant fury. The light sweeps up the ancient olive trees and the red terracotta rooftops dotting the hill lines, and through the narrow streets and alleyways and vibrant market squares. Not a cloud in the sky.

Just rich, unfettered Sicily, waking up. Cal's breath catches in his lungs as he sees it. The rugged, gorgeous landscape, its white beaches and mountains and lazuline, Baroque steeples, such a stark departure from the bleakness of prison and everything before that in Cal's life – so much so that he can hardly believe what he is seeing. What he is feeling. What he is taking in.

Something out of a dream. An old black-and-white movie – the kind he watched as a boy. Cal gazes on, watching the dawn flourish over the city and the nearby Mediterranean as the plane taxis forward, slow and steady towards the terminal buildings. After a minute or so, he pulls the shade all the way up in the opal-shaped window and dawns his new sunglasses from Damian, smiling alone to himself at the beauty.

Today's going to be a great day.

The first day of the rest of them – at last.

A new life. One where I can start over. One where we can.

Sarah and I. Our daughter. All of us.

The plane finally stops, and the lights flicker on. Cal shifts in his seat and catches Sarah staring at him with her piercing green eyes filled with the same sunlight, and something else too. Her expression is a mix of resolve and curiosity, staring back at him, searching for something of her own. He offers a small smile, and she looks away, as if suddenly realizing she's watching. He then sees she's breastfeeding.

"I'll help get the bags unloaded," Cal says, his face feeling a bit hot as he unbuckles and stands.

"You're cute," she replies. "Won't be a minute."

Cal steps down the stairs into the hot morning sunlight, walking out onto the open tarmac, correcting his blazer's fit, his eyes adjusting to the brightness even behind his shades.

Cute, she said. What's with her?

Things have been off since reuniting. It's a gap he can't quite define, filled with a mix of fear, or anxiety... maybe even regret.

Every glance, unspoken word, loaded with a weight Cal can't fully understand. The uncertainty gnaws at him, a persistent itch at the back of his mind.

Is it fear of what's coming? Or nervousness about what we've left behind? What we've done.

Whatever it is, it's palpable, an invisible wall that feels more solid with each passing kilometer spent in the plane– this necessary move that she's organized.

Wherever it may be going. However long it may last.

"No questions," she'd said in the car on the way to Heathrow. "Not until we get there. Please, Cal."

He grabs a bag from the gruff, broad-shouldered airline man.

Determined to break through it, he resolves that today, he will find out what's truly going on.

Who is after them, specifically. The begging questions.

He wipes sweat from his brow. So many damn questions – he is determined to understand Sarah again, piece together the fragments of their strained connection, the space formed since the night it all went down. Since the night he killed Sarah's husband. Figure out fully what they're facing because it all went down. Beyond the scuttlebutt and speculations of his former prison mates. Beyond his own theories and uncertainties and paranoias.

It is the only way to move forward. It's the space that's killing us.

She's been facing it alone. But now, we're together.

She couldn't talk on the plane. She wouldn't. Why?

Patience, she'd said. There'll be time. When we get there. A lifetime of time.

A lifetime. Starting today. Once we get there –

Soon.

On some level, of course he understands. These conversations needed to be in private. But there's still an unease.

Cal grabs the last of the bags and loads them in the undercarriage of the parked bus nearby. By the time it's all done, Sarah places her hand on his shoulder from behind and they wait for their turn and board. When the shuttle reaches the main terminal, they walk through the busy building to the arrivals section, and then are waived through the doors, after very little scrutiny over either passport.

Cal hails a cab and then helps the small Sicilian driver with the luggage and Sarah gets in the car with Lucy.

As Sarah promised: no customs inspection. No fuss.

Someone paid them through – as she said would happen.

His passport wasn't flagged.

Who paid, Cal hasn't the slightest idea. But considering Cal has no valid passport nor clearance to leave the United Kingdom on parole, the relief he feels as he closes the taxi door and settles into the broken leather seat is palpable, washing over him in a tidal wave.

I've done it. I'm out of there. I'm free.

Another hurl passed.

They didn't stop me. Sarah's plan is working. As she said.

"Dove stai andando?" the driver asks. Cal looks at him, unknowing, sweat dripping down his neck.

Sarah puts her hair in a ponytail, and then repositions the sleeping baby in her carrier across her chest. The driver starts the car and it stutters awake, coughing exhaust smoke. Cal takes Sarah's hand as they pull off into traffic.

"Dove stai andando?" the driver repeats, louder, flashing a look in the mirror.

"Scusa, Taormina," Sarah commands the driver. "Per favore."

"Per favore," Cal repeats, stressing the accent, smiling at her.

Sarah elbows him, flashing one of her own.

A little over three half-slept hours later, with nothing but the sound of the wind through the old Fiat's open windows, Sarah nudges Cal, softer this time, pointing ahead as the winding clifftop road that's coming up, just as a massive, soft-yellow villa appears around the bend.

"Ecco, ecco, si," Sarah says to the driver, leaning forward. "Sculla scogliera." She points to a gated entrance over the sleeping baby.

"Bene," the driver responds gruffly and slows down to turn, clicking on the blinker.

"So you speak Italian?" Cal whispers to her as she leans back beside him. She smiles and shrugs but doesn't say anything, instead telling the driver the numbers for the gate code as he slows the old car up to the keypad.

"Tre, sei, nove, due, uno, tre, tre," she says. "Perfetto."

The old gate creaks open before them, its rusted bolts crying out until both sides of the tall iron open fully inward, coming to rest beside an idyllic straightaway.

"Grazie," the driver replies, glancing in the rearview mirror at his passengers, before accelerating the car down the gravel road, flanked on either side by a tunnel of tall Italian stone pines and fig trees.

Cal breathes in deeply, putting his head out the window, savoring the citrus and the smell of the sea as it wafts over him and mingles with the distant sounds of the crashing waves far below the cliffside.

"Wait until you see it," Sarah grins, flashing a look of expectation at him.

"Bellissimo?" Cal cocks an eyebrow, the breeze feeling good in his hair.

She rolls her eyes and smirks, "To die for."

"I'm sure it'll give Belmarsh a run," Cal replies and he hears her call him an idiot or something in Italian. The driver chuckles.

The small road begins to turn beneath its sheltered canopy, and after about a hundred meters of their slow crawl, it abruptly curves right towards the house itself, arriving at a clearing in front of the sun-kissed villa that clings to the cliffside in ivy-wound stone.

The driver pulls up beside the stairs leading to the front door.

"Shall we?" Sarah asks.

Cal steps out of the car and takes it all in: the precisely maintained gardens in front of the house, bursting with bougainvillea and fragrant jasmine, filling the air with intoxicating smells; the cobblestone pathways that wind from the main gate to the side of the house, flanked by cypress and lemon trees, and the expansive veranda that comes into view as Cal follows the path around the side garden. The breathtaking panoramic view of the endless sea, the hazy horizon, resting lazy behind the house's shimmering indigo-tiled pool. A short space beyond the pool and some lounge chairs, a gazebo to the right, and there the cliffs begin Cal sees, walking up - the land falling away for a couple hundred meters into the Mediterranean.

An obscene fall. Cal peers over the edge at the rocks.

"Remind me not to get too pissed," he mutters.

"Bit hazy, but you can just see Taormina, over there," Sarah says, the wind carrying her golden hair up behind her as she comes with Lucy in her carrier, and points over his shoulder. "See it, just to the north?"

From the distance, the town appears like a little jewel along the cliffside, nestled at the base of Mount Etna with its tiled rooftops and pastel-colored buildings creating a pleasing contrast against the lushness of the slopes and the dark, imposing presence of the volcano. The expanse of the sea stretches out in vast sapphire space between the town and Sarah's villa, but he can just make out the ancient Greek ruins perched on the cliff's edge above, standing out with its grand, weathered arches in the distance.

"How old are those ruins?" Cal asks her. "Ones above the town?"

"The theater? Little over two thousand years, I think, give or take. Bloody ancient," she giggles, looking at him knowingly, his face, his eyes, as he gazes out. "What do you think of this view? It's special, isn't it? That volcano's active by the way."

"Just how I like my volcanos," he smiles to her. She continues looking at him in the sunlight.

"It's incredible, Sarah," Cal exhales. "I've never seen anything like this before. Not in my whole life. It's... breathtaking. Absolutely breathtaking."

"I'm happy you're here," Sarah says.

"Is it yours? This place?" Cal asks.

"Heavens no," she laughs. "My family's place. Still, I was hoping you'd say that about it," she beams, and he steps towards her and the way she is looking at him makes him think she might kiss him for a moment, but the moment passes, and she turns, his hand in hers, leading him back to the driveway.

"When can we talk about it, Sarah?" Cal asks her, following along the cobbles.

"Let's get this driver underway first," Sarah says, not looking back. "Then we will. Okay? I promise."

Promises again, Cal thinks.

More promises.

He returns to the car with her and helps the man with the bags before slipping him what little cash he has left to his name - what was in his wallet the night of his arrest, the night he almost died.

The change from buying the wine and lilies. That bottle of Malbec. Ouroboros, it was called.

The logo. A pair of intertwined snakes, one black and the other white, consuming each other's tails around a silver tree. An ancient symbol below it, engraved on the roots.

A feeling of cold descends over him and Cal's neck hairs bristle.

The driver speaks something back to him suddenly, rejecting the cash he realizes, and Sarah then leans in, apologetically, fetching money from her purse and handing it to the man. She extends Cal's money back to him.

"Pounds don't work here, amante," she retorts, then passes beside him, heading up the entrance stairs to the front with the baby.

"Right. Course. Scoozy," Cal says sheepishly to the man. "Not thinking."

He taps his head and feels even more silly. The driver chuckles before carrying on.

I'll have to get a job, Cal thinks after a moment, grabbing a bag.

A real one again. Maybe I can teach. Enjoyed that.

Much more than accounting. Was good at it, too. Took pride in it.

I'll have to learn Italian. No doubt about that.

Sarah can teach me, maybe... wouldn't that be nice, learning Italian in the sunshine here... a place like this.

How long will that take I wonder? To learn something like that, at my age? Weeks? Months? If I speak and hear it all day long?

And with each new thought, each new idea, each new question, Cal can't help but get more and more excited. Walking over the intricate floral tiles of the entranceway, the expansive courtyard, beneath the wrought iron balconies, desiring to take in every sculpted corner of this place – every opulent spectacle and each angle in its turn.

Through the main entrance with a bag in each hand he passes the massive oak doors with iron knockers shaped like tritons, entering the courtyard with a fountain at its center, water spilling from the mouths of the three conjoined marble dolphins.

And further still. Into the living area. Into the main house.

If one can even call it that – a house. More like a castle. A chateau. An estate. A level of wealth he's never seen up close. A level he's never seen at all.

I've died and gone to paradise, he thinks, looking around.

Another chance. Another life. Another me.

Finally – at last.

But the truth first. She owes me.

Nothing else before that.

39

C al spends far too long in the shower trying to figure out which knob is hot, which is cold, which is pressure, and which is water spread, before at last getting it to his liking. The first proper shower since preparing to see her. That night, all those months ago. Before sponge baths and hospital rinses, and prison showers. He takes his time, scrubbing every inch of his body, savoring the peace and the hot water flowing down readily over his scalp and skin.

He scratches his beard, loathing it.

The steam rises up around him and he thinks of the steam across the mirror. The words etched in her handwriting...

Bon chance.

A half hour later, he descends the curved staircase in the center of the villa, admiring the decorative risers and the paintings on the walls as he goes. Various antiques. Pictures. Photographs. Sarah's family. Sarah as a young girl by the cliffside with what looks like her grandparents. Sarah and her sister, another blonde little girl, both eight or nine or so, in the dark blue pool outside with floaty toys. Then on the bench in the gazebo. A man swimming nearby them. Older. A picture of just him, fishing off the back of a gorgeous old sailboat. The picture, black and white.

Cal leans inward. He has Sarah's eyes, but his skin looks darker - almost olive skin.

Then another taken with all of them on London Bridge. Standing shoulder to shoulder. One in Birmingham next to it, too. A school shot. Both young girls in uniforms. Then a larger one: Sarah, probably six or seven, on the shoulders of a woman that looks like an older version of her today. Her mother – must be. On a beach.

Did she grow up here? Or did she just visit?

She said she came from money, but I guess I never asked how much money.

Who is your family, Sarah?

"Cal?" her voice startles him.

She's standing at the foot of the stairs with an older man in a suit beside her. He has long silver hair combed back and a neatly trimmed beard and stares at Cal intently as he approaches.

"Hey," Cal says, coming down. He sees that Sarah's skin is glowing from her own shower. She's changed into a light blue sundress that makes Cal's heart skip as he steps down to meet them.

"This is Giovanni Russo," Sarah introduces. "Our property's caretaker. An old friend of my father's. He's been a part of our family for many years. Since I was very young, right Giovanni?"

"Five, I believe, ma'am," he says. "Yes."

His voice is a flat current with little intonation. Difficult to read. For a butler, he has quite the intimidating air about him, Cal thinks.

"Giovanni, this is the man I told you about. Cal Beckley. The man who saved my life from David. The court case you followed. You remember?"

"Of course, ma'am," he says, accepting Cal's extended hand, and Cal notes his cockney accent despite expectations. "You have our gratitude, sir."

The man's piercing dark eyes, sharp and observant, linger as Cal shakes his hand, and Cal can't help but feel slightly at a disadvantage, knowing very little about this man other than what Sarah's just told him.

She didn't even mention others being at the house.

She's still not told me anything. Despite her promises.

"Pleasure to meet you, Giovanni," Cal says.

He notices the man's tie is perfectly knotted, and he wears a very crisp white shirt beneath the suit, his ensemble a far cry from Cal's own clothes, presently rewearing the same shirt, shoes, and suit as yesterday.

"A certain pleasure, Mr. Beckley," the older man says with a voice like an accordion. "The first order shall be to acquire some new clothes, of course. May I measure you after lunch, sir?" he asks. "Or would you prefer before?"

"You may now, I guess," Cal says, and he returns Sarah's smile. Cal can't help but feel awkward by all of this.

A day ago, at this time, I was being released from one of London's more notorious prisons, he thinks.

"Splendid. Let me go get the measuring tape. I shall take the trip to town to gather clothing and essentials, leaving you for the rest of the afternoon unattended for, if that's alright, my dear?" he asks, glancing to Sarah.

"Of course," she says.

"Splendid."

Then, as the man turns, Sarah stops him.

"Giovanni, any word from my sister by the way, where she's gone?"

"Yes," he nods, "She's staying in Naples tonight. Was expecting you next week I believe, as was I in fact. I'd look for her late tomorrow evening. Ms. Ciambra."

"Perfect. That worked out for Lucy," Sarah grins. "Thank you, Giovanni."

The man turns towards the living room area and Sarah cocks her head to Cal:

"Get measured, then meet me out by the pool, okay? I've had pasta brought out. Nobody to cook here but us, so I whipped up some leftovers. Can you manage?"

"No cook? What's this?" he derides.

"Cal?"

"Look, I might get lost," Cal holds up his palms. "I'm hopeless here. Where have you taken me?"

"I'm sure you'll figure it out," she replies, smiling and brushing her hair behind her ear. "So, go get sorted, I'll meet you out there with the food."

Ten minutes later, when he at last joins her in the gazebo, sitting down across from her at a set table overlooking the sea, Cal's heart pounds like a freight train in his chest. It's the first proper moment without travel, without strangers, without legal proceedings, and subterfuge, and letters, and police, and walls, and space between them.

The moment he's been waiting for months to have with her.

The moment alone.

Cal takes her in as he sits across from her. The azure dress clings to her figure, the fabric shimmering in the hot afternoon sunlight, accentuating her eyes that seem to capture both the colors of the sea and sky as she looks at him. Her long blonde hair, still slightly damp from her shower, falls in soft waves over her shoulders, and her earrings dangle delicately, swaying as she tilts her head, lost in thought for a moment. Her fingers, slender and graceful, trace absent-minded patterns on the tablecloth.

"You go first," she says as if giving permission.

There's a faint smile on her lips, her dimples showing through, but a smirk that does not quite reach her eyes, which hold a mix of other sentiments. "Like our little game back in the restaurant. Cucina del Cuore. You remember, taking turns?"

Despite his apprehension, Cal smiles a bit, "If I'd have known your gaudy roots, this and all, may have chosen a little more carefully there."

"Cal," she smiles, shifting in her seat, crossing her legs and leaning forward, the movement fluid, deliberate. "You could have taken me anywhere."

Something in the ease of her response irritates him though. Prickles beneath his skin. The assumption woven to her flirting.

"You set me up," Cal says, ignoring her remark, his voice just above a whisper yet charged with the weight of months of tormenting over the questions to come.

Months of having this conversation in his mind. Alone, in the dark of his top bunk.

Sarah's eyes narrow, her fingers ceasing their restless tracing on the tablecloth.

"I did. I set you up to fight David," she says. "I set you up for a fight where I knew one of you might die. I did that to you. And I regret that, Cal. It was –"

"Why?" Cal interrupts, the intensity of his anger boiling to the surface. "You almost got me killed. You apologized ... so fucking what – should I accept that? Nearly got me put away for years and years of my life. Why?" The questions burn within him, demanding an answer. "Why would you do that to me, Sarah? I need you to explain it to me. I can't see it."

Sarah sighs deeply, her gaze dropping to the table for a moment before meeting his eyes again. "Really, Cal? After all these months, you don't know that yet?"

The wind picks up and the sound of the waves crashing below fills the spaces.

"Because I loved you," Cal says, and the words escape his lips before he can fully process them.

"Because you still do," Sarah replies, her voice softer now in the breeze, almost tender. "You did what I couldn't do. You killed that man. You did that for you and for me."

Cal almost thinks he sees a small smile break across her lips, but then it is gone.

"Why?" Cal demands again, his frustration mounting. "Why couldn't you do it, if that was the only way?"

She looks out over the water, considering this, as if seeking an answer in the distant hazy horizon. "Because I was afraid," she says, her voice barely audible over the sound of the waves. "As I said in court that day. I was afraid of what he would do to me if I tried to leave, as I told you, as I told all of them. Afraid of what he would do to Lucy, suspecting she was yours. I needed someone who'd care enough to stand up to him, someone who could protect both of us. Someone who loved me. It was you – someone who told me I'm not alone. Wanted to be there. Wanted me to be his. Who wouldn't be the only kind of man in my life I've ever known - someone who, for once, gave a shit about me. Who gave a shit about what I wanted."

Cal feels a surge of conflicting emotions – anger, understanding, a deep aching sadness in his chest.

"You used me," he says, the words heavy in his throat. "You nearly let me die because you lied to me about everything that brought me over to you."

"Not everything," Sarah says, her eyes glistening suddenly. Cal sees tears falling out of them, steering down her cheeks. She wipes them away with her palm.

"But I did – I needed you. I needed you to survive, Cal. And I knew that you loved me enough to fight for me, even if it meant risking everything, even your life," Sarah shakes her head, sighing. "And I needed you to know that I would fight for you. And I still have been fighting. In every way I can. Trying to see you – testifying, getting you through that awful trial. Then writing you. Then getting you out of England, chartering the plane. Making sure you were safe."

"Making sure I was safe," Cal repeats, smirking, his mind in overdrive, piecing together the fragments of the story he suspects but doesn't fully know.

"David was involved in something bigger, wasn't he?" Cal asks. "Narcotics or something like it. Wasn't he?"

Sarah stares back at him but doesn't say anything. The wind whips around the gazebo.

"He was connected," Cal continues. "I heard things in the prison about it. The Fennington brothers and all that." Cal's voice is steady despite the turmoil, the resistance inside him. "I was approached by someone from them, before our trial. He threatened me. Told me to keep my mouth shut. About what, I had no idea. But still. What was it, Sarah?"

"They approached me too," Sarah sniffs, wiping her nose with her serviette. "I was getting calls in the middle of the night. They even came to my OB. My doctor, for God's sakes. Threatened her, looking for me. That was it. That's when I decided to move back here. Staying in hotels until your trial finished and then I was gone, sold up and left for good."

"When they burned your studio down?" he asks, his tone pointed.

"I was already gone by then," she replies, her brow furrowing "Absolute fuckers. The lot of them. After everything I went through to get that. Opened up an arson case on themselves through that, the fools. Which I think angered them even more. They thought I did it, not knowing the place was already dead in the NCA's crosshairs from David's bullshit. So, the police told me anyway in the questions after. Did you know the police raided it?"

"Yes, Sarah. But who the hell are they?" Cal asks. "Answer me that. Stop avoiding it."

"The Fenningtons were David's mates," she says. "Business partners some of them, pub friends from what I could tell in the beginning of things. I didn't know much – he kept me in the dark. But several were at my wedding and my family was not pleased. A bunch of half-cocked gangsters that ran clubs and such, from my understanding," Sarah replies, nodding slowly as she explains. "It's really who runs them – that's the menace. Who supplies the dope that David was into at the end of it. Stuff he was bringing in for the Fenningtons. With them. Whatever the arrangement. The Russians, so far as David told me. Bratva types – what the police confirmed to me. And then men with Russian accents started asking around for me in the months after David died too, the months of your trial – going to my studio, going by the flat, going to my doctor – and... well, I realized David was in a lot deeper than I ever could have thought. And that he owed them money for the drugs he'd been fronted to move for them. Wherever it was he was moving it."

Cal shakes his head, struggling to keep his composure. "So, you wanted me to be the fall guy to Russian gangsters? To solve this problem of a husband?" Cal asks at last, letting it all sink in, exasperated - his words sharp and cutting as they escape his lips.

"Listen to me," Sarah says, leaning forward, "My family is involved with the Sicilian Cosa Nostra, if you haven't figured that out by this ridiculous place. This ludicrous palace on a hill. Does this seem bloody normal to you?"

Her arms motion around them at the surroundings.

"No, of course not. Was hoping for something else..." Cal shrugs, "World famous surgeon... tennis star... film director..."

"Sorry to disappoint you," Sarah says, her eyebrows cresting in a subtle smirk.

"Yeah," Cal sighs, "So what, birds of a feather, your daddy step in to help?"

"Please," Sarah dismisses him, shaking her head. "When David's criminal activities started mucking with his business is only when he cared, mixing me up in this shit, then it was a no-no – but it was my problem up until then. Honestly. And they only added petrol to the flames."

"I don't understand," Cal says, unsure if he really wants to.

"My art gallery—my hope for something different—was funded a little by what I inherited from my mom when she died – and then my dad's lawyer swooped in when we relocated, insisting I raise more equity, get investors for added distance, and then David swooped in after. I had already made something of a name for myself by then, nothing huge, but enough where I had people to ask. My own people – I didn't need my fiancé's money. I had enough of my own. But nobody trusted that I could raise enough capital to run it nor wait to find out halfway through the renovations. None of the men in my life, least of all. Even though for the most part I did. And I still had the majority stake in it. My own money I put into it. But that doesn't mean my family was okay with David's leverage when they found out he'd contributed too. Hell no they weren't."

"So David donated," Cal interjects, already knowing the truth.

"Fractionally, compared to my stake, not enough to care whether it succeeded or not," Sarah replies, sipping her wine, not taking her eyes off him and his reactions.

"What do you mean by that?" Cal asks, shifting in his chair, watching her the same. "It was big enough to concern your father."

"No, no. That wasn't it. David had bigger plans, and those are what concerned him," Sarah explains. "Plans he never told me up front until I stumbled right into them one night, coming back late to change the lock code for a subcontractor. And, lo, there he is. My husband at the studio."

"Doing what, exactly?" Cal asks, feeling uneasy with the direction this is going.

"Hiding his poison with his chums... in my paintings' frames. In quantity. Loads of it."

"What do you mean, poison?" Cal demands.

"Fentanyl. Molly. Pills. I didn't take too hard a look, mind you. Using my gallery as a bloody distribution mechanism, for whoever, to distribute that poison across Europe. Right under my nose. Right in my well-sourced fucking frames. I tried to get it out of there..."

Sarah's lips curl into a sneer as she recalls the memory, her eyes narrowing in disdain – a look Cal hasn't seen since she was on the stand.

"Well... didn't take long before I was mixed into it again," Sarah continues, her gaze distant, recalling. "Police started coming by the flat when he was gone, a couple months after that, after he'd promised he wouldn't do it again. Came looking for him, but speaking with me, nearing the time the renovations were wrapping up, claiming they had narcotics suspicions. Claiming they knew he was involved."

She shakes her head, "And David thought it had to do with domestics, catching them over one day in the house of all places, but it was about his drugs and his company," she says, disgust evident in every line of her face. "But in reality, it could have been worse... They probably had him on a wire, babbling, as he did," she continues, "if I had to guess. And I knew it was bad, too, them coming by. Didn't say anything to him, because fuck him, but I knew it was only a matter of time before our door was kicked in by someone or other. And if things escalated... well, let's put it this way. The investigators knew I was in danger," Sarah scoffs to herself.

"They bloody well knew it. Advised me to install a camera in my living room even, in case he ever tried anything, or brought some stuff back with him more likely. They called it a decree nisi or something, if that were to occur, because then I'd have him. I'd be free of him. But they didn't move in when he hit me. When I showed them. They didn't give a shit about anything but building a case on who he was supplying the drugs to, who he was getting them from. Asking me, dropping by unannounced. Endangering me. Like I knew. Then, that night happened. And the cameras were there. They were on. In the end, I guess it paid off."

"Guess it paid off... small blessings," Cal mutters, recalling the images in the courtroom, the jury's reaction to seeing something like that filmed, dispassionately, in every gory pixelated detail.

"Large blessings," Sarah corrects him, her brow furrowing, clearly getting irritated.

"So, your family didn't want to beat the police to it, that it?" Cal questions, feeling resentment rise like battery acid in his guts, every answer compounding it deeper within him.

Politicking, the underhandedness, the criminality.

"What do you mean by that?" she asks cooly. She picks at her food.

"After you told them, when the police did nothing. That's what happened right?"

"It'd be a war, they said," Sarah responds, tears beginning to well in her eyes. "My family couldn't let that happen. Just wanted it dealt with quiet – their business venture and daughter removed from it. They sent some of my father's old cronies who asked David to reveal his tiny side of the business, give up the slavs who fronted him that junk, and when he refused, right, they threatened him as I understand it, and he of course then came right home and took it out on me. Screamed at me that I'd killed him, effectively, in telling my family his charade," Sarah takes a deep breath, then continues.

"Screamed at me he'd kill me for it first. Broke our bedroom door down. Choked me unconscious on our bathroom floor. Really beat the hell out of me - well, damn it, I could take that. By then, I could take it... but then he raped me," she pauses, her breath sucking in her lungs, "And I woke up while he was raping me... and he hit me even worse. His elbows. I barely remember it now... It's strange... Closer and closer to the edge, I guess. Escalating. Him coming home in a frenzy. Just before I met you. Then it changed..." she pauses, looking at him, her eyes swollen and red. "Don't you see it, Cal?" she sniffs.

He looks at her, shaking his head – "See what, Sarah?"

"That we needed each other at the exact time. How that part wasn't a lie," she stutters. "It wasn't – not fully. It was the cold truth. Really. We needed each other. It was a beautiful accident that brought each of us in the other's life... at the worst time."

"You in your window... why?"

"Because I could," Sarah replies, "the night you were on your edge. I saw you... I lured you in... and that saved you."

The weight of her confession settles over him – thick, conflicting, oppressive. What he's always suspected, confirmed into existence.

Cal feels speechless, lingering without words, looking at Sarah, seeing her almost like a stranger... not as the manipulative woman he once thought she was, but as someone desperate and afraid and most of all involved, clinging to the only hope she had in her deadly situation – and in so doing, putting his life strategically on the line in the process.

Just a card she had to play as soon as it fell in her deck. To absolve herself from killing David. To absolve her family from needing to kill David. To absolve her of David entirely.

One way or another. However... she'd be absolved.

David would be gone. In prison or dead. And so too, not just the violence and malice he trapped on her life, but that violence and malice of his friends too. His business that he'd mixed into her life against her will. Poisoning the well of her passion.

She'd be rid of it all – forever.

But she hadn't counted on Cal surviving.

She hadn't counted on saving his life.

For the truth to come out in trial. For it being what was required to defend him. She wasn't counting on doing that.

"So, because I needed someone to fight for, is that it? After our date? Because I was down and out...and you confirmed it in me... it was just okay to use me?" he demands, pushing aside his thoughts. "I needed a lifeline; you saw the opportunity. I was the perfect score to do your dirty work, wasn't that it?"

"No, that wasn't it, you know that," Sarah replies, contempt in the sharp sound she makes as she sucks her breath in again, wiping away a tear with her elbow. "That's not what I'm saying, Cal."

"The perfect way for your family to not have to get their hands dirty killing someone connected to these Russians. Have someone do it for old fashioned love. Bloody brilliant."

"You weren't a score, Cal. I promise you that," she leans in and takes his hand but he pulls away from her.

"Please," he says. "Stop."

"Cal, you saw the way I wrote you. The way I defended you in court. The way I saved your life that night. You know that. You know how much I care for you. You must know."

"You wouldn't have had to save my life Sarah if you didn't nearly kill me!" Cal exasperates. "You think of that?"

"Of course, I've thought of that!" Sarah retorts. "But that's not why I did it. I did it because I knew I couldn't let you die. I knew that even though…"

"Even though it would have been better for you to… that these, these Russians wouldn't be coming after you –" he starts.

"No, it's more than that," she pushes her food away, frustrated. "Look, I owed you. I didn't even think about that at the time. Walking into the room. You saved my life, don't you see it, Cal? You didn't have a say. But that doesn't mean we shouldn't be together, that we shouldn't love each other as we want to. Now. Tomorrow. That you wouldn't have fought, either way. You already did… with the mace. You showed me you would. And yes, it was fucked up. And I'll never forgive myself for ly –"

"Fucked up? I don't know if I can forgive you at all! Ever, Sarah!" Cal snaps, his heart pounding even harder. "I mean, goddammit!" He shakes his head, struggling to look at her, his eyes drawn instead to the horizon.

"I don't expect you to," she replies, tears pulling at her mascara again. "But I hope you can understand at least why I did it. I thought that was the whole reason we were doing this. To move on. Press forward. You said it when I picked you up. It's worth a try. Isn't it?"

Cal takes a deep breath, the salty air filling his lungs as he tries to process everything.

I did say that. Why did I go with her at all?

I had to find out. It was the only way.

Is that the only reason?

You know it's not...

He feels sweat dripping down his back, and the familiar pull of his own tears in his eyes. The pain, the betrayal, the lingering love he still feels for her. His head feels knotted in conflicting feelings about where he can even allow himself to go from here.

Should I run? Should I leave?

"We'll see," he says at last, his voice steadying. "But now, I need some time. Please. I need to think about all of this."

Sarah sniffs. "I understand," she says.

Cal stands up, his chair scraping against the wooden floor of the gazebo, his pasta untouched, and takes a few steps away from the table, thoughts swirling with the torrent of Sarah's revelations.

He pauses then, the ocean breeze cooling his flushed face, sighing, and he turns back to Sarah, his voice tight.

"Is David Lucy's father, or is she mine?" he asks, his eyes searching hers. "Please just tell me the truth, Sarah. I need to know. I need to hear it from you."

Sarah meets his gaze steadily, a flicker of sorrow in her contemplation towards him. "Neither" she says softly. "Lucy's in vitro. She's from a random donor."

"A donor?" Cal repeats, his mind spinning.

She turns her head towards the ocean, looking out at invisible Africa somewhere across the hazy horizon. He takes a step closer, finally getting the truth he has craved since seeing the ultrasound photograph all those months ago.

"I began the sessions as soon as I knew David and I couldn't conceive. I told you I wanted a baby. It was all I wanted at the time. That was weeks before we met, Cal. Just weeks before I saw you looking at me. Saw you past my own reflection in the glass. Of course, in my mind, she's your daughter... if you'll accept that. If you'll accept me. But I can't change what's been done, only where we go. If you want to..."

Sarah starts to cry again.

"Believe me. And forgive me," she sobs, her head in her hands, before looking up at him. "Think about where you want to go. We can't stay, I know that. But I don't want to go anywhere without you. A year was long enough. I know..."

She wipes her tears away and stares at him for a long moment, continuing, her voice, direct: "I know where I want to be. Starting over, with you. Leaving this place and these sins behind us. Putting lots of distance between us and here and... and everything else. I have the means. We can do it. But I can't do it alone... I'm with you, a hundred percent in. I'm part of you. What we've been through. There's no other way... We have to try..."

"You can," Cal says, his voice low. "You can do it alone, Sarah."

"No, I can't," she says. "I won't..."

"I don't understand."

"I love you," Sarah says, her chin trembling as she says it. "Like I've never loved anyone. Cal, you alone fought for me. And you never stopped fighting for me. I'll never forget that. It's all I want. I'm sorry I dragged you into this... this horrible mess. Please believe me... I love you. That won't change."

40

I s there anything left in me? Anything?

    Have I compromised everything good about myself?

All for her? All for Sarah and her twisted, demented life...

One black and the other white.

Consuming each other's tails around a silver tree.

Around until they cannot breathe. Coiling.

Around and around and around...

... until the two...

Break.

Cal's eyes open wide.

He lies in the enormous bed, staring up at the high, frescoed ceiling. He hears the sound of the waves crashing against the cliffs below, filling the room, echoing through the open balcony doors with the breeze: a constant, deep, rhythmic pounding, like some sort of ethereal drum. A restless symphony of motion.

He looks around, the setting sun casting checkered blood red light across the eastern wall of the room. The opulence feels almost suffocating in its foreign weight: heavy drapes of deep burgundy framing the tall windows, and the floor a mosaic of polished marble that seems to glow in the fading crimson dim. Every piece of furniture is antique, dark wood with intricate carvings, and the rugs are thick and ornate. A palace, and yet it feels like a cage somehow.

He sits up, swinging his legs over the side of the bed. The hunger gnaws at his stomach, but the thought of facing Sarah again fills him with a dread he doesn't much care for. He's angry, yes, but there's something deeper—a fear that he hasn't felt in a long time. The cold realization that he's far over his head, sinking like a leaden weight in him. Perhaps long overdue.

Sticking your nose in others' business.

Business you barely understand.

It could end up even more sideways.

You're exposing yourself to this. Dipping a toe in someone else's pond...

You have no idea how deep this thing could go...

Cal stands and walks out onto the balcony thinking back to that moment when he had a choice, looking out over the expanse of the dark Mediterranean, then down at the pool and gazebo, both empty and lit nearby with torches that burn stilted in the wind. The sun is a fireball sinking into the horizon, casting a cerise glow across the water as it does.

From his side of the ivy-covered villa, he can see how rapidly the cliffs drop into the sea, the waves crashing against the rocks, spraying huge throws of water at the base by the waterline.

Beautiful and terrible all at once.

Like her.

You still have a choice, Cal. But what is it?

Go back to London?

How would I even begin to do that, even if I wanted to?

I'd be back in prison before I even knew it.

Parole violation, immediate.

Cal steps back feeling a bit dizzy, turning into the room. Beside his bed, he spots several designer bags, and within them he pulls out clothing Giovanni's evidently purchased. He places the pieces on the bed, one beside the other. Very nice clothes – far better than what he used to wearing, even before he wore prison garbs that is.

Dress shirts, casuals, jeans, slacks, trainers, and so on.

Are they buying me? Am I this cheap?

Have I forfeited every last strand of my decency? Have I forfeited any agency as well? My choice? Another direction?

My only chance at a new life?

Did you even give that life consideration?

Cal pulls on the new jeans and then a dark shirt, turning and looking around the room for the light switch. His eyes fall instead on the landline phone sitting on the desk in the corner. He walks over, hesitates, then picks it up, listening to the silence on the other end before setting it back down with a sigh.

His thoughts turn to Sarah, to everything she's told him.

The Sicilian mafia background of her violent father, David's criminal activities and his violence, the art gallery—her hope for something different—twisted into a front for drug smuggling. Violence on violence – a cycle. A world of it that Cal just stumbled into, letting his heart lead him instead of his brain.

He can't shake the image of her, the desperation in her eyes, the way she clung to him as if he were her last hope only yesterday, the day he left prison.

The day he saw her again after going to prison for her...

And the child, not David's, conceived in vitro from a bank.

So much to take in, but none of that feels especially terrible compared to other information.

I can live with that bit, I think.

As long as she's not his.

And Cal's always known, deep down, that there was more to her story. To where Lucy came from.

Of course there was, despite his delusions otherwise. Damian insisted on as much to him during the trial, his mind stuck in his ways against logic and reason.

But the strange fear remains. Knowing her connections, knowing the danger that surrounds her, and by extension, him.

Especially now.

He's a target, painted by her actions, by her decisions. And he's not sure he can trust her. Even after all her apologies and confessions.

Not completely. The thought sends a shiver down his spine. Never, perhaps...

This woman he loves, the mother of the child he's come to care for, who he's yearned to meet all these months, is also the person who's dragged him down this deadly path.

The woman who begs him to stay with her on this path. Begging not to leave her – to run with her.

She said she loved you. She meant it - this woman. She loves you. That much, he's sure of now.

He paces the room, the tension building with each step.

The grandeur of the place feels uneasy, the luxury a mocking distinction to his inner turmoil.

He looks out to the balcony again, the sea darkening fast as the last of the crimson light fades under the horizon. The sound of the waves grows louder, the wind picking up and carrying it up the cliff face. Into his room.

A porcelain moon rising through the bruise colored cloud lines...

Cal knows he must make a decision... time is running out.

To take Sarah. As she is. With everything out there. Those looking for them.

The danger accepted fully on his part.

Or leave tonight – walk away, maybe run, and never look back – save himself from any more chaos that her life will bring upon him. Inevitable as it may be.

Any more death and destruction.

And since it could arrive on her doorstep at any time, even here, he must go tonight. No allaying this. He must get out of the quicksand without lingering another moment in it. It's the only way.

But the thought of leaving Sarah, of leaving Lucy now... it fills him with a deep ache. Deep in his heart. Far deeper than he expected.

Cal can't deny it. It goes against everything.

An ache he can almost feel... like a phantom wound within him. To wait so long to be back with her again only to run away... now that she's told him the truth.

Can you do that? Can you really do that?

He takes a deep breath, collecting himself.

He must face her. He must tell her.

I know this. There's no stopping it now.

Cal steps away from the window, and the room shifts into shadows as a large cloud crosses over the sky behind him and the last light of day fades into a violet blue. He moves carefully across the room. One step at a time. He peels open the door into the hallway and then closes it behind him quietly. A few moments later, he stands in the kitchen, the room cloaked in darkness save for the faint moonlight filtering in through the massive windows that look out to the sea. The marble countertops gleam in the moon's reflection and so do the brass and copper fixtures, the other shiny objects of the kitchen. He runs his fingers over them. Heavy and intricate.

The meals I'd make here.

In the shadows, he finds an orange in a crystal bowl on the counter and peels it methodically over the trash. His eyes linger on the bowl of fruit he plucked it from, his heart pounding with the memory of finding his knife that one night.

As he eats, his gaze is drawn to the pool outside by a noise, a splash. He moves closer to the kitchen's window and presses up to the glass.

Sarah's silhouette travels in the water, her form illuminated by the soft turquoise glow of the pool's violet lights.

He watches her glide through the pool like a specter, the water rippling in her wake, her breaststroke fluid and deliberate as she peddles, up and down. Up and down.

She must have just come down here, Cal thinks. I would have seen her from the balcony. Would have heard the pool...

Then Cal stops chewing, his eyes adjusted, gasping slightly as she turns around for another lap, realizing she is swimming naked, seeing her bare skin flicker in the refractory light.

Her presence mesmerizes. Watching her, he feels like an outsider, a voyeur to her private world.

Like he did that first night when he couldn't look away.

The night I saw her touching herself through the glass.

The night she saved my life.

Stopped me from jumping. Somehow stopped me. Erased the idea for that moment. Made me forget the pain.

The way she moves through the water, so at ease, so at home in this place, contrasts starkly with his own sense of alienation.

There's an energy about it. A familiarity. A love.

He finishes the orange, the last segment bitter on his tongue and he wipes his hands on a dish towel and leans against the counter, his eyes not leaving her.

The villa, the wealth, the drugs, the connections to the underworld—it all feels like a world so far away from his own, yet now it is his reality. However, he splits it. He's been drawn into it, inextricable now as he sees it, linked to her fate.

The moment he killed David, that was sealed.

They won't let me go.

The moment he stepped into her little gambit, she and him attached to the consequence. Together.

The sight of her, so serene in the water, only deepens his resolve.

He has to get them out of here. Even here is not safe. Not with who her family is. It's only a matter of time before someone looks for her here. Maybe she knows that. Maybe she's anticipating that, too.

She is right. They need to go – together.

The darkness of the kitchen feels like a shroud, wrapping around him as he watches.

No. He knows that confronting her was inevitable, that the answers he got were never going to be the ones he wanted to hear.

But he can't turn back now.

As she said, she's a hundred percent in.

And so, I need to be. I've already made my choice. Made it a long time ago in fact.

Now, I need to follow through. No more pouting.

It's time to step up and go.

"For once in my goddamn life," Cal says to nobody but himself, stepping to the door, his hand on the handle.

Sarah turns into the pool, panting in the water, floating on her back now with her face upturned to the night's sky. The moonlight and one of the nearby torches cast a pale glow on her features, and for a moment, she looks ethereal, untouchable, almost porcelain.

Like she did that first night.

The night I began falling in love with her.

Cal's heart aches with a mix of longing and purpose.

The woman he loves will always be an enigma, with answers lying deep beneath her. A surface he may never break through, but one he'll gladly die trying to reach.

She was right about me.

He knows, beyond anything else, that is the truth. There's no going back.

And so he opens the door and starts walking. He approaches the pool in the shadows, and he sees Sarah still floating on her back, her eyes closed, the water glistening around her like liquid silver. He reaches the edge and stands there for a moment beside the baby monitor. She senses his presence and turns slowly, her eyes opening to meet his own. There's a brief flicker of surprise, followed by a calm, steady gaze.

The moonlight dances down her wet skin, highlighting the curves and lines of her body, the darkness of her nipples, the spill of her hair floating around her – the body he has ached to touch for so long.

The body he's ached to kiss, to hold, to consume.

Without breaking eye contact, Cal strips. He pulls off his shirt first, the fabric sliding over his skin and falling to the ground in a soft heap. His hands move to his belt next, unbuckling it with a slow, measured motion. He drops his jeans, standing there in just his knickers. He hesitates for a moment, the cool air prickling his skin, before finally shedding the last of his clothing.

He moves towards her, each step down the pool's stairs slow and deliberate, the warm water parting around him. Sarah remains still, her eyes following his every move. When he's close enough to touch her, he stops, the water lapping at his waist.

She faces him. For a moment neither of them speaks, the silence filled only with the distant murmur of the sea, and the ripples of the water at the edges of the pool.

"So, you've made a decision?" she asks at last, her voice barely above a whisper, yet it carries across the water with a clarity that sends a shiver down his spine. He reaches out and brushes a wet strand of golden hair from her face. Her skin is hot to his touch, smooth and inviting, her pulse up.

"I love you, Sarah," he says, low and steady. "I always have."

Sarah's eyes are alive, filled with mesmerizing affection, her gaze not leaving his. "I know it's not easy," she says.

"I'll never leave," he continues, taking her into his arms, pressing her against him. "I want more than bare minimum love. I want you – I love you, Sarah."

"Kiss me then," she whispers between them. And he does. Delicate at first, before pulling her closer, their tongues reuniting eagerly. He wraps her in his arms, pulling her tight against him. She sucks his lower lip into her mouth.

They stand, enfolded around each other in the water, there with the moonlit ripples around their waists and the weight of words heavy between them. The burning feeling of each other's skin, the signals of each other's fingertips. The world and the sounds from the cliffsides around them fading into the background, leaving just the two of them suspended in the delicate balance of their desires and fears, love and betrayals, and everything that comes next. Everything after.

Their bodies move against each other now frantically, the soft cushion of her breasts pressed into Cal's chest as her hot breath scatters across his neck, moaning, him inside of her again without effort and she starts moving with his hips, her legs wrapping tight around him, riding him, gazing into his eyes as she does. Leaning close, kissing hungrily at each other's lips, waves of pleasure rolling through each of them, their bodies moving in unison, up and down, the water splashing, her nails scratching into him; his hand on the nape of her neck, the other on her lower back, pressing her into him until Sarah comes alive with her climax.

All time and boundaries seem to vanish between them, and he feels her body swallowing him, her legs tightening, and he lets himself go clutching her, barely holding her slippery body against him. But they manage. Each anchored into one another. Each equally powerless to everything after. Him rushing into her deep and in that moment the world dissolves into nothingness. No sights or sounds surrounding them, no other presence at all. No memories, no fears or insecurities—only that pure, atavistic passion, the same they experienced the night together in Cal's old flat.

Months ago, back on that cold, snowy night.

That passion he could never forget.

They cling to one another in the vast emptiness of it, their selves fading... an unbroken flow of energy rising between them, warm and secure, seamlessly intertwined, inseparable...

As he always wished it: she and him together against it all.

41

C al awakens with her nakedness in his arms stirring against him, and he smiles at the sound of the predawn rain tapping on the tiles of the balcony nearby, barely audible above the crashing of the waves. Then he hears another sound too – Lucy's insistent cries from the adjacent room.

He reaches over, gently brushing a golden lock of hair from Sarah's face.

"I'll get her," she says, shifting the sheets away, her eyes closed.

"No, no. Sleep," he whispers back, and he hears her murmur something incoherent, turning over and settling back as he gets up.

The cold marble floor sends a shiver through him as he steps across the room, sliding on his underwear from where she pulled them off a few hours before, and then he closes the balcony doors, cutting out the rain and breeze.

Turning around and pulling on a tee shirt, he admires the bare skin of her back before crossing the room to the door.

Padding softly through the villa's grand hallways, the large statues and pieces of art stare back at him, and he follows the noise around the dim corner to Lucy's little room. He finds her in her crib, her tiny face scrunched up in distress.

"Hey little girl," he says. He lifts her up and cradles her against him, feeling her hot tears against his chest. "Did you poop?"

He takes a whiff and confirms that's not it. "Maybe just gas then," he says, and begins to walk with her, humming softly. "If it's hunger, that's your mom, okay?"

The halls are cavernous and his footsteps echo as he goes from dark room to dark room, listening to the rattling of the room's windowpanes with the distant thunder. He flicks on the lights in some of them as he goes just to look at the soaring gilded ceilings or take in another piece of colorful, striking art. He sees the shadow of a grand piano in the den and thinks of the piano in Sarah's old flat.

The chip from the crystal bowl Sarah threw at David's head. His witness to her world of violence.

Something, by that point, she'd become very used to.

Something she'd been raised in her whole life... under an opulent sheen.

Something she swore she'd escape...

And now, she simply has company in it.

Now, she simply has me. A partner to run with.

She's not alone. And neither am I.

He roams the halls.

Maybe... he thinks, her words echoing in his mind.

Take violence, for instance... any violence has a history, right? A lineage, passed from one generation to the next, one hand to another... I've felt the weight of my history pressing down on me.... My violence. My whole life, really.

Two inseparables...

Can we break the cycle, Sarah? Can we escape it now?

History... it clings to you... That deal we didn't know we were signed up for...

Starting over, with you...

Leaving this place and these sins behind us.

Putting lots of distance between us and here and...

Everything else...

I'm part of you.

It's the only way.

As he soothes Lucy, he finds himself in front of Sarah's great painting room. The heavy wooden door creaks open when he pushes, revealing the vast space filled with canvases, easels, and the scent of turpentine and linseed oil. The overcast morning light filters through the high windows and the skylight, casting shifting shapes across the floor as he steps into the room to take a closer look.

He moves slowly, Lucy's cries diminishing to soft whimpers as he rocks her gently, and finally she's falling asleep, her head resting on his shoulder, as he goes along.

She's used to this room, Cal thinks.

Where her mom spends a lot of her time, no doubt. Since fleeing the UK.

And one by one, he walks past Sarah's paintings, each a proof of her obvious talent and turmoil, colors and bold strokes telling her stories, one after the other – pain, hope, and everything in between.

Minutes go by on each one – lingering, holding Lucy.

Landscapes and hand sketches, faces and marketplaces, naked bodies intertwined; one giant one of the Sicilian cliffside, and another of a woman with a swollen belly, her palms pressed against it.

But then his eyes fasten to one particular painting at the far end of the room: a piece he recognizes from his online searches of her. The same one he saw in her place the night he was over, before David came in and shattered the room and his life in ways he could never have imagined at the time.

A figure standing alone, shoulders stooped under the weight of an unseen burden, an oppressive force above them, facing a storm on the horizon. The same intense purples and blues, dominating. The same delicate outlines of flowers beside the figure's feet in emerging light.

And the frame. The same one as he saw in her flat that night – two inches deep against the wall. Golden.

He taps it lightly with a knuckle, examining it while holding sleeping Lucy in the other arm. The canvas feels solid, the frame sturdy.

But still... I wonder...

"Something I can help you with?" a voice cuts through the silence, startling him.

Giovanni stands in the doorway, his expression polite but unreadable in the dim light of the room. Cal turns fully around, offering a faint smile.

"Just admiring the painting. Gorgeous one, isn't it?"

"Yes, indeed," Giovanni agrees, stepping in slowly, his volume adjusting after seeing Cal with Lucy. "That one in particular, one of Sarah's finest you'd agree?"

"Certainly. Something about it. Foreboding."

"Like our Sarah. You've seen it before?" he asks, stepping up beside Cal.

"Once," Cal says.

"I see. She mentioned giving it away recently," Giovanni says, stroking his well-trimmed, silver beard. "Was odd to me."

Cal asks, "Why's that?"

"Astounded me considering her fondness for it," he replies. "Most of her paintings she has no issue selling, you see, but never this one. She's had several generous offers over the years, and yet has never budged."

"I saw it in her living room once back in London," Cal says. "She must want to keep it close."

"Well, yes, of course. It was the first thing she painted after Ephemeral Lake. Her Sam's death. More to my concern, you understand, when she told me she was considering giving it as a wedding gift to someone. A gift. Of all things. Peculiar."

Cal raises an eyebrow, resisting the urge to ask him what he knows about Ireland.

What he knows about the death all those years ago.

"To whom?" he asks instead, his mind shifting.

Giovanni's icy eyes flicker at him with something Cal can't quite decipher. Perhaps a shared understanding. Cal can only guess.

"I'd ask that of Sarah directly," he says, his tone courteous but firm. "It's her business, after all."

Cal nods, sensing the undercurrent in Giovanni's words. He looks back at the painting.

"I will," he says. "Thanks."

And at breakfast – out on the terrace eating together a couple hours later in the overcast morning, each wearing bathrobes – he spits it out, not wanting it to linger on his mind and ruin the day ahead.

"This morning while with Lucy I walked into your studio room."

"Oh," Sarah says, blowing her hair away from her toast as she chews, wearing his wayfarers. "Did she paint you a masterpiece?"

"Few more years on that front, I think," Cal chuckles. "But I saw a painting I recognized."

"Did you now," she says. "The one from my flat, I imagine. The dark one?"

"That's it."

"You like it? From my Wandsworth days. Call it Ichor," she says. "For storms."

"I love it, of course," Cal says. "But that's not it."

"You want me to tell you about Ireland. About what happened to him?" Sarah asks, her eyes now curious over top of the shades.

"No. I believe you. What you say it was. A tragedy."

"That's what it was," Sarah retorts.

"But I think you know that's not it as well, Sarah. Not my meaning, anyways," Cal says, his gaze narrowing, careful as he watches her. "Come on..."

A moment passes, and she puts down her fork.

"Yes, fine, okay? I'm awful," she relents at last, "Giovanni spilled it before I could ask you. Ugh, the old bastard," Sarah sighs, looking slightly bemused as she sits back. He sees the corner of her mouth twitch as it does when she's questioning whether to say something.

He can't help but want her. Want to kiss her dimples, her neck, and elsewhere too.

"Wow," he says. "I knew it."

"Well, your thoughts on the idea? I wouldn't do it of course without your consent. It has to be your revenge. Not mine. Much as I detest what they did to you. Much as I'd just assume go do it. But I'm done with behaving like that. No more subterfuge. No more mischief."

"You're a wicked devil, you know that?" Cal says, after a moment. "But you're my wicked devil. How would you even get it there?"

"Ways and means. People don't freight good art, if that's what you're inquiring. I've developed a decent network over the years for such things. Getting art across Europe. Avoiding inspections. Taxes. I can do it quite discreetly if need be," she shrugs.

Cal chuckles, hardly believing what he's about to say. But he's done being nice. He's done his time. It's time to give a little back, perhaps.

A little treachery. A little backstabbing. A little in kind.

"Send it to them."

"Yeah?" Sarah cocks an eyebrow. "Really?"

"May they prosper in the joys of their union, all with pounds of heroin or whatever it is hanging above their mantel."

"Assuming they can get it from France after the wedding, back to England," Sarah clarifies, sipping her coffee, an impish look of satisfaction plastered across her face. "I had a private jet on my side, after all."

"Why did you leave with it?" Cal asks, curious. "Why not remove the frame?"

"I didn't know. I had to leave in a hurry, remember. They burned most of my work in their bloody fire – I wasn't letting them have Ichor. The work has seen me through a few bad places. Wasn't leaving it in one... Of course, then I came to find out, David had loaded it up, like the others. Bastard. Kept it right under my nose in the flat. Thank God I didn't take it with me, flying commercial. Would have been arrested if they found it in their search of the flat, too. It was serendipity all around. Blind luck, really. Like I said – painting has seen me through a lot."

"Look. What happens, happens," Cal says. "Serendipity might even follow it. Who knows, right? Maybe they'll stay in France."

"Maybe," Sarah nods, looking a little disappointed at the prospect.

"Send it anyway... if you're ready," Cal says. "I want you to."

"You sure?" Sarah asks, her tone more serious. "I can't unring the bell, so to speak. It's quite the little criminal offense should they ever, you know, figure out what's what."

"Another?" Cal shrugs, "Join the queue."

She peers at him over her sunglasses, her green eyes searching for his true feelings.

"Just saddens me for you to lose a painting you care about for a bit of revenge on my part," Cal says to her, taking a bite.

"Nonsense," Sarah replies. "It's my idea. I've had it the better part of a decade. It's time for it to have a new home. I'm past my storms – I've got you now," she smiles. "So, for a good cause, I can live without it. And who knows... Maybe it'll end up in some bohemian place after auction, right? Inspire someone else in some dark times."

"Or some bank will sell it to a rich twat, who will put it in their garish, lotus eater skyloft for none other than them to see," Cal volunteers, believing it likely.

"I can live with that. A devil I made peace with long ago in the art world," Sarah shrugs, flipping her hair away from her face. "That's half my clientele you're describing right there thank you very much. Rich twats."

"You really think they'll catch him with something in that frame?" Cal asks, shifting the conversation, taking a sip of his brown-sugared coffee. "I mean, really?"

"Enough to get my name thoroughly, professionally off it," she nods, "and have it sent today with your blessing, quick as can be."

She grins cheekily: "Do you want to send a note, too?"

"That seems incriminating," Cal chuckles, shaking his head, thinking of the look his ex-fiancée will have on her face one day – if it ever does happen to trigger a custom officer's canine at an airport or train station.

"I think it says enough to the bastard. Both of them, for that matter," Cal continues. "For their collective part."

"Me too," Sarah says. "But I am grateful it all led to meeting you."

"And still," Cal says. "I say do it."

She raises her coffee – "To a dish served cold then."

"Served cold," he repeats. "And overdue."

They cheers mugs. Sarah calls Giovanni over to have the painting wrapped with instructions for the afternoon. Later, the pair go for a swim before laying out, then a shower in her bathroom with the large windows swung wide open, giggling like teenagers under the patches where the sunlight reflects the mosaic tiles.

42

A couple hours later, Lucy is dressed and ready to go and Cal carries her down the stairs with his new wayfarers, new jeans and a new linen button-down on. Sarah meets them at the bottom, wearing another of her floral spring dresses that makes Cal's heart melt at the sight of her. He helps her with the clasp of her necklace, and then puts his shoes on. Sarah breastfeeds and finally they're ready.

They leave together, past the fountain, and through the great oak front door, stepping into the back of the waiting Mercedes bound for town. After a windy twenty-minute ride, Cal, Sarah, and Lucy are dropped off in the bustling heart of Taormina, at the Piazza IX Aprile, Giovanni offering a wave behind him as Cal closes the door.

The square is alive with the sounds of morning chatter, clinking cappuccinos, people laughing and chatting, cars horns, and the distant, ever-present hum of the sea. It's all quite the juxtaposition from the solitude of the villa.

Movement again. Noise. Commotion. People out enjoying life.

The sun is high in the sky shining hot on the old pastel buildings, down into the alleys and narrow streets, making the wet and crowded cobblestones gleam as the scattered puddles evaporate.

Sarah and Cal, with Lucy in her carrier, wander down an alleyway into a quaint boutique off the main square that Sarah seems fond of, its shelves lined with delicate children's clothes. Cal watches as Sarah selects outfits for Lucy, her hands moving with practiced ease through the fabrics. The shopkeeper, an elderly woman with a warm smile, coos over Lucy in Italian words, and she giggles and reaches out for a brightly colored dress just beyond her reach.

Cal feels a warmth in his chest, a contentment that has eluded him for a very long time.

It's the right choice. Of course it is.

After making their purchases, they book a charter to Gibraltar through an agency off the square that apparently specializes in private voyages. They lock-in their journey to leave the following day, sailing out of Messina on an exquisite, fifty-foot schooner.

Cal doesn't see the price but doesn't worry when Sarah seems unfazed. She pays with a huge wedge of cash, pulling each bill out in turn.

"He seemed to know you," Cal remarks, as they step out of the office and back into the busy alley.

"Not me," she replies. "My father."

"Where is he, anyways?" Cal asks, a question that's been lingering in the back of his mind for some time. Ever since he got to Sicily, in fact.

"Pagliarelli prison," she answers, watching his response from beneath the shade of her wide-brimmed hat. "Almost six years now."

"That was going to be my next guess... or first," Cal says.

She elbows him and shakes her head. He smiles at her.

"Sorry. That came off crass."

"No, I mean you aren't wrong," she says. "You're starting to see it. Guess I'm my mother's daughter. Falling for a prison rat."

"Hey!" Cal smirks incredulously, then after a moment he nods. "Okay, a little earned. But I was groomed for this life, I tell you."

With their plans settled, and her father's whereabouts ascertained, they head down the bumpy road to the beach, the salty breeze invigorating. Cal changes into swim trunks and wades into the cool Mediterranean. The waves lap against his skin, and he dives down into the water, swimming out far into the ocean, his skin brushing the sand at the bottom.

The water is clear and shimmering blue as he paddles out, and he feels a sense of liberation – the weight of the past months and years shedding off his shoulders. Slowly. Piece by piece. Part by part.

I'm a new man, he thinks.

He floats for a while, watching the clouds pass him over, feeling the kiss of the sun on his skin, listening to the waves and the gulls overhead, the conversations carrying up on the wind from the town and terraces above the seawall. The smells of the cheese and the tomato sauce and the freshly chopped garlic. Fennel and the basil and the saffron. Feeling the warm swells beneath him. Listening to the lapping of the waves. More at peace than ever before.

And when he at last returns to shore, Sarah is on the phone, her back to him, her voice low and urgent. He doesn't interrupt, and resists the urge for suspicion, instead turning his attention to Lucy. He finds a spot on the sand and begins to build a small sandcastle with her, Lucy's tiny hands helping to pat the sand into place. Her laughter is infectious and he can't help but join her in it, feeling more of that electric joy that he hasn't felt in ages.

Eventually, Sarah finishes her call and joins them, her expression softening as she watches Cal and Lucy play.

"Have a nice swim?"

"Really nice. Everything okay?" he asks.

"Tutto è perfetto," she exclaims, chortling at Lucy who is laughing at her mom. "Dry off and get dressed, amante – let's eat. There's someone I want you to meet."

They head to a nearby café for lunch. The bistro sits at the top of a steep set of stairs, overlooking the beach. Sarah glances at her watch several times and then they order some wine. At last, a darkly tanned woman approaches their table and makes to sit.

"Sofia!" Sarah calls out, standing and kissing both her cheeks. "This is Cal."

Sofia is striking, with dirty blonde hair and the same sharp features and green eyes that Sarah's face possesses – but her demeanor is much different than her sister's: cool, quiet, almost distant. Removed and observant. Cal senses a tension in her gaze, an unspoken judgment. She barely says a word to him through most of the antipasti, talking about herself and her time in Naples.

The steaming seafood pasta arrives next, the scent of the fresh herbs and lemon mingling with the salty sea air. The conversation warms, polite but stilted, and Cal can't shake the feeling that Sofia doesn't approve of him. He tries to engage her, but her responses are curt, and her eyes drift often instead to Lucy, softening only when she looks at her niece.

She asks Cal at one point how prison was, to which Sarah chastises her, groaning, but besides that the conversation is mostly shallow which is fine by Cal. The two women tell him a couple stories.

Some about the mythos of Sicily. How Demeter and her daughter Persephone picked flowers as the lore goes, before Hades stole the god's daughter away to the underworld. This forces the Greek god of harvest away from Sicily's shores in a rescue attempt, leading to the seasons of the world supposedly.

Cal can't help but sympathize with Persephone's plight and he makes a joke about the underworld only Sarah gets, Sofia throwing him a strange look.

Later, over another bottle of wine, Sofia tells him about spending time with their father during the summers down here, following their parent's split. Occasionally getting to dodge a cold Christmas in Birmingham. She tells about her tan being the subject of envy upon returning to school. She warms up a little.

But the stories get tense when talking about their father, rather than just the general memories, and Cal steers clear of asking about him too much. Instead, he simply listens, and holds Sarah's hand under the table, drinking a couple more glasses of the pale wet wine and simply enjoying the stories about their time growing up in a half-Sicilian family.

And he realizes it's evasive in its own way. How they speak around the cold truth of it: that their family is made up of bandits. A bloodline mired in the criminality of the island, seeming to go way back, judging by the fragments they drop about their grandparents, and great-grandparents. Their efforts to undermine Mussolini during the war and ancient rivalries with other names he doesn't recognize. Hints casually dropped. The outline of secrets undisclosed yet carried by both sisters.

But Cal doesn't probe further despite his curiosity at these morsels of intrigue. He simply listens. Plenty of time for that later. Alone with just Sarah. Better to just enjoy the day.

Not cast any stones from his glass house.

After lunch, Sofia offers to take Lucy with her to Messina for the night, suggesting that the lovebirds could use some time alone.

"It will be good for her to spend time with her auntie, especially if you are flying out of here so soon," Sofia says, her tone leaving little room for argument. "I've got formula."

Cal looks to Sarah, who nods in agreement.

"I have changes of clothes too, don't worry so much," her sister adds.

"We'll pick her up first thing in the morning, mia sorella, okay?" Sarah says.

"Okay, love, okay," Sofia replies and they leave the restaurant, and then she kisses Cal on each of his cheeks in a moment of rare warmth.

"Be good to her," she says, her eyes scrutinizing him.

"It's nice to meet you, Sofia," Cal replies.

"Thank you, again," Sarah says, giving her daughter a kiss and handing Lucy over. "We'll see you tomorrow my love," she coos to her, giving her another kiss. Cal does the same. And as Sofia departs with Lucy, Cal can't help but feel a pang of unease mixed with relief.

It's the first time Lucy's been out of sight with someone else. Maybe it's just that. Separation anxiety. An instinct.

The prospect of a night alone with Sarah is enticing, but the coldness of Sofia's demeanor lingers in his mind.

That will take some getting used to.

He watches her disappear into the distance of the crowded piazza, the shadows lengthening as the late afternoon wears on. Turning to Sarah, he takes her hand, feeling the warmth of her skin, and together they walk back in the direction of the villa, the horizon painted with the petitioning hues of the sun over the ocean.

"Is she always like that?" Cal asks at last after they've walked a ways.

"More or less," Sarah says. "I got all the charm in this crazy family."

He puts his arm around her, drawing her in, "Yes you did. I love it." He kisses her.

"Shave this thing before we go," Sarah commands, tugging on his beard. "I want your face again… just because we're sailing tomorrow doesn't mean I want you… looking like… a sailor, capiche?"

And they kiss some more and walk a while longer along the narrow streets and alleys, buying a suitcase in a boutique and then people-watching, gazing at the tourists and the merchants, taking in the last rays of the beautiful day - the sounds of the waiters and patrons calling; the laughter from down the cobbles to the beach. The way the sepia-hewn light collects across the old, cracked buildings, in the squares and edges of this timeless place. And when her feet begin to hurt Cal hails a taxi heading in the villa's direction, back along the cliffside road.

Excited for a last night in Sicily.

43

The sun has long since set below the horizon by the time the taxicab pulls into the driveway of the cliffside villa, the delay from Taormina traffic stretching the day into dusk. The air is cooler now, the scent of the sea more pronounced in the evening breeze. Cal and Sarah make their way inside, the courtyard shadowed with the ivy encroaching over its walls looking like a kraken's tendrils in the dark.

They head upstairs and begin to pack, Cal folding his clothes with care, placing them neatly into the new suitcase. Sarah moves across the room, gathering Lucy's things and her own, methodically filling her cases too. The space is filled with the soft rustle of fabric, the curtains swishing from the open balcony doors mixing with the muted hum of the breezy night outside.

"You think it will be difficult to get into Morrocco?" Cal asks her, folding and breaking the silence.

"No," Sarah says, zipping up a handbag. "Another bribe."

"Your father's daughter," Cal jabs.

"Oh please, sir," she says, and sticks her tongue at him like a schoolgirl, "Unless you have a better idea, that is."

"No, no," Cal grins. "Following your lead."

"We can always ship what I don't take," Sarah says after another few minutes of packing, her voice breaking the comfortable silence.

"You're the one with stuff," he says and then walks around the bed, moving towards her. "Your art... your clothes... your toys..."

"Naughty," she says back, eyebrows cresting.

He reaches out, drawing her close to him, wanting to bridge the space between them. Wanting to get her out of her dress.

Her lips part, but she pulls back slightly.

"My mouth is dry from the walk, amante," she says, a faint smile playing at her lips.

"Where's the wine?" Cal asks, eager to make the night special.

"Don't bother with the cellar," she replies. "Just check the fridge in the kitchen."

"Most don't have to specify the fridge's location, you know that?"

"Bring glasses you heathen," she says, eyes furrowing, and he makes a cowering face at her. She snorts, and Cal laughs at her. She throws a sock at him.

He leaves Sarah folding and heads downstairs into the kitchen, the familiar path through the dimly lit hallways calming his nerves rather than elevating them for once.

He opens the refrigerator, stooping and scanning for the bottle, when a loud pop resonates like a firework outside.

Somewhere back towards the road.

No. Deeper than a firework. Like someone dropping something heavy.

He looks around the dark kitchen.

BANG it rings out again, sharp and jarring, closer, shattering the night's tranquility, and Cal realizes all at once it's a gunshot.

He ducks, his head swiveling to either end of the room.

BANG BANG followed in short succession by three more shots. BANG BANG BANG

Heart pounding, Cal moves towards the front door, keeping his head low, adrenaline and pure instincts kicking in.

Peering through the window behind the palm, he sees headlights rolling down the driveway, weaving through the trees like serpents.

Cars driving fast. Several of them. Flying towards the house.

Panic seizes him, the hairs on his neck standing on end, and he sprints back through the villa calling out for Sarah.

"Sarah!" he screams, his heart pounding in his ears. "Sarah get down here!"

He finds her on the staircase, her face pale yet composed, her eyes wide with fear.

"Cal, what the hell's happening?" she asks, her voice steady despite the tremor in her hands as she comes down to him.

"They found us."

"What?"

"I think they've shot Giovanni. Either that or the gate – they're coming," he says, his heart pounding. "We have to go now, there's no time, they're right outside Sarah," he says, grabbing her hand. "I don't know how, but they found us."

"Found us," she repeats, terror in her eyes.

They move quickly, Cal leading the way, her hand in his, his mind racing with the possibilities.

"Your sister," he whispers as they reach the kitchen. "Was it her?"

"No way. It wasn't her," Sarah answers back, her face white as ash, even in the shadows. "Definitely not. She would never do that to me."

"Then they followed her," he hisses. "Can't be a coincidence. Can't be. We just saw her. Now this. How do we get out of here?"

The villa, a haven minutes ago, now feels like a trap, its opulence twisted sinisterly in the wake of the arriving danger outside. And Cal realizes it all too late.

Only one direct way off the clifftop property: the road the gunmen came in on.

"Shit" he curses, looking out to the pool. "Shit!"

"How many cars do they have?" Sarah asks, her eyes frantic. "Can we sneak through the brush past them, I mean? Hop the fence? Run to town from there?"

"No," Cal shakes his head, thinking. "No way past them. There are lots of cars, Sarah. At least three. Probably more of them back by the entrance. The whole driveway was lit up with headlights."

The pair unlocks the back door, pushing it slowly open and scans the grounds. The garden, bathed in moonlight, offers little cover, but it's their best chance. He guides Sarah outside – through the shadows, his grip on her hand firm – the urgency of their situation overriding all other thoughts.

They pass the violet lit pool, moving from shadow to shadow, and Cal recalls the morning he snuck across the road to confront David in a similar fashion.

May this go better than that, he thinks.

As they reach the edge of the gardens, Cal glances back at the villa, its silhouette stark against the night sky and the shadows.

He can still see the headlights, now stationary, casting long, eerie backlight from the front of the house. They alternate between scooting and crawling low over the open ground, past the gazebo and along the cliff line, losing a bit of visibility with the hill as they near the edge.

"We have to keep moving," she says above the wind, taking the lead closer to the bushes at the corner of the property. The night swallows them, the sounds of their pursuers fading as they plunge deeper into the darkness.

He makes out someone shouting suddenly from not far off.

Then there is a flurry of gunshots and he hears the snaps and whirring of bullets like angry insects flying near their heads, a storm of angry metal descending down upon them - the rounds smacking into tree limbs and branches nearby, thudding rocks and kicking up dirt in the half-light.

Cal grabs Sarah and they plunge to the ground in an instant as the volley streams overhead.

For several moments, the world is drowned out in the noise of gunfire.

"There has to be another way out of here," he yells to her over the shots. "Some other way!"

"There is another way down!" she screams back, her eyes locked onto his, her face pressed into the dirt. "It's dangerous, but it might be our only chance, Cal!"

The shots taper off, becoming sporadic, a few at a time as if they're probing, listening for sounds of success.

"What are you talking about?"

"The old cliff diving route," Sarah replies, scooting closer to him. "It was here. The one my sister and I used as teenagers. I told you about it on our first date. If we can get to the jump point, it's about timing that water."

Cal's mind races, thinking about that water and how little light they'd have to be able to even see it at this point in the evening. But amidst the chaos of the gunfire overhead, intervallic but concentrated in their general area, it's not the worst plan right now. At any moment, either of them could be shot dead. Jumping from a cliff doesn't seem as bad somehow, Cal thinks.

"There's a chance, at least," she screams above another wave of gunshots, the bullets hissing near them in the dark bushes.

The memory of their first date surfaces. The way Sarah spoke of the cliffs, the thrill of the jump, the exhilaration she'd felt growing up doing it...

Absolute nutter, he thinks looking at her. He swallows hard, glancing back and seeing nothing.

"It's better than getting killed here," he admits. "Maybe we can hide down on the ledge until they leave. We may not even need to jump."

"Okay, let's do it then - stay low with me," Sarah whispers as the gunfire stalls for a moment, determination flashing in her eyes. "Follow me."

They rise to hands and knees and move quickly through the underbrush, the sound of their pursuers calling out to one another growing fainter but still present on their heels. After a bit, they get up and crouch, moving quick, stopping and listening every now and again.

At last they get to the edge. The path to the cliff is narrow, wet, and overgrown, and Cal can hardly see where he is placing his steps.

His heart pounds in his chest, a mixture of fear and adrenaline propelling him forward. One wrong move, and he's tumbling down to the rocks below. He periodically glances back at the villa, but this far along the cliffside it's hard to see its outline anymore through the dark trees.

Cal hears another bullet whiz by him then hears the bang from somewhere behind, and Sarah stumbles.

"Are you okay?" he asks, his hands going to her sides.

"Scared the hell out of me. We have to move faster," she says. "They can see us somehow."

"Night vision or something. It's too accurate."

"Come on," Sarah says. "Almost there."

They reach another sheer edge, a switchback, the drop-off point looming before them, and the sound of the waves crashing against the rocks below is almost deafening.

Sarah stops, turning to face him, her expression a mix of resolve and fear in the dim.

"Stay close," she yells over the noise of the ocean's spray, her voice firm. "And be careful on this next part. It's always wet."

Cal nods, and then hear the pursuers calling somewhere in the darkness behind them – beyond the sounds of the waves, yelling something – his grip on her hand tightening.

"Russian or Italian?" she says, her eyes on him.

"Does it matter?" he asks.

"No," Sarah agrees, and she presses forward.

They begin the descent on the loose talus, judging it only by the little moonlight creeping through the clouds above them. The wind whips over their bodies in the exposure of the cliffside, and

Cal shivers. They carefully pick their way down the rocky face, the ocean's pummeling of the rocks becoming louder and louder as they descend.

Finally, after what feels like a half hour of climbing downward in the dark along the steep path, Sarah stops abruptly in front of him and Cal nearly runs into her.

"It's here," she says to him, and he can see her silhouette bending down in the darkness, reaching for something. He hunches down beside her, running his hand along her forearm to find what she's holding: the end of a wet rope.

"This will take us down to the face of the ledge, to the outcropping we'll jump from," she says to him. "It's about fifteen meters or so below if I remember correctly. Gives the best drop on the deepest part of the shallows. I used to –"

Suddenly, just above them, far closer than Cal would expect, someone calls out something that sounds like 'what's this' and then there are more voices calling out close as well from just beyond the rocks.

"We have to go," Cal says, as low as his voice allows while still being heard above the sounds of the angry sea. "Fast as we can, Sarah. We're not losing them at all."

"Just be careful," Sarah replies. "All I'm saying is this rope was never great and it feels even worse."

He can make out her squeezing the rope in the dark, looking for a particular point of weakness.

"Doubt anyone's done this for a decade. Maybe more. It was our little secret – Sofia and mine."

"Not anymore," Cal says, and he steps a bit closer to her. "I'll go first. Then I can grab you if need be."

"No," Sarah snaps, "you don't know where on the ledge to get off. If you don't get off, you'll have to pull yourself up, or just fall. Both are not good positions to be in. Not with those rocks. Please, trust me."

"Okay, okay," he says. "Just be careful. I don't want to be up here too long, Sarah. They've got to be just above us."

"Wait one minute or so, then follow me," she says. "Okay? Can't have too much weight on this rope at once."

"Okay," Cal replies, and he pulls her to him. "Bon chance."

"Bon chance," Sarah says, kissing him. "We're going to do this."

"I'll be right behind you."

Then she stoops down and carefully swings her legs over the ledge and Cal's heart flips in his chest as he watches Sarah's dark outline disappear down the edge of the cliffside, repelling slow and steady into the black.

Cal waits his turn with anticipation, the fear coiling in his chest like a snake, with nothing but the sound of the waves crashing below, a roar in his ears, his hands on the wet rope, feeling Sarah's descent in his palms.

How did I get here?

I got myself here.

Why did I stay?

I love her. There was never any other way.

He hears the faint crunch of pebbles overhead and glances up, his heart pounding. Something's moving. He looks closely and makes out a shadowed figure moving along the path, not far above him at all, maybe three or four meters, and then someone's head peers out over the outcrop. A darker patch in the black, popping up over the rock.

Now or never. Out of time.

Moments from getting shot, Cal commits to the descent, following the hold of the rope to the edge and beginning the climb down the face of the cliffside in the dark.

Step by step down. Over the ledge he goes.

His palms are covered in sweat as he grips the rope, his feet dangling on the edge, his body twisting around.

The rough texture of the stone scrapes against his shins and then the toes of his shoes as he feels for holds in the wet crevices. Every movement is deliberate, every breath measured.

Every step down a leap of faith that his trainer's grips will hold.

He can feel Sarah still on the rope below him, her progress slow but moving, the rope vibrating in his hands as he descends after her.

Cal's muscles warm up quickly with the effort, his arm and back muscles firing, his mind laser-focused on each step of the descent.

Suddenly, the sharp cracks of gunshots pierce the night; a rapid succession of them, echoing off the cliffs above.

The rope shudders ferocious in his hands, and he realizes with horror that they are shooting at it on the ledge.

Panic surges through him - white hot panic - and he fights to keep his grip as the rope shudders.

He reaches out in the blackness for a handhold in the rock nearby... and grabs one just as the rope snaps.

Then his grip fails him on the slippery surface.

The world tilts as Cal slides down the cliffside. The jagged rocks tears into his chest and arms, pain searing through him with every edge he falls against.

He claws, desperate – grabbing, snagging, sliding – his fingers searching for anything to stop his descent. The rough stone rips and cuts at his skin as he reaches for it, scratches, lunges for anything at all and then, out of nowhere – breaking a finger or two in the process with blinding snaps that radiate hot in his palms – his terrified grip latches onto a jutted outcrop above. A large bumpy rock, and his other hand copies its positioning in an instant, his body jerking to a halt.

Suspended. Floating.

Feet dangling in the blackness.

His breath comes in ragged gasps, the salty air stinging his lungs, a warmness along his chest and belly that he is certain is his own blood from sliding down the serrated rockface. Above him somewhere, the broken rope swings uselessly, and as he hangs, he hears Sarah's panicked breathing, and he knows she's still clinging to the cliff, not too far above him. He can't see her, but he can feel her fear – her desperation.

"Sarah!" he calls out into the black, his voice raw. "I'm okay!"

Although the gunshots have stopped, the silence is even more terrifying. He looks up, trying to make out any movement above them. Shadows shift in the moonlight, but he can't tell if it's the attackers or his imagination. It's all too far away. This far down the cliff.

His toes push into the rock, feeling for anything, trying to find a grip, but there's nothing on the slanted wet surfaces. All he's got is his hands.

Cal forces himself to focus, to push the fear aside. Every muscle in his body is taut with tension, every movement a milestone.

"Oh my God," he hears her yell out, "I thought you fucking died!"

"I almost did!" he calls back to her. "I fell down the cliff!"

"How far below me are you?"

"I have no idea. I'm fucking hanging. I don't think I can climb back up either. The rope's gone… I think I broke a thing or two in my hand… It doesn't feel right."

"Okay, I'm coming to you."

"No, it's too dangerous, Sarah."

"I can't jump above you, that's too dan –"

A string of gunshots sail out over their heads, going wide. Whizzing far; no longer snapping.

Not aiming anymore perhaps. Too far down the cliff. Defilade. They're getting desperate.

They're giving up – he can only hope.

"Are you okay?" he calls out after a moment.

"I'm coming down, Cal," Sarah shouts back.

"Shit!"

"What?" she calls.

"I'm losing my grip..."

He feels the fingers of his good hand knotting and beginning to weaken, and he tries to pull himself up again, getting his forearms onto the rockface, but slides back to his hands again after a moment on the slick rock. The sound of the waves is close beneath his feet, which means the rocks that will kill him aren't far either. He has no idea where to jump, his back turned, and below his feet he sees darkness punctuated only by the white froth of the sea.

Somehow, he holds on, and after several severe moments he hears pebbles falling past him, and Sarah climbs down about a meter to the right, on a side of the rock catching the moonlight, her form huddled against the jagged, steep face and her dress blowing around her.

"We're almost there," she says, clearly trying to infuse her voice with confidence she doesn't feel. He appreciates the effort.

"Remind me to do this in the daytime next time," Cal pushes out, his forearm muscles beginning to burn.

"We're never doing this again," Sarah calls back. He can only just hear her above the slamming of the waves and the gusts whipping around the face. She begins side stepping a bit closer to him along the rock. "We can't go up without a rope, so this is where it's got to be, Cal. I just need to time it."

"That a problem?" Cal asks, his breath coming in ragged gasps. He wonders if he's broken a rib or two in the fall as well.

"No running start," she says back, her voice breaking. "But let me just listen a moment... we can get this... we can kick off..."

"I can't give you too many more moments, Sarah," Cal call back to her. "My grip is killing me..."

"Hold on. Got to count the seconds of the breakers..."

The cold wind whips around them, carrying the salty tang of the sea in the swallowing blackness. Cal can feel the cold spray of the ocean below him, blowing up in the breeze across his face.

"Okay, I think I've got it," she yells back after several moments. "Yeah – think I've got it. Nearing second high tide. We can do this!"

Cal takes a deep breath, looking over at Sarah, her face illuminated by the slight of the moonlight, appearing almost porcelain like the first night he laid eyes on her from his rooftop, her naked body through the windowpane... where it all began.

He can see the determination etching across her features in the dim, the blood on her knees, the strain in her gaze. Her panting chest. The whites of her eyes aimed towards the sea, her hair furling around her in the shadows.

"Sarah," he calls out to her, his voice faltering. "I need you to know something before we do this. No matter how this ends tonight, no matter where we land in that ocean, I wouldn't change a thing. You saved me, Sarah – I'll never forget that. You brought me back from the edge when I was ready to let go."

She cocks her head, looking at him, and he thinks he sees her smile.

"Okay," Cal admits, "I can see the irony in saying something like that... in this position..."

And he thinks he hears the sweet sound of her laugh, her eyes wide, the weight of his words sinking in.

"Bad joke," she says. "But appreciated."

"When I first saw you," Cal explains, "I was broken."

"Cal..." she tries. "Look, I know -"

"But you... you changed that, Sarah. You showed me that there's still beauty, that the cycle... can break. That the worst doesn't have to cut you forever... No matter what happens tonight, no matter where we land, I just want you to know that I'm grateful for every moment with you. I wouldn't change a thing Sarah."

Cal pauses, the memories of their time flooding his mind. The moments of joy, laughter, fear, the shared pain and understanding, the fight of their lives, starting that first night, up in the icy breeze. He feels a lump in his throat, but he pushes through it, needing her to hear every word.

"I love you," he says just as the last of his grip begins failing him in his injured hand.

"We'll get through this," she calls back above the crashing of the waves, and her voice trembles with the cold or with emotion, or with fear, he doesn't know. "Together. Okay? I will see you down there," she calls to him. "I'm glad you didn't jump that night. It was the greatest thing that's ever happened to me... Seeing you past my reflection. You better survive this, Cal Beckley. Because I love you. With everything I've got left. And we have a daughter to raise – don't forget that."

Cal nods, his heart swelling despite it all.

"Yes we do," he says, almost to himself.

"Can't let my sister indoctrinate her into an Amalfi yuppie, right?"

"Never," he says, surprised by his own smile cresting across his face. He turns his gaze down to the dark churning sea below his feet.

"No matter what happens, I'm with you, Cal," Sarah calls out. "We'll jump together!"

"Okay," Cal says, looking up at her, his stomach lurching, his voice feeling distant. "I'm ready, Sarah. Tell me."

"Let's count it down."

Then, his injured hand falls away, his heart skipping a beat, and Cal dangles from the face of the rock with one hand. Clutching for anything.

"Okay!" Sarah yells above the wind. "Three!"

They exchange a look, a silent moment of understanding.

The fuse is lit.

The wave is waning out below, somewhere in the black.

"Two!" Cal calls out, his voice steady despite the terror clawing at his insides and the numbness in his last hanging arm. He plants the soles of his feet back on the rock and gets his hurt hand back up again, up above his head. Searching, he finds the grip.

This is it. This is the moment – the jump.

The only one that ever matters.

"One!" Sarah shouts, her grip tightening on the rock as she looks down as far as her neck can crane, then nods to Cal, ears piqued to the tempo of the waves.

The last seconds stretching, the world narrowing to the two of them and the crashing void of the sea – the roaring, churning black they're heading towards.

Cal takes a deep breath.

"Now!" Sarah screams, and each of them kicks into the cliffside, leaping as far back as they can go.

And he feels the biting rush of air pass him, whirling, and the water howls upward. Springing forth out of the dark.

And his thoughts go to London, inexplicably, and the winter. To the icy rooftop of his old flat in January. To his broken heart from Diane. The snowflakes falling down on his drunken, depressed head.

To the dusted binoculars, the shock of seeing her there through them, sitting with her head back, her hand moving between her open legs.

To the moments racing up there to the perch after work, following her in the market, discovering her name on the floor. On her grocery receipt.

His excitement and horror, looking through her window. His purpose restored. Night after night.

Falling in love with Sarah.

And for a moment, time seems to stop; the outline of the cliffs tumbling away as they plunge the few dozen meters towards the maw of the angry ocean. And somewhere in that fall, Cal grabs hold of her – in that last precious moment before they hit whatever it is they're meant to hit. And in that second with all his might and memory, Cal knows he is exactly where he is supposed to be, with who he is supposed to be with.

Peace washes over him with the impact – tender and welcoming – and he knows he's ready.

Cal Beckley is not afraid.

Epilogue

Detective-inspector Grant carefully makes his way under the polizia tape on the perimeter and across the courtyard to the group by the fountain. He introduces himself to the wrong detective who then directs him towards the back of the villa, to a barrel-chested Sicilian, the primary on the case, who is flanked by uniformed cops out of Taormina.

The man is lingering by the cliff's edge looking out in the sunlight at the serrated rocks and the surf below, his immaculate three-piece suit a lot of material for the climate as far as Grant is concerned.

Quite the juxtaposition from his own tired garb. But Grant doesn't care. Half the problem with these people: fatalistic... vain. Devoid of sense.

Beyond reason, wearing that in this heat.

Can't wait to get back, he thinks.

Just get this done. Get this over with.

"Bongiornu. Long way to come, Detective-inspector," the man with Furio scrawled across his badge says, eyeing Elliot Grant's disheveled appearance, a hint of amusement across his face. "Interpol already spoke with us, I'm sure you heard. No need for a visit unless you planned it – a holiday, perhaps."

"Right," the gruff Englishman says. "Detective, pleasure. Hard man to track. Been calling. So no, not for holiday."

The two shake hands and size up one another.

"What is the nature of your arrival then?" the Sicilian asks.

"Another look is all. Just thought by now something would have washed up to ID. Worth my review with my files on the suspect. Thought I'd come take a look myself."

"If you insist," Furio says with exaggerated grace, looking at him curiously.

"Nothing but the bullet casings, then?" Grant asks, looking around as if he might spot one gleaming in the sunlight. "Still?"

"Turkish bullets. Nine-millimeter. One killed," the Sicilian detective replies. "Estate's caretaker. Respected man. Known well about here – che peccato."

"Right, peccato..." Grant replies, stroking his beard, his voice hoarse, feeling the rising cost of his red-eye flight. "But other than him?"

"Other than him," Furio replies, a small hint of offense in his tone, "not much to go on, detective-inspector."

"And you identified the couple how, exactly?" Grant asks. "The ones who also died?"

"Confessions. Shooters... In the report, I'm sure you saw it, no? Few arrested that following morning. Attempting to fly out to Riga from Comiso. Stated they shot them off the cliffs."

"The arrests – a tip?" Grant asks, his eyes scrutinizing the man.

"Eight of them fitting descriptions," Furio shrugs. "Not very coordinated. Hired killers. Didn't even split away from each other after. Even we can manage something like that, down on this little isolotto."

"Didn't mean to imply..." Grant begins but Furio whips out his phone instead, swiping through and presenting Grant the headshots of a selection of tired and angry looking eastern European men. Young, pale. Early twenties maybe.

"What are they saying?" Grant asks.

"Not much, so far, beyond the target. But give it time."

And the detective-inspector thinks it through again...

Why they would have done it this way...

"Been days now," he says, looking out across the cliffs. "It's odd, yeah? Nothing coming back..."

"They'll turn up," Furio shrugs. "Everything washes up here col tempo. All the sins of the island, they say."

"But Estonia?" Grant scrunches his face. "The shooters... Seems doubtful considering these two. I mean, why the trouble, you know? Couple civilians, they were. Seems..."

"Doubtful, you say, detective-inspector?" Furio asks, his eyes searching the man, suspicions clearly sprung. "I'm sure you know well the Ciambra name is - how do you say... notu... around these parts."

"Notorious?" Grant offers. "No I wasn't sure - well off, obviously. But she was clean, far as we was concerned. An artist. And a parole hopping convict. Nobodies."

"Beh, she was not a nobody in Sicily, detective-inspector. Family members tied to the thirties with la Cosa Nostra. Low, high, middle... all down the line, mafioso. Her father's crimes... you read, no?"

"Imprisoned father," Grant adds. "Right, yes. You're checking into it, then? The father?"

"Yes."

"And how Beckley got into the country?"

"Si, non rompere le palle. Of course," Furio retorts, clearly irritated with being told how to do his job.

"Still doesn't make sense," Grant says after a moment, pressing forward, breaking into a crouch and peering over the edge at the sputtering rocks a couple hundred meters down. "To leap like that... kill themselves... over, what, some family squabbles? Bit... drama –"

Then his view lurches. The world spins and his stomach flips upside down. Vertigo hits Grant suddenly and he flails back onto his behind. Furio steps closer and offers him a hand, suppressing a grin, to which Grant waves him off, standing awkwardly, his face red.

"Hate bloody heights. Look, mate. Look. Just... Just let me know," Grant says, brushing his blazer and then his beard. "When the bodies wash ashore. When you find them. Comprende?"

"Of course, I will notify proper channels," Furio says back, a hint of impatience beneath the exactness of his response.

"No," Grant snaps, taking a step closer, and pressing his business card into the man's chest. "Call me. He was my case. Call it... a professional gesture...interdepartmental... claro? I'd appreciate that, Furio."

Detective Furio's eyes narrow, but he takes the card, looking it over.

"You know what Plato said about this place, detective-inspector?" Furio asks slowly as he reads the text of the card.

"I don't give a toss," Grant replies, "'less it has to do with the case."

"Sicilians build things like we'll live forever. And eat like we'll die tomorrow."

"What's your point?" Grant furrows his brow, his lips pursed. His tie whips across his face in the breeze. "Gluttons, are you?"

"No, no. No point," Furio chuckles looking back, his eyes detached. "A simple insight. Sicily has a way. You know? A memento, say, for your holiday – la magìa, capiscimi?"

"Bugger it," Grant scowls, waving him off, and Furio watches the man walk away, his arrogant stride almost comical as he storms towards the perimeter tape.

"And how long will you be in our lovely country, Detective-Inspector?" Furio calls after him.

"Couple limoncellos," Grant grumbles, and then says back louder, "A phone call will suffice when you find something, yeah? Thanks, mate." And he doesn't wait for a response, just makes his way under the tape and back towards his car.

"Vaffanculo," Detective Furio swears as the Englishman disappears from sight, crumpling and tossing his card over the edge of the cliffs.

A few minutes later, Grant accelerates onto the labyrinthine clifftop highways back to Palermo where his flight awaits, and while keeping his eyes on the road, slides open his prepurchased phone, pulling out the SIM with his thumbnail. Then, fishing from his breast pocket, he pulls out another card and presses it into the slot at the back of the phone. Once in place, careful to keep his eyes on the winding median and the cars passing, he puts it all back together. At last, he powers the burner on and then, thumbing through the preloaded contacts, makes the call that's been expected of him – his real reason for the trip.

"It's done," Grant says when the line picks up. A long moment of silence goes by on the other end. Grant accelerates and passes a truck around a blind bend. He then switches lanes, and while doing so, glances at the phone screen confirming it's in fact connected.

"Certain?" a voice at last says.

"Zaversheno," Grant reiterates louder. "You hear me? You got them."

"Spasibo –" is all he hears on the other end before it clicks.

Word of Sarah and Cal's bullet-riddled clifftop fall reaches London quick as any news these days, and it doesn't take long for Damian to find out too.

True to form, as the week progresses, he dives into every newspaper he can get his hands on, ordering some even straight from Sicily. Tons and tons of papers covering the ongoing investigations. His old, voracious habit: eternally at odds with the digitized age. Piles in his office in a short amount of time.

And in the more salacious ones, he reads headlines like: INFAMOUS COUPLE PULLS SICILIAN ROMEO & JULIET and FUGITIVES ON THE RUN SUICIDE PACT

And in the even more conspiratorial rags acquired lining the grocer's marts, things like:

FIRST HER HUSBAND, NOW HER: REVENGE MOTIVE REVEALED

CAL & SARAH: ARE THEY DEAD?

STILL NO BODIES OF ALLEGED CRIME DUO

WHAT POLICE AREN'T SAYING ABOUT BRITS SLAIN IN SICILY

REASONS WHY SARAH MURDERED CALVIN NOW

Damian sits in his office alone after hours with the many papers spread out before him on the floor, holding his second glass of amber, and after a while he can't help but feel himself start to weep for his friend. A deep sadness rising up within him.

A feeling that he failed him.

"Why, Cal," he says to himself, "why after all of that? Why go with her - why, mate? Why even humor it?"

But after another hour or so, and another glass of scotch, he finds no answers and so he grabs his light jacket and stumbles out of his firm's front doors in the late dusk.

He makes his way to the Tube as he seldom ever does, his car parked in the underground lot nearby – only today he's not going home, and today he's too drunk to drive. He takes the half-hour train journey instead, and by the time he ascends the stairs at Lewisham's exit, going through the turnstiles, it's already dark.

He follows Cal's old journey to the flat that Damian settled for him, all those months ago, while representing the man on trial for his life.

I tried to save his life, he thinks. I tried to help him.

And he lingers there on the corner, looking up at the building, before turning to face the adjacent one.

Where it all started for you, dear boy.

His eyes settle then on the pub at the foot of the Jones's building, glowing in the dim of the street.

The Old Hound the decaying sign reads.

"What the hell," Damian murmurs to himself, feeling low.

Stumbling across the road and through the doors, the noise and the music and the cheer warms him, and he leans up against the scarred mahogany bar and orders a stiff pint from the tattooed bartender. A moment later, she eyes him funny as she wipes the counter and serves him.

"Recognize you," she says, pushing a loc out of the way, pausing, before she turns around and takes two glasses from behind the shelf, filling them with generous pours of Glendalough.

"Very kind. But no thanks, please, had too many. No offense meant," Damian says, putting his palms up, but she slides a glass beside his pint anyways.

"On the house," she says, throwing hers back and then nodding behind her to the mirror above the bottles. "For friends."

And Damian's eyes focus on where she is looking on the mirror, where behind the vodka and gin bottles he spots a newspaper clipping taped up with a photograph taken during the trial. One of the dramatized ones stitching Sarah and Cal together, each exiting the Old Bailey at separate times but side-by-side within the edit.

Just below the clipping, a postcard is taped with a vivid painting of Marrakesh on the front of it, beautifully etched in acrylics. And then Damian sees a handprint at the corner of it. Gold and orange pressed over the card's display of the red city, like someone has guided an infant's palm from a palette of mixed colors.

"Arrived yesterday," the bartender says, her voice low, following his gaze. And Damian smiles at her, and through tears raises his glass.

She pours another and they clink.

After setting a couple more back, the young lawyer wishes Karalana farewell, attempting to pay again and being denied. She insists instead on hugging his swaying frame at the door and whispering to him, "Thank you for all you did."

"We cared about that lovesick bastard," he replies, sniffing. "It's all we could do. What we knew how."

"All anyone can. Love 'em fierce, love 'em well. With what little time there is," she sighs and gives him another squeeze. "Now get home safe, man. No more pitstops."

There's the sound of a glass smashing inside.

"Aye," he says, throwing her a slanted smile. "Thank you. I mean it."

"Don't mention it, got to run," Karalana smiles back then closes the door. Damian checks his watch, stepping out, before fetching and stoking a cigarette with a cupped hand over his lighter in the wind. It takes a moment to spark it, and sighing, he begins the slow journey back to the Tube, his steps unhurried, his body warm and loose.

And then something seizes him: a feeling he is being watched. Eyes on the back of his head, creeping up. And he looks around the street... before his gaze draws to a particular window.

Her window.

A blackened pane of glass fifteen flights above.

Damian watches, and for a fleeting moment he thinks he sees someone moving up there: ensconced in gloom, staring outwards,

peering down the rooftops and avenues and hard corners of the city. Regarding himself, at last he chuckles, pulling his collar up.

"To both of you," he nods, raising a hand to the windowpane. Then he turns towards the station without looking back, soon out of view of the streetlights. Another figure in the wind and shadows, finding their way in the darkness, heading home.

Through The Windowpane
by CS HAGON

About the Author

CS Hagon grew up with a passion for storytelling,
crafting tales from an early age that
explored the gritty allure of crime noir,
the thrilling vantages of historical drama,
and the boundless potential of science fiction.
Originally from Florida, he now resides in Colorado.
Through the Windowpane marks his debut novel.

Reader's Note

Thank you for reading my book!
If you enjoyed it, a personal review from you would be **amazing**!
And if you didn't enjoy it, you can also leave one.
But you know, *especially* if you liked it...
Okay, I'm joking. Any & all feedback is fantastic.
Writers of any stature
(particularly the newcomer variety)
live by the reviews our readers give us.

I'd be truly grateful for yours.
P.S. For book info, early-access, the newsletter, & inquiries, head
over to **cshagon.com**